DEAD POOR

A Dakota Mystery

D1518933

M.K. COKER

First Print Edition:
ISBN-13: 978-1717439741
ISBN-10: 1717439748

Editor: Red Adept
Cover and Formatting: Streetlight Graphics

This is a work of fiction. All characters, organizations, and events are the product of the author's imagination or are used fictitiously.

The Dakota Mystery Series:
Dead White
Dead Dreams
Dead Wrong
Dead Quiet
Dead News
Dead Hot
Dead Poor

In memory of Brett Wilk—homeless no more.

CHAPTER 1

BARF BUCKET DANGLING FROM ONE hand, Lori Jansen trudged up the worn trail that snaked up to the overlook of Grove Park. In the cover of gnarly old trees with bark rougher than Eda County back roads, branches grasped at her. She was just out of their reach—but not for long. Shoulders hunched, she didn't bother to glance up at the beauty shimmering around her as the crushing weight of darkness lifted—for the day, not for her.

Each footstep was a struggle as her scuffed dollar-store sneakers crunched over tattered brown leaves curled up into themselves, grinding them into the packed dirt. All she wanted was sleep. The bucket hit the side of her leg in a rhythmic throb that matched the twinges from the stitch in her side. A whip-poor-will called from somewhere deep in the darkened woods below.

Whip-poor-Lori, more like.

Look at the birds of the air, they neither sow nor reap nor gather into barns; yet your heavenly Father feeds them. Are you not of more value than they?

The answer to that verse, she'd decided years ago, was no. Any value she'd possessed had long ago been ground into the mud under her mother's heel, like the bright ribbon Lori had gotten for that long-ago feat of memorization. Her mother had used summer vacation Bible schools as free childcare.

Don't let those holy rollers mess with your mind. You gotta learn to use them before they use you. Trust nobody.

Only when Lori reached the rise into the grassy clearing of the overlook did she raise her head. Blowing bangs out of bloodshot eyes, she pushed back the hood of the gray hoodie she'd inherited from her son. Hand-me-ups, she'd told him, making him laugh, as at eleven, he was already taller than his mother.

But Bobby hadn't been laughing lately. Neither had she.

Buck up, girl, her granddad's voice told her. *A new day's a new slate.*

After rubbing the grit from her eyes, she took a moment—just a moment—to take in the new day. The blue, rose, and orange pastels were a softness she'd never known in her own life. And she realized that she had company—and not the usual dainty doe or a strutting turkey.

A stocky man with a steel-colored buzz cut sat in a lawn chair just outside a sleek silver RV. The sun nudged up over the horizon on the endless Dakota plains below and shaded it red. The man looked right through her as he sipped from a hefty ceramic mug that steamed in the cool air of the October morning. Even from the path, she could smell the scent of freshly ground coffee, and her stomach rumbled.

Maybe she'd faded right away in the night. Yeah, right. She kicked a fallen branch from off the trail. She should be used to being invisible to people like him. Sitting there like he didn't have a care in the world in a vehicle that must've cost several times more than the home she'd just lost, he saw beauty. She saw crap. Day after day. All for eight dollars and sixty-five cents an hour.

She stalked up to the closest of the two wooden vault toilets, the men's. Neither was much bigger than the outhouse at Granddad's farm. Grabbing hold of the door handle, she parted her lips to breathe through her mouth. She'd learned that trick real quick. She pulled opened the door—the creak always made her think of house of horrors at Halloween. At the screech, the RVer finally deigned to notice her, frowning deeply as if wondering if she were some kind of pervert. A trans-whatever.

She raised the bucket in answer, resisted the urge to lift a middle finger, and went inside. She reached for the cleaning supplies kept in what she called her barf bucket. That was just what it'd been when she first started this job.

Flies swarmed from the inside. She backed out in a hurry, almost gagged on a few of the critters, and wondered what they'd found to feast on so late in the season.

Whatever it was, it was more than she'd had. When had she last eaten? Dashing away flies, she went back into the—what did those old movies that Granddad had watched call it? The beach? No, the breech. He'd acted like he'd been there himself, but the truth was, he hadn't even been born until it was all over. Vietnam, that was his war, but he'd never talked about it, except once when he'd said he would have taken some pride in putting Hitler down. He wasn't sure he'd put down anything but his health on the rice paddies. Agent Orange had taken Granddad down over a decade ago—that and heartbreak.

Lori put down the bucket, pulled on her gloves, and took out the Pine-Sol and scrub brush. The toilet was little more than a covered hole in a piece of plywood, once painted white, now yellowed to the color of pee. She flipped up the cover, and the light of the single naked bulb reached down into the deep vault below.

Her high, piercing scream echoed off the concrete slab floor.

Instead of a mound of turds and soggy tissue, a bloated face stared up at her from a couple feet down, sightless eyes dulled by death, mouth gaping open and full of...

Oh, shit.

Whirling, Lori barfed into the bucket as the RVer rushed in, fists high. Turning from judge to savior, he pulled her over to his makeshift camp, called in the law, brought her a blanket when she couldn't stop shaking, and insisted she sip some of the dark, rich coffee he'd brewed in his solar-powered RV.

He was, he told her, a retired firefighter, and he'd seen a lot. But a body in a john? With its mouth stuffed full of crap?

Never.

CHAPTER 2

TIRED AND WIRED, SHERIFF KAREN Mehaffey was still reeling from the shocking news when she and her part-time detective and younger half-uncle, Marek Okerlund, drove up one of the few hills in Eda County.

She didn't know when she'd last been to Grove Park, but she'd been a kid, maybe on a Girl Scout campout or at a Sunday church picnic in the shelter of the woods on a hot summer's day. Just the thought of blackened brats and gooey s'mores made her stomach rumble loudly enough to raise her passenger's eyebrows.

"Should've picked up something at the airport," Marek said, looking rested and relaxed after their flight from Albuquerque. While she'd been strapped in and hating every immobile second, her mind speeding faster than the plane, he'd slept like the dead, along with his young daughter.

They'd left Reunion, South Dakota, a week ago for a job hunt and vacation after she'd lost a brutal election against a man who had as little care for the truth as he did for the people who'd elected him. She was returning as the duly elected sheriff after a recount, and the man she'd beaten was in the can—literally. Or so she'd heard from the last man standing—or woman, actually—on her roster when the call came in before change of shift.

Josephine Lindstrom, the longtime secretary for the Eda

County Sheriff's Office, might retire for real after being left holding the bag—or badge. But before her flight home, Karen had told Josephine to roust the day-shift deputies, and they'd cordoned off the scene and held it until the South Dakota Division of Criminal Investigation showed up.

Deputy Walter Russell, aka Walrus, with his bald pate and graying handlebar mustache, met them at the barricade at the fork in the road that led up to the overlook.

Karen rolled down her window. "Sorry I had to pull you back so early from your vacation." Walrus, his wife, and their three sons had been fishing at Lewis and Clark Lake near Yankton. "Tell Laura I'm sorry that I cut it short."

"Oh, she was happy enough to come back once Josephine spilled the recount results. Well, that and the boys were driving her crazy, and she was tired of gutting and eating fish. We're both delighted you're back on board, Sheriff. Neither of us were looking forward to me being on the night shift again at the highway patrol. Low man on the totem pole and all. Geez, they're pretty strict about things, too." He cleared his throat at her slow blink. "Not that you don't run a tight ship."

One thing about Walrus: he never held a grudge and didn't mind being ribbed. "I'm happy you put your hat back in the ring," she told him. "I haven't heard from any of the others."

"Kurt's in the campground, taking statements. He hasn't said squat about his future plans. Not to me, anyway."

Her day-shift deputies were the original odd couple, and they preferred bickering to talking whenever possible. She doubted she would have all of her roster back, though. They'd all made their plans based on her election loss. But she could hope. Finding good people willing to take low-paying jobs for long hours in a rural backwater wasn't easy.

After Walrus moved the barrier, she drove through and continued on up to the overlook parking lot, where she saw a brand-new SUV. She parked her vintage Corvette—an impractical vehicle for the Dakotas but a legacy from her deceased husband—between the black monstrosity and the DCI van. She got out, feeling like Cinderella at the ball, minus a fairy godmother to deck her out in the requisite finery. She'd had no time to change out of her vacation clothes of a frayed and faded red University of South Dakota sweatshirt and white-at-the-knee jeans. She hadn't retrieved her official vehicle, either, when they'd returned. They had only taken time to drop Marek's daughter off, along with his Silverado pickup, with Karen's father before heading for the park. Karen felt less than official for a case that she'd considered just handing over to DCI.

When a man with dirty-blond hair and gunmetal eyes met her at the path that led to the cordoned-off toilet, she hit him with her best shot. "I've got motive."

"Pathetic. Want out, say so." Agent Dirk Larson glowered at her. "Welcome home."

The ex-Chicago cop who worked out of the Sioux Falls office of the South Dakota Division of Criminal Investigation was well-known for his bullet-style conversation. "You're such a sap, Larson. But seriously, wouldn't it be better if you took the case?"

"I kissed you. Makes *me* suspect."

Karen rolled her gaze around to see if anyone other than her closemouthed half-uncle had picked up on that. But as most of her roster was out, there was little fear of being overheard except maybe by the young woman with a bucket and an older man by a silver bullet of an RV. Witnesses, she pegged them. "It still seems iffy."

"Would be stupid to kill the man before the recount. You're not stupid."

That was more than Dirk Larson had thought when they'd initially met, butting heads over a crime scene that she'd inadvertently contaminated. Who knew they would end up locking lips—though no more than that, so far, especially as she'd just come within a hair's breadth of taking a job in Albuquerque.

"Dahl filled me in," Larson went on, obviously in no hurry to return to the crime scene. "Alibi. Homicide. Balloon. Photo. Do your job."

He'd provided a succinct summary of her last several hours. She'd been up in a balloon—a giant blue chicken of a balloon—in a blue-blue sky in Albuquerque for a dawn ascension and was about to accept a job there after helping close a homicide case when the county commissioner, Harold Dahl, had called her on her cell. He'd asked her to take a photo of herself and Marek up in the balloon and send it to him. What was that? Three hours ago? No, it was less, with the time change.

They'd been able to get on a military flight directly into Sioux Falls without all the usual delays, though they'd hustled to get themselves and their luggage there in time. Being ex-Army did have its perks.

Beside her, Marek rubbed at the rough goatee that made him look like a strung-out Byzantine saint with the broad Slavic slashes of his cheekbones and dark corn-syrup hair. The pale-blue Okerlund eyes were pure Scandinavian, though. Well, that and cop, but he came by that naturally, as the county had never had anyone other than an Okerlund at the helm of justice—a link of generations that she'd nearly broken. And while she carried her deceased husband's name with pride, she'd listed herself as Karen Okerlund Mehaffey on the ballot, just in case anyone in the county didn't know. And still, she'd lost, at first count, by thirteen unlucky votes.

At the time, she'd been hurt by the unexpected backhand from people she'd worked hard for and lived among but also relieved to be rid of the vitriol flung at her. She could do better—and she had—in other jobs that didn't include being denigrated at every turn. Neither her father nor her grandfather had weathered that kind of election.

But her opponent, Robert Leonard "Baby" Bunting, was now dead. And someone had killed him. That made it her job, her duty, to find who'd committed the crime, even if she had no idea how to feel about the whole thing after the recent yo-yo of events.

"Where's Tisher?" Marek asked. Good question. The coroner should be on the scene.

Larson scowled. "Came, declared dead, got the heck out."

Tish had a lead foot, the weightiest thing in his tall, spindly body. She wasn't sure how many tickets he'd gotten—or how many had been forgiven—for speeding to the aid of the bereaved, as he was a mortician as well as the county coroner. "Cause of death?"

Larson's scowl grew. "Left us to find that out. Said he'll be back for transport."

That would be to the morgue in Sioux Falls for autopsy. Yet it had been hours since the body was discovered. She tugged on her ear, sure she'd misheard. "You haven't pulled out the body yet?"

"Waiting for you." His nose wrinkled. "Jessica!"

From inside the DCI van, a young woman with a ridged scar along one cheekbone emerged, holding a laptop. "What's your hurry?" Gone were the days when the DCI trainee walked in awe of her boss. Then she caught sight of Karen. "Oh, hi, Sheriff. How was Albuquerque?"

Karen poked her tongue into her cheek. "Getting pulled into a homicide case sort of derailed the vacation part of the program. Nice people, though, and beautiful skies."

A faint line crossed the young woman's untouched brow. "But you're glad to be home?"

"Not at the moment." Karen contemplated the ancient vault toilets that looked unchanged from her childhood memories. A place she'd never visited twice, even if she'd had to dig a pit in the woods with her hands and wipe with leaves. "Really, Larson, waiting for us wasn't necessary—or your usual MO. How do you even know it's foul play?"

Marek gave her a sidelong glance, and Jessica gave a muffled laugh before Karen's brain caught up with her mouth.

Foul. "Ha ha."

"Foul, any way you look at it." Larson's mouth twitched before turning down. "Time of reckoning."

With a groan, Jessica ditched her laptop and handed out white protective suits. They had one in Marek's towering size—eight inches over Karen's six-foot-one—but only because they'd special-ordered them. That the suits came with masks—something she'd always considered overkill—was now a blessing.

When Karen took her turn at the crime scene, she doubted she would have survived more than a few seconds if she hadn't had a barrier against the stench.

"What I want to know," Karen said as she stumbled away from the overwhelming smell of crap and death, "is how the hell someone got him in there. I mean, really, it's a small hole, right? And he's not a small man."

A shaky voice said from behind, "The cover is hinged. You can lift it."

Karen turned to the woman with a blanket around her thin, quaking shoulders. "You were the one who found him?"

"Yes, I'm Lori Jansen. I clean the johns."

Jansen was less common than Jensen and far more uncommon than Johnson in Eda County, but Karen couldn't place the woman. She looked to be in her twenties, but washed out, as if those years had put her on spin dry. Her legs looked longer than her stubbier body, as if she'd been stunted just at her growth spurt. "I went to school with a Jimmy Jansen from Dutch Corners," Karen said. "Is he a relation?"

Rather than putting the witness at ease, as Karen intended, the question made Lori tense. "I've got no relations." The phone that was clutched tightly in her hand vibrated. She didn't take the call, but if possible, she looked paler. "I've got to get to work. My boss called me five times already."

The RVer hovering behind Lori stepped forward, his lips tightened. "Threatened to fire her. Heard him loud and clear. Asshole."

"I'll try to make this as quick as possible, Ms. Jansen."

"Lori."

"All right, Lori." And taking her statement also meant Karen could delay pulling out the body. "You don't have to tell me what you saw. I saw it for myself, but can you tell me what time it was when you found the body?"

"Well, I'm not sure exactly. I mean, it was just after dawn. I always get the johns done first thing before I go off to my next job."

Next? How many did this poor woman have? Not that it was unusual for rural Dakotans to have more than one job, usually farming and something to bring in health insurance. That was often a couple's split, though, and given Lori's lack of a wedding ring, Karen guessed that Lori had no one. Marek had two jobs, detective and carpenter. She assumed he would continue with the latter considering what the county paid him. Her own was a bottom-feeder salary, and his was a mere pittance compared to that. But the job came with benefits, not all of them monetary. To be honest, she'd expected him to be as antsy as she was on the way back, wondering if he was going in the wrong direction by returning to their hometown. But he'd accepted his daughter's verdict: Reunion was home now.

The RVer tapped a watch that sported more knobs than a cockpit dash. "It was seven eleven. I was sitting right here when Lori went in there. Wondered what she was doing going into the men's side, I admit, until she lifted the bucket with the cleaning supplies. Heard her scream a minute later, and she nearly ran me over when she rushed out."

Lori hunched into the blanket. "I'm sorry."

"No, I am. For everybody." He glanced at the toilets and swallowed. "That's one nasty way to end. I don't know who that man was, but somebody really thought he was... well, crap." He looked back and held out his hand. "I'm Pat Donahue, by the way. Rover of the forgotten highways and byways of America. Former San Diego firefighter. I've been on the road for four years, two months, and five days."

"When did you get in?" Karen asked after nearly having her hand crushed. Donahue was exactly the sort of witness she loved.

"Last night. I was headed for the Palisades near Sioux Falls but decided I'd had enough. I'm always in bed by ten. It was nine-twenty-seven when I pulled into this spot. The campsites down the road were full, and all I needed was a place to park, and I like the peace and quiet."

"Did you use the facilities?" Marek asked, startling them all. Karen never figured out how a giant of a man like Marek could disappear into the woodwork—or the air, given the clearing—and be forgotten, but he did.

Donahue scuffed a shoe on the asphalt and shook his head. "I've got a composting toilet in my rig. Most of these old one-holers are crappy, dirty as hell, and stink to..." He caught sight of Lori's fallen face and cleared his throat. "Oh, sorry... I didn't mean..."

"It *is* crappy," Lori said. "But I clean it as best I can. They keep saying they're going to replace it with a new one like they've got down at the campground, but—" Her phone vibrated again. "Sorry. I gotta take this."

She winced as a man's voice bellowed out loud enough for Karen to hear, too.

"You're fired! Do you hear me? I ain't takin' no more excuses. I turned on the radio, and Nails Nelson ain't talkin' about no dead body in the park, so you're just full of it. I don't hold with bald-face liars."

Nails Nelson ran a low-power FM station and was Eda County's only version of a news reporter. If Lori had been pale before, she now looked whiter than the corpse in the john, and she seemed ready to keel over. Donahue grabbed her shoulders, and Karen snatched up the phone.

"You're talking to Sheriff Mehaffey," she said over the man's blistering tirade. "I suggest you calm down. Your employee was a witness to a serious crime. She had no choice but to stay on the scene until I arrived. Which I just have."

A short pause followed. "Who the hell are you? One of her dead-end friends?"

Karen gritted her teeth and reminded herself that she couldn't arrest the man for being an asshole, especially over the phone. "I told you who I am. Karen Okerlund Mehaffey. If you want to verify that I am on the scene of a crime at Grove Park, I suggest you call the Eda County Sheriff's Office, not Nails Nelson."

"Don't think I won't." He hung up.

She could only hope that he wouldn't think to call Nails Nelson directly with the scoop. Karen held out the phone for Lori. "Is your boss always that hot under the collar?"

Lori took the phone gingerly, as if it were a grenade. "He hates working the counter at the gas station. Makes him crazy. I think he hates people, period. Can I go now? I need that job real bad."

"Better if you get another one," Donahue said. "No cause to treat you that way."

Marek saved the woman from having to come up with something to say to that, as it was clear that she couldn't comprehend the concept of just getting another. "Notice anything odd or out of place, other than the body, Lori?"

"I don't think so... wait, I didn't see the toilet rolls. I always put out three. But that happens sometimes. Not from people using the toilet so much, as taking the rolls."

Because it was public property, people considered the rolls free game, forget that it left your neighbors with their butts hanging in the wind.

Marek adjusted the string of the mask around his neck so it didn't dig in. "Have you ever met Bob Bunting before?"

Lori looked at her feet and shook her head.

But before Karen could press, Donahue said, "Like Baby Bunting?"

"You knew him?"

"Hardly. Never been here before—came from the Black Hills most recently. Just thought of the lullaby my mother used to sing to me. 'Bye, baby Bunting, Daddy's gone a-hunting. Gone to get a rabbit skin, to wrap the baby Bunting in.'"

Karen refused to be distracted from her prey. "You knew him," she said to Lori. "Bunting."

"No, I... that is... are you saying that's him?" Shock rounded her face. "In the john?"

"Yes."

If she knew him, she didn't appear to have recognized him. Not too surprising, given the low light and his distorted features.

Lori's phone vibrated again. "I gotta go. I don't got enough hours as it is."

"Wait. How can I get ahold of you?"

Lori hesitated. "You can get me on my cell." And she spouted off her number, shed the blanket, thanked Donahue, and rushed down the worn path. For the first time, Karen wondered why Lori hadn't driven up. Then again, the park wasn't all that big, and Lori hadn't expected to be delayed by finding a body.

Or had she?

Turning, Karen looked at Marek. One of the perks of office was surely that she got to call the shots. Even if, technically, Marek worked for the county commissioners, to forestall charges of nepotism in the line of command.

She smiled winningly up at him. "You're our designated dump-ster diver."

CHAPTER 3

THE LAST TIME MAREK HAD come to Grove Park, as a senior in high school, it had been with his terminally ill mother. He wished, for her sake, that it had been her last stop. Dying weeks later in a dim windowless room in a Sioux Falls hospital, despite Marek's pleas to the staff to let him move his mother into one with natural light, had been a brutal introduction into the intransigence of bureaucracies.

That morning long ago in the park, Janina Marek Okerlund been so impossibly light as Marek had carried her to the overlook, where spring had sprung with delicate green fronds on the trees and scented the air with wild plums, in a bittersweet reminder that life went on. Her hometown of Valeska—a town of hardscrabble Czechs with few opportunities for a woman of her education and ambitions—was just a smudge on the endless horizon that spread out below.

Her fingers had twitched in his, as if for one of the cigarettes that she'd given up too late, as cancer ate at her lungs, at her every breath.

She'd told him, "It was right here in Grove Park that I really believed I could be whatever I chose to be. I was just a kid then. I'd never been to any park, ever. People like us Mareks, poor as dirt and living on the largesse of grudging family, didn't go to parks. It didn't even occur to us. Life wasn't for frivolity. Mom worked her fingers into gnarled stumps to keep us fed and clothed—when she could keep Dad from drinking her seamstress earnings down the drain."

Though Marek had known about his mother's rough childhood, she'd rarely talked about it when he was growing up. He'd learned more from his father, Sheriff Leif Okerlund, who in his official capacity had occasionally yanked the much younger Janina and her brother, Jim, out of the family home, away from their father's heavy hand. Janina had grown up idolizing the sheriff and had eventually married him after his first wife died, which had caused unending friction between Leif and his eldest son, Arne, who was Karen's father.

While Marek had cradled his mother against him as they sat at the overlook that day, she'd continued speaking when air settled into her damaged lungs. "Your father brought us up here, me and Jim, after our dad was taken to prison that first time. He said, 'Don't make his name your destiny. Make the name your own. You'll find people along the way who'll help you. Do well in school or in an honest trade, and the sky's the limit.' And we both looked out, at all that sky, and we believed, even though life had told us not to. Choices. I made mine that day, to make Sheriff Leif Okerlund proud."

And for the most part, she had. That she'd taken a long time to accept that her only son was flawed in the one area she held supreme—the life of the mind—had been one of the few bones of contention between his parents. But perhaps the yin and yang, the push of his mother's expectations and the pull of his father's compassion, had made him what he was today.

"Marek?"

He blinked himself back to the present, at Karen's half-amused, half-desperate expression, and looked down at his feet. "I'm not going down there in these boots." The battered Blunnies he'd bought in Australia in his twenties had carried him through many, many hard years. His late wife had even had them resoled for him as a birthday gift. That the short leather boots with elastic-gore sides weren't the norm for the Dakotas was just his little bid to stand apart—other than his height.

"You need some shitkickers," Karen mused.

Marek smiled faintly. Shitkickers in Australia were people who did menial work. In South Dakota, they were heavy boots... or the farmers who wore them. All of the above would work. And did. But he didn't want to work, not when it came to shit.

"I still have a job offer on ice in Albuquerque," he reminded her.

Her fjord-blue eyes narrowed. "Thin ice."

"How 'bout some Wellies?" Donahue interrupted from behind them, holding a pair of heavy-duty rubber boots, probably cadged from his firefighting career.

Marek looked at the man's feet and relaxed. "Too small for me."

"Prove it," Karen countered.

Feeling like O. J. Simpson presented with the infamous glove, Marek toed off his Blunnies and couldn't get his feet even halfway down Donahue's boots. So, with vast reluctance, the rest took turns trying them on.

"Sorta like Cinderella and the glass slipper," Donahue said with a grin as he watched the proceedings from behind the crime scene tape. "Glad I'm out of the running."

When the perfect fit was found, Marek slapped the winner on the back. "Congrats. You get to go to the ball."

Larson glared down at the black boots that fit him as if molded onto his legs.

With a flourish, Karen bowed. "May I have this dance?"

"Only if you lead. Otherwise, shove it."

When she just laughed, he stomped toward the toilets, looking like the Michelin Man with puffs of white suit bulging between tie-downs so no crap got in.

It was soon obvious that none of them was going to come out of the deal smelling like roses, though, after Larson lifted the large plywood hinged cover. The crime scene below, such as it was, was a killer.

Larson balked at the sticking point until Karen needled him. "Your scene, Larson. We amateurs wouldn't want to disturb it."

With a litany of curses, Larson allowed Marek to lower him down into the slime. He sank to his shoulders, just as Bunting had.

"Look for a weapon," Karen suggested.

"Crap hasn't gone to my head." He gave her a basilisk stare that shut her up. But after rooting around, he shook his head. "Nothing here but shit and the body."

That left them with the difficulty of removing a three-hundred-pound deadweight in tight quarters. In the end, it took heavy ropes, the firefighter's ingenuity, and all of Marek's strength to raise the heavy body. Then the rest of them had to muscle the body onto a tarp outside.

A blanket to wrap the Baby Bunting in.

Gingerly, Larson retrieved a phone and a pair of keys from Bunting's pockets. The first, he placed in an evidence bag to take back to DCI, the second, he separated. The house key, he handed to Karen. The car key, he handed to the tow truck operator who'd come to take the SUV to Sioux Falls for processing.

Looking like a doctor who'd strayed into a mud-wrestling contest on a feedlot, Larson pointed to Jessica then to Bunting's mouth. "Bag that fecal material." Maybe it made him feel that he got some of his own back as his trainee gagged. Sitting as far away as she could, she scooped up Bunting's last meal into an evidence bag.

"Interesting dental implant," Donohue observed, finding yet another euphemism for the crap stuck in Bunting's no-longer pearly whites. "Looks like it was done on purpose."

Despite what they'd all just been through, Marek's stomach churned, and his mind did the same as he finally caught up. "You're thinking the killer used his own... excrement?"

"Hey, no cause of death determined yet," Karen said, having learned her lesson well from Larson not to make assumptions. "He might've died over a Big Whopper then got stuffed in there later."

Larson gave her a sour look as he threw his heavily stained

protective suit into the nearby dumpster. "Got a good look. Homicide."

Silence descended on the clearing. Even the birds held their songs.

Larson dragged off each glove slowly, deliberately.

"Well?" Karen demanded. "Don't be a... turd."

Not until he'd disposed of the gloves and washed his hands at the water pump did the DCI agent finally look up again, grey eyes bleak. "Stabbed in the back."

CHAPTER 4

WHILE KAREN HAD SEEN SOME creative carvers in her short time in office, they'd all done their damage face-to-face. The idea of attacking a man from behind was deeply disturbing, even when it came to Baby Bunting. Who would kill in such a way? An enemy, no doubt. But it wasn't unheard of even for a so-called friend to turn treacherous. She stripped off her slimy gloves much more quickly than Larson had. "Et tu, Brute?"

The agent gave her an arch look that told her he wasn't going to forgive her anytime soon for her own treachery in making him go down into the slime. "Facts, my business," Larson told her. "Motive, yours."

Still in his protective suit, Marek looked like the Abominable Snowman with a toothache, waiting his turn for an extraction. "Single blow?"

"Looked to be," Larson hedged. "Autopsy to determine."

Without something to dry her hands on after washing under the pump, Karen flicked beads of water from her fingers onto the concrete. The wet spots evaporated in the sunlight. She wished she could remove the case as easily. Bunting was proving to be as much trouble dead as alive.

When she saw Jessica shifting from side to side like a kid trying not to pee, Karen moved aside. "You need to go? You can use the women's. Or take it in the woods—or the campground."

"I'm good. Just want to get this crap off me. Never been to a scene as bad as this. I thought dumpsters were the worst. All that stinking garbage. But this, it takes the cake." She blanched in mid-peel, her suit at her midriff. "I don't think I'll want to eat or do anything else until I've taken a proper shower."

"I'm with you there, sister." Karen began to pace the short sidewalk. "A single blow. What does that tell us? That it's a man? Have to be pretty strong, I'd think, to get through that bulk."

Marek shook his head. "All depends on the angle, the sharpness of the knife, the depth of the wound. Doesn't always take that much, so long as you hit the right spot."

"Lucky break or—" Her *Adam-12* ringtone interrupted her. As a former dispatcher, she'd thought it appropriate, but maybe the time had come to change it. Along with her phone number, she wished, as she looked at the caller's name.

"Nails," Marek deduced, no doubt from the way she'd involuntarily extended her arm. She'd rather be holding a rattlesnake than her phone.

Larson looked up from stowing evidence bags. "Better take it."

She made a face but complied. "Mr. Nelson, to what do I owe the honor of your call?"

The low-power FM radio operator was Eda County's only claim to a news channel. YRUN, his ironic call name for a legless Vietnam vet, operated out of the top floor of the converted Carnegie library, where Nails lived and rarely left. She'd saved his life once, but his thanks had been to stab her in the back. He'd pushed her to reveal her biological daughter's identity on the air, nearly igniting Marek's notoriously slow-burn temper. Her loss to Bunting, at least initially, had largely been Nails's doing, no matter how much the bigwig news reporter from the Twin Cities had contributed.

Well, that and a killer who'd masterfully manipulated both of them.

"Knock off the sarcasm, Sheriff. I apologized. On air. And

given how many times I ran that broadcast, that means I apologized over and over again. Congrats on the recount, by the way. And I mean that, swear to God, and said so in this morning's broadcast. You're the best man... woman... for the job. Bunting was a bad egg. But he didn't deserve to get stuffed into a john."

Karen quickened her pace. How had that gotten out? If she had to guess, Lori's boss had browbeaten it out of his errant employee and then called Nails. "No, he didn't."

"Murder?"

Nails knew the song and dance, so why ask? Because he could, apparently. "The autopsy hasn't been performed yet. We only just got the body out. Tish hasn't—" The squeal of tires on asphalt interrupted her. "Has just arrived to transport the body to Sioux Falls."

"Not to put your back up again, Sheriff, but if it is murder, aren't you the prime suspect?"

Because Karen wanted to nip that speculation in the bud, she gave Nails a complete rundown of her whereabouts, that of her men, and even of her father the previous night. If the killer had been planning to pin the death on any of them, they were out of luck.

"Good thing you won the recount," Nails finally said. "From what I hear, the parties nearly came to blows at the recount. In fact, I saw some pushy-shovey spill out on the courthouse steps."

Turnabout was fair play for once. She might as well use Nails as a source. Too bad he wasn't in the running for a suspect, as she wasn't the only one Bunting had targeted. But from Nails's vantage point kitty-corner from the courthouse, he might give them something. "You were following the recount?"

"Sure. It was news. Had some skin in the game, too. I wasn't looking forward to trying to get any straight answers out of Sheriff Bunting. You might play the evasion game when it suits you, but it's usually for the right reasons. Had to wait into the wee hours for the result. Finally broke up around one in the morning. Talked to Janet Dahl and got the morning broadcast ready to roll. Why?"

The register of deeds, standing in for the ailing county auditor, was high on her list of people to talk to once she'd wrapped up at the park. Karen turned her back on the sight of Marek and a wrinkle-nosed Tish wrestling the tarped body into the back of the extended-cab pickup that served as a hearse with its shell and crepe-curtained windows. "I need information, and I figure you owe me. Fill me in."

He paused. "Not like I was in the room, Sheriff. Didn't hear anything, just saw."

"But you saw who came and went?" she pressed, getting a taste of being on the other end of the evasion game.

"Sure. By the time I wheeled myself over to the window, I saw Bunting burst out of the courthouse, slapping the doors back so hard, it's a wonder they didn't fall off their hinges. One of his supporters trailed after him, nipping at his heels and grabbing at his arm, and he shoved her aside."

"What did she look like?"

"An older woman with long gray-streaked brown hair, bulky, wearing an oversized Packers sweatshirt. She followed him into the street. Bunting turned around, lifted a finger—and it wasn't the ring finger—and said something that made her stop in her tracks. She stayed there until a car honked at her. Then she lifted her own finger before she stalked over to an old beater of a truck. Red. Ford, I think."

It was Karen's lucky day for observant witnesses. Maybe they'd have this solved before the day's end, and she'd have some time to recover from the whiplash of the last twenty-four hours. "What about Bunting?"

"He stomped over to a big black SUV that he'd parked in a handicapped spot near the band shell. New sucker with chrome grills. He stopped when he saw somebody already sitting in the passenger side. I think he's going to blow, but instead, he lights up like it's Christmas. He rounds over to the driver's side with a little spring in his step, then he walks right into the fist of some big bruiser who'd been sitting on the curb. Wide face, dark hair and brows. Maybe thirty. Czech, I'd guess. One of your detective's relatives, maybe?"

Wouldn't that be swell. But it couldn't be a Marek. None were left in the county after Marek's uncle died in a car wreck. Generally speaking, Dakotans didn't lead with their fists. In a largely rural area, you needed to count on your neighbors—not take them down for the count. "Did Bunting go down?"

And why was she relishing the answer?

"That he did, Sheriff. And I can't say that didn't give me a tingle. The guy stood over him, said his piece, and then crooks his finger at the SUV. A young woman gets out of the passenger side. And before you ask, she's wearing a red-and-black-checked flannel shirt and black stockings or leggings or whatever they call them. Maybe twenty, if that. Same coloring as the man, but far prettier. I'd say sister and big brother, most likely, but could be kissin' cousins. They left in a vintage white Dodge Ram with purple and yellow stripes on the bed. Bruiser driving."

Probably a Minnesota Vikings football fan with those colors. Only surprising thing was that the Packers and Vikings fans hadn't been going at each other during the recount. "And Bunting?"

"He didn't get up until after they left. He limped into the SUV and took off in a cloud of exhaust. Probably left rubber on the road." He waited for several long seconds. "Am I forgiven yet?"

Karen pursed her lips at his wheedling tone. "We'll see how it pans out. I'd appreciate it if you kept the details to yourself until I can check them out. I don't want to tip anybody's hand."

"You know, I'm not an idiot." When she remained silent, he backtracked. "Well, okay, so I got snookered by Bunting, just like the bigwigs. But I learned my lesson. Keep it clean, keep it straight, and keep it going. That's my new motto. Just like an Okerlund."

Good thing he couldn't see her smile, because she wasn't ready to forgive him. Yet. "I'll let you know if we need a formal statement," Karen told him and rang off, just in time to see another vehicle barrel up the drive to the overlook. Some idiot had run the barricade, right into the arms of the law, who were all too ready and eager to arrest him for obstruction of justice. Then she saw the side of the Jeep Cherokee as it stopped. A big magnetized sign read PARK MANAGER.

Karen pocketed her phone and started toward the stocky man who got out, but he'd already headed for the closest man available.

"Sheriff Mehaffey?" The man wrinkled his nose at Marek. "I want a word with you."

Typical. Man's work. Women were a poor second.

CHAPTER 5

MAREK WONDERED IF THE STENCH, seeped deep into his pores, would linger forever. He'd dealt with waterlogged bloaters before, the worst of the worst, but never anything like the rank sliminess of a body in an outhouse.

But Marek knew that the park manager had just stepped in worse. Something must have alerted the man to that fact, because he faltered on the blacktop then stopped on the sidewalk, confusion plain on his square, sun-spotted face.

"I'm Detective Okerlund," Marek informed the doomed man as Karen closed in. "You'll want to—"

"Speak to me." Karen planted herself in front of the shorter man, edging into his space, guarding the scene like the basketball hoops she'd once defended. "*I* am Sheriff Mehaffey." She flashed her badge, dribbling a bit of New Mexico sand into the ever-present Dakota wind. "How did you get through the barricade?"

Obviously taken aback by both the biting question and the woman who'd issued it—granted that Karen looked like she'd just come off a soup-kitchen line—the man fumbled. "Uh... Jack. That is, Jack Biester. I'm sorry. I got the okay to come up from a deputy." He tried a smile, lightening his intent predator-on-the-hunt look. "Bald guy, big mustache? He said you'd want to talk to me." His brow furrowed as he looked past her at the cordoned-off toilets. "Uh... that's where the body was?"

Marek never quite got that, asking for the obvious, but his

old partner had done it all the time. That need to verbalize wasn't a trait native to Dakotans, except maybe Karen.

"Where were you last night? This morning?" Karen demanded.

Biester continued off-kilter. "The info was posted on my door."

Marek recalled that the park had a house for the park manager, hidden away from the road past the entrance. He'd always thought it was a good gig.

"I haven't been to your door," Karen told him. "I drove straight from the airport to the scene."

"Oh. Well, I just got here myself. I got a call from Harold Dahl, saying I'd better wrap things up in Sioux Falls and get back ASAP."

Marek could see the steam start to pour out of Karen's ears, and to save them all the aggravation, he spoke up. "Mr. Biester, what did you need to wrap up?"

"Oh, Sorry. I seem to be slow today. It's just the shock. Nothing like this has ever happened to me, and before I took this retirement gig, I was a park ranger all across the US in some of the biggest parks. I saw a lot of bad behavior, mostly from two-legged animals, and more than a few deaths—mostly amateur hikers who thought they could beat Mother Nature at her own game."

"Mr. Biester," Karen said through clenched teeth, "please answer the question."

Biester blew out a breath, nodded, and tried again. "I was at the Game, Fish, and Parks headquarters in Sioux Falls for a stakeholder meeting on converting Grove Park to a state park. I've been trying to make that happen ever since I took the job here three years ago. The meeting started yesterday afternoon and ended at noon today. Well, there were more sessions planned, but I left that in the hands of the head of the Friends of Grove Park."

"But you were here last night?" Marek asked. He couldn't see Dahl paying for a night in a hotel when it was less than an hour's drive away.

"No, I stayed at the Hilton Garden Inn. Paid out of my own pocket." The wry tone told Marek that their minds were tracking the line of thought. "There were evening sessions for the public to attend and lots of informal discussions after that. Very productive and positive. I think we've just about locked it in once we take care of the homeless issue. We've already made upgrades in the campground, and with state funding, we can make it even better." He glanced at the toilets then back at Karen. "Replacing those atrocities is first on my list. They're what knock down our ratings online, big time."

"I can get behind that." Karen finally relaxed. "What homeless issue? Do we have some survivalist types staying here?"

His jaw tightened. "Ask your Deputy Van Eck. I've had him out here often enough. Not that he ever did anything."

A good lob over Karen's head. "I haven't seen any reports on my desk from my reserve overnight deputy," she replied stiffly. "And if you had an issue with his performance, you should have contacted me."

"I did. Twice. Talked to someone called Josephine. Once you were working that media mogul case, and I was told to try again later when things calmed down. Seems we weren't high on the priority list. Then this past week, I contacted your office again and was told you were out all week. On vacation. So I talked to the sheriff-elect instead. We've agreed to work together to make sure that the riffraff don't take over the park and destroy our chance at state sponsorship."

Marek shared a sidelong glance with Karen. Biester didn't appear to be up on the latest.

"Just what do you know about what happened here?" she finally asked the park manager.

"Almost nothing other than that someone was killed at the park. Dahl said even that much had to be kept in the strictest confidence. That won't do our reputation any good, but we'll recover, so long as you catch the killer. I'll bet your man's from the trailer park. I wish to God that the county had condemned or bought that adjoining land years ago when they had the chance."

So much for the tranquil effect of Mother Nature.

"That would be Ted Jorgenson's trailer park?" Karen asked, picking up the thread.

"'Park' is a misnomer." Biester crossed his arms. "And it's no longer Ted's. He was pretty good about kicking out the really disruptive residents. And he almost single-handedly kept this place going before I got here. Established the Friends of Grove Park. Good man. He'll be missed."

Marek had been to the trailer park on a few calls in the handful of years he'd been back in Eda County. While he'd never use the term "trailer trash," not given his own roots, when people who had little money—for a myriad of reasons—were put together like that, it was a recipe for crime. But most people there worked hard and kept their noses clean. He'd guess that Lori was one of them.

"What happened to Ted?" Karen asked, her defensiveness gone. "I heard a while back he was in the hospital, but nothing since then. I assumed he was recovering."

"Had a massive stroke three months ago and never came out of it. No funeral. You knew him?"

"Most everyone did," she told him, stuffing hands in the frayed back pockets of her jeans. "He donated to charities, supported the local businesses and sports teams, and always had a smile for a kid, along with some Tootsie rolls. Too bad he never married."

"Doubly so," Biester said, finally on the same team as Karen. "His heir isn't any of those things." He frowned at her. "You haven't told me who died."

From Nails's mouth to the media's ear. Not much point in keeping it under wraps.

Obviously coming to the same conclusion, Karen told Biester, "Our body in the john was Bob Bunting."

"Damn. Really?"

When Marek confirmed, the park manager looked abruptly

drained, as if Bunting's death had tripped a circuit breaker. "So much for getting state park status."

Bunting's death was sensational, but in Marek's experience, that acted more as a lure, unless there was a random serial killer on the loose. "You might be surprised."

"Maybe. Maybe not." Biester ran a hand through his gnarled thicket of chestnut hair. "I hope you're going to let the campers go soon. When I was talking to your deputy, several of them came over, demanding to be let go. I said I'd do what I could."

Marek scratched at the beard he hadn't had time to reduce back to a goatee. "Do you keep a list of the campers?"

"No, it's a self-pay dropbox at the entrance. Honor system."

Marek had seen the dropbox next to a bulletin board but hadn't realized it included the campsites. He wasn't sure how many day visitors honored the system, and he guessed a killer probably wouldn't, though it depended on whether it was a crime of passion. He knew that teenagers often drove up to the overlook to... well, not look at anything but their chosen significant other.

Karen looked more resigned than anything. She must've known or suspected as much. "We'll need you to open the dropbox with one of my deputies present to get names and addresses."

Biester's eyes narrowed. "Are you implying that I would hold some names back?"

"It's chain of custody," she said evenly. "I'm sure, even here, you know how bureaucracies work."

That got a commiserating nod. "Sure. I had my fill of it with the feds. I thought this place, just a county park without all the hassle, would be different."

Army-trained, Karen stood a bit taller. "You put people together, you get rules."

"And rule breakers. Different in the wild. The only rule is to survive. Poor Bunting." The park manager ran his hands down his face and then walked back to his truck.

Biester drove back down the hill as Karen and Marek

followed, close on his bumper. And all the while, Marek felt an itch between his shoulder blades that, on some primal level, told him he was being watched by something out there in the wild. But was it animal or human?

Perhaps both.

CHAPTER 6

ALL KAREN HAD WANTED TO do as a kid was travel far, to mountains, to deserts, to seas... anything but the flat, boring plains in a small town hemmed in by people who seemed far too content with their lot. But one thing she'd never imagined was traveling the country on wheels. Not when the jets that crisscrossed the huge Dakota skies with trails of promise could take her so much farther.

Grove Park campground was full, just as Donahue had said, and every slot held a different home on wheels. Car campers had set up tents: a pup tent that must require the college-student-aged owners to spoon like cloves of garlic and a family rambler that billowed in the wind. The homes on wheels ranged from a DIY truck camper all the way to a top-of-the-line luxury coach.

Predictably, the owners of the last one confronted Karen and Marek, walking right past Kurt Bechtold's raised hand. Her senior deputy's tan-and-brown uniform looked less than spick-and-span, his usually pressed-to-a-killing-edge trousers rumpled and dirty. His hatchet face tightened as he moved forward to intercept the couple.

Karen opened her mouth to tell him she would deal with them herself, when a flick of movement had her yelling, "Duck, Kurt!"

Though in his sixties, Kurt was spry, and he didn't question; he just dropped.

Jumping as high as she could, Karen snagged the offending flier in restricted air space. She studied her catch. No cheap plastic doohickey made in a sweatshop overseas, the seriously rad Frisbee was one heck of a toy.

A red-haired boy of about ten, accompanied by an even-redder-faced man, hurried toward them. Kurt rose to his feet, dusting off his trousers, but the knees looked to have sustained permanent damage. Better wrecked trousers than a decapitated head. The Frisbee looked lethal.

"What a catch, lady!" the boy hooted as he reached her. "You play? I'd give you game."

The red-faced man huffed his way in front of her. "I'm so sorry about this, Miss... Ms.... um... Officer?" The way he pronounced "about" as "a-boot" gave him away as Canadian. "It got away from me."

The boy blew a raspberry. "Dad can't throw worth shi—"

"Hugh Macklin McGurdy, don't you dare say that word," said the woman trailing behind, her voice carrying. Maybe that was an ability that came with mother's milk. As always, the thought of what she'd missed in giving up her daughter, by reluctant choice but precipitated by none other than Bob Bunting, tugged at Karen's heart.

"Here's your Frisbee." Karen handed over the offending flier.

"It isn't a Frisbee," he told her solemnly. "It's a flying disc."

She kept her mouth straight—with effort. "Of course. Sorry."

"You need a ref," someone said from the crowd.

But he shook his head. "There's no refs in Ultimate."

"Sounds like it could get out of hand."

Again, the solemn shake of the head. "No, the players ref themselves. Fair-play rules."

Karen wished more people would do that, but in her world, she was the ref when it failed. As she turned, Kurt's rather harried expression finally sank in to her consciousness. He'd been riding herd on this crowd since dawn. Maybe she should have put Walrus at the campground instead, but she'd wanted Kurt's meticulous attention to detail in the statements.

Hopefully, he wouldn't quit on the spot as soon as she released the tourists to wherever their travels led next.

A florid man in a Hawaiian shirt stepped up, accompanied by a thin woman with cheekbones as sharp as her nose. Despite the rustic setting, she wore silver-and-gold jewelry draped over a white twinset.

"High time you people got here." The man nodded at Marek, his jowls quivering like a bulldog's. "Sheriff Mehaffey, you've kept us waiting far too long. Not to mention, you should arrest that kid as a danger to person and property. I told the park manager that I didn't pay good money to have dings put in my rig."

Tired of being taken as an underling to Marek, Karen took a pace forward to look down at Mr. Florid from—she checked the license plate—Florida. Figured. "I am Sheriff Mehaffey. And I am investigating a suspicious death, not property damage. I appreciate that you've been delayed, and you will be allowed to leave shortly, but I need to assess the situation before I do."

Hugh's mother intervened, putting her arms around her boy. "That poorly aimed throw came from my clumsy husband, not my son," she said, looking straight into Florid's face. "And you couldn't put a ding in that tank of yours with a sledgehammer."

Looking torn between arguing the point and what was obviously a point of pride, Florid appeared stymied. Instead, he turned on Karen. "We gave our statements. We saw nothing, heard nothing, know nothing. We're from Sarasota, on our way to Seattle."

From her perfectly coiffured hair, his wife picked a piece of browned leaf and dropped it to the ground with the distaste usually reserved for spiders or bird poop. "For our daughter's wedding. We can't be late. I planned out the route, and we had reservations made at a luxury resort in the Black Hills, but we had a wheel go flat after hitting a curb"—she glared at her husband, who also flattened—"and so got thrown off course and had to settle for this... unruly thicket on a hill that I won't dignify with the term 'park.' Further delays are unacceptable."

So, thought Karen, was murder. "Kurt, do you believe that we need to speak personally to any of these good people beyond their statements?"

Her deputy straightened from where he was trying to repair the damage to his trousers—and his dignity. "Yes, three of them. The Farleys, Akio Miles, and Mary Redbird."

Karen raked the crowd that had gathered, respectfully back but still within earshot—though a few probably couldn't hear a train's whistle blown in their ear. None of the rest of the crowd had kids with them, which wasn't surprising, given that it was October. She'd guess the Canucks were homeschoolers. The day-trippers had fortunately been turned back at the barricade.

Once she let this pool of suspects go, most of them would be in the wind, even if Kurt had collected their contact information. If their killer was amongst them, they were screwed. Unless he or she—or they, God forbid—were among those staying.

Karen glanced around, looking for Marek, and found he'd stepped back into the woods and was taking photos of the crowd and their vehicles with his phone. A good idea. At least they'd have that as evidence, even if someone lied about their identity. Too bad she couldn't fingerprint them all, on the off chance one had a feces fetish. Wasn't smearing feces a kid-against-parent thing? Did Bunting have any kids? Something to find out.

Pocketing his phone, Marek walked back to her.

"Any reason to keep them any longer?" she asked him.

He took one last long look then shook his head. A cheer went up from the majority, but a few looked vaguely disappointed, as if a garage band had been substituted at the last minute for the headliner act they'd bought tickets for. If they were looking for drama from Dakotans, they'd come to the wrong state.

Mrs. Florid said, "About time, given we pay your salaries and that of the park manager, who wasn't even on the job when we pulled in. You can be sure I'll be writing to the state parks board or whatever you have in this godforsaken county to complain about this false detainment."

Karen winced as she thought of Jack Biester's hopes to get

state sponsorship. As for her own salary, she wasn't being paid by Florida taxpayers. She had a very hard time keeping her mouth shut instead of pointing that out. As a consequence, she got nothing out at all. But Marek saved the day.

"The park is run by the county, not the state," he informed the woman with the gravitas that came with his deep voice—and his deep well of patience. "If you'll wait, I can give you the contact information for the county commissioner so you can—"

But Mrs. Florid of Florida gave him her back. She frog-marched her husband into the RV. Thirty seconds later, they were gone, the huge rig farting its last insult into the crowd.

Mrs. McGurdy waved a hand... to swipe away the exhaust. "People like that are the bad apples in a good American pie. We've been on the road for five months now, and there's always one, it seems. It's small of me, but I hope that their daughter gets jilted at the altar. Save the young man a lifetime of regrets with his future in-laws. They've done nothing but complain since they pulled up last night and took over our spot."

That made Karen blink. "Yours?"

"Yes, we played nice and moved over for them, though they more or less demanded it, as our rig is just a Class C, not an A like theirs." Her hands on her hips, she surveyed her son and husband. "Well. It's been... interesting. I'll say that for this park, which by the way, is quite nice. Deputy Bechtold has been very clear that he can't say anything about what happened, but I'm dying to know. I mean, he asked us if we knew a man named Bob Bunting, who died at the overlook. I'm assuming it wasn't an accident, given everything?"

"The way his body was left at the scene wasn't an accident," Karen hedged. "But the autopsy has yet to be performed, and it would be premature of me to tell you more than that."

Mrs. McGurdy shivered. "Well. Always heard it was more violent in the States, but I guess I got lulled into complacency these last months. People have been so friendly." She blew out a breath. "Here I was concerned about pedophiles in this park, not killers."

As Kurt frowned, Karen decided the woman hadn't relayed that tidbit before. "Care to expand on that, Mrs. McGurdy?"

She flushed. "Oh, it's nothing, I'm sure. Just an overdeveloped sense of maternal paranoia."

Her son rolled his bright-blue eyes up like pinballs. "She freaked just because I told her that I saw some guy with a long beard and old camos in the woods with a boy a little older than me when I went to get one of Dad's bad throws. Probably just taking a piss... a leak," he corrected at his mother's glare. "We meet lots of people like that, with beards and old clothes and everything." He darted a look at his mother. "Grownups don't have to take showers or brush their teeth or wear new underwear everyday just 'cause. Being a kid sucks."

His mother blipped him. "Someday, some pretty young woman is going to thank me."

"Yuck," he said, rubbing his head, then catching her glare, he grinned up at her. "The only pretty young woman in my life is you, Mom."

Her lips twitched, then she laughed, as did her husband. They walked together, arm in arm, back to their Class C, whatever that was, as their son ran with his flying disc before them. Karen guessed that, in the scheme of things, they weren't rich—except in everything that mattered.

Moments later, the stubby RV with a prominent maple leaf logo on the side meandered past with a honk and a wave, returned by pretty much all of the crowd.

Karen wished she were going with them. Playing Frisbee—correction, flying discs—aced murder any day. Heck, she would even take Old Dan Sanderson's weekly call-ins to dispatch about flying saucers. Anything but having to delve into the life, and death, of Baby Bunting.

Alas, she was going a-hunting.

CHAPTER 7

M AREK HATED THE CLOSED-IN FEEL of the campground. Like many others raised on the Great Plains, he didn't feel cosseted and protected but penned in by the tree cover, which was made up of assorted pines, oaks, and maples. A windbreak, sure, a nice, orderly row of trees around the farmhouses and barns that dotted the ex-prairie, but a forest?

No thanks.

He doubted that Gus and Marlene Farley of Chelsea, Vermont, held the same opinion, though. They were sprawled contentedly in their lawn chairs in front of a vintage Airstream trailer pulled by an aging Dodge Ram. With his white hair plastered in swirls on one side, Gus had apparently seen no need to take a comb to it after rising.

"We don't see leaving yet, just because something bad happened," the seventyish man told them from his chair. "Probably safer now than it will be for some time to come. We spent last week over in Yankton near the dam, saw the aquarium and took the tour, but it was just too crowded. You've got some nice spots here, hidden away from the beaten path."

Gus nodded his swirled head toward the stand of maples bleeding from yellow to red in the light, unfiltered, as they towered over more humble offerings. "Nothing like our own neck of the woods for sheer brilliance—that little stand there multiplied by hundreds of thousands when we got good color—but that's why we travel, so when we go home again, we'll appreciate it all the more."

His wife, wearing a baggy sweatshirt that proclaimed *Don't Take No Gus From Me* and denim capris that showed a tangle of gnarled blue veins down to the orthopedic shoes, shifted in her lawn chair. "Leave off your jawing, Gus. These people are busy. Tell 'em what you heard last night."

"Right enough," he responded without apparent rancor. "Well, my old plumbing ain't working like it used to—went on the fritz about the same time I gave up my plumbing business, which is mighty odd, don't you think? But it was time. Sold our house to the kids, bought the Airstream on the cheap, and put our Social Security checks together. Never regretted it for a minute. We've been on the road for twenty years now last Independence Day, but—"

"Get to the point," his wife interrupted.

"She's the Yankee," he informed them in a faux whisper. "Met her when she taped up my bum in 'Nam."

"Shoulda taped your mouth shut while I was at it," she countered. "They don't want your life story. They want to catch a killer."

Marek shared a sidelong glance with Karen. At this point, they could stand here waiting for the rest of the story until they were covered with snow, which might be as soon as Halloween or as late as Christmas. You could never tell in the Dakotas.

"All right, I'm getting there. Got up in the night. Don't know when, like your man asked me. No reason to know. Went over to the restrooms over there." He waved at a squat concrete building, much newer and bigger than the one-holers at the overlook. "Nicer than our own and saves having to dump the tanks. Full moon, so no need for any light. I took care of my business then decided to take a stroll. Nice cool night. I could just see the tip of Orion's belt from the top of the road. The Hunter, that's what they call him."

"Mr. Farley..." Karen began.

"Now, just hold your horses, young lady. I've got a point to make. I used to hunt, long ago in the woods of Michigan, so I recognized the sound of an animal thrashing in a snare. Don't hold with that myself. Quick kills, that's what it should be. Wondering if I could find the poor thing in the dark, use the pocketknife I carry, when I hear some yelling down the road."

Marek visualized the park and felt a letdown. "Down? Not up?"

"Down toward the picnic shelter by the river," Gus confirmed. "Not up at the overlook. Anyway, my hearing, it ain't the best—"

His wife snorted. "Talked his own ears off."

"But I'm pretty sure it was a man and a woman. He's bellowing, she's screeching. My better half and I, we've got our set-tos on occasion, but mostly, we rub along okay. These two? Admit I don't know what they was carrying on about, but I hear a slap, and the woman yells, 'You always were a piece of shit.' Pardon the language. Show was over at that point. At least for me."

From the outset, this homicide had seemed personal. But Marek doubted a woman, no matter how strong, could heft a man who hit three hundred pounds, into the john. Though she could've had help, like from that bruiser Karen had told him about after her call with Nails.

Gus reached over and grasped his wife's hand. "Thanked my lucky stars I had a warm bed to go back to and went there pronto."

Though Marlene huffed, she turned her hand to grasp her husband's, weaving their fingers together. Karen thanked them for their time and headed to the vehicle that Kurt had pointed out as the temporary abode of their next witness. On the way, they nodded at Donahue, who'd apparently not been scared off, taking a spot left by those less sanguine about their chances of ending up as compost.

"You know," Karen said as they walked to the far end of the campground, "I had a message on my answering machine, before the election, from Bunting's ex-wife. Nadine Early. She promised plenty of dirt on Bunting."

Marek blinked. "What was the dirt?"

"I don't know. I didn't return the call." She nibbled on her bottom lip. "Believe me, I was tempted, but I didn't want the job enough to stoop to Bunting's level. I didn't want to stop looking at myself in the mirror in the morning."

How did Marek tell her how much he wildly admired her for that? He jingled the keys in his pocket. "Yeah, that'd be a hardship."

"Now you make me sound vain." She socked him on the arm then, looking down at her less-than-spiffy attire, readjusted her badge on her belt as they approached a van that looked more industrial than recreational.

Akio Miles bounded out to meet them, his black hair as sleek as his Lycra-encased body. He was probably the same age as Lori but looked far younger. "I've been waiting for hours, it seems." Unlike the Florids of Florida, the young man said that with eagerness, his white smile dazzling in his tea-colored face. "I wanted so bad to post to my blog, but I don't want to cause you all any trouble."

Karen pursed her lips. "And how would you do that?"

Some of his excitement dimmed. "You mean cause trouble or upload?"

Marek smiled reassuringly. "Both."

"Oh. Well." Akio pointed at a dish set up behind the van. "I've got satellite. I need it for my work."

"Which is?" Karen asked sharply.

Akio hunched his shoulders. "Blogging and coding."

"That's a relief," she said, relaxing. "I was afraid you were going to say reporter." But she poked her tongue in her cheek. "Isn't that taking a working vacation to the extreme?"

The faintest of laugh lines appeared. "I'm always on vacation. And never. I chucked my job in Los Angeles five years ago and never looked back. All I need is an internet connection. I don't need much to live on, staying at cheap parks and boondocking on BLM land for free. I can travel with good weather and choose million-dollar views for little to nothing. Can't beat that."

"Until you get married and have kids," Karen put in.

He just beamed at her. "I met a girl online last year who's got her own rig. She's a photographer and online instructor. We're meeting up again at Quartzite in Arizona at the end of the month. You gotta be nimble these days. We like working for ourselves, without a big mortgage, going into debt. If we have kids, we'll homeschool. You gotta think outside the box these days to survive."

At not quite forty, Marek felt old. He'd done some world traveling, thought of himself as cosmopolitan, despite his current residence, but he'd still gone the traditional route. Marriage, house, kid—and lost two of the three already. And right now, Marek wanted to get back to the kid, the new-old house, and the new girlfriend. "You met the man in the picture that Deputy Bechtold showed you?"

"Bunting? Yes." Akio's curious gaze rested on Karen. "You must be Sheriff Mehaffey. I read all the news articles while I waited. Talk about a motive for murder. He did a number on you."

She grimaced. "The internet needs to die."

"Oh, don't worry. You came off golden in the end. And I'm a travel blogger, not news. No worries. But I wasn't going to upload video until I got the okay."

Video? Out here? Marek contemplated the dish. "Isn't that expensive?"

Akio shrugged. "Not cheap, but technology makes my life possible—out in the boonies, connected to the world. Pretty weird contrast, isn't it. But when I was sitting in a cubicle in a high-rise in LA, I was going crazy. I hated the traffic, the long hours, all just to pay for a tiny studio apartment that barely allowed me to tread water on my student loans. Not to mention having zero time to do any hiking, biking, anything in the great outdoors. I stumbled over a blog one day of a guy with basically nothing, living in a van."

"Seems like an extreme solution," Karen said.

"Well, I did it in stages. At first, I moved out of my studio and into the van that I fixed up myself, but they're making it illegal to park on public roads or stay in your vehicle overnight, which is unreal. Homeless sleeping under their cars, in the trunks, instead of in the cars. Just because some are bad eggs doesn't make us all that way. It's like banning people living in houses because of drug flops. Target the drugs, the trash, whatever. Eventually, it became too stressful, trying to stay off the radar. So I decided to go on the road. People make fun of living in a van down by the river, but that's what I did. My parents, they thought I'd lost my mind, but then they saw how much happier I was. And then they met my girlfriend. Thumbs-up."

People on the road seemed in no hurry to get to the point. Too bad Marek couldn't do his job on the road. Maybe he'd get some decent time with his daughter. His girlfriend, such as she was, would probably be good with it—except they would need room for her pottery. Her kiln. Her own space.

Okay, maybe a rolling life wasn't in the cards.

Karen shifted on her feet. "Can you tell us what you saw, Mr. Miles?"

"Mr. Miles. Hah. That's my dad. Mr. Button-Down Businessman." He slicked his hands down his sides. "Yeah, I can tell you. It happens now and again, but it's always a shock. Almost everyone on the road is friendly. Of course, your Mr. Bunting was a local, not a traveler. But I didn't know that. I was up late, editing some code for a client. After one o'clock in the morning, I know that."

"I thought you were fleeing long hours," Karen commented, looking faintly amused.

Akio grinned at Karen. "Only because I played before I worked. And I'm a night owl. Another benefit. My hours don't have to conform to a time clock. It's usually quiet at night, and I get a lot done. Unlike cubicle life, when I'm done, I'm done. So I work less for more. No bennies, true, but I can handle that. I finally turned my dad around when I told him I was a classic entrepreneur. Taking risks. I don't want to be the guy who spends decades being hired, laid off, hired, laid off, then having nothing to show for it at the end of the day. I want to *live*. And I've seen more of this country than most ever will, and I'm just getting started."

When Marek cleared his throat, Akio blew out a breath. "Sorry. I hate seeing people taken for a ride in the back of the bus—when they can drive the whole freaking bus. That's what my blog's about, plus what I see on the road." He pulled on his ear. "Your Mr. Bunting? Thing is, the man's dead, and it just seems... wrong. To talk about him behind his back, so to speak. But okay. I finish off the coding gig, send it off, and I realize how long it's been since I took a... uh, used the restroom."

A popular place the previous night. Then again, why else would you wander out in the middle of the night, unless you were intent on foul play? "You met him there?" Marek asked.

"Yeah, I'm... doing my business... and he barges in like he owns the place, muttering something about meddlers under his breath, along with a lot of profanity. He's at half flag at the other urinal before he notices he's not alone. He's red-faced, not like he was embarrassed, but more like he'd just blown a gasket over something. And I got to be his target. 'What are you staring at, you stinking chink?' he said."

All trace of the beaming young man was gone. "You know the rant. Told me to go back home, that I was taking all the good jobs from real Americans, that anything I'd gotten in life, I'd gotten for free."

Nothing Marek was learning about Bunting made him any more sympathetic. The man was an ass, fore and aft.

"What happened then?" Karen asked, her hands fisting on her belt. "Did you kick his butt?"

Akio sighed. "You don't engage with those kind of people. No point. I played dumb and mumbled the few Chinese words I learned from my great-grandmother and got the heck out. I went straight back to my van, locked it from the inside, and crashed. And I didn't wake up until your deputy knocked on my door. When I saw the uniform, I'll admit I was scared—afraid I'd been reported for something trumped up like drugs, just to mess with me. Deport me, maybe, except I'm fifth-generation American. I'm glad you won the recount, Sheriff Mehaffey, because Bunting's the sort who'd use the badge for his own agenda."

Neither Marek nor Karen could say anything to refute that, because it was true.

"We appreciate your candor," Karen finally told him. "I'm sorry you had such an experience. I apologize, not on Bunting's behalf, because the word 'sorry' wasn't in his vocabulary, but on behalf of my office and my county. If you think of anything else—"

"Oh, I nearly forgot." Akio bounded back into the van then came back out holding something that looked like a mechanical mosquito, an insect that any red-blooded Dakotan was all too intimately familiar with. "I don't know if it's helpful, as it was before dark yesterday, but I've got feed. If you've got a hard drive available in your office, I can download it for you."

Marek had never seen one of the contraptions in the flesh— or in metal. "A drone?"

"Yeah, makes really good footage for my blogs. Had an outstanding sunset last night from the overlook. But I got good shots of the entire park. It's not all that big, you know? And that's not a knock. I like these little parks. Makes me feel a bit like I'm on the Corps of Discovery, showing people something they've never seen before."

Karen lifted an inquiring eyebrow at Marek.

He didn't know how the footage could be of help, but he'd learned at least one thing during his years in homicide. "You take what you can, when you can."

"All right," she acceded then turned back to Akio. "Can you transport it to the Sheriff's Office?"

"Sure. Reunion, right? I don't think I'll have any difficulty keeping my camping spot here."

"Aren't you worried about a killer on the loose?" Karen asked him.

"No. And not because I killed him. I forgot him as soon as my head hit the pillow. You just have to let that stuff roll off, or it'll kill you. Anyway, I figure this must be personal. Hassling me was just a cheap shot in the dark. I got a radio feed from a local station with my booster, and it said that Bunting was stuffed in the john." He looked down at his spare frame. "He probably had a couple times my weight. So I'd guess it was more than one person. Takes a village, you know?"

The last member of their little village of witnesses sat at a picnic table in front of an old gray Toyota, her hands folded, simply sitting quietly, with the infinite patience of the elderly. They'd seen all and had little left to see but eternity.

Mary Redbird was a tiny woman with white braided hair, high cheekbones, and black eyes that seemed only a little dimmed. When they approached, she got to her feet and, in doing so, revealed she was hunchbacked. Marek was reminded strongly of the print on his wall at home, one bought and framed by his mother. "The Woodgatherer" by Sioux artist Oscar Howe. Hauling the wood through a blizzard for her family's fire, hunched with her load against the wind, she was the picture of survival with grace.

"Please, let's sit," Karen said. "It's been a long day. Even if it's not noon yet."

Though a faint uptick of the mouth told them the woman saw through the ruse, she sank back to the table, and Marek and Karen sat on the other side of her.

"I am on my way to the Black Hills, to work as a tour guide," she told them when Karen asked. "I just came from the sugar beet fields in North Dakota." She must have seen their horror, because she smiled. "I have been doing it for many years now. I can outlast many younger. And the pay is good, about twelve dollars an hour."

Not a bad wage but not an easy job, either. "Shouldn't you be retired by now?"

"On the reservation? Oh, I could be. My family worries for me. But I am married to the sun, as the saying goes among my people. No husband, no children. And our people once roamed the plains, for food, for sustenance... and for beauty. I looked at how those who were my age were dying, long before their elders had, with so little beauty to make their last days glad. You have not seen poverty until you've seen it on the reservation. No jobs, no hope. I was lucky in that I taught school, but eventually, I could not stand to see so many of my children lose their lives to hopelessness, to alcohol. So I chose this life. When I can no longer earn my living at it, I will go back home to die. Until then, I will roam as the sun does."

Marek hoped that meant that, in winter, she went south. "What did you see last night, Ms. Redbird?"

"Nothing. I saw nothing. But I heard. I had my car windows open, as I often do when the flies are gone and the air is cool with the coming winter. It reminds me of my childhood, when we still hunted, still maintained the traditions, the links, to a life now gone for good."

"What did you hear?" Karen asked, her voice low, almost hushed, as if she and Marek were sitting at an ancient campfire to hear the tales of a village elder.

"The thrashing of an animal in a snare. I felt for it, deep in my soul." She put a hand to her stomach, and Marek wondered if the gesture was the equivalent of a hand to the heart in her tribe's culture. "Because so many of my people, they are in that snare, a death snare, with no way out."

He guessed Mary Redbird came from the Crow Creek or the Pine Ridge reservation, the poorest areas in South Dakota, and possibly the entire country.

Karen looked disappointed. "And that's it?"

"No, I heard a hunter's step, stepping lightly in the woods." She gestured in the direction away from the overlook, to the other side of the hill. Her campsite was the closest to that side. "And I knew that the suffering would not last, and I lay back down. I felt... comforted... to hear a hunter again in the woods. It is a blessing of the old, when young and old merge, and I slept again with the abandon of a child, until your deputy woke me."

"I hope he didn't startle you," Karen said, probably thinking that the hatchet-faced man in a uniform might well do more than startle a woman like Mary Redbird.

"Oh, no. All I could see, at first, was light around him, and I thought, perhaps the time has come, and I go to my people sooner, rather than later. But then he spoke, and I knew he was not of my people, and I woke fully. And so I have waited to speak to you. They know, in the Hills, that I will come, and they will accept my word, that I was delayed. It is better there, now, when they let us have some small part again of our sacred lands."

When they should have had the whole.

CHAPTER 8

SURVEYING THE MEDIA OUTLETS AT the barricade, Karen wished to God she had a drone that could bring her uniform to her. She had her official jacket with her, but it was a warm, sunny fall day, and she was already wearing a sweatshirt. The combination would look ridiculous. She didn't need a mirror to know that, and she wouldn't want to look at herself in the mirror anyway. Business casual didn't stretch to encompass her current getup. But she'd already been seen, so she had no choice but to suck it up.

Cameras panned as she got out of the vintage Corvette, making her wish for that piece of crap known as the Sub, her official and even more vintage Chevy Suburban. That was the one thing she absolutely, positively had been looking forward to handing off to Bunting.

Schooling her face, something she hadn't needed to do as a dispatcher, took a huge effort of will. The press was, she told herself, not her enemy, though it had certainly felt like it of late.

Walrus and Kurt were doing a good job of keeping the ramparts from being breached. Though truth to tell, the Dakota press was generally a pretty easygoing lot, unless the nationals swooped in for the kill. Then they could get downright vicious, as Nails had.

Right now, though, she saw nobody farther afield than Sioux

Falls and Sioux City. The tale of two cities, two states—South Dakota and Iowa—led to two channels for every network.

A grizzled veteran from Sioux Falls allowed all the rest to shout out their questions, waiting as Karen did, for the eye of the storm. How could she possibly answer questions when they were all talking at once? Sometimes she wondered about their IQ.

When the hubbub finally died down, the veteran asked, "Sheriff Mehaffey, you won a recount late last night to the victim of what sources are telling us is a homicide. Robert Leonard Bunting Jr. Why are you on the scene and not a suspect in his death?"

She felt Marek's silent presence behind her. He had her back. "Along with Detective Okerlund, I was in Albuquerque, New Mexico, when Mr. Bunting was killed. I was about to sign on with APD there when I got the call. Detective Okerlund also has a standing offer with APD. As for why I'm here, DCI was first on scene. Though I offered to step back from the investigation, they declined to take the lead."

"What about your deputies?" a blond bombshell of a man from a Sioux City station asked. "Won't you have to investigate your own men?"

She took Larson's lead on that. "Killing Bunting *after* the recount? That's monumentally stupid. And I don't keep stupid on my roster. Besides, my men had leads on other jobs. None of them needed his death to advance their careers. Or in one case, retire."

"Didn't you win with Bunting's death?" he pressed.

"No, I won by seven votes in the recount. I may not have liked his election tactics—and I'm sure you'll recall his win was courtesy of a killer—but I didn't rejoice."

And that, she realized, was the honest-to-God truth. Perhaps some of that leaked out onto her face, because that angle was mercifully dropped. At least for the moment.

"Are you going to close the park?" another reporter asked.

Karen hadn't even thought that far ahead. "Not at this time."

"Can you confirm reports that Bunting's body was found dumped in a toilet at the overlook?"

Since Nails probably had that out on the airwaves by now, she confirmed. "We do not, however, have an official cause of death from the medical examiner in Sioux Falls. Word is, the autopsy will happen tomorrow morning."

In the fast-paced world of media, that was years away. The questions went downhill after that, since she could answer none of them without compromising the investigation. She'd started to step back when the veteran reporter asked, "What does it feel like to be the only elected female sheriff in South Dakota?"

Off balance, she answered without thought. "It feels scary." When that got a startled pause, she clarified, mentally kicking herself. "Scary to know that the people I serve have put their trust, sometimes even their lives, in my hands and that of my men. It's a heavy responsibility. I don't take it lightly. Anyone who does, doesn't really get this job."

"Like Bunting?" As if talking of feelings had opened the floodgates, the bombshell said, "You didn't like him."

She gritted her teeth. "Whether I liked him or not has no bearing on the job."

"We had a complaint from a couple who were detained for hours, waiting for you to show up." Another reporter had muscled in with a grating gotcha tone. "Do you really believe that Bunting was killed by a visitor to the park?"

Karen felt her fingers tighten, wanting to strangle the Class A assholes from Florida. Behind her, Marek cleared his throat, a rare occurrence of him wanting to speak on camera. Perhaps he knew just how close she was to saying something she'd later regret. She hadn't eaten a bite since sometime the previous day, and that was making her lightheaded. Not a good time to be spouting sound bites. She moved aside.

Marek introduced himself then said calmly, in that laconic way of Dakotans who weren't her, "Recall, we have a potential killer on the loose, and keeping the campers together, with our deputies, protected them. And in a case like this, you can't make any assumptions about what, or who, might be important. People may not even know what they know until we interview them. And we have just finished. We have now released the campers with our apologies for the delay. Any complaints should be directed toward the Eda County commissioners and will be promptly addressed."

It seemed ludicrous, said like that. Marek's deep, almost subsonic voice seemed to have lulled the press into a trancelike state, as they didn't try to stop Karen and Marek from leaving.

With the press in her rearview mirror, Karen said, "That was boneheaded."

He frowned at her. "What did I say?"

"Not you, me. *Scary.* Talk about a poor choice of words."

"Oh." He rubbed at his knee. "It *is* scary. If you don't get that, you've no business in the job."

"But guys don't say that on air. And for me, as the lone female sheriff in this state, to say it was just idiotic. Makes people think I can't handle the scary stuff. I can pretty much guarantee that's what they'll run with, not anything else either of us said, or even Bunting's death."

"After you burned them last month, getting an apology in print from no less than a Pulitzer-prize-winning Twin Cities reporter?" He shook his head. "No, I think they'll give you the whole sound bite."

"Maybe... but only after they lead with something like 'Lone Female Sheriff Afraid of the Job.' Maybe with a Halloween theme and little ghosties. But enough about my fat mouth. What about the investigation? What's next?" She glanced down at her frayed jeans. "That is, after we stop to change cars and clothes."

Marek blinked as if such mundane matters had been far from his mind, even though his knees were practically under his chin in the bucket seats of the Corvette. "We need to go to Aleford to talk to the aunt. She may know what was going on in his personal life."

Josephine had let them know that Bunting's next of kin and only known blood relative was his mother's sister.

"And to see the ex-wife," Karen reminded him. "Last address Josephine found for Nadine Early was there. Speaking of our long-suffering secretary, maybe we'd better stop at the office before she has time to type up her resignation letter."

He frowned, as well he might, since Josephine typed up his dictations. His dyslexia had been a sticking point when he'd first been hired, and Josephine had ridden to the rescue by offering to type up his verbal reports. "At her speed? If she was set on it, it's been done since yesterday."

Karen sank farther down into her seat. Would she even have a roster other than Walrus, when all was said and done?

CHAPTER 9

A S SHE PULLED INTO THE drive in front of her bungalow at 22 Okerlund Road, mirrored across the street at Marek's at number 21, she sniffed and smelled... nothing. But she wasn't sure if that was because there wasn't anything to smell or if her olfactory senses had been obliterated. She feared the latter. "I'll meet you back in twenty. Shower first."

She entered her house, hoping to see her recently found daughter, but Eyre was apparently out. Karen's young Brethren cousin, Mary Hannah, would be back home with her parents in Eder over the weekend. So Karen dumped her filthy clothes in the washer and ran up to the shower in the attic room in her birthday suit.

Half an hour later, scrubbed to the pores and back in uniform, Karen pulled the Sub into her reserved slot behind the courthouse, something she'd done many times over the last couple of years as the acting sheriff.

Why, then, did it suddenly feel different?

Beside her, in the passenger seat, Marek wore a new pair of jeans, a chambray shirt, and over his damp hair, his official Eda County Detective cap, his one concession to a uniform. He hadn't tamed his beard yet, though. But that sort of rough look didn't reflect as badly on a man as it did on a woman. Unfair but true. For a man, it said he had more important things, more important work, on his mind. For a woman, it meant she couldn't even manage to get herself together. So how was she going to manage the job?

"Bridal jitters?" Marek asked, making no motion to get out of the Sub.

Nodding, Karen laid her head back and looked up at the fanciful turrets on the Richardsonian Romanesque courthouse. Constructed of Sioux quartzite and rose-colored optimism, it was built to last, unlike the county, which was still declining in population.

"Why did I want this job again?" She ran her hands down her face. "No, don't answer that. Family, that's the biggie. Except we're sitting right here, in Reunion, home of the brave and true Okerlunds, and we might as well be in Albuquerque. Or heck, we could be road warriors like the campers. Why not? Most had better rides than this piece of—" She stopped herself and patted the dash. "This loyal, dedicated work of ingenuity."

Marek snorted but didn't contradict her. Typical Dakotan. A snort, a huff, a faint rise of the eyebrow... but nothing more to tempt fate. Rural communities lived far too close to the bone, to the whims of the weather and winds of economic change, to say something aloud that might be construed by the gods as bragging—and hence require a sharp putdown.

"Do you think we've been doing this too long, us Okerlunds?" she asked him. "Are we hidebound, or are we just bound to this place? I mean, I love it. It's our town. But if it wasn't ours..."

"It wouldn't be ours," he said simply. "But it is."

She let that settle—and it settled her. She put her hand on the door handle.

Then he spoke again, so softly that she barely heard it, and she wasn't sure she was supposed to. "I promised my mother I'd never come back."

Her hand dropped as she debated whether she should reply.

"She had her reasons," he said then opened the door.

And that was on her father. The famous Okerlund feud had eventually run Janina Marek out of town, not on a rail, as the railroads were long gone, but with a pink slip from her beloved teaching position at Reunion High.

He'd broken his promise for one reason, and that reason was why they were all still here. Becca De Baca Okerlund. Marek's seven-year-old daughter was the bridge between all of the remaining Okerlunds. Karen and Marek were only children who should've grown up like siblings, across the street from each other, but the gulf had been too far to cross back then, courtesy of Arne Okerlund's frosty feud with his father and—for at least a while since the return—with Marek.

Thinking of her father, she wondered just what had happened between him and Marek, something that made Marek look weary and a bit grim when he saw his much-older half-brother. For a gentle man like Marek, a forgiving one, whatever had happened, it had gone deep, though she'd seen a lightening of his grimness—and the disdain of her father—of late. Mareks were trouble, Arne had always said, but Marek was now in the Okerlund camp, a sight she thought she'd never see.

"Are you ever going to tell me what happened between you and my father?" she asked his back, taking a stab. Though not quite in the dark, it was close, as she had nothing but a gut feeling to go on. His shoulders tensed, then he slowly turned.

For a long time, he just looked down at her from his Olympian height. "No, that's a promise I'll keep."

At one time, she'd have picked at him until he spilled—or swatted her down, to both their hurt. But she'd learned sometimes you just didn't need to know. "Okay. I'm just glad you two aren't at each other's throats. Are you going to open that door?"

After a slow blink, he turned, opened the door, and bowed. "Your carriage awaits, m'lady."

Would it turn into a pumpkin at midnight? She breezed past with a sniff, lady-of-the-manor to peasant, but not entirely for effect. He smelled clean. "You're supposed to pull a forelock."

"Did someone say pulled ham hocks?" A head poked out from a side door, then the rest of Janet Dahl followed, ensconced in a rolling office chair. She had moved from the register of deeds to the county auditor spot over the summer to pinch hit for the incumbent, who was at the Mayo Clinic, battling kidney disease. "Oh, hi. Welcome home, Sheriff. You don't know how absolutely, positively delighted I am to say that. Sorry that Harold had to bring you back from vacation, though." She wheeled herself right out into the hallway. "You two just can't catch a break. You should try something with regular hours."

"Like running elections?" Karen asked her.

Janet threw back her head and laughed. "Got me there. Still, only one very long night, even if it will live on in infamy. I fully intended to sleep in. Then Harold got the phone call from Josephine at the break of day." Janet sobered, beckoning them into her office. "You'll want to talk to me."

Karen looked at Marek, who nodded. They walked into what looked like a frat house the day after a party, with chairs overturned and pizza boxes and half-filled plastic beverage containers littered over any available surface. As pizza wasn't normally available from Reunion, Karen guessed some unlucky soul must have been sent to Aleford for it.

Janet surveyed the office with bleary resignation. "Sorry about the mess. I just haven't had the energy to attack it as yet. I think I need a wrecking crew." Given that Janet, at least compared to her husband, Harold, was the Energizer Bunny, that was saying something. Janet wheeled herself back behind her temporary desk. "I know one shouldn't speak ill of the dead, but Bob Bunting would've destroyed the reputation of the Sheriff's Office within months, if not days. He cared nothing about this county or its citizens, only himself and how he could profit."

Deciding that she didn't want any sticky residue on her clean uniform, Karen remained standing, her preferred default setting anyway. "Then he'd have been in for a rude surprise, given how little this job pays."

"It wasn't the pay, but the power. Oh, I don't mean he didn't care about the money. Did you see that big black SUV he bought the day after he won?" Janet shook her head sadly. "He'd have been paying on it until he was old and gray."

Like all Dahls, even one by marriage, Janet could pinch a pound from a penny. Frugality was a blood sport to them.

Marek righted a chair and sat down. Brave soul. "When did you last see Bunting?"

"Just before one in the morning, when he stormed out of the office, vowing he'd see us all jailed for corruption. Even his supporters, what few remained, were pretty disgusted at that point."

If Bunting thought a Dahl was corruptible, then he'd really flown the coop. "Who was with him?"

"Let's see..." Janet laid her head back and stared up at the ceiling as if it held the answer. "On your side, we had a passel of Forsgrens."

Karen closed her eyes. Her great-grandmother on her father's side had been a Forsgren, and the county was littered with them, but they could be more than a little trying, especially Bill Forsgren. He was one of the patriarchs, and a drunk to boot. Still, Bill had been the one to spearhead the recount, even though he didn't hold with female sheriffs. Fortunately for her, he hated Bunting more than he valued his own principles. "My apologies."

Janet waved a listless hand. "They were jewels in comparison. Let me tell you, I get that people want to win..." She looked around at the spoils of public service. "Or I did until last night. But I talked to Roland from his hospital bed, and he said he'd never encountered anything like what I described. He sounded kind of disappointed he'd missed it, the one big race with people breathing down your neck, challenging every single vote, and trying to make it sound like those overseas military folk with absentee ballots were somehow imposters. Even though I showed them their bona fides, the post office marks, everything. We checked and double-checked... and triple-checked... before they finally conceded."

Karen decided that Janet was well and truly beat, because

she didn't usually go off the rails when asked a direct question. "Bunting's supporters?"

"Oh, yeah. Five of them. Women outnumbered the men, three to two, which doesn't say much for our fair sex, does it. But the idea of sleeping with power seems to attract a certain type." Her lips pursed, and she glanced out the door. "I shouldn't have said that. My brain is mush."

Karen blew out a breath. Maybe this was going to be a slam dunk. "Bunting had a significant other?"

"Well, he had at least two vying for that spot from my cynical gaze, but I don't actually know the details, nor do I want to know. A young woman who should know better—and have much better with her looks—was hanging on him until the bitter end. Though I'll admit she wasn't... quite there. When all was said and done, she abandoned Bunting and ran out, phone clutched in her hand like it was the lifeline to God Almighty. Didn't catch her name. And I don't recognize her people, but I'm guessing Valeska by coloring." Janet closed her eyes. "The other woman was more what you'd expect of Bunting, maybe fifty, looked much older, with a look about her... how do I say this politely?"

Marek saved her. "Well used? Overweight, wearing a Packers sweatshirt and a sour expression?"

Janet peeled back an eyelid to look over at Marek. "I see you've already got her number. One of the others called her Nadine, and I think, if I'm not mistaken, she works or worked at the truck stop in Aleford. I rarely go in now that you can just swipe for gas, so I can't swear to it, but that's where I'd start. Funny. I know a lot of people, meet a lot of people, in this county, but I didn't recognize four of the five. Too bad I wasn't checking *their* bona fides."

Nadine was almost certainly Bunting's ex-wife. That explained a few things, except why she was backing him at the recount when she'd tried to sabotage his election.

"So that's the two female hangers-on." Karen knew that even if Janet didn't know the young woman, others would know people who did. And some were likely related to her, to boot, which sometimes made things dicey. "What of the last woman?"

Janet cleared her throat. "Mindy Hansen Bullard."

It took a second, but Karen got the connection. Mindy was the wife of Cal Bullard, who was doing twenty to life in the state pen in Sioux Falls. That had been Karen's first homicide case and Marek's first in Reunion. While she personally would have given him a lesser sentence for what he'd initially done, that he'd held Marek's daughter at gunpoint wasn't something she could easily forgive. "I get that. I had to evict Mindy off their farm a couple months ago. The bank wouldn't hold off any longer."

And the bruised, lost looks of the huddled mother and children had ripped at her. Evictions were one aspect of the job she truly hated, but like her father and grandfather, she refused to hand them off to anyone else. She always took business cards along for various public services and charities that might help, but they usually went into the trash—sometimes right there in any convenient mudhole or even manure. Dakotans were a proud bunch. Karen respected that, tried to make it sound like neighbors helping neighbors, but there was no good way to kick a family out of their home.

Still, why was Mindy using her energy to fight for a man like Bunting? It made no sense, except maybe on an emotional level, which was plain stupid. Getting even with Karen for doing her job wouldn't do squat. Mindy's kids needed her. Bunting didn't.

"Who were the men?" Marek asked.

Janet consulted the ceiling again. "One wore a muscle shirt. Arms as big around as hams. He left after the absentee ballots came out. I think he might have been ex-military? Had a tattoo of an anchor on one arm. Left. I think."

Marek and Karen exchanged a look. "Did he resemble the young woman?"

Janet's unpainted mouth rounded into an O. "Now that you mention it, yes, and he kept looking at her with that come-hither look, like he was trying to get her to go with him, but she wasn't having any of it, so he left. Here I was thinking that was a come-on, and she was an idiot for hanging on Bunting, but you're right—they must be related. After the last vote was tallied, she screamed at Bunting, 'It was all for nothing,' and ran out. And that really riled our erstwhile sheriff. I thought he was actually going to strike one of my workers. I stepped between them. After blowing a lot of hot air, he went out, with Nadine."

That tallied with what Nails had observed. "And the last man?"

"Ah, the last man standing. Now, he was a real puzzle. He seemed... disconnected... from the rest. And talk about put together. Looked slick, with money and connections, and when he left, when it became obvious to anyone with an eye to spare that Bunting was going to lose, he whispered something to Bunting that made me pity our wannabe sheriff. For at least a second. Bunting went white then red and said, 'We'll see about that.' But Mr. Slick just said, 'Don't let the door hit you on your way out.' And out Mr. Slick went... and I can bet you, those old doors didn't dare touch his mighty fine butt. Ah... don't tell Harold I said that."

Karen grinned. "Wouldn't dream of it."

Janet groaned. "What do I need to do?"

"Find his name for us." Karen shot a wad of napkins into the trash. "We've got a lot of irons in the fire. That would help a lot."

"Let me see if I can brand him for you, then. Now, shoo. Josephine was looking for your hide this morning. Make sure you don't get lassoed and pinned to the wall."

Despite that dire warning, Karen eased herself through the side door into the office, an open bullpen with wooden desks facing large windows with a view of Main Street. Talk about transparency in government. Right then, Karen would have preferred a little less transparency as the sole occupant of the office stood waiting, hands on hips, stance wide. Her rhinestone-studded orange-and-purple paisley shirt descended into skinny jeans and purple boots with tassels. If you thought dude rancher, you were dead wrong. The belt buckle proclaimed one of her many wins as a champion barrel racer.

Deciding to be the barrel, Karen stood stock still as the sixtyish secretary advanced, while Marek, coward that he was, disappeared into the wallpaper... a phenomenal accomplishment given there was none on the boring cream walls studded with sheriffs of the past, all Okerlunds. Looked like she'd be joining their ranks sooner rather than later. Hers would be the shortest stint for a sheriff on record.

The hit came hard, the wrap up, suffocating.

"Josephine... I can't breathe."

"Good. Congrats, Sheriff. Don't ever, ever leave me holding the badge again."

"I... promise." One last squeeze, and she was released. Gingerly, Karen checked her ribs. Josephine hadn't worked on a West River ranch throwing hay bales in decades, but you'd never know it. "Really, I'm sorry. I left Kurt and Bork in charge. And my dad as backup." Then Kurt's sister had suffered a serious panic attack, Bork had fallen victim to appendicitis, and her father's adopted grandson had swallowed a penny and almost suffocated. Emergency surgery in Sioux Falls had taken care of the rest—and provided a rock-solid alibi. "How is Bork, by the way?"

"Still woozy. Idiot. He should've called the ambulance."

Travis Bjorkland, their native Minnesotan from just over the border, had driven himself to Sioux Falls with his sirens going the entire way.

"That would've taken too long, and they needed the ambulance for Joey later," Marek said, startling Josephine, who turned and treated him to the same crushing wraparound—but with far less effect.

"Are you here to stay?" she demanded, thumbs hooked in her belt, her forefingers in the ready and locked position to shoot him if she didn't like the answer.

He waited a beat. A bit of Okerlund payback. "Becca says yes."

"Thank God for sensible women." Josephine turned on Karen. "Speaking of which, and speaking of myself, I've secured your roster for you, other than Kurt, who said he'd tell you himself. Well, except..."

Josephine could do payback with a vengeance when she chose. But the Okerlunds fought back with their usual tactic: silence. Though it killed Karen to wait, as she hadn't gotten that closemouthed gene.

"Two Fingers said he'd have to think about it."

Since Josephine wasn't smiling, Karen was pretty sure that was straight shooting, not a pulled ham. Her swing-shift deputy had an offer to work at the tiny reservation at Flandreau, north of Sioux Falls. That he didn't meet the blood quantum was a sticking point for tribal enrollment, but not, apparently, employment. Still, family was a powerful draw, and he had a mother, stepfather, and two young half-sisters there. "I'll just have to convince him, then."

"You do that. First priority. After that, you've got a pile of evictions waiting, and I'm getting tired of being nagged about them."

"I'll get to it, when I have time." That was one plus for the current investigation. "I've got Bunting to clear up first."

"So far as I'm concerned, you can let Bunting stew in his own shit for eternity." Josephine's eyes narrowed. "Don't you glare at me, Karen Okerlund Mehaffey. That man was a menace. And he's going to give me nightmares that I won't be able to ride out to the buzzer. Do you know yet if it's a homicide?"

Karen wished it wasn't. So that she could shut the door on Bunting and forget him.

"Stabbed in the back, according to Larson," Karen began just before the doors burst open.

Walrus stomped into the room with a curious crunching sound, like boots on twice-frozen snow. He dropped himself into his chair, jerked off his boots, and turned them up. The soles glittered like ice pellets. "Geez, these boots are new, too."

Trailing in after his partner, Kurt pursed his lips into a line thin enough to cut ice—or glass. "I told you not to step there."

"*After* I'd stepped. That doesn't count. It's going to be a bear to get these out. It's disgusting."

"That you have to work at it?" Kurt shot back.

"Geez. Get a clue. That people litter public parks like it's their own backyard."

"People don't litter their own backyard. They litter public grounds because they don't have to clean it up. Biester said it's become a real problem."

"Get real, Kurt. Broken glass has always been a problem, from way back when that's all we had. Now it's usually cans and plastic, not glass. Point is, people have no respect anymore for Mother Nature."

Used to the bickering, even reveling in it as a return to normality, Karen nonetheless had work to do, and time was ticking. They needed to get to Aleford. But they needed evidence more. "You got the list of payments dropped in the box?"

"Yep, we did. Kurt's got it." Walrus banged his boots together, creating a shower of small pellets over the marble floor. Kurt glared at him, handed off the list, and disappeared into the break room. A minute later, Kurt returned with a dustpan and sweeper while Walrus obligingly lifted his de-glassed boots for his partner to sweep under them. After sharing an amused glance with Marek, Karen left them to it.

The only good thing about this homicide was that it hadn't gotten anyone down. While they might not be glad, they certainly weren't sad.

CHAPTER 10

ALEFORD, TO THE NORTH OF Reunion, was primarily known for its truck stop, and unlike the majority of Scandinavian, Slav, or German towns in Eda County, the town was primarily populated by English and Irish settlers like Walrus.

Karen pulled the Sub into the drive of a white vinyl-sided ranch home that barely fit in its tiny spot between two larger homes whose incomes, she guessed, were earned by commuting to Sioux Falls. Zoning laws weren't as strict in the country as in cities.

Personally, Karen liked that, that you had a good mix of the haves and the not-so-haves, but she doubted that the sentiment was echoed by the raker-of-leaves in the right-hand house. The woman eyed the official vehicle with grim satisfaction, as if she'd predicted that the neighborhood would go to rack and ruin if one lone woman of seventy years was allowed to live amongst them.

That woman, Alice Dutton, turned out to be nothing like the overbearing female version of Bunting that Karen had expected. Instead, she was immensely petite, almost nonexistent, at least compared to Karen and Marek.

Her red-rimmed eyes peered up at them with a resignation, even an acceptance of something long feared, which told Karen that Alice Dutton had held no illusions as to her nephew's character.

After Karen and Marek were seated on an afghan-draped sofa that creaked under their combined weight, Alice spoke first. She perched on a wood-slatted chair. Only the toes of her sensible shoes touched the floor. "I feel as if I should apologize to you, Sheriff Mehaffey, for what my nephew did to you during the election. I told him that he'd made a pact with the devil, but he just said that he hadn't been born with a silver spoon, but when he won, he'd buy a really long one."

Her hands twisted a soaked handkerchief. "Josephine Lindstrom told me you'd be by, and I've been trying to think what to say." She sighed, a whisper of sound that barely ruffled the air. "I still don't know. But I hope you find his killer, not for the man he became, but for the boy he was."

Ready for an angry, vituperative interview, Karen wasn't quite sure how to handle this sad, faded woman. "We will do our best to find his killer, no matter who or what he was, Ms. Dutton."

"Miss, please. I never went for Ms. It seemed too outrageous at the time. I'm afraid that once I made it out into the work world, I was so afraid to lose my position there that I never rocked the boat. So I'm Miss Alice or just Alice." She repeated that last under her breath. "Just Alice."

Wanting to pace, Karen wished she hadn't sat down. "When did you last hear from or see your nephew?"

Alice glanced at an old radio on the settee. "I stayed up to hear the recount. When I heard he lost, I didn't rightly know what to feel, given how he'd conducted himself, but I called him. Isn't that what they always say, to just be there for your kids? He was all I had, even though he paid me little attention. He was in the car. At least, I could hear road noise. He was furious. He said it wasn't over, that the whole county was corrupt. I'm afraid that I... how do you say it? Tuned out? Until I heard him turn onto gravel—you know that sound it makes, with the rocks hitting underneath? Then he... well, uttered an oath...

and said something about the last straw. He hung up on me. That's the last words we had between us. I wish I'd said I loved him. Because I did."

Yet Karen would've bet Bunting was one of those people not even a mother could love. "You were close, then?"

A faint smile ghosted over the pale, almost translucent face. "A long time ago, yes, when I babysat for him. He was such a sweet little boy, bringing me little gifts, like dandelions and rocks and bottle caps, even a ragged red ribbon once for my hair, and I wore it. He'd snuggle in my lap like I was his blanket in the night. I blame my sister and her parade of men for how he turned out."

A tear spilled down, disappearing into a deep line, and finally dropping down onto her blue-veined hand, unnoticed. "I wanted to adopt him after his father split and Rachel took to the bottle. But she resented me, even though she didn't want to be saddled with the brat, as she called him. Can you believe it? That's what he thought his name was, until I told him, no, it was Robert, and he cried because the other kids taunted him with 'brat,' and he didn't know why they thought it was so funny. Later, they called him Baby, and it stuck, much as I hated it. I made sure I always, always called him Robert, to remind him that it was a good name, a solid name, and that he could live up to it. It means 'bright fame,' and I told him he had a famous future. Back then, I believed it."

More like infamous. Karen didn't really want to hear this, but she needed to, because knowing Bunting might lead them to his killer. "I take it you were unsuccessful in getting custody."

Wringing her handkerchief, Alice got up, went to a drawer, and pulled out a photograph, which she handed to Karen. A much-younger Alice Dutton in a neat white blouse and modest gray skirt held a beaming baby with a smeared face and a cowlick. Baby Bunting in the flesh. Bookending them, both standing with arms crossed, must be the sister and one of her men. Rachel was taller and broader than Alice, as if she'd been pulled like taffy out of the neat shape of her sister. The dark-blond, mustached man on the other side towered over them all, his jaw jutting, as if he'd just been asked to take a hit, not a photo.

"Rachel cleaned up her act just enough to satisfy social services. And her husband at the time, Ed Johnson, was in your line of work, and that was that."

Karen imagined that Ed was a man's man, a cop of the old school, who'd expected to be kowtowed to, and for Alice Dutton to have challenged him must have taken more than a little courage.

Alice's lips compressed to invisibility. "The judge ruled that, as a single woman, I had no claim, even though I'd spent more time with Robert than Rachel had by that time. The judge told me to go snare my own man and have my own kids if I wanted them so bad. After that, I only saw Robert rarely. By the time Rachel got done with him, he'd not only lost any sweetness, he didn't trust anyone, not even me. Not that I can blame him. He had a terrible childhood, worse than mine and Rachel's, being our father's punching bags." She took the photo back, cradled it in her worn hands, then put it back in the drawer and shut it with a sharp click. "But I comfort myself that, while Robert was undoubtedly... less than ethical... he wasn't violent."

Marek finally spoke, his voice gentle, "What about your nephew's ex-wife? Nadine Early. She had a restraining order out on him, didn't she?"

A deep, anguished rage lit her faded face. "It should've been the other way around. Nadine was the worst thing that happened to him." Her toes went *en pointe* on the floor. "Robert wanted kids. Did you know that? So I could be their granny, he said, and we would have the life we should've had together. He'd finally escaped his mother, was living in my spare room, and was working for... your father, I believe, Sheriff Mehaffey? Arne Okerlund. A good man, if a bit abrupt."

Her lips trembled. "I had such high hopes for Robert then. I told him, after he proudly brought his new girlfriend around to meet me, that Nadine was his mother all over again. A drunk, a manipulator, and a backstabber. Maybe I shouldn't have been so blunt, because it just put his back up. I didn't see him again for a long time after that. Often, I didn't even know where he was, as he moved around a lot, from job to job. But I was right. She dumped him, then she'd come back and hit him up for money, promising him they'd reconcile, have kids, and she'd stop drinking. Cheated on him the whole time. He finally divorced her, and she married Jim Early on the rebound. That didn't last any longer than you can hold your breath, and he fled to Mexico. So she went right back to her old ways with my nephew. I never did understand why he couldn't stand up to her, but I guess, if he had, he might've killed her."

"Do you know where Nadine is now?" Marek asked.

"No, I haven't seen her for a long while. In a town this size, that's unusual, but I'm grateful. We had an unspoken agreement, you might say, to look right through each other. Of course, most look through me anyway, always did. Rachel was the looker, 'til she lost it to the bottle."

Alice looked down at her handkerchief blankly, then with a stiff, determined movement, she wiped away the fallow tears. "Alone of the Duttons, I escaped. I took typing and shorthand in high school and got hired as a secretary for Milt Logan, the lawyer. I still have no idea why he took me on. He taught me how to dress, how to act, how to talk, even." She glanced around her neat little home, without a single family photo or anything else on the white walls. Though one bookcase did hold a large, framed photo of a man in a suit. His salt-and-pepper hair, wide smile, and pronounced jowls rang a bell with Karen—she'd seen Milt Logan in the courthouse hallways when she was growing up and visiting her grandfather or father, and he'd always given her a friendly nod.

When Alice looked back at them, her eyes—blue fading into the whites—looked as empty as her walls. "I'm the last of my family. Maybe it's for the best."

CHAPTER 11

I N HIGH SCHOOL, MAREK HAD once taken a job as a busboy at the Early Diner in Valeska. He'd hated every one-thousand-two-hundred minutes of it before he and the owner, Eldon Early, had decided to part ways. He'd spent the rest of that summer detasseling corn for Curry Seed. When you finished a field, you felt you'd done something, unlike the never-ending parade of dirty dishes at the diner.

While Marek often ate out, or at least got takeout from Mex-Mix or The Café in Reunion, the clink of dishes, the clatter of utensils, and the slosh of water in bussing tubs always made him feel closed in, trapped, and faintly nauseous.

The Aleford truck stop was no different.

Unfortunately, they'd struck out on Nadine Early's last known address, a dilapidated Section 8 apartment building that had been razed to the ground after a fire caused by someone using an upside-down iron as a cooktop. So Marek took a deep breath to settle the memories before he walked in behind Karen, who'd apparently never had a phobia in her life.

After a quick survey, Karen headed straight for the roly-poly waitress by the counter. The woman wore a pinstripe polyester dress with a blue apron and heavy-duty support stockings that ended in a pair of bright-blue sneakers. "Hi, Mrs. Bridges. Can we have a word?"

Looking up from where she mulled over an order, Nancy

Kubicek Bridges blanched. "Is it Tanner?" Her son was the light of her life, or had been, last Marek knew.

"No, nothing wrong," Karen assured her. "We're looking for someone who used to work here."

"Oh. You gave me a fright." Nancy rubbed at a liver spot on her chin as she looked around the room with its low-level hum of midafternoon. "Well, it's a lull. Should be okay. Fred! I'm taking fifteen!"

"Make it ten!" a smoke-graveled voice rumbled back from the bowels of the kitchen.

Nancy rolled her eyes. "He doesn't believe in breaks. Says it's a lazy habit, not to be encouraged. Let's go outside. If I stay in here, somebody'll flag me down."

She moved more slowly than Marek recalled, and he wondered just how long she'd spent on her feet over the years. Far more than he had, he'd bet. She went out and sat down on a concrete divider that separated the gas from the diesel lines. She heaved a big sigh. "I feel 'bout ninety today. Doctor says I need my veins stripped. I keep hoping to put it off." She rubbed her thigh. "Tanner is after me to do it while I still qualify for subsidies for insurance."

"Smart kid," Karen said. "He still in school to be a vet?"

Nancy's lips compressed. "The insurance company twisted like a ball on a string, trying to get out of paying Leo's life insurance claim, but they finally paid out the day before Tanner's college bills came due. Thought that boy's heart was going to break, when it looked for sure like he'd have to drop out, even with the scholarship he got. Just not enough. Never enough. I offered to mortgage the house, though it still would've come up short in the long haul, but Tanner said no. Leo paid his premiums, fair and square, and the company should've done the same. Playing with people's lives like that, it's criminal."

Marek had barely made it through high school, but he'd heard an earful over the years from financially strapped coworkers about the cost of college. Gone were the days that a summer job could cover tuition and a side job could cover room and board.

Nancy raked her hand through limp brown hair. "Now, who're you looking for? I figured you'd be working the murder at the park. That was the big buzz this morning. But maybe you already solved it. We've had a few light-fingered waitresses over the years, but Fred grinds them up and spits them out. Can't say I ever got to know any of 'em well enough to know where they ended up. In jail, I'd guess. Once you start down that road, you ain't likely to do a U-turn."

When Karen glanced at Marek with a raised eyebrow, he knew that he'd been far too quiet, even for him. He cleared his throat. "We're looking for Bob Bunting's ex-wife. Nadine Early."

Nancy's lips parted. "Well, you should know, Marek Okerlund. She's closer kin to you than me." When he just stared down at her, trying to process that unexpected answer, she blew out a breath. "Okay, so maybe you wouldn't know. Your mother was pretty standoffish when she came back to Valeska, even though it was the Kubiceks gave her a roof over her head growing up. But I don't want to rehash old hurts. You're my cousin. I've said it before. I'll say it again. Whatever went on before, with hard feelings both ways, that's water under the bridge. When you've got nothing else, you've got family. My sister Lola's been a godsend to me since Leo died. We used to fight like cats and dogs as kids. Now we're closer than two catfish in a skillet. Even if she does nag me about getting my hair done up right. Who has time?"

A truck honked as it pulled out. Nancy gave the driver a wave. "That's Henry Dill. One of Leo's friends. Nice man. Good tipper." She gave them a sad smile, as if resigned to the idea that tips were all she would ever get from a man again. She rubbed her thigh again. "I'd better get back soon if I don't want to be thumbing for a ride."

As if trying to spare Marek from having to ask, Karen did it for him. "How is Nadine Early related to the Kubiceks, and where might we find her? Is she still working at the truck stop?"

Nancy gave a mirthless laugh. "Nadine? She worked the gas station, not the diner. And only when it pleased her, which wasn't often. Fred took her measure first time he saw her. Same as your grandmother did, Marek. 'That girl's gonna be trouble,' she told my ma when Nadine was just a tyke. And boy, was she right. Let's see. She was your grandmother's brother Frank's youngest. Spoiled rotten, if you ask me, just 'cause she was one of those surprises you sometimes get when you think the fat lady's sung her last. Her father got his own back, you might say, when he cut her right out of his will. And he had a fair amount of prime farmland, so it wasn't chump change. 'To my daughter Nadine, I leave nothing, not even my name for her to further shame.' What a cut-up that was, her trying to make it out like her father was batty in his old age and that she'd been the one to take care of him. Think that's what finally banded that family together again after she'd done her best to destroy it. If anyone should've been in that toilet at the park, it was her, not Bob Bunting. Always felt sorry for him. He had no clue what he'd walked into when he walked her down the aisle with that gaudy diamond on her greedy finger."

A voice grated out over the truck engines. "Nancy, you want a paycheck, or what?"

As Nancy rubbed her thigh again, Marek held out his hand. After a second, Nancy accepted it, and he hauled her to her feet. "Any idea where we can find Nadine?"

"You might try your grandma's place on the old Kubicek farm. Now I'd better get back, or Fred really will dock my paycheck. He don't make any threats he don't follow through." She headed back to work, her shoulders rounded, her steps faltering.

"Nancy?"

She turned with difficulty. "Yeah?"

Marek rubbed his temples. "Your son is a smart kid. I'd listen to him. Get the surgery."

"Yeah, he's smart, my boy," She gave him a real smile that took years off her face, though the smile was quickly suffocated by anxiety. "Fred will fire me if I took that much time off. He works through bad hip pain, you see, and refuses to get it replaced. Says original equipment is always the best, no matter what. Doesn't trust doctors."

Karen said, "You're too good to lose. If he's got a brain cell left, he'll know that. He'll grumble, no doubt, but as far as I'm concerned? He's the wimp, refusing to go under the knife."

Her head tilted, then she nodded. She disappeared into the truck stop with her shoulders braced, and Marek guessed she was going to wage war. He hoped she was the victor.

When they got back into the Sub, Karen sat for a moment before turning the ignition. "We take it for granted. Need surgery like Bork did? Take sick leave and do it. Health insurance picks up most of the tab. But for the Nancys and Loris? It's work hard, don't get sick, or work sick. Different world with different rules."

"Survival of the fittest," Marek murmured and got the fisheye. "Just remembering what Biester said. My take is, if you work, you get benefits. Nancy puts in more hours, I'm sure, than I do. And I'm no smarter, just luckier."

Karen pulled out, slowing to drive over a series of potholes made worse by the summer rains. "You don't give yourself enough credit, Marek. You've got dyslexia, not a low IQ. That's why your mother..." She pursed her lips. "So, your grandmother's place, where is it?"

Thankful she'd aborted the subject of his mother, Marek gave her the instructions. They would never see eye to eye on what Janina Marek Okerlund had done one fateful evening that had forever tainted Karen's view of the woman. He couldn't really blame Karen—and owed her that it hadn't been worse.

The Sub hit a pothole, rattling Marek's gritted teeth. He'd always hated this road, the same one he'd traveled with his mother after she'd lost her job, after his father died, right before high school. He'd always associated Valeska with the Mareks, with the man he'd desperately tried to be the opposite of, despite sharing Lenny Marek's face. Returning to Valeska had been a desperate move at the last minute, and neither had thought it would be Janina's last residence.

Her ashes had been buried at the Catholic church, near her

mother's, with a simple headstone she'd ordered ahead of time. Her father's ashes, also nearby, had not been memorialized. Marek hadn't gone with his mother to that funeral, which had been short and anything but sweet, according to his mother. But Marek had gone to his grandmother's service. A worn, gnarl-handed seamstress, she'd gone out as in life, quietly and efficiently, without a peep of complaint.

Don't expect anything in life, and you won't be disappointed.

That had been her favorite saying, one she'd lived by—and nearly died by—if the tales were true. In those days, a man's fist easily weighed down the scales of justice. But Leif Okerlund had been the exception to looking the other way. When the law itself couldn't help, he'd taken the Marek kids, Jim and Janina, into his own home, at least a few times.

As Marek and Karen bumped off the main road onto a deeply rutted dirt road that led to the Kubicek homestead, Marek felt his shoulders hunch, waiting for the inevitable slide into disaster. Once you were in a rut, it was hard to get out. But Karen kept clear, a neat feat, until right near the house. The Sub's wheel rims screeched against the rut in protest, before Karen rocked the vehicle and gently accelerated, launching them out and onto the weed-infested lawn.

Pools of stagnant rainwater, filled with leaves and the dead of summer past, reflected nothing but decay and an overcast gray sky. The fair day had turned foul in a hurry. The skeletons of rusted cars, farm implements, and assorted outbuildings stood around like an old-timey set piece.

The dilapidated two-story clapboard farmhouse that rose from the muck, once a proud marker of survival on a harsh prairie, had been abandoned well before his grandmother had moved there. Later, it had been her prison, a "gift" from her father, a hard-nosed farmer who'd warned her not to marry her chosen mate. She'd made her bed, and he'd made her lie in it. She'd almost died in it.

Even knowing that Lenny Marek most likely had the same severe dyslexia that Marek did, he didn't feel any closer to the man, even if he could feel sorry for the young man Lenny must have been. By all accounts, he'd tried hard to make a go of it, moved from town to town for a new start, tried taking classes to try new trades, but eventually, his frustration had led to his drinking, which made him unreliable.

The jobs dried up—and his fists came up. He'd been forced to accept the charity of his in-laws, and that just fueled more rage, more brawls, more assaults—until it'd ended in death.

Thinking of his own life, Marek wondered, not for the first time, how he would have responded in his grandfather's gargantuan shoes. He'd never know. Courtesy of his mother's promise—and his half-brother's forceful kick in the rear to make sure it happened—he'd left Eda County. He'd started over with a clean slate in a city that had never heard the Marek name.

"Looks abandoned." Karen didn't move to get out. "I should have saved myself that excuse for a road. I may not be as lucky on the way back out. Talk about getting in a rut."

He didn't move, either. "You got out."

"Only because my dad made me do a lot of driving on the worst roads in the county. He wanted me able to take care of myself. I took it as a challenge—but, boy, did I have to learn the hard way. More often than not, I gunned the engine and ended up in the ditch or axle deep in mud. The trick is a light hand on the wheel, slow and steady." She nodded at the house. "Is this really where your grandparents lived? Looks like it wouldn't stand up to a Dakota winter—certainly its inhabitants wouldn't."

"Wood stove," he said shortly. "And lots of blankets."

"When was the last time you were here?"

"After my grandmother's funeral. Mom and Uncle Jim came out to see if there was anything worth keeping. I got dragged along for the ride."

Karen pursed her lips. "Did they find anything?"

Marek remembered the shuttered expressions of his mother and uncle as they'd walked into the small, cramped parlor and kitchen, and the way their gaze had scanned over the worn plank floors, the ancient potbelly stove, then each other. Weighted. That was what he'd felt from them both, that they could barely keep their heads up against the bad memories. His uncle had simply walked out without a word. His mother had taken a little longer, fingering a few tattered quilts and embroidered pillowcases then going up to the second floor, where she'd slept in a tiny room not much bigger than a walk-in closet, but ultimately, she'd walked out, as well. "Nothing. Mom said later that the only warm thing in that house was the stove. It was the only thing she would've taken, if she could've."

With obvious reluctance, Karen reached for the door latch. "Well, somebody made those ruts. Just because it looks abandoned doesn't mean—"

On cue, the door of the house banged open, nearly falling off its hinges.

CHAPTER 12

OTHER THAN NANCY KUBICEK BRIDGES, the only Kubicek relation Marek had met since returning to Eda County had been his mother's first cousin, Blaise, who'd been disowned by his father for cultivating the life of the mind, not the soil. Unlike the rest of the family, Blaise hadn't looked down on his poor Marek relations and had, in fact, blazed Janina Marek's path out.

Marek hadn't seen Blaise for several months, though they'd sent texts. Blaise wanted him to come down to Vermillion and talk to one of the professor's master's degree classes about how Marek's undiagnosed dyslexia had affected him growing up. Marek was of two minds. He owed Blaise. But he also didn't want to dredge too deep into his own past, or that of his mother or grandfather.

Fact was, though, the Kubiceks and Mareks had never been close, and if anything, it had been worse when Janina returned to Valeska. Marek didn't think they'd ever really forgiven her for going from a dirt-poor relation living on their grudging charity to a South Dakota teacher of the year and wife of arguably the most respected man in the county.

Instantly, Marek could tell the woman whose wide body brushed the doorframe was not someone he would ever connect with, no matter the blood tie. But he did recognize her. He'd seen that face looking out at him in endless mug shots over the years: the sagging, sallow skin of old age no matter the actual number on the driver's license, the lank hair greased with neglect, the bloodshot eyes of abuse, and the permanent sneer turned toward a world that didn't go their way.

"Get the hell off my land, or I'll call the cops," Nadine yelled from the doorway, her voice slurred but more than loud enough to carry through Karen's cracked-open side window.

Predictably, Karen pushed open the door and got out, her hand hovering above her open holster. Marek followed.

"Are you blind, Ms. Early?" Karen challenged. "I am the law. We want to talk to you."

"I ain't talking to no pigs..." Her head tilted back as she looked up at Marek, and the whiskey bottle in her hand slipped and sloshed onto the warped steps. The nauseating smell rose in the dead air. "You're dead. Long way dead. Did a header into the courthouse steps. I was there. What's in this shit?" She looked down at her hand, swore, then rescued what was left in the bottle, holding it against her sagging but ample bosom like a child. "I ain't that drunk. You ain't Lenny Marek."

"No, I'm Marek Okerlund."

For a long moment, she just looked blank. Then her sneer deepened into a yawning chasm. "Sissy-ass teacher's son. Halfwit. Even the hoity-toity Okerlunds said so."

Karen flinched beside him and not, he guessed, at the elitist jab. Her father had been the one to cultivate the "halfwit" tag—along with the oft-repeated "Mareks are trouble." But Arne had been at least half right. Marek had been short of wit and in trouble—with his teachers and his mother—because of his bad grades. But he'd taken Nadine Early's measure. "You afraid to talk to a halfwit?"

Her chin came up, just as he'd predicted. "Hell, no. Even half-pissed, I can outwit a Marek."

Nadine stumbled back into the house, leaving the door open. He took that as an invitation and walked in, Karen on his heels, simmering but quiet. The two of them had found their rhythm, more or less, and she'd silently acceded the floor—a plank floor

with several missing nails and upended boards here and there—
to him. He didn't relish the job, but he didn't see another option.

All Nadine Early had given Karen was lip and the finger,
but to him, she'd want to play the dominance game. A stand-
in for the hard-nosed father who'd disowned her, he guessed.
He only vaguely recalled the overalled man and his mouse of
a wife who'd brought boatloads of stroganoff to the few family
gatherings, mostly funerals.

What Marek did happen to know, his trump card, was that
the Kubiceks, if duly informed by the law of a trespasser on their
property, would no longer turn a blind eye to their wayward
relation. The land and house belonged to Blaise's younger
brother, Don, who planted corn and soybeans up to the fence
line to the east and grazed a small herd of cattle to the west.
That Don hadn't razed the place to the ground was the only
surprise. But it was, after all, the family homestead, so perhaps
he hadn't wanted to hear the hue and cry from sundry relations
who revered such things as a testament to their hardscrabble
roots.

Personally, Marek hoped the place would fall down, crushed
by its own weight, even if some of the carpentry work inside was
his. He'd worked his first jobs here under his Uncle Jim's eye,
helping to patch up the worst as his grandmother had aged in
place, refusing to leave for better, as if staying was a penance
only death could sever.

As Marek walked into the kitchen, where the potbelly stove
appeared to be the only thing that was indestructible, he could
feel the tackiness of a long-unwashed floor, smell the alcohol
that seeped into the very structure, and see the litter of bottles
outnumbering the food cartoons. With an arm that dangled
flesh like a milked udder, Nadine swept them all off the table.

"Welcome to my humble abode," she said with vast
insincerity, sitting down heavily into the only decent chair.
Though Marek preferred to stand, he knew that wouldn't help
his cause, so he gingerly sat down on a metal folding chair that

creaked dangerously, making him grip the table, which didn't go unnoticed. Nadine was already taking points.

Karen moved out of the line of sight to lean against a far wall, but Nadine seemed to have wiped the sheriff from her world anyway. All her focus was on her target.

"Heard tell you was back. Didn't think you was *that* dumb. Guess I was wrong. Then again, your mother always had a swelled head. Got her comeuppance once her baby daddy got himself dead, though. Served her right. What goes up, must come down." She laughed, an entirely humorless and faintly chilling cackle that might have come out of a B-grade horror flick.

Marek didn't blink at the whiskey-soaked wave of insults, even if the urban slang was jarring—she must've picked it up from the idiot box that sat on the peeling counter, where an antenna cable snaked between discarded gin, whiskey, and vodka bottles. Though the setting was far different from his digs in Albuquerque, he'd met her like, and much worse, in the interview room. That didn't mean he thought this interview would be easy, as it was a delicate balance between letting her think she had the upper hand and actually giving it to her. But she'd expect pushback.

"You've certainly come down in the world," he told her. "Living on Marek castoffs."

Nadine pushed a lank gray lock out of her eyes so she could give him the beady—and bloody—eye. "Living on the Kubicek homestead that the Mareks trashed."

"He's an Okerlund," Karen pointed out before she compressed her lips.

But Nadine either didn't hear or didn't take note. "Far as I'm concerned, you Mareks owe me. Heard you ain't good enough to get hired on full-time, so you do odd jobs on the side, just like Lenny. Might as well put that to good use, paying off his debt."

Almost admiring the woman's unmitigated gall in suggesting a master carpenter give away his valuable time for some imagined debt, he refused to be baited. "Did you treat Bob Bunting like this after he lost the election last night?"

She scowled at him. "You won't get out of your debt that easy. You play, you pay." She rubbed her fingers together in the classic give-me-money gesture. To her, the debt was now set in stone, a marker to be pulled.

"And if I did some work here to pay that debt, you'd answer my questions?" Ignoring the fierce glare from Karen, hotter than the potbelly stove, he kept eye contact with Nadine.

She took his capitulation with a hint of disappointment, but more satisfaction, and a gloating smile temporarily disabled the sneer. "That's the deal."

"You were with Bunting last night."

Nadine pouched out her chapped lips as she pondered that, looking for a trap. "Yeah, at the so-called recount. What of it? He's my ex, and while we ain't looking to get hitched again, I supported him. I was a good wife to him while it lasted. He's the one who catted around on me. Broke my heart. Drove me to drink. Not that I can't hold my liquor."

As if to prove it, she tipped back the broken whiskey bottle and downed the remains in a swallow. Marek himself had to swallow back bile. Was this what it had been like for his grandmother, living with Lenny Marek all those years? Yet even Lenny, despite his violence, hadn't had any illusions about himself. When he'd come up dry, he'd often been sorry. Too little, too late. With hands the size of platters, he'd never known his own strength.

With effort, Marek unfisted hands of the same size. "I meant when you saw Bunting after the recount, at Grove Park."

Nadine slammed down the empty bottle. "What the hell are you talking about? Why would I go to some piss-poor excuse of a park?"

Marek heard truth there, but if it was truth in wine, *in vino veritas*, or actual truth, he wasn't sure. "We have a witness who said you slapped him and called him a piece of shit."

Her bloodshot eyes narrowed until they disappeared into folds. "You're trying to frame me, that's what you're doing. Talk about a piece of work. So much for the high and mighty. 'Okerlunds don't lie.'" Nadine mimicked the informal campaign motto. "Always knew that was a crock. But you ain't gonna pin nothing on me. I can prove it. I went to drown my sorrows at The Shaft—and old Martin let me stay after hours. Slept it off on one of the tables until he rolled me this morning, to tell me Bob was dead."

Although Marek had no illusions about the owner of the off-color bar beyond town limits, he had the sinking feeling that her alibi would hold up. Sensing the win, Nadine grinned at him, showing only one front tooth.

Time to stop playing nice. "Bunting gave you the finger after the recount. And you just stood there in the street and took it. All but crushed, our witness said."

"Nothing of the sort." That raised color in Nadine's face. "Bunting had nothing. Was nothing."

"So why were you pulling for him to win?"

"To get you lot out. Okerlunds and Mareks. Even nothing's better than that."

Whatever she saw in his eyes, in the hands that had fisted again on the table, must've spooked her, because she hissed out what sounded like truth. "Damn man finally had something worth something, and a blind eye when a body just wanted some fun. Then he fucked it up, just like always, just like forever. I'm pleased as punch he's dead. No use, no-account dead weight. Now get out—and don't come back without a tool belt on."

Marek rose to his feet, ready to leave—with nothing—but Karen headed for the table, not the door.

"You called me before the election and left a message. Said you had dirt on Bunting."

For a moment, Marek thought that Nadine simply wouldn't respond. Finally, though, she tipped her head back with her sneer at full wattage. "And you didn't have the wit to call me back. You'd have paid good money for the dirt I could've dished, 'stead of buying off the election after. I know how it goes. You grease the wheels of those Dahls, and they grease yours. I ain't telling you nothing."

"You don't have to. You filed a restraining order. That'll tell me all I need to know."

"A restraining... what?" Her sneer faltered. "Oh. That. Just surface. I got more. You pay, you play."

Karen's face was colder than a Dakota winter. "I wouldn't play you if you were Elton John's best instrument. You can keep your lies." Karen turned on her booted heel and marched out, stepping perfectly on the uneven flooring so as not to ruin her exit. A born athlete.

"Okerlunds lie!" Nancy screamed after her.

"Yes, they do," Marek said down to her. "To liars."

Her gaze swung back to him. "We had a deal."

"No, I asked 'what if.' I didn't seal a deal." As she gathered breath, he told her, deadly serious, "You try anything to smear Karen or anyone else that belongs to me and mine, and I'll go straight to Don, and you'll lose this place."

She choked a laugh. "Don won't give a Marek the time of day."

"Maybe not. But all Karen's got to do is tell Don a concerned citizen's filed a complaint about a homeless drunk who might well set fire to the whole prairie one night." Marek let that sink in. "You'll be gone before the snow flies."

Marek didn't take satisfaction in her reaction—the glazed look of an animal caught in its last bolt-hole. That he'd seen that naked look of fear would never be forgiven, but it wouldn't be forgotten, either.

"You have a debt to pay," Nadine finally sputtered. "You're family."

"I don't owe you anything. And the only thing I'd ever pay a penny for based on blood, Nadine, is rehab."

"Don't need your pennies. And I'm no drunk."

As Marek shut the door of the house behind him, her empty whiskey bottle shattered against it. Let her clean up the mess. Like his mother and uncle, he left the Kubicek homestead with nothing.

Except pity for Bob Bunting.

CHAPTER 13

KAREN HAD TO WORK HARD to keep her hand light and her wheels out of the ruts on the way out. When she'd stormed out, Karen had actually been more pissed at her detective than at Nadine. But they both were what they were. Marek, soft. Nadine, a user. "You better not have promised to fix up anything in that godforsaken house."

"No," Marek said shortly.

"Good. Glad you made that clear." So maybe she'd been off there, imbibing too much of her father's bias. Karen relaxed onto the bad but drivable county road. "I hope that place falls down around her ears. Alice Dutton was spot on. A drunk, a manipulator, and a backstabber." After a few miles of grim silence, she asked, "Do you think she knows anything worth knowing?"

He shook his head, not in the negative, she decided, but to clear it. "Maybe, maybe not, but whatever she was selling, I wouldn't buy. You buy once, you never stop. That was Bunting's mistake."

"Yeah, I got that. I have to say, the idea of a young Bob Bunting falling into her clutches just when he'd escaped his mother's makes me feel a lot more sorry for the man. And that's a good thing. Makes me want to find his killer. Just wish it was her. She's poison, through and through. What now?" Her stomach rumbled. "What time is it?"

He pulled his phone from his shirt pocket and looked at it far longer than she would've thought necessary. That told her that he was seriously upset—because that was when his dyslexia was at its worst. "Just going four. I suggest we search Bunting's place."

Too early for supper, despite her stomach's protest. "Okay, I'll get a warrant. Judge Rudibaugh shouldn't have a problem with that, given the man's dead, and I got Alice Dutton's okay before we left."

While Judge Rudy wasn't quite so easily—or at least as quickly—persuaded as she'd hoped, he did issue the warrant, along with his congratulations. "Justice under Robert Bunting would have been a travesty. While regrettably inexperienced in the field that you have been elected to, you are still a far more welcome addition to the forces of law in our county."

Damned with that faint praise, she'd taken the warrant and called in her remaining swing-shift deputy. Two Fingers met them just behind Grove Park in the trailer park. While Ted Jorgenson kept up what he could, it was obvious that within the last year, the place had deteriorated.

"I didn't even know Bunting lived out here until I ran the address for the warrant," Karen told her companions as they picked their way through weedy grass grown too tall and littered with trash. "I'd have guessed something far more ritzy, given his ride."

"All he had was his ride," Two Fingers said. "He's filed bankruptcy twice. Had another pending and creditors at the door. I don't know who gave him the loan, but they'll be repossessing the truck."

Karen took it as a plus that her career-wavering deputy was interested enough in the case to do some of his own sleuthing. "Good to know." She filled him in on their progress as curtains twitched and lights were extinguished. The majority, in fact, were dark. Though, to be fair, at about five o'clock, their residents were likely at work. A few occupants bravely stared out at them, but more were oblivious, mesmerized by the glare of the boob tube.

Karen checked the address on the warrant again then stopped in front of a rusted once-white trailer with a twisted skirt of corrugated aluminum that looked as though a giant had gnawed on it. "I'd have thought the man had a pension—or pensions—to keep the wolf from the door."

Marek finally spoke. "Never lasted long enough to get one."

Two Fingers gave him a sidelong glance, as if that was a not-so-subtle dig at the deputy's undecided plans for the future, but Marek didn't notice. Her detective had disappeared into himself, into his own world, something he hadn't done often in the last year. But she'd seen far too much of it when he'd first returned to Reunion after his wife's death.

Karen mouthed at Two Fingers, "Bad day."

That got the barest of nods. Karen took out the house key that Larson had given her. She pushed open the door with gloved hands and flicked on the lights.

"What a pig," Two Fingers said.

Over every available surface, Bud Lights intermixed with takeout from The Café and empty Spaghetti-O's cans. She didn't see anything from Mex-Mix, which didn't surprise her. He would have seen it as the domain of illegals, no matter the quite-legal, American-born owner. Probably thought he'd be poisoned if he ordered anything there.

"It's a wonder Bunting didn't die of botulism or something worse." Karen poked through the remains of many days and nights. "I swear, I see things growing. Disgusting. I'd say something about typical bachelor digs, but I'm pretty sure you both have neater homes than I do. So I won't."

When she got no response, she looked up. Marek and Two Fingers had disappeared down the hallway. She heard drawers being pulled open and presumed they'd started on the other rooms. She looked through mail on the coffee table. All looked to be bills—utilities, mostly—and plenty were stamped *Final Notice.*

She just hoped the electric company didn't pull the plug while they were in the trailer. When she saw nothing more but mold in the kitchen, she moved into the hallway. Both of her men had avoided the dark, dank bathroom. As their putative boss, she did the same. She passed Two Fingers rifling through a battered desk in a room used as a study.

"Anything?" she asked Marek as she stepped into the final room, the bedroom, with sudden reluctance. The dead man's most intimate area was not something she wanted to think about.

Marek's answer was a shake of the head. She turned to look around and saw a photograph, the only one in the room, and it was the same photo that resided in Alice Dutton's drawer.

A happy baby, a happy woman, all gone down the toilet.

"You can't hate a man too much who'll display that in his bedroom. I'm guessing it's probably the only photo he had from his childhood."

Leaving the nightstand for Marek, she went to the closet. Bunting had a number of duty shirts in progressively larger sizes, a slideshow in fabric of his career, starting with Eda County, to the South Dakota Highway Patrol, then crisscrossing the state in county jobs, going over the border into Nebraska once, back to the patrol, Iowa twice, then back to the patrol and... she stopped. That one didn't fit. The patrol duty shirt was for a slimmer man, and the insignia was quite dated behind its plastic covering.

And the surname on the tag? Not Bunting but Johnson.

Could it be? She could think of only one possible reason that Bunting would keep a duty shirt of his hated stepfather, Ed Johnson. Back in the day, Bunting could have worn that shirt, as he'd been much slimmer when he'd worked for her father. All sympathy for Baby Bunting disappeared in instant revulsion. "Marek."

She had to say it twice before he looked up from his perusal of a box of condoms. If she was right, Bunting hadn't been so conscientious in the past. Over two decades in the past. She raised the shirt and watched her detective's eyes narrow, pop wide, then narrow again. Like her, he hadn't forgotten. "Don't tell Two Fingers," she told him.

"Don't tell me what?" her deputy asked from the doorway.

Karen closed her eyes and cursed her big mouth. Slowly, reluctantly, she turned, still holding up the duty shirt on its hanger. She waited a long beat. When she opened her eyes again, her deputy's face, with its classic high cheekbones, looked hollow. Scooped out from the inside.

Dropping the papers in his hand onto the floor, he slowly came in, reached out, and brought the front tails up into the light. Old stains stood out like black marks on the light fabric. The kind of stains one would expect from a violent rape. But why keep it? A trophy? If her own stomach churned, she couldn't imagine what she'd just stirred up in her deputy's gut.

Surprisingly, Marek spoke first. "Johnson's a common surname."

Two Fingers's head snapped up, and Marek fell silent. A common name, yes. It was the surname, after all, of Karen's daughter. But if you coupled Johnson with the South Dakota Highway Patrol and the stains, the story became an age-old one of power over right.

Karen let out a breath. Whatever she'd expected to find here, it wasn't this. Different case. Personal case. About as personal as it got. And as cold. "Deputy, it's your call. I can turn this over to the FBI in Sioux Falls. You could take a DNA test..." He dropped the shirttails as if burned, and the black holes of his eyes swallowed her words.

Surprisingly, he said, "I already took a DNA test. To see if the tribal council might change their ruling if I tested over fifty percent Native. It was forty-seven percent."

And that number would have been comfortably close to a hundred if his mother had made the choice of her son's father. "We'll have Dr. White send a sample from Bunting over to the FBI, if that's what you want. Your decision. You'll want to talk to your mother."

CHAPTER 14

TWO FINGERS JUST STOOD THERE. Karen thought she understood the dilemma. Justice or privacy. Probably even more than that. Was it better to have an unknown rapist father or a known one? Just how long had Bunting been playing the good guy when he was, in all likelihood, the worst of the worst? It certainly put a different spin on their current investigation. Had a victim—or a victim's brother, father, or son—killed Bunting?

"Your mother probably wasn't his only victim," Marek said flatly. "Never are for that type."

The words seemed to shake Two Fingers out of his stasis. "The last reported with that MO."

The familiar give and take of facts, speculation, of detective work, seemed to have been the right approach. Keeping her tone brisk, Karen asked, "And what MO was that?"

"Pull over a single female driver in the middle of the night, plant drugs on her, then spread-eagle her over the hood, rape from behind. Let her go with the warning if she reports, no one will believe her. That she'll go down for years on the drug charge." His rage, as dark and deep as his eyes, surfaced for a moment before he controlled it. "Kept his hat low and shined his light in their eyes. My mother was the only one who saw the name tag."

Karen could barely get the words out. So much for emotionless. "How many victims?"

"Three that reported. DCI did the initial investigation. Checked the active duty roster. No Johnson on duty. Thirteen on the roster. Interviewed by phone, all denied knowledge, all came up with alibis from significant others. No further investigation. Nothing done with the rape kits. Deemed pointless. One of the women was a drunk, one was a stripper, and the other…"

Was an Indian. On, as Karen recalled, reservation land. "And that's when the FBI took it over?" They had jurisdiction along with the Bureau of Indian Affairs.

"Yes, but they didn't touch the case until a few years ago. They got a lot of bad press, national press, over all the unsolveds on the reservations. So they ran all three of the rape kits. No hits."

"Was Bunting in the patrol way back then?" Marek asked.

Karen didn't need to think. She knew exactly when he'd left her father's employ. She hadn't wanted to face him again after the riot act he'd read her as she'd idled in the ditch with an open beer can in her car—and though he hadn't known it, a baby in her belly. That lecture had made her decide to give up that child instead of telling her parents and risking her father's job during a difficult election. "Yes, he was. He quit my dad's roster by leaving a note stuck under the windshield wiper of his squad. I knew the man was an ass. I never guessed he was much worse. I realize you have to ask your—"

"No. I don't need to. She's always wanted him found." And with that, he seemed to settle. "We need to get that to the FBI."

She held it out. "Then take it. I'll call and tell them to expect it."

He frowned, not taking it. "But with Bork out…"

"Marek and I will handle any calls. I need to talk to Adam anyway when he comes on shift at midnight." When Two Fingers didn't move, she glared. "You think we can't handle it?"

He saw right through the move, but it got him moving—with the duty shirt.

"So much for feeling sorry for Bunting." Karen turned her

back on the bouncing baby boy and scooped up the papers on the floor. "Nadine was too good for him."

Marek didn't answer. He'd disappeared again into himself, but this time, she suspected that was because he was thinking hard about the case, not about the emotional minefield of Two Fingers's father or his own checkered ancestry.

"We might as well head home for supper then meet back up to talk to Mindy Bullard. See if she can ID the bruiser and his knockout relation." When Marek's shoulders braced, Karen sighed. He'd had a hard day already. Facing the wife of the man who'd nearly killed his child might break his back. "I can talk to Mindy myself. No need for you to go."

He shook his head. "If I start avoiding people related to people we arrest, I'll soon be out of a job."

"Isn't that the truth." After one last look around, Karen locked the door of the trailer and turned to see a slim blond man in his early thirties walking gingerly over the muck toward her.

"About time you got here. Guess when you get around to it, you really get to it fast, seeing this is Bunting's unit." The man started right up the stairs. "No need to lock it. I'll have it cleaned out before the night's done. I've got a crew who'll do it for me for a reduction in rent. I assume you've finished with the rest already?"

Marek kept walking down the steps so that Mr. Slick, for who else could it be with his natty suit and tie, had to stumble back or be flattened. "Hey, watch it. You blind as well as dumb?"

"Just dumb, I guess," Marek said, stopping on the last step, an unmovable barrier.

"Go get the tape for the door," Karen told him.

Mr. Slick frowned up at her. "Tape? What tape? Did Bunting break the door?"

Marek moved, and Mr. Slick scrambled back, stumbling into a mudhole. He lost his cool enough to stick out his middle finger at Marek's back. "Is that the best you can get? At least Bunting would have hired someone with a few brain cells to go with that brawn."

Karen let him think so. "Is that why you supported Bunting to the bitter end, staying for the recount, Mr....?"

"Digges. Alan Digges." He didn't try to deny he'd been there. "I supported Bunting because, unlike some I could name, he promised to get things done. I called your office numerous times this past week and got the runaround."

Uneasily, Karen thought of Biester, who'd said much the same.

Sensing the upper hand, Digges smirked. "I've got tenants lined up, money in hand, waiting for those trailers. All you've got to do is show up with the eviction notice, and we'll do the work. But since you're here now, we'll let bygones be bygones. I expect you'll see lots of me in the future. That's how you make a profit." Like Nadine Early, he rubbed thumb and fingers together in a money gesture. "Churn, baby, churn."

He might be from a higher social strata than Nadine, but not a moral one.

"You must be Ted Jorgenson's heir."

Digges managed a sorrowful look. "Dear Uncle Ted. I'm just trying to do his memory proud. Make sure we've got good tenants here that won't cause trouble for you."

Tenants who wouldn't cause trouble for *him*, more like. She couldn't imagine how this man shared even a drop of blood with the unpretentious Ted Jorgenson. Marek returned with the crime-scene tape, but Digges blocked the way, puffing out his nonexistent chest.

"Hey, hey, hey. You aren't putting that up there. There's no crime here except that an airhead like you carries a badge. Your boss and I just came to an understanding. She shows up with the paperwork, and we do the work. You won't have to lift a finger, though you look like that's about all you're good for."

Marek took a step then another, and Digges cursed him and moved back.

While Marek applied the tape, Karen applied her tongue. "What we have, Mr. Digges, is murder."

That brought his head around. "What? What are you talking about?"

"Bunting. Don't tell me you haven't heard."

"Are you serious? He's been murdered?"

She wasn't green enough to take Digges's surprise at face value. "Where did you go after the recount last night?"

"You want *my* alibi?" He fingered the knot of a tie that had probably cost more than Karen's monthly pay. "I'm a respected businessman, not a killer. My wife has connections in the statehouse. And after this latest insult, you better believe I'll be using them."

Though he might well have such connections, Karen wasn't going to let him shake her. First Biester, now Digges, had threatened to take their complaints to a higher level. Took three strikes, not two, for an out, she hoped. "Just answer the question."

"Under protest."

"So noted."

"Very well. I stopped by here to see if any progress had been made on the evictions, which none had, and to start the process on several more. I then returned home to Sioux Falls. You can check with my wife, Michelle Bayton." He said that as if it were supposed to mean something, and when he got nothing but blank faces, he shook his head sadly. "You really are out in the boonies. Baytons? Big-time real estate tycoons. We own millions, probably billions, in property in this state."

Anyone who needed to brag about their money hadn't always had it. What was his story? She was willing to bet her bottom dollar that he'd married into that money. The only surprise was that he hadn't taken the name Bayton, at least hyphenated.

"What did you say to Bunting after the recount that made him turn white?" Marek asked.

Digges blinked at her detective as if surprised to hear the dumb speak. As if only then remembering the piece of paper he held in his hand, he lifted it and slapped it against Marek's chest. "Here. Read that. If you can."

Marek trapped the paper before it could fall then tilted his head down to read. It took him a second, if that, before he handed it back to Karen. She recognized the form, though it was a homemade version, not one issued by her office. Perfectly legal, even if it said as little as legally possible.

Three Day Notice to Vacate.

Bunting was being evicted from his trailer.

Digges gave a satisfied nod at their silence. "I expect action on those prior evictions within the required window, Sheriff Mehaffey, or I will contact Judge Rudibaugh, who issued them, and let him deal with you. By the way, that means by tomorrow, since Friday was the third day, and Monday is the next official business day."

As threats went, it was a good one, but fortunately, he didn't see her flinch. He'd turned to stalk his way back to his sleek, slick Benz, though his exit was marred by the sucking sounds of his loafers.

"Looks like I've added one more thing to tomorrow's agenda. Joy." Karen stuffed the eviction notice on the dash of the Sub. "Why did I want this job again?"

This time, Marek didn't answer.

CHAPTER 15

PULLING UP IN FRONT OF her bungalow, Karen felt her spirits lift. During her quick shower earlier, her mind had been focused on the case, so she hadn't really settled into what this place meant to her. Here, finally, was home. Her home for at least the next four years, assuming Digges didn't get her impeached or whatever. Home for her, home for the Okerlunds for generations, home for now. Home for her daughter.

Eyre was going to turn twenty-two in just another day. The same age Karen had been when Eyre was born. But Karen had given up the right to be called mother. Her daughter had been raised by a very good mother—a gracious and seriously smart mother who was a professor of English down in Vermilion. It had been her idea for Eyre to live with Karen after Eyre's apartment was burned to the ground. Neither had expected to be so different from each other, and they were still treading cautiously.

Still, after taking her temporary leave from a brooding Marek, Karen opened her front door with a bubble of happiness she hadn't felt in a good long while. The smell of German pot roast, the same recipe that her mother had served on numerous weekends, scented the air with good memories. Eyre must have heated up leftovers.

Karen stowed her gun and followed her nose into the kitchen. Only to stop short. The two young women sitting at the old oak table before untouched plates looked like sisters, not cousins.

Their rounded faces were as long as possible. And their long brunette hair unadorned.

That wasn't right. The younger, only fourteen, was a member of the Eder Brethren. Mary Hannah had been baptized into the faith only the past spring and wore a bonnet and dress with a short cape as a badge of identity, much as Karen did her uniform.

But the bonnet was gone.

Had Mary Hannah abandoned her faith after little more than a month as a freshman at Reunion High? That would be a real barn-burner, razing right down to the ground the tentative ties that Karen was building with the Eder Brethren and its leader, her mother's brother, Sander Mock. But when Karen saw the ice in Eyre's Okerlund eyes and the downcast hazel of Mary Hannah's, she knew something else was afoot.

"What happened?" Karen demanded, food forgotten. "Why are you still here on a Saturday when you should be with your family, Mary Hannah? Is something wrong at home?"

Mary Hannah grabbed a new plate and began filling it up. "No, they're fine. Nothing happened. Please, eat. I had Eyre call Mr. Hahn to let my parents know that I would not return this weekend. We need to celebrate Eyre's birthday tomorrow and your homecoming. I know it's just pot roast, but..."

Karen understood babbling to hide a hurt, as her mother had done, as Karen still did on occasion. "Mary Hannah, I appreciate any and all food that you choose to put before me. I'm a terrible cook, and you know it." She took the proffered plate and set it down on the table but didn't pull up a chair. "But I am responsible for you while you live here. I need to know what's happened to you, to your bonnet."

Mary Hannah's chin rose, a bit of spirit that Karen took in with secret pleasure, as the Mock women had never, despite their supposedly submissive beliefs, been meek and mild. "The Brethren do not speak of those who wrong them. It is of no import."

"No import?" Eyre pushed away her own plate. "After school

yesterday, a boy named Sean snatched her bonnet off her head and stomped on it in the mud. Told her that she must be dirt poor, wearing the same clothes every day, never taking a bath. Said she was nothing but a ho to a bunch of randy little cowards." Dots of color appeared on her cheeks. "I had to explain to Mary Hannah what a ho was."

With simple dignity, and not a little bewilderment, Mary Hannah said, "I am not a prostitute. Why would I ever wish to be? All I want to do is to bring children into the world. Why would this boy, who I barely know, accuse me of such a thing?" Her hand went to her head as if to search for a vital body part. "Why would he take and ruin my bonnet?"

"It wasn't the first time he's taunted her, either," Eyre said darkly. "Always after school as she walks back home. He's the coward, not her."

Karen closed her eyes. "And you said nothing, Mary Hannah? Have you told your father?"

Sander Mock had experienced his own culture clash after being drafted into the Army during Vietnam, despite his religious stance against violence.

"No, I don't want to distress him. And... he might pull me out of school, and then I cannot be a midwife." That clearly distressed her young cousin most of all. "Besides, Father said it would be hard sometimes. He told me not to judge all by one, that the one—and there's always one—will try to make my life miserable, just because they can. And that's what nonresistance is about. You pray for your enemies, you love them, and you forgive them."

And the sky was blue. It was that simple for the Brethren. But Karen's mother had broken that cardinal rule by calling in the police—and she'd been placed under the ban. The Brethren didn't have a mechanism to deal with evil. At least, not in this life.

But Karen did. "I'll take care of it."

Mary Hannah looked alarmed. "I don't want you to put him in jail."

If only she could. "I won't. Look, what would you do if that had happened at Eder?"

She blinked. "Tell my parents."

"How do you think they'd handle it? Just tell you to forget it?"

"Oh, no, they'd talk to the boy's parents, and he'd be punished... but it's not the same."

"Isn't it? Consider me *in loco parentis*. Substitute parent." Karen ignored Eyre's flinch. She could be a parent to Mary Hannah, but not to her own daughter? Karen sighed inwardly. She went to the closet and retrieved a small chest that had belonged to her mother. She hadn't opened the lid since she was a kid. And her father had always feared the contents would lead Hannah Mock Okerlund away from him.

But they never had. All that she'd left Eder with was in that chest. The modest blue dress, looking no different in style from the one her namesake wore, lay on top. Removing that and the cape, Karen found the bonnet underneath, still stark white, not a bit yellowed. Why her mother had kept the clothes of her former life, despite her husband's silent disapproval, Karen was never really sure. Had they been a security blanket, knowing that if things didn't turn out, she could always return to the Eder, make her penance? Or were they a reminder of what she'd lost—or what she'd gained?

Whatever the case, Karen didn't think her mother would mind that the bonnet would at last return home to Eder. "Here you go, Mary Hannah. I don't think your parents will notice the difference. After dinner, Mr. Hahn can drive you home."

Her young cousin took the bonnet as though it were a crown, with awe, with responsibility. "Thank you. I will treasure it. And I will bring my other bonnets with me so that the boy does not ruin this one."

"He won't be ruining any more, regardless," Karen told her. "Now, let's all dig into this excellent pot roast before it goes cold. Waste not, want not."

By the time Karen went out to meet Marek at the Sub, she

and the girls had laid waste to the roast. Marek looked a bit more substantial, as well, as if he'd re-centered himself with his supper. Mex-Mix, she guessed, from the faint lingering scent of green chile. A faint twinge of guilt surfaced that she hadn't asked him over to partake of the roast, as she knew that Becca was over at Arne's until Marek picked her up for the night. The arrangement suited all parties, even if that was never officially acknowledged. Karen opened her mouth to apologize then caught sight of Nikki, Marek's sort-of significant other, heading out from the back of Marek's bungalow toward her bluff-side home. So he'd had company. Good for him. At least his life was progressing. Hers? Not so much.

"Where does Mindy live now?" Marek asked as he got into the Sub.

Karen pulled away from the curb. "With her brother's family near Fink. Jeff Hansen. He married Ann Schwartz and farms her father's land. I don't expect a warm welcome."

As they pulled up in front of the cheap modular home on a section line, Karen's prognostication was proven true. She'd barely gotten out of the Sub when a man stepped in her path. Jeff had been a year ahead of her in school, while his sister, Mindy, had been three years ahead. A hard worker, Jeff wore grease-stained jeans and a torn flannel shirt.

He re-seated his seed cap on his head. "You got something to say, say it to me, then get out. My sister don't need any more grief from you."

Because she saw grief as well as anger, Karen tamped down on her own. She turned her head away to regain control and saw the faces behind the front window. Mindy and her kids... and Ann and her kids... all huddled together in little windbreaks of hurt. How did they all fit in that place? Just a cheap home on a concrete slab, it had no basement or second story. Why couldn't they make those things homier? Her own bungalow, after all, was a Sears model, yet it looked like a home.

"I don't intend to give her any grief," she told Jeff when she looked back. "I just have some questions for her about Bob Bunting."

He crossed his arms. "She had every right to support the man against you. If you think you can pin his murder on her, just for payback—"

"Don't go there," Marek said with an uncharacteristic edge.

Karen wasn't sure who was more surprised by the interruption, her or Jeff. But she was even more surprised at Jeff Hansen's reaction.

He dropped his head and kicked at the gravel with a work boot that was on its last tread. "Sorry. I just... it eats away at me. I go from hating Cal to hating meth to hating me, that I couldn't have seen it coming, couldn't have helped Mindy keep the farm, but I can barely keep my own head above water. And Cal had mortgaged the farm to the hilt, supporting his habit, not his family."

He scuffed the gravel again. "Mindy... she's messed up with the shame of it, the anger of it, and needed a target... and you Okerlunds ended up being in the crosshairs." He raised his head, his eyes pleading. "Look, Mindy told me what happened last night. Let me answer your questions. My sister... well, she's on a new med to keep her upright and out of the dumps, and it's starting to work. She's interviewing tomorrow for a job at that new grocery co-op that's going to start up in Reunion. I don't want to upset the apple cart. If she can get back on her feet, it'll be the best thing for her, for her kids, and, well, for my sanity— and my marriage." He put his hands into empty pockets. "I got no trouble helping family in trouble, happy to do so, but there comes a time..."

When too many people in too little space would backfire, leaving them all scorched.

"Fair enough." Karen relaxed her shoulders, not realizing until then just how tense she'd been. "What we're really after is the players at the recount and any motivation they might have had to kill Bunting. We've identified Alan Digges, Mindy, and Nadine Early as three of the five who were in Bunting's corner. We need to know the other two: a young woman and what looked to be an older male relation, described as a big bruiser, perhaps a bro—"

"That would be Kaylee Early and her big brother, Kyle." The disgust in his voice rang clear. "You want to be looking for a motive for murder? Take that Dud-amic Duo. Kaylee's half a brain short of full—some difficulty with her birth—and her brother is basically her pimp. He's a dealer in whatever vice you care to indulge in. I'm surprised he isn't on your radar. I told Mindy that if those two were backing Bunting, your victim was on the take, and she'd better get out or get taken down with him."

Karen mulled that. "Are the Earlys related to Jim Early, who married Nadine Kubicek?"

"Cousins, I think, though they take after their mother, a Rezac. But Jim's a good man. Dumb to fall for Nadine, yeah, but smart enough to kick her to the curb within the year—and run off to Mexico to make sure he wouldn't get pulled into her nasty little games. Have you talked to her? She's the sort who'd enjoy stuffing a man's mouth with her own shit."

Karen felt her own mouth fall open. "Where did you hear that detail?"

He raised his eyebrows. "YRUN."

Great. So much for playing it straight, Nails. "Okay, I think that's all we need to know." Karen hesitated and hooked her thumbs into her belt. "I'm sorry about Mindy, her kids. I hated to kick them off the farm. Evictions are my least favorite thing to do, other than death notifications."

He shot an uneasy glance at the window then back. "Look, I know you served that eviction personally because that's the way you Okerlunds operate. You don't hand off the hard stuff. But Mindy? She took it as another slap. I'd appreciate it if you go through me if you've got more questions."

"Will do." She started for the Sub then turned. "Oh... I've seen a large fifth wheel for sale in Reunion dirt cheap by Maggie Dietrich now that her husband's gone. Just a thought. Looked structurally sound, and you could hook it up here without much difficulty."

Jeff pursed his lips then nodded. "Thanks for the tip."

Turning back, Karen risked a quick look at the window. The elder Bullard kid, the boy, gave her the finger. Almost, she let it go. Then she flashed him another gesture, a comeback learned on her last trip. The Vulcan salute. She prayed it would come true, for his sake, as well as hers—she didn't want to see his name on an eviction notice or a court reporter's docket.

Live long and prosper.

CHAPTER 16

BACK DOWN BAD-MEMORY LANE.

Marek stood on the leaf-and-dirt-littered porch of the battered brick bungalow. Figured that the wayward Earlys would live in the same house where he'd spent his four long years in Valeska, a stone's throw from the high school where he'd struggled to pass class after class in a gauntlet far more grueling than the gridiron where he'd found more success.

He'd spent many, many nights up in that attic room behind the now-shuttered window with the lights burning late, his mother downstairs, waiting to grill him after she'd finished her grading. That he'd finally been diagnosed with dyslexia by then had helped, as he'd been allowed to take many of his exams verbally or given extra time on the written, though the mutters about favoritism and special breaks had followed him throughout school. He'd been drafted into football based solely on size, not talent, and mostly against his mother's wishes. But it had been his ticket to acceptance. Or at least tolerance.

The name of Marek certainly hadn't helped endear him to this town where two of its not-so-upstanding citizens had lost their lives to the heavy-fisted Lenny at the Barstool Bar down the street.

Both Valeska and the house looked like they'd taken more than a few hits in the years he'd been gone. Lawns once groomed and porches once broomed had gone to seed and weed. He wondered how many more years the high school would hold out against the siren call of consolidation.

Karen leaned on the doorbell. An anemic buzz sounded inside. With no vehicle in the driveway, he doubted anyone was home to answer. But the door screeched open with a hard pull.

A stunner of a young woman in a lacy pink peignoir stood in the doorway. Her gaze went straight to Marek as if Karen weren't there. "Oh. Hi. You aren't Ned. Kyle said Ned was coming tonight."

Had to be Kaylee Early. The words were simple, the gaze guileless, and the body easy. But made so, Marek had no doubt, by the facilitation of her brother. That made him sick. "Is Kyle home?"

"Oh. No. He went to Sioux Falls for more pills. Did you want to pay him?" She held out a soft-scented hand. "I'll take it. I can do that. We have a lock box. Only Kyle has the key."

Marek felt torn between getting the information they needed from someone clearly of legal age and getting the young woman a court-appointed guardian to look after her rights. She was a danger to herself.

"Money for what?" Karen asked from the dim shadows.

"Oh. You scared me." Kaylee's flawless porcelain brow furrowed as she took in Karen's uniform. "You're the police. I'm not supposed to talk to the police without Kyle."

"We're from the Sheriff's Office," Karen told her gravely.

"Oh. That's okay, then. Do you want pills or sex?" Her gaze went from Karen to Marek with a faint frown. "Manage a tree? But if Ned shows up, he gets to go first, okay?"

Ménage à trois? Marek felt his hands fist. "No, we just want to talk."

"Oh. I don't charge for that. I don't think. I'll ask Kyle. Come on in." Kaylee turned and sashayed back inside. A diva with a child's mind. Marek followed into a gaudy living room, a stark difference in tone from his mother's Arts and Crafts–era affinities. A huge sectional couch in red velvet dominated the room in front of an even bigger wraparound TV. He didn't want to think about what lay beyond in the master bedroom. If that was what it still was. Maybe the business side ran out of the second-story room, which made him never, ever wish to revisit it.

Kaylee swooped down into the sectional into a pose that showed swells of breast and length of leg. "I like when people come to visit. Mostly, they just want sex, you know? But it gets kind of boring. That's why I was so mad when Bobby lost the votes. It was all for nothing, Kyle said, letting him have sex without money." Her lower lip trembled. "We were going to get a big house with a big bed and have lots of babies. I like babies, don't you?"

Just how, Marek wondered, had this woman-child made it through school, through her brother's machinations, and through Bunting's less than pure embrace, with such innocence intact? "Um... yes. I have a daughter. She's seven."

Kaylee clapped her hands together. "You have to bring her to see me. I love kids, too, not just babies. Oh, but I have to make sure it's okay with Kyle." She gave them a serious look. "He says that little kids shouldn't be around sex."

Except when it came to his woman-child sister. Carefully, Marek probed. "The agreement you had with Bob Bunting, what was it for? What was Kyle going to get out of it?"

She frowned, and for a moment, Marek thought that some bit of wiliness had seeped into her dove mind. Then she smiled. "I had to think. Kyle said that it was win-win. I get babies, and he gets a... a blind eye. Isn't that weird? Who'd want a blind eye? Kyle just laughed. He said it was just an expression but not to worry—he'd get paid, and we'd all get rich." She fingered the cheap velvet. "I made Bobby promise I could take the couch. I like it." She actually bounced on it, her body jiggling, and Marek sighed. He just couldn't deal with the juxtaposition.

"What kind of pills do you sell, Kaylee?"

Until Karen spoke, Marek didn't know she was back in the room. He figured she'd been walking around, looking for anything that might help the case.

"I don't sell them. Kyle does. He had to go get more. He helps people. They hurt, you know? Really bad sometimes. He gives them pills that make it go away. He's like a doctor."

Opioids, most likely. Not the worst drug out there, at least in theory, but they were laying waste to rural America's workforce. Just take a painkiller and get back to work. No problem. That lie had been going around for millennia. Take this, cure that, and you'll be rich, young, on top of the world.

What in the world would become of this child if—or most likely *when*—her brother was jailed?

Karen asked, "When did you last see Bob Bunting?"

Kaylee pouted. "Kyle hit him. I'm sorry because he looked so happy to see me in his truck. I was mad, but I got over it. I wanted babies, you know? They look at you like you aren't stupid. But Kyle says he wasn't the right man for me, and he wasn't very...well, you know, good looking. But he was sweet. He'd bring me things." She grabbed a gaudy pink teddy bear. "Like this. Isn't it great?"

With a girl toy like Kaylee, Bunting must've been high in hog heaven. But still, the MO didn't quite jibe for Marek. He'd met Bunting. He'd disliked Bunting. But a cold-blooded rapist? That still didn't gel for him. Though the stains might well tell the tale—or shirttail.

"What about Kyle? What did he do after he hit Bobby?" Karen asked evenly.

"Oh. He bought me a big tub of rocky road ice cream at Casey's. Then we came back here. He went out to the bar. Then he came home and went down to the basement and hit things. He likes to hit things when he's mad."

"Has he hit you?" Marek asked.

The puzzled look thankfully answered that in the negative. "Why would he hit me? He's my big brother. He protects me. That's why he says he has to work out. He's got lots of guy stuff in the basement that I'm not allowed to touch because he says it could be dangerous. He looks after me, you know? My mom died when I was born, and we had a stepmom for a while, but she didn't like us. She called me a ninny. Then we lived with Grandma until she went to heaven when I was fourteen. Kyle took care of me after that. I love him."

The roar of a truck engine made her squeal. "He's home!"

Marek rose to his feet just as the door burst open. Kyle sounded much like his engine as he roared, "Get the hell out of my house!"

Kaylee squealed again but in distress. "Kyle, he's got a daughter. She's seven. Don't yell at him."

With obvious effort, Kyle Early turned on his sister and said through gritted teeth, "I told you never to talk to the police without me here."

"But they aren't police. They're... Sheriff's Office. Right?"

Kyle closed his eyes, and when he opened them again, Marek felt an unexpected pang of pity, because what he saw was a man determined to protect his sister from the sharks, in his own less-than-legal way.

"That was dirty pool," Kyle said.

"We don't have a pool," his sister replied with a pout. "Bobby said we'd get one with the new house." Abruptly, she turned sheet white and ran from the room. The sound of retching came through loud and clear a few seconds later.

Karen was the first to ask. "Is she...?"

The bruiser's big shoulders slumped. "Pregnant? Yeah. Bunting convinced her to stop the pill. She doesn't really get it, getting sick, getting more... well...." He flushed and made a cupping gesture over his chest. "I haven't told her yet that she's going to have a baby. I don't know what to do. She'd love the kid. Heck, so would I. People look down on her, always have, but when I'm at my downdest? She's there to cheer me up. She's a sweetheart. But..."

But Kyle Early was in the business of vice. And he could get busted at any time.

"I'll do what I gotta do to pay the bills. But I'm out of your territory as of next week. Going to Sioux Falls. I just need to break it to her. Fingers crossed she'll be so damn happy about the baby that she won't care where she is, as long as she has her couch."

Though Marek had stepped back from his initial judgment of Kyle Early, Karen hadn't. "What you've turned your sister into, Mr. Early, is criminal."

Kyle only sighed. "I didn't pimp her like people say. Heck, I'd drag her away from guys who took advantage of her and pop their cork. But she'd just go back to them. And then she'd get her heart broken when they told her they just wanted sex, not babies. Finally, I told her she should make something from the deal, so at least she'd get something to take home with her. It sort of... took off... from there. I've never forced her to do anything she didn't want. Ever. But I could see it was getting old. Then... Bunting. I thought I had the answer to both our problems."

"A blind eye," Marek murmured. "And a baby."

In the coolness of the evening, the blue anchor rippled on the bared arm. "Yeah. And I know what you're going to ask me next if you haven't already of my sister. Where I was after I picked her up at the courthouse. Bought some ice cream for Kaylee, brought her home, went to the Barstool until closing, then I came home and beat the shit out of a punching bag. Then I hit the sack."

Karen shifted, making the floor creak. "You hit Bunting."

"I did. He made Kaylee mad enough to hit the panic button on her phone. That's our signal for me to come get her ASAP. I really do try to keep her out of trouble. God knows what'll happen to her if..."

He couldn't end that sentence because it wouldn't end well. Marek could feel the waves of anxiety coming off the man. "Do you have any idea why someone would kill Bunting?"

"I'd look into Bunting's side deals," he said with a cynical eye that his sister lacked. "I got the feeling mine wasn't the only one he'd set up, seeing as he was talking how he'd build Kaylee a big house. But I don't know anything more. You might try the trailer park. Something fishy there."

Kaylee came back in, looking as if she hadn't just been sick, and the glow about her was now obvious. Marek understood Kyle's dilemma. What kind of life would that child have, raised by a child? Taking it away from her, as the law might well do, might do what nothing else had—kill the innocence.

As if on the same page, Karen pursed her lips. "Honest work is the only way out, Kyle."

"You think I haven't tried?" He tapped his anchor. "That was supposed to be my ticket out of this godforsaken place. I thought I had it made, like the recruiter told me, that I could see the world, make money, get on the GI Bill, and get medical care and a pension if I stuck it out for twenty years. But I ran up against a bent officer who threw a trumped-up insubordination charge at me and got me dishonorably discharged. That was twenty years ago. With that on my record, I've worked nothing but scut jobs since."

Honestly, anyway, was the subtext.

Karen wasn't so easily dissuaded. "You've got impressive muscles and a work ethic to keep them that way. Try a gym in Sioux Falls. Or hire yourself out as a personal trainer." When he blinked at her as if she'd just told him to take a shuttle to Mars, she let out a breath. "If you used as much creativity in thinking of new ways to make money honestly instead of otherwise, you could spend the rest of your life taking care of your sister." Karen checked her watch then headed for the door. "I noted some suspicious packages on the kitchen counter, Marek. I won't have time to get a warrant until next week, most likely. Put it on my list."

With that, she exited, leaving two dropped jaws in her wake.

She'd just given Kyle Early a green light to get the hell out before she took him down. Bent? You couldn't bend Karen Okerlund Mehaffey with a crowbar. But she'd let out just enough rope to let the man hang himself—or climb out of the hole he'd made.

Marek went to the door. "Kyle?"

Kyle managed to get his jaw working. "What?"

"If you ever need to park Kaylee somewhere?"

Suspicion warred with desperation. Suspicion won. "Don't tell me. You'll take care of her?"

Marek stood in the doorway that he'd last seen when he'd piled all his belongings into his mother's sedan and headed away from Eda County. Never, he'd promised himself and his mother, to return.

If he'd had a little sister like Kaylee to support, not just himself, what would he have done? How far, really, was he from a man like this—or even his grandfather? His mother had pushed him harder than a Dakota wind, but his father had given him roots deep enough to keep him upright. He owed both. Big time. What did Kaylee's child have?

"Look up Alice Dutton in Aleford. She's Bunting's maiden aunt. She's got a nice little house there with nothing to do now that she's retired. She likes kids. You might want to meet her before you head out—babysitter if nothing else."

Kyle seemed to be waiting for the punch line, the payout, the deal. Finally, he nodded. "Okay. Thanks. I know it seems I'm nothing but a loser as a brother. But all I've ever wanted was a good man for her. Bob Bunting was bent, but he wasn't bad, not to her."

An interesting eulogy, but was it true? Was Bunting bent, bad, or pure evil?

With effort, Marek shut the door behind him. Hopefully, for the last time.

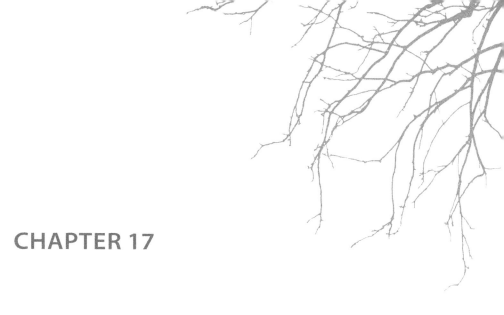

CHAPTER 17

C ALLS IN THE MIDDLE OF night always woke Marek with the shakes—as if his brain had already knocked back a good shot of adrenaline before waking him. Ready to fight or flee whatever threat lurked in the dark. His first thought: Becca. Then the strains of the *Lone Ranger* pinged. The cold shock of the metal of his phone against his fingers told him that he needed to make sure the furnace was ready for winter.

He rolled over onto his back. "What's up?"

"Fire at Nadine Early's."

Karen's tone, detached and brisk, told him all he needed to know. He closed his eyes. "She's dead."

"We don't know that yet. Jordan tells me that the fire hasn't been contained. It's engulfed the house and threatening the nearby fields. I'm heading out the door. We'll take the Sub."

He ran a hand down his face, feeling the scruff. "I need to take Becca to Arne's."

"Already called him. He'll expect her. We can drop her off. Not like it's far."

Marek could easily walk her over. He had in the past, but the night was cold, and the urge to get to the fire was powerful. So after he pulled on discarded clothes, he rushed up to the attic room, automatically adjusting his step to avoid the worst creaks—a talent honed early in life, especially on report card day.

The night-light glowed softly, like a tiny fire. His daughter was curled into a blanketed ball underneath the dark Hispanic gaze of Madonna and Child wearing the faces of her mother and her dead brother. While newer *retablos* had joined the painted wood icon that his old partner had made for Becca, and still more awaited their place from their most recent trip, that older one took prime place on her wall. He'd always thought it morbid—and it always gave him a stab—but that was not how she saw it.

His daughter believed in angels. He believed in devils.

Carefully, Marek scooped her up, blankets and all, and heard her voiceless protest. It needed no translation. "Sorry, sweet pea. Karen needs me. I'm taking you over to Arne's."

After they made the short trip down the road, he was thankful to see the porch light on at Arne's, or he might have spilled his precious load on the uneven walk.

Clumsy. That was one tag he'd earned the hard way.

Arne met him at the door but didn't take Becca. He worried he would drop her with his stroke-weakened arm. So in the proverbial Okerlund silence, the two of them did their usual dance. Slitted eyes from Arne. Stiff nod in return. Follow on silent steps and place his precious bundle on the bed across from Joey's crib.

Marek took a moment to note that both children, in their half-sleep, rolled toward each other as if drawn by an invisible bond. A bond not of familial blood but of blood, nonetheless. Children of violence. Joey had lost his mother, Becca her brother and her mother.

Nod of transfer made, nod of transfer accepted, and Marek rushed back out to the waiting Sub. He slid in, and Karen floored it.

Unlike the woods, on the plains, trouble was easily spotted, from tornadoes to blizzards to fire. Long before they arrived at the Kubicek homestead, Marek could see the huge plume of smoke from a voracious base of bright flame roiling the night. His dyslexic mind went to 'bright fame,' the meaning of the name Robert, and he had a brief flight of fancy that Bunting was enjoying a last bit of mischief before the afterlife... or afterdeath.

Once on Kubicek land, Karen pulled up behind a battalion of vehicles.

When Mother Nature couldn't be trusted, neighbors could. A tractor pulling a disc plow had already made a firebreak to one side of the house, starving the fire of fuel as the dark, damp earth was turned in its wake. Shadowy figures in hastily donned coveralls shoveled another firebreak near an unharvested field to the east, where there was no room for the plow, while volunteer firefighters from Valeska and Reunion blasted the structure, which glowed orange and ash-black like a cheap plastic Halloween haunted house.

While Marek waited beside the Sub, Karen wound her way through the vehicles to talk to the fire marshal. The sounds of bawling cattle being herded into trailers at least meant they'd been saved.

When Karen returned, she handed Marek a shovel.

"Nadine?" he asked.

"Nothing yet. Follow me. We're going to start a new firebreak." Karen led him away from the house, toward the fence line. The earth was not easy to turn, but Marek's weight on the shovel helped make the initial cut, and Karen followed up. They made a decent pair of prairie dogs, leaving mounds of dirt in their wake. Marek only looked up when the building collapsed with a great whoosh. Beside him, Karen put her boot on the lip of the shovel.

"I said I hoped the place would fall down around her ears," Karen got out in a low, hoarse voice. "But not like this."

Marek turned his back as the wave of smoke and ash hit them, all that was left of his mother's childhood home. Vaporized. He had no doubt what she would've said. Good riddance. "You didn't say it to Nadine's face. I did." At least in so many words. He'd threatened to evict her from her last bolt-hole. With luck, she'd bolted instead.

Karen pushed sweat-damped bangs away from her face. "Most likely she's at The Shaft, getting drunk. Maybe she set the fire herself and left." Karen attacked the stubborn soil again. He fell back to the rhythm.

He didn't know how long they worked before a cheer went up. The fire was officially out.

Karen jiggled her shovel, looked at her blistered hands, then waited as Jordan Fike, their night dispatcher-jailer and a volunteer firefighter, approached on heavy feet.

"We found the car out back and a body by the stove. Not much doubt it's Nadine Early."

Marek's last hope collapsed. She probably hadn't moved since he'd left her to stew in her own juice.

Jordan removed his helmet. "Preliminary from the fire marshal is that it looks accidental. Sparks from the open stove. She must've stoked it, had a good long toot, and passed out. Doubt she knew what hit her. If that helps."

Not much. And Marek had been through enough notifications that he recognized the soft landing—the victim didn't feel it—meant to protect the loved ones from the specter of suffering. As Karen went with Jordan to get more details from the fire marshal, Marek heard shovel hit sod.

"Well. Looks like a good night. A good fight."

Marek turned to find Pat Donahue leaning on a shovel, his grin almost feral. "Surprised to find me here? Don't be. I have insomnia. Normally, I take something for it, but not since what happened at the park. I want to be able to respond if needed. I saw the plume from the park and figured I could help out. I do miss that."

"Fires?"

"No, helping out, being part of the collective." He gestured to the people piling into pickups, tractors, and fire trucks. "Everybody unites against fire."

Marek's antenna went up. "Are you aware someone died?"

His face fell. "Someone lived in that old house? I thought we were saving the farmer's harvest, the cattle. You know how to ruin a man's high, Detective. Anyone you know?"

"Nadine Kubicek Bunting Early. A shirttail relative."

Donahue didn't blink at the name, not even Bunting. "That sucks. Close?"

Marek shook his head.

"There's that, at least." With a long sigh, Donahue handed the shovel over to its owner. "Well, I'm still going to take the win and see if I can get some shuteye. All those years living, working, on an adrenaline high—it takes its toll."

As Donahue headed out, Karen returned. "Was that...?"

"Yes, it was," and Marek filled her in.

Karen watched Donahue pull out in his fancy rig, getting a few puzzled stares but plenty of friendly waves. "A firefighter like him would know how to make it look accidental. Though what he'd have to do with Nadine Early, I have no idea."

Nor did he. Marek picked his way through the ruts that had been dug deeper by the trucks. Karen led him toward the remains: the cracked, blackened foundation, the potbelly stove, and the sheet-draped body that awaited a ride in Tish's hearse.

What made someone like Nadine turn out like she had? Did she have some fatal genetic flaw? She'd certainly had a better start in life than her female cousins, Janina Marek Okerlund and Nancy Kubicek Bridges. One became a respected teacher, the other a hardworking if low-earning waitress, but her? She'd used others to avoid making herself into anything—except a dead end.

That didn't, however, make him feel any better or help shake the feeling that he'd somehow caused her death.

"Marek? We're good to go. The fire marshal will let us know if anything changes."

He didn't move. "After you left, I threatened to have Don Kubicek oust her from her last hope for a home."

She shrugged. "Knowing you, you paired that threat with an offer for rehab." At his involuntary flinch, she smiled. "Yeah, that's what I thought. Nadine didn't want your help, didn't want to change her life. She just wanted. Now she's dead, most likely through her own stupidity." Karen tugged at his arm. "Let's go home."

On the way, Marek was haunted by the sound of shattered glass raining down behind a closed door. Hard tears for a hard life.

CHAPTER 18

O NCE BACK AT HOME, MAREK couldn't settle. Like Donahue had said, insomnia was a common hazard of first responders, but Marek didn't think an adrenaline rush was keeping him awake. Usually, Becca kept him grounded in the present, but she was at Arne's, and he wasn't going to disturb her sleep a second time. So he sat in the rocker by the empty hearth and thought of Bunting, of Nadine, of his mother, and of Becca.

The specter of Lenny Marek had haunted Marek's mother all her life—and her fear had become Marek's fear. That he might do something—or not do something—that might cause his daughter's life to turn out badly. Bunting had been terribly abused by the adults in his life. No big surprise that he'd turned out as he had. Becca had also faced abuse, if for different reasons than Bunting had. Nothing that left a physical mark, thankfully, but would it leave some mental scar, causing her to be less than she could've been otherwise?

What about his own brush with abuse? Memories of that night rose along with the winds that caused the sturdy bungalow to creak. That fateful night when his mother had tried to beat the Lenny Marek out of him. After Leif Okerlund had stopped her, by physically pulling her away, the silence had lasted forever.

When she'd dropped the bloodied belt, the buckle rang like a death knell. Janina Marek Okerlund had collapsed with a keening sound he'd never heard before. His father had been torn over whom to help first. After a moment's hesitation, he'd taken Janina downstairs then returned to clean up Marek. Then he'd taken him in his arms, even as big as Marek was at age ten, and rocked him by this very hearth, in this very chair, telling him the words that he'd tried to hold on to through all else.

If you try hard, work hard, that's good enough for me. You'll find your place in this world, and it will be the better for it.

When his mother had come up to his room later, he'd shied away from her touch. She'd taken that with stoic acceptance— that she'd damaged not only his flesh, but their relationship, forever. She'd sunk down in the desk chair by his bed and cradled her arms about herself instead of him. And it had all spilled out. The years of abuse, verbal and physical, that had undercut and underlain life in the old Kubicek homestead that was never a home. Nights of terror, days of vicious drudgery.

I will never forgive myself for turning into my father, and I don't expect you to do so. Just don't make it turn you, either. I couldn't bear that, that what I did, turned you into him.

With patience and his father's quiet encouragement, Marek had eventually forgiven his mother, because the scenes she'd painted for him that night... of going to bed not knowing if she'd even be alive the next morning... had seared deeper than any physical scar. Her fear for her brother and mother had been even worse, she'd said. To the end of her life, she'd suffered from insomnia.

When Marek had failed his mother's expectations, his Uncle Jim Marek, a hardworking man who spoke only when spoken to, had put a hammer in Marek's hands and guided him over the making of his first project: a bookcase for his mother. That had, Marek realized later, been the moment he'd truly forgiven her, when he'd seen his ever-stoic mother cry—in big, hiccupping gasps.

If only she'd made one other choice: not to smoke. He'd had enough of smoke and fire to last a lifetime—it only led to death in his world.

When Marek had left Valeska with what little he'd kept from their rental home—the house in Reunion had been let, and his mother's cousin Blaise had agreed to take care of that—all he had was a thousand dollars. And he thought he was rich. He'd driven west then south, not knowing, not caring, really, where he would end up.

In Albuquerque, he'd started out dry walling, switched to adobe, and eventually hooked up with Joseph De Baca to finish out his carpenter's apprenticeship. It had never really occurred to Marek that life wouldn't turn up something, roses or otherwise. Times had been easier. Jobs better paid. He still regretted not keeping in touch with Jim or Blaise. They'd been part of the past, along with his mother. With Blaise, he'd mended bridges, but Jim had died on an icy bridge before Marek returned.

But his uncle had at least known, after hiring a private investigator, that Marek was okay, married and working as a homicide detective in Albuquerque. And Jim Marek had been part of that solid foundation. He could only hope that even if he failed Becca, Karen—and, yes, even Arne—would shore up his fractured attempts at laying one that would hold for her.

Marek rubbed at his eyes, looked at his watch, and saw it wasn't even two in the morning yet. He walked into the kitchen, looking for some tonic that would put him back to sleep. He paused as he caught a welcome sight out the back windows. A warm glow of lights spilled out from the old schoolhouse he was renovating in his spare time. Nikki was still up.

A better tonic.

Snagging his jacket from the peg by the door, he went outside. An inquiring woof and scrabble of nails reminded him that he was not, after all, alone. His daughter's field-bred and field-failed spaniel, Gun Shy, snuffled up to him, pulling hard at the end of his tether. *We're going hunting, right, right? For rabbits.*

What was it with dogs? Marek rubbed the long, silky ears. "Sorry, Gunny. People time."

The dog shot him a look of sheer betrayal before slinking back into his luxurious doghouse.

Was "home" to a dog the people, not the place? He'd guess cats were the opposite. Territorial. Take away their home, and they'd rake you to the bone. Maybe people were divided the same way. You either needed the place or the people. Cat or dog. Marek guessed he was dog, as he'd been led back to Reunion by his daughter's wishes and her needs, not his own. She was home. So he was.

Nikki Forsgren Solberg, on the other hand, was definitely a cat, with her witchy green eyes under a careless mop of hair. She liked her own space. If he was lucky, she might one day share a bit of it. After he knocked, the door was cracked open, no doubt to give Nikki time to slam it shut if she didn't like what she saw. Then she flung it open.

Her hand went to his arm in a fierce grip. "Becca?"

Only then did he realize he probably looked like an escaped convict from a chain gang. "At Arne's. She's fine. We had a callout to a fire—and a death. Probably accidental, but... I just... if it's a bad time..."

"No, a good time." Nikki pulled him inside, where his heart nearly stopped. A bunch of boxes were stacked on the partially renovated plank floor. Was she leaving?

She patted his arm. "I just finished packaging up a big order that I got from a woman in Brookings who saw my table settings and wanted a whole spread."

Marek let out a breath. He knew she'd struggled to get any traction for her pottery, her artwork, in the Dakotas. California had been her natural home—until the economy crashed for those on the lower rungs and rents went through the roof. "Congrats."

Nikki gave him a wry smile. "Thanks. It's like now that I've got a full-time job, benefits, my pots are starting to take off. Figures." She tugged on his arm. "Tell me what's got you looking sucker punched."

She sat down on her potter's stool, and quietly prodding, she got it out of him, each halting word by halting word.

While she didn't shrug like Karen had, she did look resigned. "The Nadine Earlys can't be helped, Marek. Nothing you can say, or said, makes any difference to the outcome. I met many of them on the streets when I did my chalk art, my portraits, for the tourists. Oh, some few will help themselves, eventually, but most? They're just too far gone. Mental issues, addiction, what have you. You put out a hand, they'll bite you."

Dogs again. "Were you ever that poor? Homeless, I mean?"

"No..." Nikki tilted her head. "Well, technically, yes, I guess. I lived in my car on and off over the years, when I needed to or wanted to, or both, but that was by choice. As long as I had somewhere to sleep that I felt safe, I was good. Growing up, I never felt I had a home." She looked around the single-room schoolhouse that had come close to collapsing around her before he'd started working on it. "Except here. Here on the bluff, alone, where Grandpa Stan made sure I wasn't disturbed." She flashed him a smile. "By an overgrown puppy of a boy with humongous feet that he kept tripping over."

Marek was four years her junior. And Stan Forsgren, despite being a relative, had been clear on the territorial lines: the bluff was fair game, but the schoolhouse was Nikki's. And Marek had never intruded. Not that he'd ever felt a desire to enter any schoolhouse.

Until she'd returned. The long-haired girl, a silent ghost on the bluff of his childhood, had been replaced by a confident, alluring witch who'd stolen his heart—but nothing more. They'd kissed, they'd teased, and he'd even offered to marry her to save her teaching job. She'd turned him down flat. Because she was a cat. Her place. His place. And never the twain to meet.

Nikki sank down on the futon she'd loaded with blankets. "Your mother was home. To me. Her books, her love of art, her support. Right at the age I needed her. When all the little siblings started to show their true Forsgren colors and mine went wonky, she was there for me. Even after I left, after she died, she was there in my head. Quoting. Always quoting. Emily Dickinson once wrote, when her mother's deteriorating health required all of her time, that 'Home is so far from Home.' That's what it felt like, growing up as a Forsgren. That's why I took a new name, one for my own, when I left at eighteen."

Nikki was his first cousin, but she'd been adopted, her parents having been told they'd never conceive their own. Though he felt for that girl who'd been displaced, never supported for her artsy ways, he was glad she'd been adopted. "So you're a dog."

Her hand that had been smoothing a plump pillow rose as a fist. "Say again?"

Hurriedly, he explained his theory. Cats. Dogs.

"Oh. That's a weird way to look at it." She drew up her legs and began untying her shoelaces. "I'd say I'm a cat, always landing on my feet, independent... perhaps to a fault. But people do matter to me. Some, anyway. You. Becca. My students. I have a special one. In middle school right now. He's not Becca's equal in sheer artistic talent, but he's a wizard with computer graphics. Not my thing, but I've encouraged him, and he's really blossomed. But I'm afraid he really is homeless. I recognize the signs. And I fear one day, he just won't be there, and I'll never know what happened to him."

They shared a long, silent moment. Both of them had disappeared. Few had known what had happened to them, only those like his Uncle Jim or, in her case, her Grandpa Stan, who'd made a point of finding out.

Kicking off her shoes, Nikki held out a hand. She smiled her witchy smile. "We've danced long enough, Marek."

His heart started to pound as he let her draw him down.

"As long as you continue to fix my roof," she told him, "it can rain cats and dogs."

CHAPTER 19

KAREN HATED ONE THING MORE than notifications and evictions.

The final eviction—or evisceration—of the dead. An autopsy.

The tarp-wrapped body of Robert Leonard Bunting lay under a stained white sheet on a stainless-steel table that she wasn't entirely sure was up to the job. She wasn't entirely sure *she* was up to the job this morning. Maybe she could sleep through it all and Marek could fill her in later. Of the two of them, he not only seemed awake, but he also had a gleam in his eye that told her he'd likely not spent the rest of the night alone. Or, strictly, asleep. Lucky bastard.

"Late night?" Dr. White asked her as he came in, catching her mid-yawn.

Karen caught the yawn and stuffed it back. She'd gotten little sleep. "Had a fire in the wee hours. And before that, I had to tag team my night-shift deputy at midnight."

Her memory of that encounter was typical of many with her theatrical deputy. Adam Van Eck had entered the Sheriff's Office wearing a long black cape lined with fur, with his shoulder-length hair unbound—and glinting silver instead of its usual blond—along with a trim beard of the same hue.

She hated Shakespeare season. King Lear, she thought. Maybe. One of those old mad kings of England. But she didn't care if he was the King of Siam—she was going to have his head. "What the hell is going on at Grove Park, and why haven't you reported it?"

He stuck a finger in his ear and twirled it. "'Nothing will come of nothing: speak again.'" It always took him a while to come down off a theatrical high.

Through gritted teeth, she got out, "Homeless. In. Grove. Park."

He pursed his lips, stroked his beard, and nodded. "Nothing to report. I found some people living in their cars and in tents down by the creek. But I can't arrest people who claim they paid the camping fee in the dropbox. I told Biester to get me proof, and I'd do something about it. I suggested he put up some trail monitors. I couldn't justify staking out a park. Was I wrong?"

His weighted tone said no, but she said, "Yes. I want a report. Biester is on my ass about it. He's not as heated up or as socially connected as Alan Digges, but I—"

"Digges?" With a twinkle of eye and a quick laugh, Adam discarded the mad king for the class clown of Reunion High. "The Boy Toy of the Bayton Babe? What's he got to do with anything in Eda County? Wouldn't think he'd step one Italian-shod toe in the muck. No, don't tell me. His wife's got property here."

Six degrees of separation—or fewer. "You know him?"

"Digges schmoozed up to me for a while at The Pavilion, when he'd heard I was a big-name star on Broadway. Until someone clued him in that my headliner was decades ago. Then he started making snide comments about has-beens. Don't worry, boss. I survived New York critics. I can survive Digges."

And with a swirl of his fur-lined cape, he flew downstairs to his locker. A quick-change artist, he returned in the role of reserve deputy before Karen got out the door.

"Sheriff Mehaffey, shall we begin?"

Karen blinked back to the present. Unfortunately. She pulled on a white surgical mask from the dispenser that Dr. White thoughtfully provided near the door—along with barf bags. "Go ahead."

Dr. White gestured to the body. "Detective? Will you give me a hand with the tarp?"

With obvious reluctance, Marek moved forward. She didn't blame him. The stench that arose once the tarp was peeled back was enough to make her gag. Even Dr. White, who'd undoubtedly had far more experience with bodies in more decomposed states, rushed over to the far wall, flicked a switch, and turned a knob. Air handlers roared to life, sucking up the odor.

"That..." Dr. White said after a long pause, "was truly foul." He grabbed his own mask and slipped it on, dark fingers searching for any gaps. "Your coroner said your victim was a stinker when he brought him in. I laughed at the quaint wording, but he was apparently being quite literal. Where was the body found, a treatment plant?"

"Vault toilet," Marek said.

"Well. That's one for the books." Cautiously, the pathologist approached the half-tarped body and grabbed a water nozzle. "Have swabs already been taken from the hands and any other extremity of interest?"

Karen nodded. "Larson did what he could. He said that Bunting was stabbed in the back."

"Then I'll need help turning Mr. Bunting, when it comes to that. Your vic is a big boy." The pathologist began to peel off the stained shirt and stopped abruptly. "Who is your vic, again?"

"Robert Leonard Bunting," Karen said and saw the pathologist's chocolate-colored eyes widen. "Yes, the very same Bob Bunting who beat me in the special election... and then lost it again after the recount on Friday night. And before you ask, Marek and I were in New Mexico when it happened. We're not suspects per DCI."

He smiled at her. "That's very welcome news. On the win, I mean. I wouldn't have even thought of you and your estimable uncle as suspects. Congratulations. I wasn't aware of any of this, though I'm sure it's been in the news. I walked my eldest daughter down the aisle yesterday. It's been nothing but frills and bonbons at our house for months. Years, it seems."

"Congratulations back at you." As the father of the bride, he'd probably shelled out more than his time. "I hope the wedding didn't set you back too much."

"My job isn't always fun, but it does pay for some fun, at least for my family." Dr. White's expression turned grave. "Your erstwhile opponent, however, had little fun and games growing up. These injuries are old."

Karen sucked in a breath as Dr. White exposed the upper torso. Dots and lines. Cigarette burns. And... what? "Whip?"

"Belt," Marek murmured. "Dual-track edges."

That made her jerk and look at Marek—but he dropped his gaze. Personal knowledge or professional?

"Yes, Detective Okerlund, you're right." Dr. White, his head down, missed the byplay. "Very unusual, and very bad, for this kind of thing to be found on the torso."

Off balance, Karen asked, "How so?" Then as she instinctively crossed her arms over her midsection, she got it. "Oh. You curl up when you're being attacked. So..." She swallowed hard. "He was unconscious?"

"That or tied down." He touched a boxed-in cigarette-butt burn. "Noughts and crosses."

Karen wrinkled her nose. "Excuse me?"

"Sorry, I had a kindergarten teacher from the UK. That's their version of—"

"Tic-tac-toe." That was exactly what it looked like, or a sloppy version thereof. "Noughts. Isn't that zeros? Really, really sick. I'm guessing his zero of a mother did that, going from the aunt's report, but..."

"But Rachel Dutton had lots of men," Marek finished. "Any or all could've contributed. Still, she had to have known."

"So that's how you create a monster, with a belt and a butt," Karen said under her breath, or so she'd thought, then kicked herself when Marek winced.

"A monster?" Dr. White paused as he tackled Bunting's belt buckle. "I thought Bunting was in your business."

Karen got herself under control. "We're looking at him for a cold case. Serial rapist. We need you to take samples for DNA for the FBI to compare against a... a possible child."

The pathologist glanced thoughtfully between the two of them, probably noting that they looked nothing alike, and thinking one of them wasn't a real Okerlund.

"No, not one of us. It's a confidential matter, or I'd tell you. And as Marek keeps reminding me, I can't assume anything until we have the data in hand. But some of the evidence is... damning."

The pathologist resumed his work, this time at the feet. "Very well. I can tell you that, based on these shoes, the condition of the clothing, I believe he was dragged—in a wooded area." He dropped a few pine needles, a yellow-brown leaf, some bark, and mud into an evidence bag.

Once the body was stripped and all the clothing bagged for transport to DCI, Dr. White hosed down the blue-tinged flesh that showed even more evidence of abuse. "I am rarely shocked anymore by the depravity of man—or woman—but this does. Deeply."

Karen thought of Alice Dutton. "His aunt tried to get custody, but the judge turned her down flat. I can't imagine the man didn't know about the abuse—unless these all came after."

"How old was Bunting when the case went before the judge?"

"I don't actually know. But I'm guessing under five."

A flicker of relief crossed the pathologist's face. "Then your judge wasn't entirely incompetent. I'd say these were inflicted from age five to ten. Oh, a few of these cigarette burns"—he pointed to a series of faint elongated ones along an arm—"may have been there already. But people weren't as knowledgeable about signs of abuse, or were more likely to overlook it, back then. I will never, ever, understand what compels a person to inflict abuse on a child. When I think of how I was afraid to even hold my daughter after she was born, that I'd somehow damage her... Well." He blew out a breath and nodded at Marek. "If you would, Detective?" He paused. "Detective Okerlund?"

Marek, his brooding gaze on the body, started. "Yes?"

"Your help would be appreciated." When he got a blank look, Dr. White cleared his throat. "Turning the body. I do lift some weights, believe it or not, but I'm not up to lifting twice my weight."

After a second's immobility, Marek stepped forward, though Karen thought his gloved hands shook a bit as they closed over pale legs tracked with belt marks. If this barrage of bad memories continued, she would lose her detective—mentally, if not physically. She needed him on his A-game.

Once turned, the body revealed the endgame: a shockingly small entry wound.

"A single-bladed blow," Dr. White said with interest. "That would be an unusual cause of death. But... yes, you see this defect? One side with a sharp angle, the other more blunt?"

Karen moved forward to inspect the puckered wound. "What does it tell you?"

"Pocketknife," Marek answered, proving he hadn't checked out quite yet. "You can see the indentation from the locking mechanism, so it's not a kitchen knife."

"Very good. Curiouser and curiouser." He made a humming sound. "I am not yet convinced that this blow was the cause of death. Very unusual." He leaned in for a better view. "Looks like the blade was twisted slightly on exit. Or the body fell. Let's see if we can determine trajectory and depth."

He powered up his saw, and Marek moved back, his gaze swinging high. Karen joined him in staring at the cabinetry across the room. Fingernails on chalkboard had nothing on saw on bone.

"Well. That's interesting."

Karen wondered if her eyes fell at the same time as Marek's. Puppets on a string. "What's that?"

"Mr. Bunting wasn't long for this world, no matter that stab in the back. Advanced heart disease. A heart attack waiting to happen. Now... yes... yes. The blow appears to have gone mostly straight with a slight downward trajectory and... hmm..."

Karen groaned. "You're killing me here, Doc."

"What? Oh. Sorry. The depth of penetration is about six inches, longer than most pocketknives. I've heard about this happening but haven't seen it as yet. Textbook case."

"Of what?" Karen prompted.

The pathologist straightened, still looking down at Bunting as if he were a fascinating specimen from the far-off Amazon. "Of a wound longer than the knife. Due to the elasticity of the skin, you usually can't give exact dimensions of a penetrating object. But most pocketknives are no more than four inches. Yes, there are exceptions, but I don't think that's what we're dealing with here."

"And that is?" Karen asked.

He looked up. "Compression. A track or depth longer than the blade. Most often, you're going to get compression in the abdominal area, but the chest cavity is also collapsible due to the rib cage. Either that was a very lucky strike, or someone had a good grasp of human anatomy. A powerful thrust, I'd say. Lots of muscle or emotion behind it."

Karen picked her way through his words. "So... that *is* the cause of death? He didn't suffocate or anything?"

The dark eyebrows winged up. "Suffocate?"

"His mouth was full of... fecal matter."

"Ah. Yes. I noted that earlier. Postmortem. Do I need to take a sample?"

"No, it's been done. Larson has it. Though he said fecal material is devilishly difficult to get DNA from. You have to hope the outside layer scrapes off cells from the colon." Fishing for those cells, thankfully, wasn't her job. Karen pulled off her mask. "What is your ruling, Mr. Pathologist?"

"Homicide." Dr. White stripped off his gloves and dropped them into the trash. "Cause of death is cardiac tamponade from a penetrating blow to the pericardium. Given Mr. Bunting's physical conditioning and advanced state of heart disease,

I suspect he dropped where he was struck, though he may have lived some long minutes beyond that point, most likely unconscious."

As Dr. White surveyed the massive body, his professional interest—and tone—faded. "Whether or not your victim was a monster, he lived with one for far too many years. I hope that whoever that is, or was, is tasting the fire of everlasting hell."

Amen.

CHAPTER 20

K AREN FELT AS IF SHE were still on that rutted road, ripe with muck-sucking gotchas, even though she'd just traveled a well-maintained Interstate-29. She turned down the exit ramp and headed for Grove Park with her brooding passenger more oppressive than the breaking clouds above.

She and Marek had left the morgue, taken the evidence bags directly to DCI, and logged them in with the clerk there. Karen had been disappointed to find that neither the workaholic Larson nor his long-suffering sidekick were there. They'd been called to a homicide scene up north in the Lake region.

So she'd called up Biester to show them the homeless encampment. He'd been more than happy to agree. At least one fence mended, she hoped, with the evictions scheduled for later in the day.

As Karen drove onto a county road that rapped to the beat of the tarred cracks under her wheels, she decided she'd had enough. "Look, Marek, I know it's been a rough welcome home for you. Some bad memories, from Valeska yesterday to today's reminder of your mother's abuse..." She bit her lip as Marek stirred like a waking bear from his slump against the Sub's worn upholstery.

"My mother was no Rachel Dutton," he said tightly. "And I'm no Bunting. One belting does not equal abuse."

As far as Karen was concerned, any belting was abuse, but

she wasn't talking about just a swat or two. She'd been home that day, in her attic room across the street from his, with her window open. He'd been only ten years old, on report-card day, and he'd screamed, "I'll try harder." Over and over again. "That belting went on and on... and if I hadn't called Grandpa, you'd still have the scars."

When he didn't respond, she let out a breath. "You *do* have scars. I wondered. I'm sorry. Really, really sorry. But that's abuse. I just don't know how you can defend it. Or her."

He kept his eyes straight out the windshield. "Because I know what tripped her. Not hate, love. She was scared spitless that I was going to turn into her father, who *did* abuse her and Uncle Jim. With many scars, physical and mental. Yes, it was overkill. Yes, it was wrong. I would never condone it, any more than I do with what Val did to Becca, but—"

"Wait. What?" Karen jerked the wheel along with her head and almost ran off the road. Letting off the gas, she steadied the Sub—and herself. "Your wife hit Becca? When?"

Marek turned his head, and she didn't think she'd ever seen such a bleak look. "Hit her anytime she drew anything. Because Val didn't want Becca growing up to be like the mother who abandoned her for the lure of art. Same reason, same fear, same overkill."

How many generations would that excuse hold? She didn't buy it. "Scars?"

"Nothing that left a mark. Physically. Mentally? Another story." He cradled his head. "I should have seen the signs. I was trained to see them. But I left all the discipline to Val, because I thought..."

"That history repeats. Have you ever touched Becca?"

His voice came out muffled. "Timeouts. That's all I can manage. Kills me."

"Because you're not your grandfather. And you're not your mother, who refused to see that you were trying as hard as any kid possibly could to make her happy, to get good grades. She was an educator, for Pete's sake, and should've seen the signs of dyslexia. She's lucky that you didn't turn on her, turn into your grandfather, just to spite her. To be honest, I thought you'd gone that way, after you disappeared."

He raised his head, rubbed hands down his face, and looked back out. "We've just passed the park."

"What? Oh." She stopped on the deserted road, did a Y-turn, and doubled back. "Does my dad know what happened with Val?"

"No. I didn't know myself until after we got to Reunion and Becca started talking again." Marek's profile looked bleaker, if that was possible. "Arne gave my daughter what I didn't, didn't know I had to: permission to draw, to be herself."

"Stop beating yourself up, Marek." Karen drove past the dropbox, past the dumping station, and turned right down the drive to the park residence, almost hidden amongst the trees. "I'm sick about what happened to Becca, to you, to your mother, even to Bunting as a kid, but we have a job to do right now." She parked the Sub behind the park manager's truck. "I need you focused."

Marek rubbed his face again, nodded, and got out. Jack Biester met them in front of his ranch home. His ruddy, square face was surprisingly cheerful. He seemed... freer... as though some weight had been lifted. And all she'd needed to do was show up and listen. Obviously, what she thought of as a relatively minor problem was, to him, major.

"Glad you could make it, Sheriff. Detective." He squinted up at a sky that had shed the downcast gray for a deep blue that presaged the last hurrah before winter. "Up for a hike? We could drive over, but I'd prefer not to alert anyone to our arrival. I want to catch them red-handed."

"Why not," Karen said after getting a shrug from Marek. The park wasn't all that big, after all. She retrieved her radio from the Sub, wishing she had a shoulder unit instead. One more thing to add to her wish list that Dahl would deep-six. "I could stretch my legs."

Though as they ascended the asphalt road that meandered

upward to the campground, she wished she'd grabbed some sunscreen. Her nose was undoubtedly turning as red as the sumac beside the road.

Trying to make nice, Karen asked Biester, "How did you end up here? Didn't you say you worked for the feds? We're not exactly on the nation's top-ten list here. Not even the state's."

With a smile, Biester stopped at the campground entrance, shaded his eyes, and pointed to the loose snarl of gnarly brown-and-yellow-leafed trees on the far side of the road, nipping at the campsites like ill-disciplined, stunted trolls. "That's what brought me here. Bur oaks. I did my master's thesis on their adaptations in northern climes. As this park is basically a bur oak forest, it was, you might say, a return to my roots."

Karen tilted her head to look at the ugly trees then glanced at the small stand of maples. Tall and symmetrical, they were stunning with their pure-yellow leaves rapidly turning red. "Okay."

He gave her a wry smile. "Bur oaks are a very resilient species, if not as pretty as some." He started walking down the gravel circle of the small campground, waving at Donahue and a few new campers, who were either oblivious to the news or brave. "In southern climes, bur oaks can grow much taller, more symmetrical. But to survive the Dakota winters, the long droughts, they've adapted, growing large taproots, and growing more wide than tall." He gestured at the maples. "Those? Nothing but looks over substance. Have to be pampered. I'd rather see them die off, along with the other non-native species planted here, but people like to come for the fall color, so that'll never happen."

Karen preferred the color. "Well, I can say this for your bur oaks—they're probably the poster child for Halloween. Creepy."

They approached the very solid, very new restrooms, or "comfort station" as a discreet sign attested.

Karen asked, "How'd you get Dahl to cough up the money for that? I can't even get him to sign off on a new vehicle unless I give up a deputy. Who or what did you sacrifice?"

"Nothing," was the faintly gloating response. "I simply

brought him here and pointed him toward the original vault toilets—not much better than the ones at the overlook—and told him to be my guest. He went in and, a second later, flew back out—pursued by a swarm of mosquitoes, a pack of flies, more grasshoppers than a plague, and one very angry hornet that got him by the eye. He released the money that very day."

"So all I need is to put a hornet's nest in the Sub? Good to know."

With a laugh, Biester led them down a leaf-strewn trail that gave slightly underfoot. The rich smell of earth and decay arose to distract her sunburned nose. Though it wasn't impenetrable forest, the tree cover still cut down dramatically on the light. Birds chirped and alerted. Aviary alarms.

She should get out more to tango with Mother Nature, especially in her own county. But as they descended into a hollow, something approaching tension leached into Karen's enjoyment. For no apparent reason. She looked around but saw nothing in the denser undergrowth. They didn't have bears or mountain lions. Right?

"You feel it, don't you?"

Karen glanced over at the park manager, who'd stopped at a fork in the trail. "You a mind reader, Mr. Biester?"

"No, just observant. It's primal. That awareness. That something out there in the wild can kill you. I worked at Yellowstone for several summers when I was in college. Bear country. Those first few nights out in the open, with nothing more than the thin protection of a pup tent, I was scared to death. I heard every twig snap as death incarnate. I finally had an epiphany: we're just part of the food chain. Animals, all. If we have the might, the wile, to survive, then we will. I learned how to live with death at the door. It gives you an edge, a heightened appreciation for each day, knowing it can be your last."

Behind her, Marek slipped on the trail, nearly crashing into her, a grizzly bear of a man whose sheer size and strength could kill without meaning to, just like his grandfather. But he grabbed one long, twisted arm of a bur oak, which to its credit, held his considerable weight.

With cheekbones reddened by more than the sun, Marek asked, "Do you have poachers, Mr. Biester?"

Karen remembered Mary Redbird's claim of an unseen hunter. And Hugh McGurdy's bearded man in camos.

Biester's lips parted in surprise. "Yes, how... oh." He followed Marek's finger to a bowed piece of wood and a dangling hoop of wire set well back from the trail. "A snare. Good eye. Yes, we have a poacher. Well, more than one, if it comes to that. Though legal hunting started earlier this month. I don't mind the poachers, or the hunters, frankly. They eat what they kill and clean up after themselves. That's living with nature, as part of it. The homeless down by the river? They don't have a clue."

Biester led them down to a small clearing with a parking lot, where a number of cars huddled together despite the absence of anyone at the picnic tables or shelter nearby. Karen grimaced as she crunched over fine glass near a post. Walrus was right. People didn't have any respect anymore.

Biester held a finger to his mouth as he skirted the parking lot and led them down another trail, wider, with lots of footprints—and not a little trash. The soft earth turned mucky under her boots. A gurgling, sloughing sound told Karen they were approaching what the trailhead map called Connor Creek. She'd never, to her memory, come down this path before, and as they descended, the undergrowth grew more impenetrable.

And just behind that barrier, as they carefully took a side path, was another clearing, filled with about a dozen makeshift homes. Most were pup tents, but one was made of plywood, and another looked like an earth-bermed structure. And in the air, a smog of smoke lingered with the scent of brats on a grill.

Taking an involuntary step toward that siren song of late summer, Karen brushed against a post and felt the grind of glass under her boot. Again. She looked down. Not just glass but bent metal and plastic. For the first time, she understood just what she was looking at.

When she glanced back up, she saw Biester nod. "Trail monitor. Or was."

CHAPTER 21

MAREK HAD DEALT WITH URBAN homeless—squatting under bridges, panhandling along tourist strips, and drifting in and out of trouble or running from it. At night, they slept in doorways or stayed in shelters, cars, and abandoned RVs. And yes, in city parks. Whenever the issue hit critical and cops were sent in to clear the homeless, an interagency system was set in place to deal with it, from emergency shelters to job training, though the social services were never adequate.

But he never imagined he'd find a mini-Hooverville in Grove Park.

On the surface of things, it could be any lazy Indian summer Saturday, a last-ditch camping trip before the hard frost.

From his vantage point, Marek could see a man flip sausages on a grill, and a cutoff-jeans-clad boy, a fishing pole in his hands, swing his feet off a makeshift bridge of fallen logs over a surprisingly wide and deep creek. At a picnic table, an older woman sat reading a paperback, swatting at flies absently as she turned a page. Most of the encampment, though, seemed abandoned. But he imagined, come nightfall, it would fill up, as would the parking lot. Sundays were rarely days of rest for the working poor.

Barely above the spit of animal grease on the grill, Biester said, "I paid for those trail monitors out of my own pocket. Six of them. A sweet system with online monitoring and recording connected wirelessly to my phone. But almost as soon as my back was turned after the last installation, someone with a scarf over their face took a hammer to every last one. That proof your deputy demanded went poof. *Now* do you understand?"

His voice had risen, and with it, so had the heads of those in the clearing. Marek could see them make a quick calculation of their chances to evade detection, and they decided to stay put.

Seeing the same, Karen stepped into the clearing, her thumbs hooked into her belt, her gun unholstered. The grizzled, paunchy man of about fifty by the grill hefted his spatula in what could be a hello—or a threat. "Sheriff. A good day to you."

"And to you," she said evenly. "May I see your camping fee permit?"

He didn't break his gaze from hers but patted his shirt pocket then his cargo shorts pocket. "Seems I've misplaced it. Sorry. But no doubt you'll find it in the dropbox." He gave her a smile that didn't touch his wary eyes. "Though I'll warn you now, my handwriting's been called chicken scratch."

Marek heard Biester's low snort. "That's their game. One fills out the form, drops it in the box with the money, and they all claim that's them—and I can't prove otherwise. All of them put the tear-off permits on their windshields up in the parking lot then throw away the pay stub. When I point out that the numbers don't match, they claim that someone obviously broke into the dropbox and took their money."

Homeless encampments were, in Marek's urban experience, inhabited by those who had nothing more to lose. Often they'd lost their minds, to addiction or mental illness. But he didn't get the same vibe here, though he kept alert, with his hand resting on the gun holstered at the small of his back.

"Your name?" Karen grilled the griller.

"John Johnson."

"I see... Mr. Not-Johnson. Let's cut to the chase. You and your... neighbors... have been living here in the park, illegally, for some time."

"You have no proof of that," he returned, just as evenly,

impressing Marek. "I just came down for a Sunday grill after a hard week's work. That ain't a crime. You like brats? I've got plenty."

Karen's eyes didn't so much as flick down. "Where do you work... Mr. Not-Johnson?"

"Well, I'm what you might call an independent contractor. I take work as I can find it. And I can't find enough of it because I'm not as nimble as I used to be." He turned one bared-below-the-knee leg to show her a deep, twisted scar. Marek wondered just how he'd gotten up and down the trail. Maybe he used the log bridge instead. "Lucky to keep that leg at all, doctors told me. Wasn't able to keep the job that caused it, and I lost everything from the hospital bills the company wouldn't pay just because I had a beer with lunch. Said I was drunk. And from there, the shit hit the fan, after decades of hard work. No family to take me in—I admit I burned those bridges. Too young for Social Security, too mobile for disability, and too—"

"Tell your sob stories to Social Services," Biester cut in as he stepped out from the woods to stand beside Karen. "This isn't a charity. It's a public park. You need help? Fine. Get yourself on welfare, on food stamps, on Section 8—"

"Have you tried any of those, Mr. Biester?" Not-Johnson challenged. "I have. Got nowhere. You can get Section 8 in this county, yes, but only if you're a senior. Under sixty-five, and you're a risk, apparently. For the other programs, you need a fixed address, lots of paperwork, lots of free time, and a huge tolerance for bullshit. Many of us are on waiting lists. All of us work. That's the rule here. You work, you stay. You don't, you go. Surprised?"

"Your brats are burning," Karen murmured.

Not-Johnson blinked then hurriedly moved the blackened brats onto a paper towel before he turned back to Karen. "I'm telling you my story, but I'm not sobbing, just looking for some understanding. Yes, I came down in the world from when I made good money, but I still had work, and I had a home—a fifty-year-old trailer just across the creek there." He waved his spatula toward the log bridge. "And I thanked God every day for a landlord like Ted Jorgenson. He knew I was good for the month's rent, even if it was a bit late when my hours got cut. You want someone to blame for our little home away from home, on public land that we pay taxes to support? You go looking for a man named Alan Digges. Ah, I see you know that name, and let me guess, he's just given you a big new stack of evictions to serve." Karen's expression must have registered the hit because he seemed to deflate. "Expect to see more of us, not less. That man's your one-man wrecking crew here, not us."

As Biester sucked in a breath to speak, or more likely spew, his face reddening like the coals in the grill, Karen took a step forward. "I'm sorry that things have taken such a bad turn for you. And I'll do whatever I can to help you find housing. But my job is to uphold the law. You are breaking it. I'm afraid you will have to leave. Now."

He just gave her a sad smile as he put down the spatula. "Sure. We'll leave." At a few dissenting sounds from the tents, he went on. "We'll pack up what little we have left to our names into our shitty cars, and we'll drive off with a hefty fine in our pockets that we can't pay. But we'll be back. Because we've got nowhere else to go. You can, of course, lock us up. Believe me, once the snow flies, we'll be glad for three square meals and a heated cell. All I've tried to do here is keep us all fed, clothed, and protected until something better shows up. That means pooling our resources, looking after each other, and keeping the women and children safe. Can you find us the same?"

Biester made a sound deep in his throat. "Don't make it sound like you're some kind of saint, Johnson, or whatever your name is. Have you forgotten about those dopeheads who smashed a brick through a couple vans at the campground and stole hundreds' worth of electronics?"

"They weren't part of our group. Transients. Ted kicked them out six months ago."

But Biester was on a roll. "You people have trashed this place. You use the water, the restrooms. You destroyed my trail monitors, worth hundreds of dollars. But worst of all, you've disrupted the native habitat, upset the entire ecosystem."

Not-Johnson just stared at Biester. "All we're trying to do is survive, same as the animals you put so much stock by, but they seem to be better protected than us."

Seeing no end to the argument between two men with violently opposed aims, Marek stepped into the clearing. Brawn, enter stage right. The spatula came up, and Biester gave Marek a tight nod of approval, at least until Marek spoke to Not-Johnson.

"You were here last night." Because Marek had made it a statement, Not-Johnson seemed stymied as to how to answer, so he remained silent. Marek raised his voice. "I want to hear what, if anything, you or your neighbors saw or heard last night. And I want the truth."

Birds chirped, the boy jerked as his lure bobbed, and the woman with the book rose. As she did, a German shepherd slunk from under the pilfered picnic table and shot out into the clearing with a growl.

"Don't make me shoot your dog," Karen warned, snatching her gun out of the holster.

"Quiet, Daisy."

Remarkably, the dog quieted, pink tongue lolling, a silly grin on its face as the woman caught up and grabbed hold of the collar.

"She's a big softie, really." The woman patted Daisy's sleek head. "But she's protective and the only family I've got, other than... Mr. Johnson... and the others. I'm not saying we're all saints, 'cause we aren't, but we're not bad people. Just unlucky, mostly. I got laid off from working in the school cafeteria at Dutch Corners when it closed and haven't found much else but part-time work at the Reunion cafeteria—but it's all outsourced now, so I don't get a pension or nothing."

She looked around at the tents. "All of us lived in the trailer park, and all of us were evicted in the last two months since Ted had his stroke. Digges plays dirty. Said I hadn't paid, but I had the money. And do you know who helped him throw us out?

Who threw his weight around, backed up Digges with his lies? Yeah. Bob Bunting."

The boy on the bridge, head down, jerked again, but without the bob of the lure. Marek changed course as his antennae quivered. "Who is the boy?"

"My son," Not-Johnson said without blinking, but his head jerked, and the boy reeled in his line. "Andy."

Surprisingly, Karen countered. "I don't think so. I've seen him before. That ball cap..." Karen snapped her fingers. "Baseball boy. Little League. Bobby. Bobby... begins with J."

"Johnson," Not-Johnson insisted. "Like I told you. Andy's his middle name. How I call him."

The boy hopped to his feet and ran lightly across the logs toward the trailer park. Interesting. Marek wondered if he was the boy young Hugh McCurdy had seen. And if so, who had his companion been? Not-Johnson certainly didn't fit Hugh's description.

As if to head off further questioning on that tender head, the woman blurted, "He was here that night. Bunting, I mean. You may not believe it, but we were all pulling for you to win, Sheriff Mehaffey. I stayed up to listen for the recount. I don't sleep so good with a bad back on the uneven ground. So I was still awake, keyed up to think Bunting finally got what he was owed, when I heard that big SUV of his roar into the lot up the trail. We try to be as quiet as mice, not disturb nobody." She shot a heated look at Biester. "Bunch of us work late hours, or early, and don't want no trouble."

"That's all you've been to me," he shot back. "Trouble. Trouble for me, trouble for the park, trouble for the paying campers. Do you know how hard I worked, early and late, to get the state interested in this park? And you're risking it all."

"No, Bunting was the one to stir up trouble. He was your lackey, though, wasn't he? He told us you had an 'agreement' between you. Said he was going to set fire to our tents. Once he had a badge, he'd be able to do whatever he pleased."

Biester's eyes bugged. "You think I'd risk burning down

my own park? That's insane. I just wanted him to do the job that I thought he'd been elected to do. Enforce the laws. No more, no less." He shot Karen another heated look. "I'm not the lawbreaker here. You do your job; I'll do mine."

Marek stepped up again. "What did you hear that night, Ms....?"

She gave him a twisted smile. "Johnson. Mary Johnson. What I heard? Some kind of argument. Yelling. Engines starting. Cars leaving. Lots of people just stay in their cars and never even come down here, especially when it's raining. After, it got quiet, so I tried to go back to sleep. Then I heard some crashing and cursing. I'm thinking Bunting's coming down the trail and gonna do what he said. I pulled the flap, ready to sic Daisy on him, take a bite outta his nasty butt." Her chin trembled, but she firmed it, looking at them straight on. "And... you'll say I'm seeing things... but I saw... the evil eye. All red, burning. Looking right at me. I pulled Daisy right back into the tent and waited for Armageddon."

CHAPTER 22

KAREN HAD HEARD A LOT of strange claims in her tenure as acting sheriff. Aliens in the attic, bombs in the basement, but not an evil eye. And not from someone who seemed, on the surface of things, sane.

Even Biester was silenced.

"Mary..." Not-Johnson heaved a long-suffering sigh. "I told you. I'm pretty sure Bunting must've had an infrared scope. I don't know just what he intended to do... shoot us all?" He swatted absently at the flies that'd scented fresh meat. "Whoever killed him did us a favor. I won't say otherwise, though I slept through the entire thing, as did everyone else, so far as I know."

Any one of these people had motive for murder. Self-defense, even, if Bunting was hunting them. "Do you have a... knife?" Karen stopped herself, just in time, from saying pocketknife.

"Is that what did him in? Yes, I do." He turned sideways, slapped a hunter's knife attached to his belt. "Hunting's legal. I eat what I kill. And believe me, I wouldn't take a bite of Bunting. Rotten, through and through. But word was you found him up at the overlook. None of us go up there. We try to stay out of sight—we know we're the prey here. You want to find your killer? Take a walk on the wild side." He nodded, not into the woods as Karen expected, but across the creek toward the trailer park. "Go serve your evictions and find out just what's been going on there."

Though she wanted to, Karen didn't move. "That's what I'm doing next. But I can't let you stay here. I'm sorry. But you know as well as I do, your little encampment isn't a long-term solution."

"You got a better one?" he asked.

Karen wanted to say it wasn't her problem, but of course, it was. This man, at least, appeared to be simply down on his luck. He'd done what he could, not only for himself, but others. To reward that effort by destroying the small community—family, really—he'd built against long odds went against the grain. She admired their resilience. "We've got a number of empty houses in Reunion. I've seen the rental signs. There's got to be somewhere you can afford, if not individually, collectively."

Not-Johnson wrapped up his brats with a slow, deliberate motion. "None of the landlords will touch any of us from the trailer park, because thanks to Digges, we've all got an eviction on our record. We can't come up with all the security deposits, the two months' rent and references, and who knows what else. Do you think we're stupid? We've all been looking. We've signed up for every program we've heard of, private or public. And we're just the first wave. Easy pickings, the compliant ones, the scared ones. We went without a fight and tried to make the best of it. If we could afford justice, you'd be putting Digges and Bunting in the Big House for years, not throwing us out of our last digs."

He stared down at his ruined brats, his shoulders slumping. He dropped the bundle, to Karen's stomach's rumbling dismay, into a trash can. A crowd of flies rose then descended, readying for a feast at the expense of a man, putatively higher on the food chain.

"*Lord of the Flies,*" he murmured, drawing blanks from most in the clearing, but Karen had been taught high school English by Marek's exacting mother. What she'd taken from the tale of the teenage boys stranded on an island was that boys were shit at governing themselves. And she wondered just what this man's history was, who he really was, but she felt a deep reluctance to unmask him. Was she really cut out to be sheriff, after all?

She'd given Kyle Early the green light to skip town to become someone else's problem, and here she was, doing it again.

Steeling her spine, Karen turned to Biester. "Do you want me to get a warrant to hunt for the scarf?" As the park manager blinked, she wished she hadn't said anything. But now that it was out there, she had to follow through. "You said you had a picture of a scarfed figure destroying your trail monitors. On your phone. We can look for the scarf and question the owner."

"Oh, yeah." Biester pulled out his phone from his shirt pocket, then with a glance at the huddle of people who'd silently come out of their tents to surround their leader, he slid it back. "Just go. Take your tents. Your plywood. Your trash. And we'll call it even."

To give him credit, Biester not only called it even, he helped cart collapsed tents, plywood, and bags of trash up to the parking lot for those unable to do so. They stuffed the tents into cars already bulging to capacity with evicted belongings. And Karen and Marek took down license plates as furtively as they could, making Karen feel as guilty as hell. But they needed identities. One blurry-eyed couple who worked night shifts said they would stay with the rest of the pitiful stack of belongings owned by those arriving later.

Blowing sweat-soaked bangs out of her eyes, Karen knocked on the top of the battered gray Honda in the lead position. Not-Johnson poked his head out.

"There's a Lions Club park just outside Reunion. Go through town and turn right then hook left. You can camp there for free for three days." She might ruffle some feathers, but the park had no restrictions. "I'll ask around and see what I can do after that. I know Marsha Schaeffer, the social services rep for this county."

He stared at her then nodded. "Thank you. That'll give us a breather, at least."

She forced herself to ask the hard question before she let him go. "Does your... the boy... have a responsible guardian? Does he go to school?"

"Yes, and yes. Don't worry. He's in good hands." He held her gaze until she had to believe him. She stepped back.

He rolled up his window, honked, and led the little band of battered lives out of the park—to a temporary promised land.

She almost envied him. He had a reprieve and the rest of his Sunday. She got to throw more joy around. Mary Johnson was right. The devil was loose in Eda County.

Armageddon had arrived.

CHAPTER 23

THE HARDEST SCALE FOR JUSTICE to balance wasn't right against wrong, Marek's father had liked to say, but right against wronged.

Leif Okerlund had served a number of evictions over his long tenure as the sheriff of Eda County. But Marek doubted that even in the gloomiest days of farm foreclosures had he evicted so many people who lived on the precarious margins of a hardscrabble life. A baker's dozen, an unlucky thirteen whom Alan Digges had deemed irredeemable, kicked to the crumbling concrete curb.

With only two left to serve, Marek decided that every evicted family was evicted in their own way. The easy ones, as Not-Johnson had intimated, had already gone. Those who remained were the desperate, the despondent, and those in deep denial.

He'd quickly learned that, despite his first impressions, the condition of the trailer didn't indicate which were the evictions. They'd evicted an immigrant family who'd meticulously maintained and upgraded theirs so it glittered like a pearl before swine. Meanwhile, a disabled man had just handed over the keys to Digges's lockout crew and said, "Have at it, boys," before limping away from the swill with a lighter step. Marek had watched him head for the woods.

At their next-to-last trailer, an overweight girl of maybe thirteen sat on the last rickety step of a dingy rust-colored trailer.

With a sneer that reminded Marek far too much of Nadine Early, the girl blew smoke from a limp cigarette across a huge puddle that reflected nothing but a bleak future.

"Is your mother at home?" Karen asked in the monotone she'd adopted after they'd evicted the struggling young Guatemalan family that she'd once helped rescue. Victims of human trafficking and newly minted American citizens, they'd lost first their meatpacking jobs when PBI left town in the middle of the night, then lost their meager wages with the agricultural jobs winding down for winter. They'd been scared to death that they were being deported, but at least Marek, who spoke Spanish fluently, had been able to reassure them on that head.

After they made a hasty call to a Bosnian family who'd befriended them back in their mutual PBI days, Marek was able to tell Karen that they had a good place to go. Those same Bosnians had once found shelter in Karen's own basement, so it was nice to see the gesture being paid forward.

Both Marek and Karen had helped them move their belongings. Unlike in Albuquerque, where companies had sprung up to clean out houses for hands-off landlords, Eda County had never seen mass evictions on such a scale, and it had no mechanism to deal with them. One family had just gotten into their car and driven away, telling the kids they were going to drive to Disneyland. Marek doubted they'd go more than a few miles on a nearly empty gas tank.

Finally answering Karen's question, the girl on the trailer step said, "My mother's dead."

The girl might as well have said, "My pet mosquito is dead." In other words: good riddance.

"Who, then, is Doris Harkness?"

Another blow across the bow. "Gran."

"And is she home?"

"She's always home. She doesn't go anywhere. Ever. You wanna move her, be my guest. She's, like, five hundred pounds."

Though she'd exaggerated by a factor of two, the girl was otherwise correct. Doris Harkness flat-out refused to move from her Kleenex-and-paper-plate-littered recliner in a trailer barely a step up from the homeless encampment—and likely kept up only by the girl.

With dark circles under her rheumy eyes, the woman glared up at them like a raccoon that had staked its claim. The claim might be to garbage, but it was her garbage. "You're only taking me out in a coffin. I've been in this trailer for thirteen years. And I've paid my rent on time for every one of those years. Comes straight outta my disability—I got diabetes something fierce—and the stipend I get for taking in my granddaughter. Had Zoe pretty much since she was born. Her mother got herself killed in a high-speed car crash with that good-for-nothing boyfriend of hers at the wheel—both of 'em had no more sense than a gnat—when Zoe wasn't even a year old."

Though the words were dismissive, Marek heard the emotion underneath. He knew the pain of losing a child, and his son hadn't even been properly born when Marek lost him.

"I'm sorry for your loss." Karen looked frustrated but resolute, just as she had when faced with all the previous pleas, excuses, and accusations. "As for the trailer, if you'd paid on time, you'd be fine, but—"

A snort cut Karen off. "I'm the one who takes the check over." Zoe stepped inside from where she'd been sitting on the steps, giving every appearance of not giving a damn. "Every first of the month. I got ears. I know what happens if you don't pay on time. Mr. Jorgenson, he was cool. He never looked at me like Mr. Digges did, like he'd scrape me off the bottom of his snazzy shoes. I handed him our check, just like always."

A residual outrage rose on the girl's face, making Marek wonder if perhaps a seed of hope still survived in her that the world could be fair, or should be. "Mr. Digges wouldn't take the check. Said something was wrong with it. So I took it back to Gran, and she says there's nothing wrong but the man's eyes. The money was in the bank, just like always. Not like we ever go anywhere, do anything. So I go back, and he's already filled out that stupid notice. Hands it to me and says, 'If you can't read, that says you've got three days to get out—or we'll do it for you.' Then he sniffs. 'Might be good for you, force you to skip a few meals.' And then he got in that badass car and left me standing there."

Marek had quickly learned that the eviction rules in Eda County heavily favored the landlord, but if the allegation were true and not just... blowing smoke... that was beyond the pale. But why would Digges piss a reliable paycheck into the wind? They'd heard this story already, and Karen hadn't bought it.

"Can I see the check?" Karen asked.

Marek wasn't sure who was more surprised: the girl, the grandmother, or him. But maybe she'd seen the same thing he had in the girl's face—and didn't want to snuff out that last bit of irrational trust in the system.

Doris reached into a little cubbyhole in her recliner and handed over the check. Karen took it by the corner. "Have you made out any checks since then?" When handed the checkbook, Karen thumbed through the mimeographed copies and looked at Marek. "Sewage and electricity paid same day but after the rent. We can track that, can't we? See if it holds up?"

"You calling me a liar?" Doris challenged.

Karen looked over at her. "No, I'm looking for evidence that will hold up in court."

Lips sank in over missing teeth. "We don't have money for no lawyers."

When Karen glanced at the flat-screen TV and the cell phone in the cubbyhole, Doris glared at her. "That TV cost me a hundred. See that corner? It was dropped in the store. It's cracked. But it works. Only way I'm ever going places again is through that TV. Only way I keep in touch with my granddaughter and get my meds taken care of with Doc Hudson is through that phone. It hooks up to that net thing that's all over the airwaves. I got a right to enjoy a bit of life. Pursuit of happiness, right? A couple hundred a year ain't gonna make a difference to anything. You prefer I just sit here and die?"

Marek wondered if the woman had just sunk her last ship

out. While Marek had been raised by Leif Okerlund, who'd lived his life with the mantra of *Judge not, lest you be judged*, Karen had been raised by Arne Okerlund, who followed the more popular, if non-biblical, *God helps those who help themselves.*

Karen's jaw tightened, and Marek held his breath.

Widening her stance, his niece glared at Doris over the open checkbook in her hand. "Are you going to let me take these?"

Suspicion narrowed the raccoon eyes. "Why?"

Between gritted teeth, Karen said, "To see if I can get a print off the check to match Digges. The judge could put a hold on the eviction."

Doris's sunken lips parted. "Oh. Well, I suppose. I ain't going anywheres." She cleared her throat as if unsure just how to handle the situation, of the law extending help rather than a slap. "Leastways Bunting ain't here to back up Digges."

Marek took the baggie that Zoe produced from a broken drawer in the tiny kitchen, and Karen slipped the evidence in. "Bunting lied for Digges?" Marek asked Doris.

Still looking faintly suspicious, Doris nodded. "Lied, intimidated, whatever it took. In exchange for living rent-free. Talk about someone who lived large when he had less than nothing in the bank. You get a load of that monster truck? Got some real good folk kicked out of their homes. People been here for years. Good neighbors."

Marek still wasn't sure what the endgame was, if the accusations were true. "Why would Digges want to get rid of good tenants who paid on time?"

"Alan Digges has grand plans for this place. Thinks he's gonna raise rents hundreds of dollars. And he doesn't care if they stay 'cause then he can take their deposits." She looked over at her granddaughter. "What'd he call that?"

Zoe screwed up her round face in a passable, even dead-on, mimic of Digges. "'Churn, baby, churn. Out with the old, in with the new.'" She blew out a blast. "Bunting said the same thing after he won the election the first time—that he and Digges were gonna clean up in Eda County."

The fine grammatical distinction between cleaning up any supposed corruption and cleaning up monetarily by aiding and abetting corruption was indicative of Bunting's viewpoint on the world.

"And you better clean up your act." Doris pointed at her granddaughter's cigarette. "Put that out. I keep telling you, girl. You keep at that, you'll never make old bones."

That elicited a shrug. "You smoke all the time."

"And look at me. If the diabetes don't kill me, the lungs will. Doc Hudson says I got to start on oxygen soon. That'll cost money we can't spare. And, yeah, I know. Gotta stop. I tried damn hard." Her rheumy eyes blurred. "You know I did, but this eviction stuff, it's got me puffing away again. I gotta last me five more years 'fore you're legal."

Zoe stabbed the butt into an overflowing ashtray. "I'm *glad* Bunting's dead. And I got to see—"

"Zoe!" For the first time, Doris Harkness moved her bulk up in the recliner. "Don't make trouble."

The girl's chin wobbled as she looked up at Karen then at Marek. "I saw him dead. And I was glad."

CHAPTER 24

J   UST BEYOND THE LAST TRAILER, the late-afternoon light filtered through the oak trees like an alchemist's autumnal elixir, turning the bloodstains on the bent grass into the dark red of the sumac that edged the woods beyond. Bunting's fall had been camouflaged in fall color.

From where Karen stood, she could just barely see the end of the makeshift bridge into Not-Johnson's encampment. Turning her head back toward the trailer park, she watched the curtain in the last trailer on the lot twitch like a nervous tic. With good reason. Witness or perpetrator, the man who lived there would soon find himself on the hot seat.

Zoe gloated from the gravel road, where she'd been sternly commanded to stay. "See. I told you. Bunting was just lying there, dead."

What had Karen's father said, about how he'd once tracked down an FBI most wanted in a bolt-hole on Bandit Ridge? *If you want the best recon, ask a kid.*

Karen had withheld judgment on this particular kid, as she wasn't entirely sure whether Zoe was taking her for a ride. But apparently, it was Bunting who'd been taken for one, from the kill site here up to the overlook. The grass that grew long up to the gravel was tamped down with foot traffic to the log bridge, but didn't hold a print. So they were out of luck when it came to forensics. If Larson were free, she could still get him down here to see what magic he could pull out from his investigative hat, but he was still in the Lake region. So they made do. Marek photographed the trampled grass and stains before kneeling to take samples.

Karen turned back to Zoe, who met her gaze with an expression torn between a told-you-so sneer and an excited delight that turned her into a kid again.

"Tell me again," Karen told the girl. "What, when, where."

Though they'd done it all in the trailer, with very grudging permission from Doris, Karen wanted it spelled out again on the scene, where it might jog a new memory. Zoe rolled her eyes, but more for form, Karen thought, than anything. This girl had probably never had such a rapt audience. And that was incredibly sad.

"Told you, I woke up when I heard a car pass, going to Mr. Peterson's." She nodded toward the last trailer. "And I came out to take a smoke. Gran gets on me, otherwise. Clock on the wall said one-fifty-three."

At thirteen, Karen would've been sound asleep at that time, even on a weekend—or at the most, under the covers, listening to banned rock music on her Walkman. But she'd been so busy with school and sports that she'd never had time to get into trouble. And the one cigarette she'd cadged with another girl had convinced her that breathing ash wasn't something she wanted to continue doing. She needed her lungs to catch up with the star of eighth-grade basketball, Joanie Harrah, a Southern transplant who'd moved on before high school rolled around. What, Karen wondered, had ever become of Joanie? Like Zoe, she'd been the product of a broken home. Had she made it out, perhaps courtesy of her talent? Karen hoped so.

Zoe scuffed her toe in the gravel. "Like I told you, I saw Mr. Bunting's SUV parked on the road across from Mr. Peterson's trailer. Thick as thieves, those two, Gran says. 'Cause that's just what they were."

Marek rose to his feet, bagged swabs in hand. "Was Mr. Peterson's trailer lit up?"

"Oh, yeah. I was... well, I was gonna see if I could hear anything. Like find out who else they were planning to kick out so I could warn 'em. So I start tiptoeing over to the open window, and I can hear somebody talking real low, and I see Mr. Peterson's sitting like this..." She put her head in her hands. "But then I tripped over... Bunting." Her excitement drained, leaving her face as faded and pocked as Eda County's backcountry roads. "I split after that. Told Gran. She said not to tell anybody."

In Doris Harkness's own words, she'd told her granddaughter to keep her flapping trap shut tighter than Fort Knox. Staying off a cop's radar was an understandable, if frustrating, defense mechanism for those in precarious circumstances.

Almost to herself, Zoe continued, "Well, I told Bobby, but he wouldn't tell. But I—"

"Bobby?" Karen asked, more sharply than she'd intended. "Who is he?"

Zoe's chin lifted. "Just a boy I know. He's nice. He doesn't call me Zero Zoe like the other boys."

Karen felt that like a sucker punch to the gut, so she imagined how much worse it must feel for this girl who would never win even a point in the beauty sweepstakes. Puberty hadn't, and wouldn't, rescue her, but a good diet might clear the acne, at least.

"Don't listen to them, Zoe," Marek said in his gentle way, with such a wealth of understanding that the girl teared up. Karen forgot sometimes that her half-uncle had been taunted mercilessly on the playgrounds of Reunion. *Dumb Polack.* Hell, she herself had thought he was slow—and when he'd first appeared again in Reunion as her sight-unseen part-time detective, she'd wanted to let him go because she couldn't imagine he would be any good at it or be able to deal with the endless paperwork required. How wrong she'd been—at least about the job. The paperwork was, thankfully, Josephine's problem.

Dashing her tears away, Zoe looked up at them with a fierceness that brooked no comment. "I've only got eighth grade to get through, then I can drop out. Gran says I have to go to high school, but I know the law. I don't have to. She can't make me. Not like she went, and she still had a job 'til she got sick. People like us, we work until we can't. That's just how it is."

How different this child, with her cynical adult eyes, was from Mary Hannah, with her innocent child's eyes. Only a year older than Zoe, the latter was already an adult by Brethren standards. The Brethren had made an exception in Mary Hannah's case, to let her go beyond the eighth grade, and she'd jumped at the chance. Though objectively poor in material things, Mary Hannah wasn't poor in any other way that mattered.

Karen scrambled for a way to change Zoe's mind. A high school diploma might be the girl's only ticket out. She stuck her thumbs in her belt. "Dropping out means they win, Zoe. Don't give their puny egos the satisfaction. Get your diploma and prove them all wrong."

The girl tilted her head, as if trying to wrap her head around that reversion of the usual power structure, with her at the bottom. Winning wasn't likely something she'd experienced often, if ever, in her short life. Hoping she'd given the girl something to think about, at least, Karen asked, "What's your friend Bobby's last name?"

Zoe's eyes dropped to the gravel. "Just Bobby."

That was another thing about kids, Karen recalled. They ran in packs and could be fiercely loyal. But Bobby's welfare concerned Karen. Perhaps if she pressed a bit, played the concern card—

A car door slammed shut, breaking the moment. Karen turned to see Alan Digges saunter up the gravel road. The war of sneer versus gloat on his face was as fierce as it had been on Zoe's, but Karen much preferred the teenager's. Zoe had reason—and was a child. What was his excuse?

"My lockout crew tells me you finally showed up and did your job. Looks like I won't have to call in the cavalry. Yet. They're still waiting to clean out the last two. What's the holdup?"

Karen turned her back on Marek as he quietly took the grass and blood samples to the Sub. She didn't want to let the cat out of the bag just yet. She wanted Mr. Peterson—and who else could it be, still twitching away at the curtains—under wraps first. "Doris Harkness's eviction is on hold."

Startled, Zoe looked at her sideways, but she didn't look pleased—or displeased, for that matter. Just held a breathless stillness, like cornered prey. Would death come swiftly, or did the predator want to play first?

"What do you mean 'on hold'?" The gloat, at least, had melted off his face. "Judge Rudibaugh signed off on it. It's all legal."

"Maybe, maybe not. Allegations have been made."

"Allegations? From people being evicted?" He snorted. "These people couldn't find their way out of their own ass. Are you stupid?"

Karen wasn't, but he was. Too stupid to see the crew behind him, while ostensibly working for him, were rolling up shirtsleeves, no doubt to kick his very white ass. Though she'd love to see it, she had a scene—and a girl—to protect. So she named names, just to see his spin. "According to Doris Harkness, she had the money right on time like always, but you wouldn't take the check."

A helicoptering brown leaf caught in his hair. He picked it off with distaste. "And you believed that overweight piece of white trash?"

"Don't you call my Gran names," Zoe said, fists balling. "She's not trash. You are."

For the first time, Digges deigned to acknowledge Zoe. "Trailer trash, white trash, you've heard it all before, I'll bet. And worse." As the hit went home, he sniffed. "Maybe if you stop stuffing your face and start using the legs God gave you—instead of spreading them for any—"

Marek's hand came down hard on Digges' shoulder from behind, making the man let out a squeal, which delighted Zoe—and Karen. What planet had this man come from, that he thought speaking like that to a child was fair game?

As Marek held Digges in place, Karen got in his face. "If you ever, *ever* speak to a child like that again in my hearing, or if

I hear of it, I will arrest you for child endangerment. Do you understand me?"

His wide-eyed look of panic lasted about three unsatisfying seconds. "Don't tell me you didn't think the same. Though, now that I recall from the election chatter, I heard you spread your own—"

"What do they call you?" Karen interrupted, barely keeping her fisted hands at her sides. "Let's see... the Boy Toy of the Bayton Babe?"

At the snickers at his back, Digges shook off Marek's relaxed hand, straightened his tie, and stalked back to his car with stiff legs that probably wouldn't have held him otherwise. Once he was safely in his luxurious cage, he rolled down the window. "You'll hear about this from our lawyers. When they're done with you, you'll be cleaning crap out of prison drains."

The car spit gravel as it sped away.

"What a zero," Zoe said into the silence. And her audience raised a cheer.

CHAPTER 25

AREK TOOK NO PLEASURE IN having one of his past tormentors on the hot seat. With the air conditioning off for the season, the still, stifling air of the filing-cum-interview room in the Sheriff's Office seemed to suck all the life out of their suspect. Taylor Peterson sat, balding head in his hands, at the scarred table.

After they'd brought him in from the trailer park, he'd requested privacy for his one phone call, which they'd given him, after a recitation of his rights. Though with the undoubted lawyer soon to arrive, they would be lucky to get anything out of him.

Peterson had never been the ringleader of the playground taunts, even though he'd been almost as big as Marek and could pack a wallop when so directed by those up higher in the pecking order. But Peterson seemed to have no fight left in him. When they'd taken him in, he'd kept his eyes downcast, his cheekbones high with color, the rest of his face gray with stubble.

Truth be told, Marek had never felt that Peterson's heart was in the playground taunting. As they'd moved from elementary into middle school, Peterson had saved his wallopings for the gridiron, where he'd enjoyed a storied career as a defensive lineman at Reunion High. Vaguely, Marek recalled talk in the locker room in Valeska that Peterson had taken a scholarship to play football at South Dakota State University in Brookings.

What had happened from there, Marek had no clue, but he'd never have guessed the son of Reunion's most well-respected building contractor would end up in a poorly built trailer at Ted's.

At Karen's nod, Marek hit the record key on the cassette recorder that, by all rights, should be in a museum, even if it was only a few years old. Progress came slowly to Eda County. They had, however, recently acquired a makeshift video feed as a somewhat glitchy backup for the recorder.

"Mr. Peterson," Karen began.

"Taylor," he mumbled. "Not like we don't know each other."

Marek had taken longer to recognize the man who'd hunched through the trailer door than Karen had. Her jaw had dropped, and they'd all stood there with their bated-breath audience, waiting for Peterson's response. In the end, it had been anticlimactic, as he'd just shuffled down into the Sub like a carnival bear into his cage, away from the scary humans who jeered him.

Karen let out a breath. "Taylor, then, will you tell us what happened on Friday night at your trailer?"

He didn't look up. "I... had a visitor."

"Bunting," Karen said.

The balding spot reddened. "No, a... a woman. Doesn't matter. She left."

When silence fell, Marek picked up the thread. "You were in bed with Bunting."

Peterson's head shot up.

"Figuratively," Marek clarified. "Not literally."

After he held Marek's gaze for a long moment, Taylor nodded. "I deserved that dig and more. You were always the better man, Marek Okerlund. You took whatever we shelled out on the playground. Didn't run crying to the teachers, didn't taunt us back, just took it, picked yourself up, and tried harder at school than anyone I've ever seen before or since. It made me... ashamed. And I feel just like that now."

Taylor slid his hands down his face then braced his shoulders. "Yeah, I helped Bunting do his dirty work, until he stabbed me in the back." Determined to tell his story to Marek, he didn't notice Karen flinch at the wording. "I'm not proud of it, but you do what you have to. I lost everything in the divorce last year even though I didn't want it in the first place. Supporting Maggie and the kids on what I make with new construction way down, with our mortgage on the house that she got in the split, and just trying to keep my head above water. Ted gave me a reduced rate for doing handyman work around the place. He knew I was good, reliable, getting back on my feet as best I could. I thought of you, y'know, Marek. Just pick yourself up like that halfwit Okerlund kid. If he could, I could. Go about my business, and eventually things'll look up."

That Taylor Peterson had given the boy Marek had been another thought after all this time floored him. Marek figured it was just the normal bullying of that era—and likely still went on. Plenty of it went on in boardrooms and on golf courses, for that matter. Case in point: Alan Digges.

"Just what did you do for Bunting?" Marek asked.

Peterson sighed. "You know all those evictions? If Digges played by the rules, by the ones Ted did with letting the tenants know they could contest the eviction in court with a hearing, it would've taken months, but Digges didn't want months. And he didn't want to pay for my time, either. Said the trailer park could fall to pieces for all he cared, because no one else would care— and the poor would still come knocking, with their vouchers, their charity-paid deposits. He could get what little work he needed just from lowering rents—or not raising them. Or...lie for him. So the deal was, if I backed up Bunting, swearing that rents weren't paid, that tenants broke the rules of the lease, I'd get to stay. Should've known not to get in bed with a two-faced liar. Told myself, 'Just hold on, and somebody's gonna take them both down.' Should've been me, because I have some connections in Eda County, but I was... too ashamed... and afraid I'd lose what contracts I still had."

He slid his hands down his face again. "Y'know, we used to look after each other at the trailer park, fixing stuff, bartering, loaning a floater, whatever it took. Then Digges set us against each other... and I fell right in line. I should've come to you guys right away. I knew it was wrong, pushing hardworking people out of their homes, but I just felt... helpless. You always wonder what you'd do if you were in something like the Holocaust. You got a choice either to live or to die at one of those camps—but to live, you gotta betray your own."

A tic spasmed in his stubbled cheek, but he didn't look away. "Well, now I know. I'm one of the cowards. And I can't ever take back what I did. But I want to be a man my son can be proud of. So I told Bunting I wasn't going to be his lackey anymore... and next thing I know, I'm on his shit list, with a notice to vacate. Last night... I'd had enough."

Marek barely breathed as the tape recorder whirred in the silence. Thankfully, Peterson was too deep in his story to hear it.

"When I went out to see my... visitor ... off, I felt like I'd taken my first deep breath since the divorce." The tic smoothed as he smiled. "Moon was out, you know? Stars galore. When was the last time I looked up at the stars? You forget they're even there." His smile dimmed. "So I walked around the trailer toward the woods, away from all the lights, and..."

Marek waited. Karen twitched beside him, probably pacing madly in her mind, like Gunny twitching in his sleep, chasing rabbits.

"And there he was. Just lying there."

Marek's shoulders slumped from a height he hadn't known they'd risen to. "Who?"

Peterson blinked then frowned at him, as if once again reassessing Marek's mental capacity. "Bunting, of course. Who else?"

Karen got to her feet then leaned back against the closed door. "Alive?"

"No, dead. Near as I could figure, anyway. He wasn't breathing."

Marek pushed back in his chair. "What about Bunting's SUV?"

"Ah... it was parked there, across the road. And... I'm not proud of it, but I panicked. We were on the outs, you know? Everybody knew I'd been booted. And I got thinking, even being dead, he was giving me shit. All I could think was, here I'd decided to start over, to get my life back on track somehow, and there he was—just tripping me up again. I figured I had to move him somewhere that I wouldn't be looked at as a suspect. Found the keys on him and took his body up to the overlook. Almost gave up my plan when I saw an RV parked there, but it was all dark. I'd cut the headlights of the SUV from the get-go, drove by the light of the moon. Bunting was one hell of a load to get into the toilet, but I've been trying to work off some of my mad, after getting dumped for no reason, so I managed. Seemed appropriate."

"No reason for the divorce? What about your lady friend?" Karen pushed back from the door. "Just who was this mystery woman you keep alluding to?"

He reddened to a beet color.

A hard knock had them all jumping. Turning, Karen jerked open the door, and Marek pitied whoever walked through—even a lawyer.

And his jaw unhinged. Check that. Not a lawyer.

Of all the women in all the world, Marek would have bet good money that this particular one wouldn't have diddled with their suspect. Or any man, for that matter, given what she'd gone through in the last few years, losing all of her family on a freakish snowy night. She'd lost some weight, of the poundage variety if not the grief, but she still had about two decades on Peterson.

Pastor Tricia Cantor rushed over to Peterson and put her

hand on his shoulder. "I got here as soon as I could, Taylor. Are you all right?"

Hearing genuine worry, genuine caring, Marek decided that age had no boundaries when it came to love, but still, he admitted that even though few things shocked him anymore, this did. The Chicago psychiatrist turned Congregationalist preacher had become an informal profiler and a friend of sorts.

Karen, on the other hand, hadn't felt the same connection, though even she had a hard time coming up with a response—a testament to her shock. "Ms. Cantor, were you with Mr. Peterson last night?"

"Why, yes, didn't he tell you already?"

Marek cleared his throat. "He was... reticent... about your relationship."

"Ashamed, more like," Karen muttered.

After squeezing Peterson's shoulder, Tricia sank down in Karen's vacated chair. "It's nothing to be ashamed of, Taylor. I told you that."

Tricia seemed to be taking his obvious embarrassment rather well. Although as a fairly new pastor in town, even if a widow, she'd probably wanted the romance under wraps, as well. Ashamed, no. Secretive, yes.

"Your... relationship... has gone on how long?" Marek asked.

"Oh, well, quite some time," Tricia answered serenely. "Taylor and Maggie hosted me for lunch during my first month here. What a red-letter day that was." She dimpled, looking over at Taylor. "Just too delicious to resist. I came back for more."

Karen made at T with her hands. "Wait. Time out. You cheated on Taylor's wife, starting that far back?"

Both stared at Karen, then at each other, and both descended into hysterical laughter.

"Oh, my. Oh, my." Tricia slipped off her glasses to wipe away tears. "Goodness, Karen, I could be his mother. You really thought..." She laughed again, more ruefully. "I think somewhere in there was a compliment to me, but hardly to Taylor."

"You're... a wonderful woman..." her parishioner stammered. "But..."

"But I'm his pastor, not his lover," she finished. "Really, Marek, I thought you had a better handle on human dynamics than that."

"I didn't want to think it," he mumbled, sure his own cheeks were red now. "He kept avoiding our questions about you, about what you were doing at his place at that hour."

"Ah, I see." Tricia slipped her glasses back on. "Well, it was pretty serious. He called me just before one in the morning, said that he needed to talk to someone or he thought he might finish it."

"Finish what?" Karen demanded.

Marek finally got it. "Finish himself."

The balding head fell back into the big scarred hands. Tricia reached over to pat his back. "You did exactly right, Taylor, calling me. Losing a bit of sleep is nothing compared to losing you. Suicide isn't the answer. Life isn't over, not for me, not for you. Don't forget everything I told you, just because all this"— she looked around the interview room—"happened ahead of schedule."

Marek slumped in his chair. Their slam dunk had just turned into a clunker. Bunting had been killed after one o'clock, after Taylor had called her. And Tricia Cantor was golden as a witness. Her presence in the trailer dovetailed with what Zoe had told them.

"Ahead of schedule?" Marek asked, trying to salvage something from the interview.

"Yes, tomorrow morning, first thing, I was going to come in with Taylor to talk to you and Karen about cutting him a deal to testify against Alan Digges. About what he did to get the others kicked out of their trailers. That's what we hammered out last night: a way out of the mess."

Karen swept a stray blond bang back up to her hairline. "So you're his alibi."

"What do you mean 'his alibi'?" Tricia looked betrayed, but not by her parishioner. "Marek? What's going on here?"

Marek simply nodded toward Taylor, who mumbled out what he'd done. With Bunting's body. After. He did deny leaving the fecal dental implant in Bunting's mouth, though, which wasn't surprising, given his audience.

"Well. That wasn't the wisest thing to do, but it doesn't change the fact that Taylor isn't your killer." Tricia swept her hands into her hair. "I got there about one-twenty, after I threw on some clothes. I didn't stop to do anything else, not with a life on the line."

If Taylor wasn't the killer, then who was? Had the killer come from the encampment, the trailer park, or from elsewhere? Marek rubbed his temples. "Did you see anything on the grass beyond Taylor's trailer? Or anything parked by the road there?"

"Other than Taylor's truck? Nothing. And I was looking because I thought it was really creepy how the road just ended right there. Taylor said that it was the end of the road. For the trailer. For him. We talked for over an hour until I left around two-thirty."

"Did you hear anything? A vehicle? A thud?"

"No, I'm afraid not. My entire focus was on Taylor." She leaned forward, a plea on her face. "Taylor has kids, a job, and just needs to get his feet under him again. I'd think, even with this new information, that his testimony would be worth something. Going to jail wouldn't help anyone."

"He's already told us about Bunting and Digges's eviction game," Karen began. "So—"

"Not everything," Taylor interrupted. "Though I can't hand you a killer on a silver platter, because I honestly don't know who killed Bunting. But I need a deal. Not for me. Please. My kids don't deserve to be ragged on for having a dad in prison..." His gaze lit on Marek. No doubt he was thinking of the taunts flung at Marek for being the grandson of a murderer. He sighed. "We were cruel little shits. Do you believe in karma, Marek? I've just handed you my head."

Marek glanced over at Karen, who raised her eyebrows at him. So she was letting him decide Taylor Peterson's fate. All he felt was the heavy weight of it. Finally, he said, "I don't eat my kills." Though Taylor's shoulders slumped in relief, Tricia looked befuddled. "Hunter's lingo," Marek told her. "Yes, we'll work with the state's attorney to get him a deal, as long as he follows through and testifies against Digges and gives us everything he has."

"Which is pretty much nothing, at this point," Taylor said morosely. "Materially, that is. They'll have cleaned out my trailer by now. Truck'll be repossessed and—"

Tricia laid a hand over her parishioner's. "I told you, Taylor, we'll work all that out. We've got a fund set up at the bank that all the ministers in town can draw on, for just this kind of situation. So take the deal and start over. The right way."

Peterson nodded, and for the first time, he sat up straight, his hands rubbing up and down his worn jeans, leaving dark stains. "Okay. I've got one more thing for you. And I hope like hell... sorry, Pastor Tricia... I hope like all get out that it leads you straight to Digges. Ted wasn't even cold before Digges was in Judge Rudy's chambers, laying claim to the estate. Now *that's* cold."

"But not illegal," Marek pointed out, disappointed he'd given the man a get-out-of-jail pass for so little. They'd just have to hope that Judge Rudibaugh would see things their way on the allegations of a man who had everything to gain by making a deal.

"Not illegal if Ted died without naming an heir. But Bunting told me that Ted wrote a will only a few days before he had the stroke. Digges knew it. He found it in the trailer after Ted was hospitalized in Sioux Falls."

As Marek let out a soundless whistle, Tricia smiled fully for the first time and folded her hands. "Alan Digges wasn't named. At all."

CHAPTER 26

THE TWIN PORCHLIGHTS OF HER old Arts and Crafts bungalow drew Karen homeward.

For all her life, she'd taken that home, and her welcome in it, for granted. Rock solid, with a foundation of Sioux quartzite, the bungalow had stood for generations of Okerlunds. It had never occurred to her, growing up, that she could lose it to the quicksand of economic catastrophe.

She'd grown up delighting in the crabapple trees that bloomed in spring, cursing their bitter fruit that splatted all over the concrete walk and driveway in summer, and raking their leaves from browning grass in the fall. Her father had put up the basketball hoop on the garage after she'd outgrown the little play hoop that her Uncle Sig had given her, forging her path on the basketball court to a national championship game, which she'd lost on her last shot.

That was her first real loss, a harbinger of many to follow.

But at every step, at every loss, this place had still been there for her.

The lights meant someone was home, because she hadn't left them on when she'd left that morning. But as she didn't see Eyre's little import, that must be Mary Hannah, back to face another gauntlet.

That reminded her she needed to talk to the principal tomorrow. *In loco parentis.* Loco. Didn't that mean crazy in

Spanish? Marek would know. For the first time, she really appreciated how difficult it was for him to juggle his jobs and his daughter's schedule. She'd just about fired him on their first homicide for leaving an incident meeting without a word, to pick Becca up at school, which she hadn't considered a valid excuse at the time.

The only wonder was that Marek hadn't kicked Karen to the curb long ago.

She pulled to her own curb, noted the hiccup of the engine with resignation, knowing that sooner or later, the Sub would die on her. Again. And be resurrected. Again.

Karen turned off the ignition, and wrapping her arms around the steering wheel, she let the emotions of the day catch up with her. Never in her life had she felt so much like a traitor to her badge. She'd dearly, dearly love to arrest Alan Digges for the misery he'd caused—and for making her inflict it on his behalf. Was she really any different from Peterson? Or even Bunting?

With nothing but hearsay about the purported will, Karen had decided that the matter of Alan Digges could wait until morning. She needed to talk to Judge Rudibaugh and the state's attorney about the litany of allegations. Unfortunately, Bunting hadn't told Peterson who inherited the trailer park, only that Digges hadn't, and that was all she—or Ted—wrote.

Karen also needed to talk to Not-Johnson about those allegations. If nothing else, to let him know that the flood of evictions would likely be stemmed until the courts sorted out the wronged from the wrong. Maybe some of them would be able to return to their trailers.

With that upbeat thought, Karen went inside.

And found, not Mary Hannah, but her father. He'd taken his recliner with him to the house down the road that he shared with his new wife, Clara. So he sat uncomfortably straight on a kitchen chair, a huge wrapped present on the table where Karen had eaten, been lectured, and done homework until deemed old enough and self-disciplined enough to do it on her own.

Karen blinked at him. It wasn't her birthday. It was... oh,

crap. Eyre's. October ninth, her daughter's true birthday, not October fourth, Karen's own birthday and the one that Eyre's biological father had inked in on the so-called "original" birth certificate, in an attempt to deflect possible repercussions to his coaching career.

"You forgot."

So much for the warm fuzzies. Fortunately, she hadn't forgotten—earlier. "I've got Eyre's present upstairs." Not wrapped, still in her duffel bag, but bought. "Where is she?"

"With the woman who adopted her. In Vermillion."

Another not-so-veiled accusation. Her father would never forgive Karen for depriving him of the opportunity to raise his granddaughter.

Because he'd taught her not to back down, no matter the opposition, Karen held his gaze.

To her surprise, he looked away first. "Any progress on Bunting?"

Well. That was a gigantic olive branch from a man like Arne Okerlund. She sank down into a chair across from him. She missed being able to talk to him about her cases. "Yes and no." And it all came out. He didn't blink, didn't speak, until she was done.

"Shouldn't have given Taylor Peterson a pass," he told her.

"I didn't."

"Marek did, then," he said with grim satisfaction. Arne considered his half-brother to be too soft for the job, just like their father, Leif. But Marek wasn't soft, not really. He hadn't stopped her, not once, during the evictions. He'd just gotten more and more—not there.

But Karen refused to throw Marek under the bus, even to score points with her father. "Give him a break. Especially after all the evictions we served today. That was brutal. I don't like being the hammer for an asshole's greed. I just wish I'd run into Doris Harkness in the first trailer, not next to the last, or I'd have stopped it all right there. Dad, did you have a lot? I mean, all at once? It just about killed me."

He extended one long forefinger and poked the present on the table, neatly and expertly wrapped with bow and streamers, which showed Clara's handiwork. After her mother had died, Karen had still gotten presents, but they'd rarely been wrapped. And when they were, the Sunday cartoon section of the *Argus Leader* served as the wrapping. "Not like what you did today. Pretty rare all around to have more than a few a year. Worst were family farms back in the 90s. People I grew up with, respected."

She thought of Mindy Hansen Bullard. "What happened?"

"Big banks in the Twin Cities did the foreclosing after buying up the local ones. Didn't understand agricultural loans at all. Most people around here were upset, did what they could to help out, let them move in on their property as hired hands, whatever it took. Some moved away for jobs, and a few others I lost up..." He must have seen her quick frown. Like Marek's dyslexia, her father's stroke-induced brain farts came on when emotions were high. "Locked up or buried. But... the trailer park? Hands down, with Ted, they got what they earned—or didn't. Choices. Bad ones."

Karen's glance fell to the present. "And the kids?"

She didn't need to look up to see the spittle fly. "People that bad off shouldn't have kids, shouldn't have 'em outta wedlock. Bad for them. Bad for the kids. Bad, period. Better choices, better life."

That rant came courtesy, she had no doubt, of his soft spot. Kids.

Karen heard a car pull into the drive. That would be her daughter. "So you're saying that I made the right decision giving up Eyre? Or that I shouldn't have had her at all?"

That got a typical Dakotan and Okerlund answer: silence.

She'd made poor choices. And she'd been very lucky that it hadn't all blown up in her face. "It's easy to armchair quarterback the lives of strangers." Karen got to her feet to go get Eyre's present. "Hits harder when it's your own. I'm not perfect. You've let me know that, loud and clear."

"Made better choices… after," he said gruffly, fingers playing with the streamers.

On the steps up to her attic room, Karen turned back, some of her pent-up emotion bursting out. "You don't know who's going to turn it around, or when. I don't blame the people in Grove Park for banding together to make it their home. It hurt like hell to oust them, because if I didn't have you, didn't have Mom, didn't have this base, this home, I might've been right there with them. I admire their resilience."

She heard the front door open below as she reached her attic room then her father's gruff "Happy Birthday" and Eyre's wavery "You shouldn't have." A chair scraped back, and she imagined they were sharing an awkward hug. Then she heard a gasp that said, from what she could gather, her father—or Clara—had hit it big.

Though it had been twenty-two years later than it should have been, Karen had at least given her father what he'd always wanted: another Okerlund at 22 Okerlund Road. That Karen wasn't part of that picture? Her choice. Bad? Good? It didn't matter. It just was.

She opened the duffel she'd thrown on the floor. Had she really been in Albuquerque less than forty-eight hours ago? After rummaging around, she pulled out the bright-silver necklace with a pale-blue stone the color of Okerlund eyes that her father, her daughter, and Marek all shared. She didn't. The necklace had been made not by family but family of family. Becca's great-aunt's son.

As Karen debated whether to wait for another time rather than adding an awkward third wheel to the reunion downstairs, her father's voice rose up from the vents from below, just as it had many times in the past, "Get down here, girl! We've got a birthday to celebrate!"

CHAPTER 27

KAREN'S RADIO BLARED, WAKING HER only hours after she'd finished off the last of the double-chocolate cake that Clara had brought over, along with a batter-smeared Joey. Becca and Marek had shown up from across the street, as well, with more gifts. Minutes later, Mary Hannah had arrived in the Brethren's rented limo with a hamper full of intricate pastries and a huge pot roast, hauled in by her personal chauffeur, Mr. Hahn of the denim overalls and gruff manner.

That always struck her as the oddest coupling of cultures: the buggy-driving Brethren didn't own or drive cars, but when one was needed, they hired a local farmer with his luxury SUV.

All in all, the impromptu party was a success, even if Eyre had seemed a little overwhelmed. Once Karen had told her that the proper Okerlund response to a surprise birthday party was a lot of grumbling, which got a knowing laugh from Clara and a mock glare from Arne, that seemed to have settled Eyre's nerves.

Karen rolled over in bed, cracked her jaw on a huge yawn, and took the call. Getting woken up in the wee hours for two nights running, with a deficit of sleep to start with, was a definite downside to her job. "Go ahead, Jordan. Sheriff Mehaffey here."

Her night dispatcher-jailer, Jordan Fike, spoke over the airwaves with an uncharacteristic detachment, though he'd never been as chatty as the day dispatcher. "Incident at Grove Park. Possible assault. See the deputy at the scene."

Karen blinked. He must've been reading one of her old dispatching manuals during a long, boring night. Or watching old *Adam-12* reruns. Though she'd been initially annoyed at the much laxer conversational tone of her county dispatchers versus the unit she'd run in Sioux Falls, she'd come to prefer it. She had to dredge up her own mental manual. "Copy that. ETA fifteen minutes. Mehaffey out."

The call had actually come at a good time, as her overworked brain had started mashing together a real Frankenstein of a nightmare. It involved a screaming baby—Bunting with his noughts and crosses—thrown out with the bathwater by Digges and rescued, strangely enough, by Zoe Harkness while Kaylee Early cheered her on with pompoms.

Wherever that'd been leading, it wasn't good.

Deciding to wait on calling in Marek, Karen drove the dark road alone, cupping yawns in one hand, driving with the other. After texting Adam at the park entrance, she was directed to the Connor Creek parking lot above Not-Johnson's former encampment.

Had they been stupid enough to return, despite her warning that the area was going to be patrolled? Because despite her misgivings about removing them, she would side with Biester in a hurry if callouts to the park continued.

As Karen turned in, the alternating red and blue lights of Adam's squad seemed strangely alien, even inappropriate, in the park, like disco strobe lights in a Victorian ballroom. The lights flashed over an old beater of a sedan at the trailhead. When she got out of the Sub, Karen saw Biester and Donahue standing near the squad, hands in pockets, looking helpless—or as though they would've liked to find someone to mash up.

"Sheriff." Adam popped out of the squad where Karen could see the outline of a smaller person, probably female, in the passenger seat—not in the cage. "We've got a possible attempted sexual assault."

No wonder Adam was so formal and looked so inordinately relieved to see her. Karen felt her brain grind to a complete stop.

Assault. She'd assumed fisticuffs, perhaps involving the newly evicted.

"Nothing possible about it," Biester said, dabbing at his face. Now that she was closer, Karen could see he had a split lip. "Bastard got away from me, or I'd gladly hand him off to you. Animal."

Karen pulled in her emotions, wished desperately for coffee, and settled for squaring her shoulders and mentally slapping herself awake. "Victim?"

Donahue answered before Biester. "Lori, that poor girl who cleans the toilets."

At two in the morning? Then again, given the uncertain hours of her other job, perhaps the woman often did her work in the wee hours. Here Karen had been thinking that her own job was the worst, getting woken up two nights in a row.

She really, really did not need another major investigation on her plate. Did they have a rapist and a killer loose in Grove Park or a rapist-killer? "Do we have any idea who the attacker was?"

Biester stared at his hand, stained with his own blood. "It's my fault. I should've told you... I never imagined..."

"Get over it," Donahue said with the bracing tone of a first responder. "You saved her. I was too far away to catch the guy, but you saved her before he got anywhere with her. That's the important thing."

Karen's shoulders came down from her ears. "She's not... hurt?"

"Bumps and bruises. And I think her wrist might be broken," Adam said grimly. "But she denies that he got any further."

"All right. I need you to take statements from Mr. Biester and Mr. Donahue. I'll take Lori with me to the office for the formal interview. Do we have a scene to protect?"

Adam shook his head. "He knocked her down on the trail. With all the leaves, there's no good footprints. She was lucky. I heard her scream as I pulled into the parking lot for my patrol, and so did Mr. Donahue from his campsite." Adam waved up the hill a short way where Karen could see glowing lights from a few campers. "Biester got there first, as he was already on site, making sure the last of the stragglers got the message that the encampment was closed. The attacker bolted down the trail, toward the creek and the trailer park, after tussling with Biester. As for any danger..." He looked at Biester.

"We can alert the remaining campers. They can choose to go or stay, and I dare say most will go. If you stay to patrol, though, I'd say there's little danger now he's been run off." He looked into the darkness, into the woods. "He'll go to ground."

Karen's brain finally booted up. "You know his identity?"

Biester hesitated. "Actually, no, I can't be sure. It's been dark as a coal mine tonight with the cloud cover. I ran blindly down the trail from memory, crashed into him—tripped, really. So much for heroics. Your deputy came rushing down with his flashlight, and Donahue with his, blinding me, and Lori screaming bloody murder. So I can't swear to anything, really, it happened so fast."

She heard the next word, unspoken. "But?"

"But I might... I might know who it was." He spiked his bloodied fingers through his gnarled hair. "I don't know his real name. He's a poacher who lives in the woods. Calls himself Mountain Man. I've sort of... turned a blind eye. I shouldn't have."

Too many blind eyes in this thing. "Wears camos and has a beard?" Karen asked, thinking she would need to rouse Marek after all. Had Mountain Man killed Bunting? If so, why?

Biester stopped dabbing his lip. "You've met him?"

"Only heard of him." And she'd felt his creepy gaze on her at the overlook. "Do you know his bolt-hole?"

"Used to be that earth-berm shelter he made down by the creek. He planned to live here during the winter. But he moved out when the trailer trash moved in. I don't know where. But... I could look."

Karen shook her head. "No. Don't. I can set up an official search, come daylight. In fact, the county commissioners will,

I'm sure, demand it, once word gets out that there's a rapist in the park."

She was surprised when he didn't protest that it would scare off the state parks board.

"Finding that animal is more important than upgrading the park status," he said stiffly. "Lori is my employee. A good one. I don't want to lose her. Anything I can do, just let me know. Her wrist…"

Karen nodded. "I'll take care of her. Adam?"

Her deputy walked silently with her over to the squad. Rain began to fall lightly, and a coyote howled somewhere down in the woods. She opened the squad door. "Lori? Sheriff Mehaffey. I'll drive you down to my office."

The hunched-over figure straightened. "Oh, no, that's not necessary."

Karen blinked at the unexpected response. "Pardon?"

"I can drive. I need my car."

"You're shaken."

"I can drive," she insisted.

"All right. We're headed for the clinic first."

"No. No need." After a slight pause, Lori got out, cradling her wrist against her body. "I'm okay. It's just sprained. I'd… I'd just like to get this all over with. The statement, I mean. I haven't cleaned the johns yet."

"You don't need to do it tonight," Biester said. "In fact, you can take some time off, heal up."

"I need the money," she said tightly. "But I'll wait for daylight." She hurried over to her little hatchback.

Donahue said, "Girl's got backbone. Well… I guess we're going to wake up some people at the campground. Deputy? Mr. Biester?"

With a final glance at the silhouetted figure in the hatchback, the men moved off, leaving Karen to lead Lori out of the parking lot in a much smaller procession, but still reminiscent of Not-Johnson's journey out of the wilderness.

CHAPTER 28

I N THE WELL-LIT BUT EERILY silent Sheriff's Office, Karen
set two steaming cups of coffee on the scarred table in the
interview room.

Lori slipped her phone into her pocket with her good hand.
"Um... thanks. I could've made it."

"Not a problem. It's my personal brand. Sisters' Blend."

Apparently thinking Karen had taken offense, she stammered,
"Oh, I didn't mean... only that I've made a lot of coffee..."

Without warning, Lori started to shake then put her head
down on the table and bawled.

Dammit. Karen should've called in Marek. He did better with
weepers, in his silent, gentle way. Well, she could do the silent.
Barely. She wanted to lay a reassuring hand on the woman's
arm but decided against it. Touchy-feely could go wrong with an
assault victim. She remembered that much from her training.

So she waited it out until Lori hiccupped. "I'm... I'm sorry. It
wasn't that bad, really, but... it's been a shitty day." She cupped
the mug in one hand and looked down into the dark liquid. "You
see, I... I lost my job."

Karen frowned. "Biester praised your—"

"No, not him."

Karen cast her mind back. Right. The boss from hell. "I
thought you went back to work for him."

Lori sniffed and looked up, eye sockets a purple so deep they looked almost black on her white face. "I did. He fired me at the end of my shift. Paid me in cash from the till." She dabbed at her tears with the sleeve of her dirty flannel shirt. "Do you ever feel like... like you're in molasses... or like those bugs that Bob... that are trapped in amber?"

"Yes, I've felt like that," Karen said. About her current case. About her years of marriage to a man who had been essentially dead. About the long months waiting to give up Eyre. "I'd speak to your boss, but I think Donahue had it right. You need a better boss."

Lori's mouth twisted. "Mr. Donahue was really nice to me. But he doesn't get it. Jobs don't grow on trees out here." She gave a watery if real smile. "Not enough trees."

There'd been plenty in Grove Park. Karen took a deep breath. Time to get down to business. "All right. Take another good sip. I need to take your statement."

Lori started to cup the mug with both hands then hissed out a gasp of pain. "Yes. Please."

"Start from the beginning. You came from your other job, I take it?"

"Yeah. I was crying my eyeballs out. Wondering what I did to deserve having my life go to shit again. I drove down to the creek parking lot. No one was there. That really surprised me. Usually, there's a bunch of cars from... well... the homeless." She spoke slowly, as if picking her way through the night and memories she didn't want to recall. "They don't bother me. I just go about my business. Some bad apples, but most are good. Work hard. Then I... I heard, or felt, someone behind me. Like needles pricking you in the neck, you know? Then I heard this sound, almost like an animal, like deep in their throat? I panicked and screamed. I ran down the trail to... to find help."

As Lori had given her an address in Ted's trailer park, Karen thought that the woman must know most if not all the people who'd been evicted. Would Lori be next? Karen hoped it wouldn't come to that. That added incentive to grill Digges in the morning. "We know about the encampment that was there."

"Was?"

"We cleared it out today."

"Oh. That's... that's sad."

Karen wanted to ask her about Mountain Man, but she pulled herself up short. *Don't lead the witness,* she reminded herself. "Did you recognize your attacker? Note any distinguishing marks, facial hair, or clothing?"

Lori lifted her head. "I never saw him. He hit me from behind."

Too bad that Bunting was dead. Because he would be her prime suspect in the attack. Taken from behind. The MO of Two Fingers's mother's attacker.

"He laid me out flat then pulled me up." She crossed her good arm across her midsection. Then, with a little gasping shake, she moved it until her hand stopped at the snap of her jeans. "After that, it all happened so fast. I heard someone running, crashing through stuff, jiggling lights. Then I heard a big 'oof.' That must've been him running into Mr. Biester. Is he all right?"

"Just a split lip," Karen assured her. "And a blow to his pride, maybe, in not being able to bring down your attacker. Now you... I want to take you to the clinic. I don't think that's just a sprain."

Color rose on Lori's face as her eyes fell. "I don't have any money. Can't you just... set it?"

Karen rose to her feet, feeling more than a little helpless, more than a little angry. This woman worked, worked hard, and had taken a lot of abuse in a short time. They had a social services rep who would be in Reunion tomorrow afternoon, she thought. "I can contact Marsha Schaeffer, our social serv—"

"No! No. Never."

Though she'd expected pushback, Karen hadn't expected such a violent reaction. But an assault victim's emotions could be unpredictable. Processing the unfathomable, to have your own body be violated, was the worst sort of home invasion. "I know it can seem like a handout, but if you need a hand up—or a wrist set, then Medicaid—"

"Just...no."

"Let's see if Doc Hudson can do it for..." Karen stopped herself. She'd almost said *free*. "Pro bono."

Lori glanced at her wrist. "Pro... bone?"

"Write it off."

The tired face brightened. "Oh. For taxes, you mean?" Fortunately, she took Karen's tilted head for assent and got to her feet. "Okay. Can we go do that now?"

"Sure. We can do that."

Half an hour later, after Karen had carried out a hurried undertone discussion with the family doctor, Lori sported a new cast on one hand and carried a bottle of painkillers with the other. Even though Karen had had to roust him from his bed, Doc Hudson refused to let her contribute to the cost, saying he'd known Lori since she was a babe and that he was happy to... ha ha... give her a break.

In the clinic parking lot, the single street light flicked off as dawn shot out fireworks on the far horizon. Karen hesitated. "You sure you'll be okay, Lori? I can follow you back to the trailer park."

"No! No..." Lori cleared her throat. "Thanks. For everything. I'm good. He shook me up, you know, but he didn't actually... I'm good. And I've got to get to... to work."

"But your wrist. Doc said to rest it."

Lori transferred the painkillers to her jeans and tugged open the dented door of her hatchback. "I got two hands."

Karen just hoped she had a fraction of the woman's resilience. She faced another long day, with a to-do list a mile long, but at least finances weren't on her radar. Though, come to think of it, she did have to pay some bills. But she was good for it and could afford any late fees.

Paycheck to paycheck was a hard way to live. Paycheck to nothing, though?

A killer.

CHAPTER 29

A S HER MEN GATHERED INTO the room at eight o'clock sharp that morning for an incident meeting, Karen dropped down into the well-bottomed armchair that had held only Okerlunds—and would no doubt have been discarded immediately by Bunting for some leather monstrosity with a thousand massage settings. He'd have sacrificed a roster spot to do it, too. In fact, he might have just dispensed with the roster altogether, given Bunting had put out a call for applications— and netted a big fat zero.

Tilting back, Karen reached out to the short filing cabinet and snapped on the radio on top.

—your low-power FM out of Reunion, South Dakota. YRUN when you can't walk? From your legless connection, Rusty 'Nails' Nelson. Well, folks, we've got some troubling news out of Grove Park this morning. Sheriff Mehaffey contacted me bright and early to give me the rundown.

All eyes went to her. Marek's were slitted. She just gestured back toward the radio.

In the early hours last night, a female park employee was attacked in what is believed to be an attempted sexual assault. Fortunately, her screams brought the park manager and a camper to the rescue, and the attacker fled. However, as you might imagine, after Bunting's death, this additional attack has escalated concerns that the killer might still be in the park. Turns out, a poacher known simply as Mountain Man has been living there. Sheriff Mehaffey is setting up a search to flush him out and question him. She emphasized that he may well be an innocent man, so keep that in mind. We don't want any lynching parties. If you wish to take part in the search, meet at the park entrance at one o'clock this afternoon.

She'd been willing to broadcast that because the low-power FM range didn't reach the park. Nor did she expect Mountain Man to have a radio. She snapped off her own radio and filled her men in on the details, which didn't take long. "Comments?"

Predictably, Walrus was the first to speak. "Mountain Man? Geez. Talk about delusions of grandeur. That park may be the highest point in the Eastern Dakotas—heck, my wife's family used to own that land—but it's no mountain. A hill. Barely. I mean, think Black Hills. You ever been to the Rockies? Now *those* are mountains."

So saying, Walrus attacked the hill—nay, mountain—of kolaches on the tray that Kurt had brought, courtesy of his sister, Eva Bechtold. Since Kurt had told Karen that morning he wasn't going to retire after all, they could continue to enjoy such culinary largesse. Only Two Fingers still hadn't committed to returning. He was a lone man, standing off to the side, without his swing-shift partner. Bork had gone home to Minnesota to be babied by his mother until he got cleared to return to work.

"Are you sure it was a sexual assault?" Marek asked into the pastry-gorging.

Karen blinked at him. "As opposed to what?"

"Different MO, different type," he said.

"You're suggesting it's two different people?" Kurt whisked away the tray before Walrus could take another handful. And that went over as well as such things usually did.

"Indian giver," Walrus accused his partner.

Before Walrus ended up pinned to his desk by the twin spears of Two Fingers's glare, Karen stepped in to clue in the clueless. "That was an offensive remark, Deputy Russell."

Walrus looked honestly baffled. "Really? Sorry, Two Fingers, but... how? I mean, we gave you guys the Black Hills, then we took it back. Isn't that what it means? We're the Indian givers. It's our bad."

"You didn't *give* us the Hills. It was already ours. Then you all got gold dust in your eyes. We're still waiting to get it back." Some of the glare diminished. "Usually Indian giver is flung at us, because of Native American customs going back to the Pilgrims—when we gave out of our riches, we expected to also receive of yours when you thrived... and got everything taken from us."

"Well, okay. I get that. But that's not the same as I meant..." Seeing Karen's set face, Walrus subsided back into his stashed kolaches. "Sorry. Truly. No offense meant."

Two Fingers granted him absolution with a slight nod.

Cultural war averted, Karen glanced at her list, which she'd drawn up after driving over from the clinic. The first was, unfortunately, a no-show. "DCI was going to give us an update on their progress this morning, but Larson texted me that he won't make it until later, so we don't know yet if there's any relevant forensic evidence." Next man up. "Walrus, what do you have for us from the dropbox?"

His lost kolaches apparently forgotten, Walrus got to his feet and fished out a piece of paper from his back pocket. "Got the names here. And, yeah, the encampment, they weren't paying, just like Biester said. One completely illegible ticket with the right date, right amount of money. Pretty good deal. Fifteen bucks for all of them a night."

Kurt swept crumbs into a trash can. "People expect everything handed to them these days."

"Not exactly," Karen mused. "Fifteen bucks times thirty days in a month is..."

"Four hundred and fifty," Marek answered. The man did more in his head than she'd ever done with her pen in school. Near perfect recall, honed by years of learning with his ears—and the reason his mother had refused to believe anything was wrong with him. "That's more than their trailer rent was at Ted's."

"You play, you pay," Kurt returned.

"Give it a rest," Walrus groused. "The encampment is no more." He handed Karen the list. "One of your camp visitors didn't pay."

Karen cast her mind back. "The Farleys, perhaps? They didn't look like they had more than a few pennies to rub together. Living on Social Security. Or maybe Mary Redbird?"

"Bzzz. Sorry, you lose." Walrus nudged Kurt. "You'll like this one."

Kurt stepped back with a set face. "I don't like anyone who doesn't carry their own weight."

"The day I can't carry mine, you can bury me." Walrus looked at Karen. "No, boss. The Reicharts."

"Who are?"

"The Floridians who reported us to Commissioner Dahl," Kurt answered.

"Oh, that's rich." Karen shook her head. "Kurt, you look into the fines for that, will you?"

Her senior deputy looked torn between the desire to do just that—and his innate sense of justice that he should also be writing up fines for every member of the encampment. "You can't get blood from a stone," she told him. "Did you two check the license plates I gave you?"

Walrus answered. "Yep. Not-Johnson? Get this. Albert Cram Bayton. Yeah. One of those Baytons, though a shirttail relative. He was hurt on a job on one of their construction sites, lost a lawsuit against the company because he'd been drinking. After that, he really went off the rails. But he's been sober for a number of years now, a gold-plated AA member. Surprisingly, he never had a DWI."

While that was an interesting connection to Digges's wife, Karen couldn't see how that related to Bunting. "Any others we should know about?"

Walrus grinned. "Well, not unless you want to know that your Mary Johnson is, actually, Mary Johnson. Came from Aleford, worked in Dutch Corners, now in Reunion. No record."

"Most of the homeless are at Lions Park," Kurt told her. "Before I forget, Commissioner Dahl said to tell you. He's gotten calls from the Lions Club about the homeless staying at their park."

"They've got three days—unless the Lions decide to close the park to everybody. Otherwise, that's just discrimination." Karen didn't want to argue the point with Kurt, so she asked him, "Can we eliminate anybody yet?"

"Well, Nadine Early's story checks out. Old Man Martin says she was passed out cold at The Shaft. So she wasn't the woman at the park who slapped Bunting. And Jack Biester's alibi holds. He was there late, talking with the state people. And he checked out of the Garden Inn at six the next morning."

"Good. We can eliminate him and the campground visitors from our—"

"Not yet," Kurt interrupted uncharacteristically. "One of the campers filed a complaint against Bunting. Got him fired from his last job."

Karen pushed up from her desk. "Oh, really. That's interesting. Who was it?"

"Pat Donahue."

Their helpful first responder. Always around. At the body. At the fire. And the assault. And still sticking around. "He denied knowing Bunting. Good work. Marek and I will follow up on that." She nodded at her detective. "What about the drone footage from Akio Miles?"

Marek fiddled with his mouse and brought up the stilled scene. Karen leaned over. The drone was released before sunset at the park entrance, where it hovered for a moment, showing the clearly posted rules, regulations, and fees with the dropbox. From there, the drone swooped up the hill then up even farther. The footage made the hill look flatter than it actually was—and showed plenty of farmland on the margins. It wouldn't make a *National Geographic* cut, that was for sure, though the small stand of maples in the campground was pretty enough.

"With the tree cover, there's not much to see," Marek told the others as it ended. "Campsites. Parking lots. A bit of the trailer park. No sign of Bunting's SUV in the evening shot."

"Any sign of Mountain Man's bolt-hole?" Karen asked him.

"Not that I can see. But then, I couldn't see much of the encampment, either, even knowing where it was—just some unnatural color from the tents."

With a sigh, Karen looked down at her list. The stained duty shirt. Though the whole purpose of an incident meeting was to share information, not keep a lid on it, that was just too sensitive. "All right. Next up. We've got a statement from Taylor Peterson that Bunting told him Ted wrote a will. That Digges found the will and that he wasn't in it. At all."

Walrus blew out the windsocks of his mustache. "Taylor? What does he have to do with this? He's a good guy. Goes to my church. He got the rug pulled out from under him this past year, but he's solid."

Karen explained and watched Walrus's windsocks deflate. "Geez. That sucks. He should've said something. His boy is friends with Junior. We'd have given him our granny flat. Still can. Where is he?"

Whatever else you could say about Walter Russell, he was a very generous man. "Still at the trailer park, at the moment. If we take his statement at face value—"

"You can take it to the bank," Walrus insisted.

"—then we need to add Alan Digges to our suspect list."

An agitated Walrus shook his head. "If Digges found the will, why not just destroy it right then and there? Why bring Bunting into it? It doesn't make any sense."

With obvious reluctance, Kurt backed up his partner. "If Bunting had that kind of leverage on Digges, he'd have used it to prevent himself from being evicted."

Marek pushed back from his computer. "Doesn't a will require witnesses? Maybe Bunting was one."

"Something else to ask Judge Rudy." Karen's list of appointments that day was bulging beyond her time limits.

"Though I'm sure he's going to tell us it's all hearsay anyway, so—"

"No."

That brought Karen around to stare at Two Fingers. "No?"

"In the trailer, in the desk drawer..." His face tightened. "I found some papers that I thought might be relevant. I had them in my hand when..."

When they'd found the duty shirt. Dammit. "I picked them up... what did I do with them?"

"You put them in an evidence bag," Marek said. "I'll get it."

She paced while he went downstairs to the evidence room. She didn't even remember that. Marek must have taken it from her.

When Marek returned, she nearly pounced on him. "Well? Is it the will?"

His eyebrow quirked. "Can't read it."

Karen snatched the evidence bag from his hand. And sank down to her desk. No wonder.

"Well?" Walrus demanded. "What's wrong? It isn't the will?"

"Oh, it's *a* will," she returned. "That's printed legibly enough at the top in capital letters. And I think... yes... it's signed. First name too long for Ted. Wait. T-H-E-O—yes, okay, we're back in business. I think that's Theodore. And that has to be a J, no matter the rest of the squiggle. But I don't see any witnesses."

Walrus crowded her. "Oh. Wow. That's bad."

Kurt, who hadn't moved from his upright and locked position, said crankily, "What's bad? Who got the trailer park?"

Karen looked up. "No clue. Ted should have spent more time in penmanship class. But whatever the case, I think Alan Digges just moved up on my appointment list for the morning. Right after Judge Rudy."

She turned to go up to the judge's chambers but found Two Fingers in her way.

"What about the duty shirt?" he asked.

Her heart fell. "You want to bring that up?"

"It's relevant."

"All right." She wouldn't blame Two Fingers for putting Eda County in his rearview mirror once this was done. She took a deep breath and turned back to her men. "When we were searching Bunting's trailer, we found an old duty shirt from the highway patrol with the name Johnson on it, presumably swiped from Bunting's stepfather, Ed Johnson, but it... had stains... on the front shirttails. Looked pretty old. Trophy, perhaps."

Kurt seemed unable to even breathe, one rigid exclamation point, while Walrus heaved to his feet, started toward Two Fingers as if to envelop him in a bear hug, then thought better of it.

"Oh, geez." Walrus nearly blew the windsocks right off his face. "Johnson? Like... your..." Even Walter Russell wasn't clueless enough to finish that with *father*.

"My mother's rapist." Two Fingers's mouth twisted. "Yet another take on Indian giver."

"Couldn't it be Johnson, not Bunting?" Kurt asked.

"I suppose," Karen mused. "But how did it end up in Bunting's hands, and why keep it?"

"Leverage?" Marek suggested.

"But Bunting was gone from the household. And if he had evidence against his stepfather, who he hated, by all accounts, why not just turn it in?"

All they had were questions. When the kolaches—and her men, except for Marek—were gone, she went to get some answers from Judge Rudibaugh.

CHAPTER 30

J UDGE JOHN FRANKLIN RUDIBAUGH SAT through Karen's long list of tenant allegations without a single indication of his thoughts. His hands were threaded together just below his black robes as he sat in his huge leather chair. The only thing that marred the gravity of his visage was his nose. Bulbous and red, it had led more than one outside lawyer to take him for a drunk—and an easy mark.

But Judge Rudy was no one's mark, nor did he give or take markers. But he often left one on those in his courtroom—or his chambers. Karen admired him like she admired the grizzlies that Biester talked about. When in his presence, you felt the adrenaline churn—and hoped like hell to live for another day. One wrong step, one whiff of weakness, and it was over.

She laid down the will in its evidence bag. "We found this in Bunting's trailer, substantiating Taylor Peterson's allegations. While I can't read most of it, I believe that's Ted Jorgenson's signature."

The judge picked up his reading glasses and peered down.

"Yes, I'm surprised you do not recognize it, Sheriff." He looked back up, weaving his hands back together on top of his desk. "Ted did not trust the vagaries of computers. Every document he filed in court, he wrote by hand. Though I suppose that, since he started to slow down in the last year or two before his death, Ted may not have had any evictions for you to serve.

Frankly, I was relieved that Alan Digges was going to take over the reins. You should be, also, since I believe a couple of your more serious cases involved residents of the trailer park."

A burglary, drug dealing, and a domestic. Two of the three miscreants were currently doing time at the Big House in Sioux Falls. The last had taken a plea deal and was in court-ordered therapy with Pastor Tricia. "Digges was the only relative?"

The judge narrowed his eyes.

She hadn't meant it to sound accusing. A misstep.

"Ted had no wife, no children, only one older sibling—a deceased sister who left one child. Alan Digges was the sole heir per statute and had all the proper documentation to prove it." For the first time, Karen caught a whiff of emotion in his sonorous voice. "Believing that no will was to be found, I granted him the administration on the estate and power to manage the assets thereof."

Though the end might have been the same, that Digges had bypassed the judge would not go unnoticed—or unpunished. Karen cleared her throat. "Can you read the will?"

He looked back down at the papers. "Even for Ted, this is cramped, uneven handwriting. It appears to have been written only days before his death, but as I saw him the day after this date, I can attest that he was of sound and disposing mind. His Ds are quite distinct, so yes, it appears Digges is not mentioned at all. I do see a legatee whose name begins with R or B?"

That brought her up short. "Bunting?"

"No. The surname begins with J and ends with an n."

"Jorgenson? Might be a distant relative."

"One not legally competent, I believe, as a trustee is mentioned. Con—Conway? It will take some time to decipher the will. I will let you know when I do." He pushed the will to the side. "Whatever the actual contents, Alan Digges subverted the cause of justice. He well knew that I, not Bunting, was the arbiter of probate matters. I dislike being used as a tool against the very thing I am sworn to protect. Justice. Digges will not find my court a lenient haven, no matter his lawyers. I presume you and your laconic detective have taken all the required and necessary steps to ensure that the evidence is unassailable?"

Karen thanked her lucky stars that she'd placed the papers in an evidence bag and that Marek had logged them in as evidence. "Yes, Judge. Chain of custody was preserved. It's too bad the will wasn't legal without witnesses. Still, Bunting may have told him otherwise later, after he had the will in his possession as leverage, and that caused Digges to snap."

Judge Rudy creaked back in his leather chair as he looked up at her—and down his nose at her. "And this is why probate matters are best left for those who actually know what they are doing." His tone left papercuts in her ego. He tapped the bag. "This, Sheriff, is a holographic will—in the testator's own handwriting." He swiveled, plucked a thick volume of state statutes out of the wall-to-wall bookcase, and thumbed through it, then with an evil eye, he handed her the open book. "For your edification—and my satisfaction."

CHAPTER 31

K AREN COULD SAY ONE NICE thing about Digges's lawyer. She rocked the color red.

Sweeping into the interview room, Michelle Bayton was one of those polished titanium blondes who could wear bright red without diminishing her aura of authority one iota. No one would leer or risk being frozen in place with her ice-blue eyes. While Karen had never met her, or any of her powerful family, the Baytons were big time, she'd discovered. Their lips to the statehouse's ear.

Alan Digges sauntered in on her heels, looking around the dingy, crowded room with a sneer. Karen was getting tired of seeing that particular expression on his face.

After the formalities were completed, Michelle Bayton tapped red-painted fingernails against the scarred surface of the table. Unlike her husband, she didn't seem to care about her surroundings or even notice them. And despite her flawless face, Karen judged her at about her own age, early- to mid-forties, at least a decade older than her boy toy. Her concentration was all on Karen and, showing her to be more astute than most, on Marek.

"Very well, Sheriff. Detective. We've taken a precious chunk out of our busy day to drive down to talk to you. I put a flight to Pierre on hold to be here. Just what is this about? Irregularities in the eviction process, I believe you said?"

"That's right. We served a large number of evictions yesterday and—"

"Late," Digges interrupted.

Karen gritted her teeth. "Not late. I had, and have, a killer to catch. I finished the evictions in the allotted time."

"Only because I threatened to have your ass in a—"

"Alan," Bayton interrupted. "Leave this to me."

He sulked then muttered, "Sic 'em, babe."

A tic appeared on that flawless face. "Continue, Sheriff."

"Allegations have been made. Tenants were locked out of their homes before the required notice time, checks not accepted, rents raised without proper notice as stated in the leases."

"Is that all?" Bayton's tapping fingernails stilled. "You must be new to the game. That's standard fare for this level of tenant. Landlords have a right to their profits. I realize that Ted Jorgenson did not maximize his profits, so you may not be aware. That dump of a trailer park is a goldmine if properly managed. Now, you may not like Alan's tactics, but they're legal. If there were any concerns about proper procedure, the tenants should have brought up their concerns before the judge during an eviction hearing, not after the fact."

Marek spoke up. "We have a check signed by the tenant, dated before several others that went through after that, that wasn't accepted by Mr. Digges. Several tenants witnessed this and will testify—"

"Oh, come on," Digges cut in. "I'll bet you made that all up, just because I called you a dumb—"

"Alan, shut up." His wife crossed her arms. "Checks can be written but not presented. Tenants will often lie for each other. Mutual survival, tit for tat." She started to rise, looking almost disappointed—maybe she liked a better challenge. "If that's all—"

"We have Alan Digges's fingerprints on Ted's will," Karen told her. They'd been fortunate that Digges had been booked for drunk and disorderly one fine night before he'd married a lawyer.

"What will?" she snapped after Digges froze beside her.

"A will that your husband found in Ted's trailer while Ted was still hospitalized." Karen placed a photocopy of the will on the table. The judge still had the original.

Michelle Bayton sank back down, her gaze locking with Karen's for a very long moment, then she turned on her boy toy. "What the hell is she talking about?"

The man crumbled. "It wasn't valid. Bunting said so."

That name swept an arctic cold into the room.

"Bunting. The man who was murdered?" Her voice barely rose, but that must've taken considerable control. "You assured me that you had nothing to do with him. Whatsoever."

Digges actually started to babble. "I don't. I didn't, but he was... he was at that point the duly elected sheriff of Eda County, and I couldn't get Mehaffey on the phone. She was off joy-larking in the sunny Southwest—"

"She was helping to solve a homicide of international interest," his wife said, to Karen's surprise. "Do not drag down others to pull yourself up, Alan. It's unbecoming."

Well. Karen didn't have to wonder who was top dog in their relationship.

Digges tugged on his tie. "I just... Bunting was the law. Or about to be. I asked him, purely in a professional capacity, if the will was valid. Bunting took the will, looked at it, and said it wasn't, because that required two witnesses." Digges pointed to the will. "Just look. No witnesses."

Marek asked him, "Was Bunting holding that over your head, to keep from being evicted? Is that why you killed him at the trailer park?"

Rather than end the interview right there, as Karen had half expected, Michelle Bayton leaned back in her chair, her gaze hooded, her fingernails tapping.

Apparently taking that as support, Digges sneered again, a full, ripe one this time. "Read my lips, idiot. The. Will. Was. Not. Valid."

Karen snagged the heavy volume on the filing cabinet and

dropped it onto the table in front of Digges, making him jump. His wife, on the other hand, just raised a perfectly plucked eyebrow.

"That, Mr. Digges, is a copy of the revised statutes of South Dakota."

"I can read. Unlike some. So what?"

"So, Mr. Digges, that will? This one here? The one you admit you found, admit you did not hand over to the proper official? The one that does not, in fact, mention you at all?" Karen noted the fingernails stopped, at the high point, in a deadly claw. "That will is valid."

"Bull. That's just bull. You're just trying to get a rise out of me. I watch cop shows. You're not going to trick me into saying something I didn't do, like some retard, like your so-called detective. You're just trying to pin Bunting on me because you're too incompetent to find the real killer."

Karen just shook her head. "It is a holographic will. In Ted's own handwriting. All it requires is a date. As you can see, it has one. No witnesses required." She pushed the book toward him. "Read it and weep, Mr. Digges. Judge Rudibaugh says the will is perfectly legal. He will be reversing his grant of letters of administration immediately. He will stand in as administrator of Ted's estate until the legatee or legatees can be found." Karen allowed herself a small, tight smile. "Yeah. Don't like being evicted, do you? Churn, baby, churn."

"No. No. No! That cannot be true." Digges turned in his chair, his hands out, pleading. "Right, honey? They're just jerking my chain. Right?"

Unfortunately for the investigation, his shock was far too real to be feigned. Karen shared a disappointed look with Marek. Digges hadn't known the will was valid. Hence, it wasn't a motive for murder. Maybe they could get him on an obstruction charge, but his wife would probably spin that as simply trusting the word of a man who'd been elected to office in a county he wasn't familiar with.

Michelle Bayton tugged on the law book, turning it so she

could read, which she did easily and quickly, and without a single demur. "We could sue on grounds of unsound mind..." she started to say, more for form, Karen thought, than anything. An automatic, lawyerly sort of answer.

Karen countered just as automatically, just as easily. "The judge saw Ted the day after he wrote that will and said he was fine. Ted died of a massive stroke, not dementia."

A faint smile curved her lips. "Very good, Sheriff. Detective. You played that just right. Alan is many things, but he is no actor. Nor, I will add, a killer, much as that might satisfy you and, I'll admit, me."

That came out of left field, shocking Karen and, if she read her detective right, Marek.

"Michelle..." Digges got out.

Recovering first, Marek asked Michelle Bayton, "You can vouch for your husband's whereabouts from about one to two in the morning last Friday night?"

"Normally, no. We have separate rooms. He tends to come in late, drunk and disorderly. I found that endearing. For about two weeks. Unfortunately, last Friday night, I was up drafting a deal for new construction near the Falls, and he did, in fact, come in at one-twenty-three by my phone clock. I reamed him out for it, as he was supposed to be home much earlier, for a charity gig at the Pavilion." She gave Karen a bright smile, more than a hint of shark in her gleaming white teeth. "That was, in fact, when I decided to file for divorce."

Every last drop of color drained out of Alan Digges's face. "Michelle..."

She turned on him. "You always were full of it. You just dressed it up so well, I missed it. But I wasn't stupid enough to take you on without a prenup. And that will stand." She stripped off her impressive diamond and plunked it on the open book before him. "I bought that. You can take it as the last thing you'll ever have from me."

While he stared at it, she turned back to Karen. "Sheriff, I'd appreciate it if you kept my name out of this, just as I kept mine out of his. We Baytons may play hard, but we play within the rules." She gave Karen a genuine smile. "I was, by the way, at USD the same time you were. I was a fan girl. Sobbed my eyes out when you got fouled on that last shot and the idiot refs didn't call it. And I've followed you in the news ever since you took over here, against a lot of opposition. I admire grit—and smarts."

She turned her high wattage smile next on Marek. "Detective, I believe you have more than enough evidence to lay obstruction charges on my soon-to-be ex. And if the other allegations hold— and they likely will without me and my legal team's help—he may well be facing jail time. Alan, if you play nice, I'll keep you out. But I don't want to hear so much as a peep out of you over the divorce."

When Digges raised his head, eyes watering, Karen actually felt sorry for the man, until he said, "Go to hell, Michelle. That prenup won't stand. And you're not going to get anyone better than me at your age. Live with me, or fork it over, babe."

His wife's smile just got wider. "You always did underestimate me. And you know what?" She reached over and fingered the lapel of his silk shirt. "I think you would look wonderful in Day-Glo orange. I look forward to making sure that happens. See you in court."

She swept out, leaving Digges with a diamond, and Karen and Marek with coal.

A win on minor charges... but a loss on the major. No killer, just a loser.

CHAPTER 32

KAREN NUDGED THE REMAINS OF the egg-salad sandwich she'd picked up at the gas station and regretted as soon as she took a bite. "Do you think we laid an egg on this one?"

Marek looked up from perusing the drone footage of Grove Park again. He'd been trying, without success, to narrow their search area. "An egg?"

"A big fat zero. Our batting average on homicides has been perfect so far. And while Bunting may have been a zero, we need to clear this one, for obvious reasons."

Marek rolled back from his computer to look at her. "Because people might still suspect you were involved, just because of the history between you?"

The two of them were alone in the office. Josephine had typed up all of Marek's oral reports in record time and flown off to her grandson's debut on the rodeo circuit.

Karen nodded. "Conspiracy theorists are thriving these days. And Bunting played a pivotal role in two of my biggest losses: Eyre and the election."

Marek played with a paperweight on his desk, one of those snow globes that made her want to tell him not to tempt the weather gods. "You got both back."

"Did I?" Karen sighed as he looked up with what she thought of as his Byzantine look—long-faced, cheekbones straining. "No, nothing's happened with Eyre. I'm just... disoriented. Not sure where I stand anymore, what I want, where I'm going. Beware of getting what you ask for, I guess. We haven't had time to really let everything sink in, now that I'm back in town, that I'm the elected sheriff. But... you have. It didn't matter so much to you, did it, where you ended up? If Becca had chosen Albuquerque instead of Reunion, you'd have accepted that."

He shrugged. "Easier to accept with you poised to take the job there and Nikki willing to make the jump once she finished out her contract. Even..."

"Even my dad, Clara, and Joey. Wholesale Okerlund going-out-of-business sale. Or as Digges would say, 'Churn, baby, churn.' We just needed to get Eyre on board."

He quirked his brow. "And Larson?"

The door opened on cue. "Speaking of the devil."

Dirk Larson would never win Mr. Personality awards. He walked right up to her desk, stole what was left of her sandwich, and chomped down. "Disgusting."

"Succinct. True. Gas station fodder."

Like Marek, this Chicago-bred cop wasn't easy to read, unless you knew the signs, and a tic at the side of his mouth told her he was amused. "Fuel."

Karen gave up the exchange of bullets. "You'll need fuel to get all those big words out in a coherent fashion. Where is your sidekick and interpreter, by the way? Out to lunch? Or out to get lunch?"

"Still in Aberdeen. Let her fly solo."

Good for Jessica.

"Need coffee," Larson told her.

When Karen brought out the mugs, Larson had pulled up to Marek's monitor. The drone footage ended, and he pushed back, cupped the mug, and sipped. "Thanks. Cooling fast."

She frowned at him. "Not that fast. Unless you drink your coffee like a society diva."

Lips already on the lip of the mug, he managed, "Outside."

With a sinking feeling, Karen walked over to the large picture window. The forecasted day, sunny and warm in the high fifties, had turned nasty. Leaves were jaywalking the street with wild abandon. "Darn it." She glanced at the clock. "We start the search in an hour. Cough up your report, Larson. I need to get out there to round up the troops."

He took another sip. "Going with you."

"Why?"

He jerked his head at the window. "Bad weather. Low turnout."

She didn't think so, but she wouldn't mind another set of eyes, even though Larson was unused to searching for bad guys in the real wilderness, as opposed to the urban jungle. "Sure. We can use you. But what do you have for us? Anything we can use, now that we've lost Digges as a suspect?"

Larson settled down with his mug in Walrus's chair. "Bunting's SUV. Blood, grass, leaves in the back. Blood insufficient to suggest your vic was still alive."

No big surprise there. "Consistent with Taylor Peterson's story, then. Bunting was dead when Peterson transported him to the overlook and dumped the body into the john." Karen got up and paced from pillar to pillar. She had so many stray details crowded in her head—and traffic jams were rare in this part of the country—that she needed to get moving again. "Good to have confirmation on that point, as Mr. Merciful here gave Peterson a ride on those charges in exchange for testifying against Digges. Much less satisfying when that deal is for probate fraud and eviction irregularities rather than murder, but so be it."

Marek shifted in his chair. "What about the rifle?"

Karen turned to stare at him. "What rifle?"

Amusement creased Larson's forehead. "Bunting's. Scope. In the SUV."

"Oh, yeah. The evil eye. Was it infrared?"

"Only the best."

Karen rubbed the back of her neck. "So who was Bunting going to shoot? Peterson? No, wait, we're back at the encampment now, not the trailer park. I need a drink." She grabbed her coffee and saw Marek staring off into space. "Okay, what's going on in that head of yours, Marek?"

"Was the rifle dirty or clean?" he asked Larson.

"No dirt. Only his prints."

Marek's gaze focused again. "Not wiped clean, then."

Larson tilted his head then swiped a finger in the air. "Point to Okerlund."

"When did we start taking points? And just what are you two... oh. I get it. If Bunting was stabbed when holding the rifle, you'd expect the rifle to fall to the ground and pick up grass, soil, whatever. And that you'd get the killer's prints, too, if it weren't wiped clean. Maybe he wore gloves?"

"Stretching it," Larson told her.

"Not that much of a stretch. Nights are getting cold. Or... the evil eye thing was just a distraction, the original red herring, or the ravings of an unsound mind. The mentally ill make up some significant fraction of homeless, and Mary Johnson could be just that. We need to get a better handle on her. Marek, can you—"

"Not done yet," Larson interrupted. "Bunting's phone. Last call. One-thirteen. From Alice Dutton. Aleford."

"His aunt. We knew about that. Texts?"

"Plenty of texts to a Kaylee. Some pretty hot. Lots of others to sort through." He jerked his head to where he'd placed a folder. "But nothing close to TOD."

While Marek retrieved the folder, Karen glanced at the clock. They didn't have much time. "Kaylee Early was his girlfriend—who is pregnant, though she doesn't realize it yet." Seeing the brows shoot up, she went back to bullets. "Sweet. Clueless. Brother an opioid dealer. Side hustle with Bunting."

"Gotcha." Larson didn't even blink. "Shoes. Bits of glass in soles."

"From trail monitors that Biester set up that the homeless destroyed."

"Heels more productive. Leaves. Pine needles. Mud. Bark."

Marek sat straight up.

"What did you find?" she demanded.

"Bark on top of the mud?" he asked Larson and got another point.

"Will you two stop doing that?" She yanked at her hair. "Bark is all over the place. It comes from... logs. You think Bunting was dragged over the creek? That the trailer park wasn't the kill site, after all?"

Larson gave her half a point. "Didn't see the scene. Can't say."

"Oh, right. Bunting was found on the grass by the last trailer. Taylor Peterson's trailer. The grass was tamped down but no footprints."

The finger went all the way up.

"Not the kill site. Wow. Okay. We're back in the woods." Karen sank down on her desk, dislodging another eviction notice. At least she could ignore that. "So... we've got the encampment, and we've got Mountain Man out there somewhere. Maybe he killed Bunting and dragged him over to the trailer park. Dumped him just enough into the grass that we think the killer is from the trailers. Whoever Mountain Man is, he has to have some muscle to drag that load." She noticed that Marek was looking off into space again. "Think out loud."

Marek glanced at Larson. "Bunting's SUV. Steering wheel?"

Another point given. "Wiped clean."

Karen tried to keep up. "Ah. The SUV wasn't there when Pastor Tricia went to see Peterson. So either Bunting drove the SUV to the trailer park and went into the woods, where he got killed... or the killer dragged him over then realized the SUV was still in the encampment parking lot, which would lead back to him, so the killer drove it over with the lights off, just like Peterson did later when he went to the overlook. Two dumps." When she saw the amusement in her companions' faces, she backed up. She groaned and swiped her jacket and her cap, tugging it on. "Stop it with the sophomoric humor."

"Anal," Larson muttered.

She ignored that, and him, as she stabbed Marek with her

finger. "You'd better hope we can find the pocketknife engraved with *I Am the Killer*. Taylor Peterson wiped the steering wheel and the door handles. We're so screwed for evidence. And I want Peterson's hide, no matter the deal, if that keeps us from nailing our killer. Let's go find Mountain Man."

"Wait." Larson leapt to his feet. "Crap."

"Don't get started again," she warned.

"No, really. Feces."

She turned with her hand on the door. "The dental implant?"

"We've got cells. But DNA will take time."

That reminded her that they had another suspect to wrangle besides Mountain Man. "Marek, take your pickup and see if you can round up Donahue before the search. He's not out of the woods yet."

Marek went out the back way while Karen followed Larson out the front. A huge gust blew him back into her. She shoved him back. "Windy City wimp."

"That was a move." Before she could pitch a comeback, he whirled her, dipped her, and kissed her. When he released her, her legs nearly gave out.

Just where was this going, she wondered. She knew very little, really, about the DCI agent. He had baggage. His childhood, his marriage and divorce, the kids who'd turned on him—or been turned on him. None of which he talked much about. Like Bunting, he'd married a woman who'd made his life a living hell. Like Jim Early, he'd finally moved to get away from her. For a Chicagoan, South Dakota might as well be Mexico. "Larson...?"

His bullet-gray eyes hooded. "Yes?"

She wanted to ask, "Where is this going?" But what came out was, "You were poor growing up, right? But not homeless."

His eyes widened again, as if that wasn't the question he'd been expecting. Good. That kept them both off balance. "Might've been better if we had been. Projects always were a bad idea. Concentrate poverty, and it just gets worse. You need to sprinkle it around."

From a recruiting trip, Karen remembered the towering

concrete, the decay of the projects—one of the reasons she'd decided to stay in South Dakota to play hoops. His life and hers were poles apart. "You grew up on the South Side, right? How many got out like you?"

He leaned into the wind as he walked down the steps toward his car. "Not many. Not always ones you'd expect, the talented ones."

"Like you?"

"Got lucky. Got picked up for purse snatching by a young cop that wasn't jaded yet—and had a passion for basketball. Worked my ass off on the court. Got me a scholarship to a ritzy Catholic high school. College scholarship from there. Without it? Probably dead, honestly."

"What was it like, growing up there?"

"Terror and boredom—like being a cop." He opened the door. "Park might be both."

After he got in and shut the door, her phone rang. Snatching it up, she groaned. Nails.

"I saw that kiss," he told her. She glanced kitty-corner at the top floor of the old library, and he waved at her.

While Larson drove off toward the park, she circled back around the courthouse to the Sub, wishing she hadn't yielded to the impulse to spend a few minutes alone with Larson. Hardly alone. *Never* alone. Why had she agreed to having her home overrun? She yanked open the door to the Sub. "Don't poke into my personal life, Nails."

"Ha, finally got you to call me Nails."

She bared her teeth, thankful he couldn't see that. "I thought we came to an understanding this morning that some things remain under wraps." She'd accused him of leaking the dental implant, and he'd told her it had already made the rounds from several sources in the park.

"Don't worry, I won't broadcast it. Don't have to. I wasn't the only one who got treated to that fine dip and kiss."

Unfortunately, that might well be true—and Larson had

apparently cast to the wind any of his concerns over airing their relationship. If it could be called that. "I'm not ashamed of it."

"Good. About time you moved on. Speaking of which… you'd better move on. Wish I could join you on the search. I'm looking forward to an update on Mountain Man."

Tit for tat. "So am I."

CHAPTER 33

M AREK DROVE THROUGH A GAUNTLET of pickups to get up to the Grove Park campground, which was deserted, except for one lone solar-powered RV parked next to the comfort station.

Pat Donahue emerged wearing camos as Marek pulled up into the next spot. "Hey, there. You might not realize it, but there's a—oh, it's you. Hello, Detective. Just wanted to warn off any clueless campers who wandered in. But if you're here to warn me off, you're wasting breath—and with this wind, it's better not to, as it might get snatched." He patted the gun at his belt. "I'm legal to carry. And I'm ready to help."

Killers often liked to "help" the police in their inquiries. Marek made sure his own gun was out—and out of sight below the open window of his Silverado. "How did you hear?"

The call that went out on low-power FM had included instructions to park on the road and gather at the park manager's residence, under tree cover on the side of the hill away from where they believed Mountain Man was hiding out.

Donahue shrugged. "Biester told me. He tried to get me to go. Everyone else did. But I want to see it through."

"You like to finish things?" Marek asked conversationally, as if he had all the time in the world.

Donahue glanced at his watch. "Always have, always will."

"Like finishing Bunting's last job?"

That brought his head up. "Pardon?"

"You filed a complaint in the Hills last year with the highway patrol."

"Yes, I did. What does that have to do with... wait." Donahue looked thunderstruck. "Are you telling me that asshole in the Black Hills who tried to bum a bribe off me for pulling a speeding ticket—which I wasn't guilty of in the first place—was Bunting? The same man you pulled out of the john? Wow. I had no idea."

Marek did the silent treatment well. He used it on Donahue.

"I didn't know him from Joe Blow," the ex-firefighter insisted. "I had my dash cam going. Taped the entire thing, along with the plate of his squad, and emailed the video from my rig that same night. No way would I have recognized him. Just a bloated idiot with a badge." Donahue finally seemed to get that he was a suspect. "You're looking at me? Seriously? Why would I kill a man who'd been fired from his job? I got a personal reply from the regional commander, who said the situation had been dealt with, that I could shred the ticket with their compliments, and that I'd helped get a bad cop off the road."

All of that, Marek knew. He'd talked to the commander and gotten an earful. "Maybe Bunting remembered you. Maybe he confronted you."

"I take things head on, Detective." His helpful, open face closed with a snap. "I don't stab people in the back."

Marek took one last stab at a dying lead. "We were able to recover cells from the feces we found. DNA is scheduled. Care to give us a sample to compare with?"

Now that hit the mark. "I... okay." The man blew out a breath. "Damn. You've got me there. And I apologize for not being up-front. I don't know if my... contribution... hit the jackpot, but yes, I did use the facilities when I got up. Just before Lori arrived."

"Why lie to us?"

"I try not to load up my composting toilet too much with a... well, a big load. So... yeah. I was going to complain to the park manager about the state of that john. I got in, got out, as fast as humanly possible. My next rig will have a black tank.

And I'm real sorry about what happened, with Lori finding the body, when I should've been the one. It's embarrassing to admit I missed seeing it. I did what I could after, to make up for it. And I'll do what I can to find this Mountain Man. Are you going to stop me?"

Marek saw a man who had exacting requirements of himself, and of others. "No."

"Good. Thanks. Detective? If he's any kind of actual mountain man, he'll know we're coming. Those survivalists have an uncanny animal sense."

Nodding, Marek shifted his Silverado into reverse. "But will he flee or fight?"

"Don't know. But I'm keeping a good grip on my gun." His eyes dipped to the invisible gun behind the door. "You do the same." He smiled faintly as Marek sighed and holstered it. "You telegraph with your shoulder—slightly away from your body. When I noticed that, I knew you were serious."

"Hop in. I'll take you down."

By the time they made it back to Biester's residence, Marek found Karen in the middle of a swirling pack—a female alpha in all her glory. Standing beside her was a shell-shocked Larson, looking like a lost accountant in his button-down shirt and khakis amongst all the camos offset by bright-orange vests. That sort of summed up the schizoid priorities that Karen was underlining: be stealthy to avoid alerting the prey, but be highly visible so you don't get yourself shot by your trigger-happy neighbor.

Walrus was there, and to Marek's surprise, so was Adam Van Eck.

"We don't know if Mountain Man is armed, but he's never used a gun for his poaching, only a snare and a knife," Karen went on. "But if you catch sight of him, stop immediately and call us in. Or should I say text. Please turn your phones on silent or vibrate." She gave out her cell number and those of the group leaders. Phones, from flips to the latest smartphones, were pulled out of cargo pockets. A few old-timers frowned at such newfangled nonsense, but their younger counterparts paired off with them, so all was settled, without a word.

"Remember that Mountain Man may not, in fact, be a killer or a rapist. He may be with a young boy, about ten or eleven, possibly his son. Keep within eyesight of each other and be aware. Unfortunately, we won't have helicopter support—the weather is too iffy. Ready?"

A sea of nods greeted her, along with a few squats and shoulder rolls.

"Let's go, then."

An ominous roll of thunder greeted them as they spread out to their assigned locations. Walrus and Biester headed one group toward the creek, Karen went toward the south side, and Adam took the far side. Marek followed him, and Donahue followed Marek. "Should've just stayed up there," the retired firefighter grumbled and hunched as a brutal wind pregnant with rain hit his face.

Adam cinched up his deputy's jacket and gripped his shotgun. "'Poor naked wretches, wheresoe'er you are, that bide the pelting of this pitiless storm. How shall your houseless heads and unfed sides, your loop'd and window'd raggedness, defend you from seasons such as these?'"

Most ignored him, a few snorted, and a few shook their heads. But all of them followed the man who would be king as he headed out.

Beside Marek, Donahue whispered, "Is he... not quite there?"

Eyes on the path so he didn't trip and become a liability, Marek said in a low voice, "He's King Lear."

Donahue stopped. "He's mad?"

"Some think so. He's an actor. He moonlights as a reserve deputy. Right now, he's King Lear."

Relief crossed the man's face. "Oh. Okay."

As a Californian, Donahue apparently thought that entirely reasonable. The rest of the way, they kept their heads down and their ears to the ground, until Adam had them where he wanted them. Then he got them spread out and made a release-the-cavalry gesture.

Still shaking their heads, they went. Marek found himself picking his way through a tangle of low-lying bur oaks, with Donahue on one side and Adam on the other. The good thing was, the tree cover helped cut down on the rain—and the thunder covered the noise of their search. The bad thing was, the temperature continued to drop. Not cold enough to snow, but Marek much preferred a dry cold to wet.

Grove Park might not be very big, but Marek still felt like he'd entered a foreign land, which wasn't laid out for his big feet, his height, or anything else. He wondered how Karen was faring. Being far more athletic, she was probably just fine. He stumbled over a leaf-covered rock, grabbed a tree limb, then heard a crashing noise and saw a flash of movement.

He and Donahue raised their guns in unison.

Their quarry flushed, white flag up. Not in surrender. A white-tailed deer bounded away.

"City boys," Adam mouthed, bumping out a hip like a waitress at a 50s diner, batting her—his—eyes at them. Donahue gave him the finger, but with a smile.

After his heart stopped pounding, Marek continued on his trek. Watching his feet as much as the terrain, he almost missed the ping in the back of his brain—the primal part that said: you have company. Tracks. Army boots, he thought. Could be a hunter's, as it was hunting season, but as he slowly raised his eyes, he saw that the tracks led into a thicket against the hill.

Only when he heard the faintest snap of a branch underfoot did he realize that his companions were converging on the same spot with guns drawn, both looking intently at something just beyond his vision. Moving as silently as he could, Marek rounded the natural windbreak and saw a lean-to, a fire ring, and several rabbit carcasses strung up nearby. He could hear, in the break between thunder claps, the sound of running water.

Pulling out his phone, Marek texted Karen. *Found bolt-hole. No MM. Far side of hill down from campground near creek.*

At least that was what he thought he'd texted. With his dyslexia, he wasn't always sure. Lots of times he got *???* back or a head-scratching emoticon. After a delay, he got a text.

Stay put. Very near you. Walrus with me. Best tracker.

Walrus must've already cleared his section. Figured. Marek showed the others her instructions. Donahue looked disappointed but resigned to the wait. He settled on a tree stump. Adam, on the other hand, struck a mad king pose and began mouthing lines that Marek couldn't hope to follow, even when they were spoken.

Marek looked around. The Spartan campsite held no bedroll, no duffel, nothing that could ID the man. He looked down at the ground, finding a few more tracks. One in particular held his interest. A sneaker. Woman or boy.

Maybe fifteen minutes later, Karen, Larson, and Walrus emerged into Mountain Man's little home away from home. Or maybe a home without a home.

"Walrus tracked him to the creek," Karen announced, nearly breaking Marek's eardrums, poised for any little sound—yet somehow canceling out the thunderclaps. "Tracks on the other side go to the road. He's gone. I'll put out the APB for a hitchhiker, but... we still have no idea who he is."

The air went out of them all.

"I'll bet young Bobby knows, assuming he's the boy who was seen with Mountain Man." Marek pointed at the sneaker impression. The others converged on the imprint, as if it held the answers to all their questions. Maybe it did.

"Well, I have to make a stop to talk to Principal Hageman," Karen said. "Maybe she'll ID him for us. I'd rather not put the thumbscrews to Zoe. Bobby seems to be her only friend."

Larson squatted near a fallen log on the far perimeter. "May not need him at all."

"Why? What did you find?" Karen got to him first. Marek could, thankfully, see over her head. Mountain Man must have been sitting on the log, in the midst of making or repairing a snare, when he'd been spooked. A partially whittled branch and a wire lay on the ground.

And a KA-BAR pocketknife, bloodied, was sticking out of the log.

CHAPTER 34

PRINCIPAL BLANCHE HAGEMAN PEERED AT Karen over her half-moon reading glasses.

"I was not aware of your young cousin's difficulties. She should have come to me or another teacher."

Once happily running herd on the munchkin crowd at the elementary school, the overworked educator now had all of kindergarten through twelfth grade to worry about and a budget that, like Karen's own, never stretched far enough. Through hook or crook, the principal managed to claw back some of the programs she'd been forced to cut, like art and music, but only by paying peanuts and leaning heavily on volunteers. Karen herself was on call to help out with the basketball program, though she'd found little time for it of late.

Karen's own volunteers at Grove Park had done admirably—and she'd thanked them all—but they'd all left with that gnawing hunger of failure. Larson had left with his precious cargo and said he would call ASAP if he was able to lift a fingerprint from the pocketknife.

She'd sent Walrus and Adam to the trailer park to warn residents and to keep an eye out for anyone hiding Mountain Man. At least Not-Johnson—she couldn't think of him as Albert Cram Bayton—and his followers still at Lions Park weren't likely to have picked up Mountain Man.

Forcing her mind back to her young cousin, Karen said,

"Mary Hannah won't come to you. Ever. Her beliefs are to take whatever is dished out. She'll tell me, or she'll tell Eyre, but she won't tell anyone who has the power to make it stop. This kid. Sean. He's taunting her."

"Off school grounds." When Karen opened her mouth to reply, the principal lifted a hand. "I am not ignoring the seriousness of what she's endured. It needs to stop. But Sean..." She rubbed at her temples. "He's been in and out of our school system, in and out of trouble, not serious but troubling. As the saying goes, he's acting out, turning the taunts he's endured over the years, about bad grooming, ill-fitting clothes, things he has no control over given his home situation, against a target who won't fight back."

Karen resisted the urge to tell Principal Hageman to hand Sean over to her to straighten out. "I told Mary Hannah that I would report it to you, and you would do whatever you could. If it continues, her parents may pull her out of school, which would break her heart, but there are other ways to get her GED."

The principal pursed her lips. "Mary Hannah is an impressive student, from what I've heard. She wants to learn and seems to be earning some respect from her classmates for standing up for what she believes in. I will talk to Sean, but I can make no guarantees that it will stop him when we aren't around. Can someone perhaps give her a ride?"

"That might work," Karen conceded. She'd been so determined that the school would take care of it that she hadn't considered that simple solution. "They've got Henry Hahn on call. He'd have come from Fink, but he could probably pick her up."

"Or other parents could."

Thinking about parents, Karen asked, "What about Sean's parents?"

"Deadbeat dad. Mother works sporadically but has some mental health issues so keeps losing jobs. The Dakotas are actually pretty good about launching kids like Sean into a better life, similar to some Scandinavian countries for social mobility. But more and more, we're being asked to be parents when parents aren't doing the job. Either they won't or can't, having to work long hours, just trying to keep a roof over their heads."

Karen tried to think back to her own school experiences. "I just don't remember that kind of thing growing up, other than maybe a handful of kids. You knew that they had it rough and felt kind of sorry for them. Parents were parents. Kids were kids."

"A lot has changed. Good and bad. But what I'm seeing now, I haven't seen in all my years in teaching. We supply breakfast and lunch for over half our students. And I'm talking about kids with stable, working parents who just can't keep up with the bills. We've talked about getting donations to send food home over the weekends. Can you believe the Forsgrens shot that down, saying it was good for a kid to go hungry? That it'd make them work harder to claw their way out. Just the opposite, in my experience. They can't concentrate, then they get in trouble. Punishing the kids, even the cases of parental screw-ups, that's a complete lack of empathy. Throwing a kid away just so you can say, 'I told you so,' isn't a civilized strategy."

Karen grimaced. "No one has ever accused a Forsgren of empathy. Not even for their own."

Blanche Hageman was no dummy. She knew who Karen was referring to, as she'd fought to hire Nikki Forsgren Solberg over the Forsgrens' protests—or at least that of the patriarch. "Nikki has plenty for all of them. She's a wonderful teacher, and I know how lucky we are to have her. I hope she sticks around."

That sounded like a question. "Marek goes where Becca leads him. Becca wants to stay here. And if I am reading things rightly, that means Nikki stays. At least for the next four years. Unless revenues plummet."

The principal let out a breath and nodded. "The new recycling center has brought back some of that. Or should I say, their workers have, and people have been trying to shop more in town. Whether we can maintain that level, who knows?"

Karen thought of Valeska. "We're in better shape than a lot of towns in Eda County."

"Consolidation. It hurts to shutter a school. But it's what we have to do to survive."

The school bell jangled, making Karen start and the principal laugh. "Awful sound, isn't it?"

"Hasn't changed. It makes me want to rush out. Which I do have to do." She had an appointment with Marsha Schaeffer at the end of the social worker's workday.

"Very well. I'll talk to Sean, threaten him with more detention if I hear of more incidents, but I suggest you line up the more practical solution. And if that's not going to work, as it is a long way to come just to ferry her over to your place, I may be able to lean on a boy or two who might want to play the hero and walk her home. It'll make her safer and make them feel like they've done something important. Two birds, one stone."

Karen felt her face heat. Two reasonable, even obvious, solutions. "I should've figured it out myself. I'm not doing very well on the *in loco parentis* thing."

"Oh, I wouldn't say that. You hit the trifecta." One finger went up. "You're here." The second finger. "You're concerned." The third finger with a triumphant whirl. "And you didn't threaten to have me fired."

They shared a wry smile. The public was a fickle boss. Karen walked out of the office, nearly running into a worried-looking parent with a sullen kid in tow. Karen didn't want any part of that. She waded out into the hallway and got carried away with the after-school tide outside.

She'd walked over from the courthouse and headed back that way, only to see a familiar head—or bonnet. "Mary Hannah!"

The bonnet stopped like a stone in the midst of the stream of kids. Almost as if bracing herself, her young cousin took a moment then turned. Then she let out a big breath as Karen came up to her.

"I'll walk you to the courthouse, at least," Karen said easily. "Should be home free from there."

Mary Hannah's gaze went to the other side of the street, where a reed-thin boy with a lean face covered with pockmarks mirrored their route. Like a young wolf kicked out of his pack, slinking around on the edges of a new one, he was looking for an opening, a quick kill—someone he could dominate... or someone who'd accept him.

When Karen shot him a hard look, Sean hunched into his too-small windbreaker, flipped up his hood like a gangsta wannabe, and slouched away down an alleyway on huge feet that made her think he still had a lot of growing to do—if he was fed. She was still the alpha. Give him a few years and an attitude, and that would change. Fortunately, a gun and a badge made up for many deficiencies. But maybe he'd get his act together and kick ass in the game of life. Military, perhaps. No better place for an attitude adjustment—and you were part of the pack as long as you didn't get yourself thrown out.

"Trailer trash, trailer trash!" a voice jeered from around the corner, causing Karen to jerk her head back around. Mary Hannah slowed, instinctively moving closer to Karen. Feeling the distinct need to pound on someone since her prey had slunk off, Karen rounded the corner, fully expecting to find Zoe Harkness at the center of the taunt.

Instead, she found Zoe's only friend—baseball boy, fishing boy, and the key, perhaps, to the puzzle of Mountain Man.

Bobby.

Unlike Sean, Bobby wore well-fitting clothes and was well-groomed. She saw nothing to indicate that he was neglected. But he was no longer the carefree Tom-Sawyerish boy she'd seen fishing from Connor Creek. His Little League ball cap lay on the ground as if flicked there, and his heavy backpack, no doubt originally slung on one shoulder, had fallen to the crook of his arm, hampering him as he raised his fists.

"Nah, he ain't even got a trailer no more," a tow-headed teen with a cowlick said, giving Bobby a push. "He's livin' in the woods, like a wild thing. Raised by wolves."

One of them gave a howl. The other two joined in, though one's voice broke, and the others laughed, doubling over, almost choking. Bobby looked uncertain whether to flee, fight—or join them. She remembered from when she'd first met him at a Little League game, that he had a knack of pulling in others when given a chance.

Karen decided for him. "Very funny." She reached down to pick up the cap. "Yours... Bobby?"

His startled gaze went from the baseball hat... to hers with its sheriff's insignia. She didn't expect him to be overjoyed. No young man wanted a woman coming to his rescue, but she didn't expect what she saw: overwhelming fear. He just nodded. She put it back on his head and put a friendly hand on his arm, sliding up the backpack onto his shoulder and keeping a grip there so he wouldn't bolt. "Did you ever get out on the diamond, slugger?"

He didn't answer.

"Slug," one of the wolves said, jabbing his mate. "Don't they live in the woods? All slimy and—"

"Don't you three have a pack meeting or something to go to?" she asked the wolves pointedly. "Because if not, I have a nice, comfortable den for you, complete with three meals a day, a bunk, and... no? Well, darn. I was looking for some fresh meat. Now, Bobby... what's your last name?"

He pressed his mouth into a line.

One of the quickly departing wolves turned. "Bobble-head? Got a girly name." In a singsong voice, he dragged it out even as Bobby tried to pull away. "Jaaaaansen."

CHAPTER 35

HER BUFFALO-CHECK FLANNEL SHIRT BILLOWING out like
a witch's cape behind her, Lori Jansen flew into the
office and straight for the boy sitting in Walrus's chair,
scuffing his Nikes on the marble floor.

Karen had told Walrus to sit on the boy while she and
Marek had discussed the new development—and a possible
new theory. Then she'd sent her detective to retrieve Lori. Karen
wasn't looking forward to working the scenario she and Marek
had outlined between them, but it made sense. The instant
she'd heard the name Jansen, a lot had become clear about
Lori's reluctance to leave the park, to file charges, or to draw
any attention to herself.

Marek trailed in after Lori, looking tired and sad. Anytime
you involved a minor in an investigation, the potential for hurt
was great. Emotions ran high. Case in point: Lori Jansen.

Gone was the submissive, washed-out woman. Her cheeks
were dotted red. "You had no right to drag my son here like a
prisoner."

Well, that took care of any lingering question mark as to
the relationship between the two Jansens. Not that Karen had
harbored any real doubt. "I didn't drag him, Lori. I asked him to
come with me and answer some questions. He did." Reluctantly,
without a word, but he'd done so. He was on that teeter-totter
between childhood and teen that still weighed toward the child.

"Right. The law asks. The law takes. Screw the law."

Lori's over-the-top response had even her son looking at her. "Chill out, Mom. I'm okay. Mr. Russell gave me props for hitting that single in the game last week."

Lori wrapped her arms around her son and glared at Karen. "I'm a good mother. I don't neglect him. You can't take him just because I lost my job."

Karen raised an eyebrow at Marek. "Just what did you tell her?"

"That you had Bobby with you. And we had some questions about him living in the park." He pursed his lips, more thoughtfully than otherwise, as if something had just clicked. "Until now, I hadn't realized she'd been evicted from the trailer park. And I didn't say anything about removing him from her custody."

That might, effectively, be what happened, though, depending on the outcome.

Lori Jansen held his gaze then Karen's, and her fire died. "Sorry. I just... I know it looks bad. Him living with me at Grove Park and at the Lions. But if we can't find anything else soon, I have a distant cousin who'll take us in until I can get back on my feet. Her son, Tom, and Bobby are buddies."

Relaxing, Bobby nodded. "Yeah, Tom's cool. We play Little League together. He taught me stuff, and I got to start. Coach says I've got a good bat." His young face glowed, with health, with excitement, with all the right things, and if Karen had to turn off that light... well, at least there was cousin Tom and his parent—or parents.

Lori still looked wary, if less combative. "So what did you want to ask him? Bobby didn't see anybody kill Bunting. I would've told you."

Not under their scenario, she wouldn't, though she might be telling the truth about her son's lack of knowledge. Karen tried to sound reassuring. "But Bobby may have seen or heard something that may help us. We've actually been looking for him. We just didn't know he was your son. Only that he spent a lot of time in the woods. Ask a kid, my dad always said, when you want recon."

Lori didn't move her hands. "You want to get my son tangled up in all this? No way."

Karen didn't like that Lori was stalling.

Bobby twisted out of his mother's grasp to look up at her. "You said talking to the cops was the right thing to do, even if you lost your job. And they aren't gonna take me away from you. They said so."

And that made it true? Karen hoped that her sinking feeling didn't show on her face—or that Lori noticed that Marek had all but disappeared into himself again. Sometimes the job sucked.

Finally, Lori tapped the boy's nose. "All right, buddy. Your call. For now." Lori's tone, her face, said it would end in a hurry if she didn't like where it was going.

After moving to the interview room, they finished the formalities, for both mother and son. The latter seemed to find it all fascinating, not intimidating, unlike his mother. Then they began.

Marek took the lead. "Bobby, when did you meet Mountain Man?"

They'd agreed to go after that information first, whatever came of the rest. Mountain Man had a lot to answer for, but until Larson came through with a fingerprint or DNA results, they were up a creek. Literally. Connor Creek was the dividing line between the barely haves and the have-nots.

Bobby looked puzzled, but at a nod from his mom, he answered, "After we moved back from Sioux Falls."

"June third," Lori put in.

"Mountain Man wasn't there when we left last year. And the log bridge wasn't there. But when Ted said we could come back to the trailer park, Mom said it was okay if I went into the woods by myself."

As if she took that as another accusation of neglect, Lori said, "He's old enough. We used to play by ourselves even younger than him. I'm not going to shut him up in the trailer all the time just because I'm at work. It's good for a kid to get outside, get some fresh air, and exercise, right? Not sitting on his ass like... some."

Zoe? Or her grandmother? Even the boy was feeling the undercurrents. His mother covered her face then patted her son's shoulder. "Sorry. Venting. Go on, honey."

"Okay, well, I didn't see him right away. I was... well, I was pretending I was an Indian." He flushed. "Not like playing make-believe, just trying to see if I could be real quiet. Real stealthy. So I went down the riverbank and then stopped and stood there by a tree, like they say if you're patient, you'll flush out the animals? And there's this guy, doing the same thing, just watching. I don't see him for like a long time, until he moves. He meant to move. To see if I'd see him, and I did. Just about shit my pants. Sorry, Mom. Crapped. But he was cool. He just stood there. Said people called him Mountain Man. I asked him what mountain, and he said it was far away—and very near. That was weird, but then he asked me about Ted."

That made Karen blink. "He knew Ted?"

"Said he used to know him, like a long time ago. In the trailer park. Just like me."

That bit of info on Mountain Man could be helpful if anyone in the trailer park went that far back, which was doubtful.

"So you became friends, then, with Mountain Man?" Marek asked.

"I guess. I mean, he's old, but... sort of like a dad, I guess. He talked to me about stuff. Guy stuff."

His mother stiffened. "Like what?"

Bobby shrugged, looking, for the first time, more adult than kid. "Like getting picked on for stuff you can't change. How to keep from getting beat up, or if you can't, how to win."

Lori looked torn between relief—telling Karen where her mind had gone—and self-incrimination. "You've never said anything about that."

"Mostly, I can get out of it." He shot a quick glance at Karen, a pleading look that she interpreted as asking her not to spill the beans. "No biggy. I got it a lot less than Zoe."

For all Karen knew, Bobby would've gotten the best of the wolves, either by laughing with them, at himself, or with a lucky hit.

Marek continued his patient, low-key questioning. "Bobby, on the night your mother was... hurt... did you see Mountain Man?"

Bobby frowned at his mother, who waved him on. "Yeah, he woke me up."

"Where were you? All the tents were taken down."

"In the earth berm. Mountain Man made it himself. But he gave it to us after we got kicked out from our trailer. He said he'd make another one if he needed it for the winter."

"What did he say when he woke you up?"

"He said my mom was okay, but someone knocked her over on the trail. She was going to go talk to the police for a little while before she came back to get me. That he'd make sure we had a place to live even though you guys made everyone leave." His lip trembled. "I hate moving."

Mountain Man seemed to have a nice little family fantasy going. Maybe he'd decided to take a mate in the way of nature, with or without consent. Mental, perhaps? Or just evil. Like Bunting. Perhaps. They couldn't hope to hear back from the FBI on the stained duty shirt yet. Karen was waiting on lots of DNA results she'd love to have right now. But none of it would be relevant if the scenario turned out like they'd sketched.

Marek shifted in his seat, and Karen tensed, knowing what was coming.

"Bobby, I know you like Mountain Man, but we believe that he was likely the man who hurt your mom."

"No!" Bobby leapt to his feet. "He'd never... he wouldn't!"

His mother, on the other hand, looked not stunned but wide-eyed, her mouth rounding in an O. She, apparently, had no problem seeing that scenario.

"Mountain Man was there. You've just told us that," Marek

told Bobby gently. "He got away from the deputy, from the park manager, and a camper, and he ran down the trail, straight for the earth berm... and you."

"No. No way!" Bobby bolted from the room into the office, where Walrus corralled him with a look toward Karen.

"Just keep him occupied."

That had, actually, been the desired result, even if it felt low. Very low. Now came the hard part. Karen closed the door and leaned back against it.

"He hasn't learned yet," Lori said wearily into the silence.

"Learned what?"

"Trust nobody. I didn't want to raise him that way. But maybe my mother was right all along. She said that all the time—and she'd know. I couldn't trust her." Lori looked down at her casted wrist. "Mountain Man. All this time, I thought Bobby was safe with him."

"So far as we know, he was," Karen reminded her. "You've raised a good kid, there."

Lori blinked at her, as though Karen had spoken in a foreign language. Then it hit. A real smile wreathed the plain face, and Karen finally saw a resemblance to her son. "Thanks. He's great."

Then her smile dimmed. "People say, 'You should never have had him,' like that would've made it all better. He made me what I am, Sheriff Mehaffey. He *made* me. I just want to return the favor. That's why we went to Sioux Falls last year. I told him it was an adventure, that we'd both do better, and for a little while, we did. I found a job at the mall. Nothing much, but it was work. Then they cut hours, made weird hours, and I couldn't get childcare. Then the car broke down. I tried job training, and it only got me more debt. They told me at the food pantry I went to—and I always ditched the box and used grocery bags so Bobby wouldn't know it was charity—that Sioux Falls had plenty of jobs, but none of them paid enough. So there were more poor people there, not less, and they could barely keep the pantry stocked. Crazy. I did everything I could to make it there, but it was like climbing out of one of those vault toilets. Shit kept piling up on top of me."

Karen let her talk. The more comfortable Lori was, the better.

"So we came home. Ted let me come back to the trailer park without a deposit, and I started all over again. Bobby's been a trouper. And he just sort of took off all at once, with baseball, with Mountain Man, and even at school. For the first time, he's got something in his life that makes his eyes shine, that gives him hope for his future."

"What's that?" Karen asked, genuinely interested.

"That new art teacher. Ms. Solberg?" She didn't notice Marek start. "She says he's got real talent. He wants to work on movies. Animalations. No, wait. Animations. Like *Toy Story*? He loves that movie. And he does amazing stuff that he shows me on his phone. I just wish I could afford a computer for him."

Once again, her face dimmed. "But we may lose even his phone. It all went to hell when Digges took over. And it got worse. I didn't think it could, but it did. Ted... he was solid. He never treated us like trash. You know what Digges did? He left the eviction notice on my door. Bobby found it when he got home from school. Do you know what it does to a kid? Do you have any idea? I'll bet you don't. I do. It's hell. You feel like you don't matter. And Bobby matters. He *matters*. He's not invisible, like I am. People like him. They pull for him."

"And that's why," Marek said gently, "Ted left him the trailer park."

Karen held her breath. One of the first things she'd done after getting back to the courthouse with Bobby was to ditch him on Walrus and hike up to see Judge Rudy, who'd allowed that yes, after another long look at the will, that Bobby Jansen did appear to be the legatee in question.

Dashing a hot tear away with the back of her sweatshirt-covered right hand, Lori didn't react for a long moment. "Left Bobby what? Our trailer? Did he?" Hope dawned.

Well, that wasn't the reaction they'd been looking for, but perhaps Lori Jansen had some as-yet-untapped talent as an actress. "Not just your trailer. The trailer park in its entirety, in trust. But you knew that, didn't you? That's why Bunting kept the will, why he threatened you that night, threatened Bobby, by taking his inheritance."

Lori's head went up and back, chin tucked. "What are you talking about? A will? Bunting?"

Karen pressed hard, not letting her catch up. "Bobby was named for his father, wasn't he? Bunting. Did he rape you? Is that why you killed him? He threatened you and Bobby, he turned his back, and you did what a mother bear does—you protected your cub. Self-defense."

"What? Where the hell do you get this stuff?" Like her son had earlier, she leapt to her feet, a fire rekindled on her drawn face. "I can't believe this. No, I take that back. I do. Dangling a bit of hope in my face then accusing me of murder? Backstabbers, that's what you people are, acting all nice and helpful—then wham! My mother was right. Trust nobody. You want to know about me? About Bobby? Ask Marsha Schaeffer."

Lori Jansen slammed the door on her way out.

CHAPTER 36

THAT WENT WELL. NOT.

But at least Karen had already scheduled a meeting with Marsha over the fate of the evictees, so they would have their answers in... she checked her watch. Five minutes. In the meantime, she sat down in Lori's chair across from Marek. He had his head in his hands, fingers massaging his scalp, as if his brain hurt.

"I'm thinking... not guilty," she told him. "Too shocked, too angry."

"I agree." He looked at her. "But it was a good angle. One we had to spring on her."

"Dragging a three-hundred-pound man across the log bridge was always a dicey proposition, even with mother-bear adrenaline. And, yeah, we didn't know if Mountain Man helped her. But you know what? I'm glad. I mean, I'm not glad that I feel like crap. But I'm glad it's not her. We don't have to separate her and Bobby. They may hate us for the rest of their, and our, natural lives, but they're still a team. Down, but not yet out. Unlike us. Or me, at least. That was my brain fart, that Lori killed Bunting."

Marek just shook his head. "We've still got Mountain Man and the pocketknife."

A sharp knock had Karen pushing back to her feet. Marsha Schaeffer, with her long, curly gray hair and flowing gossamer top over leggings and boots, looked like a flower child gone millennial. An itinerant social services rep based out of Sioux Falls, Marsha was only in the county one day a week, which was more than some rural counties that only got a visit once a month. Stretched thin was stretching it. Nothing left but gossamer of the safety net.

"Oh, sorry, am I interrupting?" Marsha asked, looking at their long faces.

"Only in a good way. Marek, do you know Marsha?"

"Only in passing." He got to his feet, enveloped the social worker's long fingers in his thicker mitt of a hand, and shook. "I've referred some of my cases to you, I believe. Never heard anything but good."

"Ditto. But we all have our failures." Marsha turned back to Karen. "I've got a pretty good idea what you're going to ask me about, Sheriff, and I'm afraid I will have to disappoint you."

Talk about a letdown. "You can't tell us about Lori and Bobby Jansen?"

With a jerk of fingers, Marsha gripped Karen's arm. "What's happened to them? Are they in trouble?"

Interesting. Like Lori, the woman was overreacting. Big time. "What did you think I was talking about?"

Marsha released Karen. "The homeless from the trailer park. Harold Dahl has already talked to me about it. He's getting pressure from the Lions to move them along." Then it hit. "Oh, no. Are the Jansens in that group?"

At Karen's nod, the social worker sank down into Karen's vacated chair. "I really want to help them out. Truly. Most of the evictees are on waiting lists for what little is available in Eda County. But I've run out of placements, of stopgaps, of—"

"Baling wire?" Marek suggested.

"Exactly. We had Section 8 housing in Aleford but lost that to fire. The owners chose not to rebuild. Ted's was my last bit of baling wire. He knew these people, knew which ones would do whatever they could to pay him back, even if it took months, years in a few cases. He gave second, even third, chances. After that, he'd give them my name, tell them to try to find something in Sioux Falls or Sioux City, find a shelter there to take them, whatever he could. People would apologize to him when they were evicted, say they'd send the money when they could. Several did, that I know of. Ted wasn't poor. Even with what some would say was a too lenient policy, he made a tidy profit, though you'd never know it to look at him. He never flaunted it like Alan Digges."

Her earnest face turned sharp. "From the grapevine in Sioux Falls, I hear that Michelle Bayton is dumping her boy toy—and that he's no longer in charge of the trailer park and, in fact, facing charges here in Eda County. Is that true?"

Karen took pleasure in saying, "When we get around to it, yes, he'll be facing charges, assuming the state's attorney goes for it."

"With the Baytons baying for his blood? You can take that to the bank." The social worker's satisfaction turned thoughtful. "As for the evictees, who is administering Ted's estate? Maybe I can appeal to their better nature, if they have one."

Karen smiled wryly. "Judge Rudibaugh."

"Oh. Well. That's going to be an... interesting... discussion." Though the social worker looked like a do-gooder pushover, Marsha Schaeffer had a steel-plated backbone. "I'll talk to him before I leave. Is that all? I need to decide how to approach—"

"That's not all." Karen gave Marsha the Cliffs Notes version of what had just transpired in the room. "What did Lori mean, to ask you?"

Marsha had both hands pressed against her long face, her mouth open in an O, not unlike that famous painting. "The Scream"? Maybe. Karen wasn't big on art history. Nikki would know.

Then Marsha slipped her hands into her hair, roiling it like some witch in a Halloween flick. "Lori Jansen was my first major failure, and my worst by far."

"Doesn't seem like a failure to me," Marek said.

Karen nodded. "She's down, but she's not out. Yet."

"My failure, not hers." Marsha roiled more strands. "Let me give you the short version, because I've got a file an inch thick. Her mother was, shall we say, a bit too fond of chemical enhancements. Dabbled first then went hardcore, and it eventually killed her, but not before she'd hauled Lori all over the county and the state, in a long line of Section 8 placements ending in evictions."

Ouch. No wonder Lori was so sensitive about the issue.

"That was all before I got on board. By then, the state had removed Lori from her mother's so-called care and placed her with her only remaining relative who'd take her, her seventy-two-year-old grandfather, who farmed a few acres outside of Dutch Corners."

A town that hadn't survived a recent flood. Only the Sub had. Karen would much prefer it the other way around. "He died?" she hazarded.

"Yes, of a broken heart. After I yanked Lori out after a home visit." Marsha pulled on her curly hair as if she could tug out the memories that obviously haunted her. "Typical newbie. Thought I knew everything and was saving the world, one kid at a time. Her grandfather didn't have two nickels to rub together, with an outhouse for plumbing and no running water, just a well. A stove for heating and lots of blankets. Appalling, I thought, with my city upbringing."

Karen managed, barely, not to look at Marek. She was describing Janina Marek's home.

"And old Bob Jansen didn't take any more kindly to me than I did to him when I started to make demands about upgrading his home. When he didn't follow through, I wrote up my report highlighting all the deficiencies. Leaving out the minor fact that he loved his granddaughter and vice versa. I was sure that removing Lori was for the best. She was thirteen. But you'd have thought I'd kidnapped her—and in a very real sense, I had."

Karen had heard of Indian children being pulled from their homes due to simple poverty but didn't realize it had happened to whites in her own county.

Marsha went on, "I placed her with a nice foster family in Reunion—but it turned out the brother-in-law from Sioux City who liked to visit on the weekends also liked young girls. He molested her for years without my knowledge, because she had zero trust in me. I lost my rose-colored glasses—and she lost far more. Only when she got pregnant when she was seventeen did it all come spilling out. I did what I could to make it right. The brother-in-law is still in jail, I believe. I arranged for an abortion, but Lori didn't want it, said she'd finally have a real family. When I asked her what else I could do, she told me that she never wanted to see me again. And while I've seen her several times at the trailer park, she hasn't seen me. I'm invisible to her. Nothing I can do will ever make up for what I did. With the best intentions, of course, but that road leads you know where."

To hell. Karen had been there. In the trailer park.

Marek finally said, "Lori said that Bobby made her what she is."

"Maybe he did. I didn't give her any chance of surviving on her own, but from watching from afar—very far—she did it. Oh, she's had it hard. And I itched, absolutely itched, to help her, but I not only burned that bridge, I vaporized the creek right along with it."

So Bobby was not Bunting's son. And he'd been named for his grandfather. And Karen and Marek had, even if unintentionally, pressed all of Lori Jansen's hot buttons in exactly the wrong way. No wonder she'd tried to hide that Bobby was her son. The wonder was that Lori felt she'd had to do the right thing at the overlook, losing her job in the process. Just how much more damage had they done?

Karen suspected that she and Marek were now on the Jansens' shit list. Instant invisibility. And in the Dakotas, a mantra of "trust nobody" was a very poor way to survive.

"Looks like we've all got a hand in landing her there," Karen finally said. "I always wondered how you can do your job, day after day. How do you keep going? Just not care?"

"If I didn't care, I'd give it up. But I no longer expect. I cajole,

I reward, I do what I can. But mostly? If I have the resources—which in the case of the evictees, looks like I don't, unless I can twist the judge's arm—then I can make a real difference. That's rewarding. To give a break to people who go through bad luck and, yes, sometimes poor choices—and boy, have I made some of those—to get back on their feet. And teaching people the basics of how to navigate the work world, the kind of things we learned by osmosis. Dress a certain way for an interview. How to avoid diploma mills, payday loans, predatory lending."

Marsha lowered her hands, leaving her hair disheveled. "But some of my clients? They don't change. The cycle just rolls around, generation after short generation. If you expect people to change, you'll just get frustrated. So I do what I can and let it go. Maybe one thing I did, or said, will turn one of them around. That's the only thing that still surprises me, who makes it and who doesn't, because it's often not who you'd guess."

Larson had said something similar. "Like the Jansens," Karen said. "If it helps, before we pissed Lori off, she said she's got a distant cousin to stay with, after Lions Park."

"Ah. That's good. I know that cousin. Pam Jansen. I've helped her get some job training so she could work on the computers at the new recycling center, though Lori doesn't know that."

Marek said, his eyes on her face, "It's not just her you've helped, is it? You've arranged for other jobs, other situations, for Lori. In Sioux Falls. Here. With Ted."

Marsha Schaeffer flushed right up to her curly hair. "All right, yes. Guilty as charged. If Lori ever knew, she'd quit, she'd leave. Anything I had a hand in, she'd reject just on principle. It's been my penance, looking after them in what little ways I can. Don't ever tell her."

"We won't have a chance, most likely. Talk about burned bridges." Karen rolled her shoulders. "Though someone will have to tell Lori that her son is inheriting the trailer park. At least, in trust. I don't know the details yet. We did tell her, but she didn't believe us."

The dawning hope mirrored Lori's. "You're serious?"

"It looks like it. Judge Rudibaugh is still deciphering the will. Ted's handwriting is atrocious. We do know that a trustee is involved."

"Lori? Oh." Marsha looked uncertain. "Well, that would be... awkward. I mean, for me. I have a number of clients in the trailer park. Or did. I hope she wouldn't kick them out, just on my account. It's all such a muddle. One bad choice, and... it ripples out for years. I yanked her out, so she can yank my people out, to hurt me, and in the process, hurt others."

Karen thought about that. "She's angry. She's hurt. But... I don't think she's heartless. She may mouth the hard line when it comes to those who aren't working as hard as she is, but when it comes down to it, I don't think she'd turn out the Doris and Zoe Harknesses of the world."

Those names got, as Karen had expected, a knowing nod. For all their dysfunction, Doris and Zoe were tight. She'd seen it in their byplay, for all it sounded more like bickering. What happened to Zoe after Doris was gone would be another story.

"If you can get the judge to let the evictees back in the trailer park before he hands over the reins, that might be a more achievable goal," Karen told the social worker. "Face-saving is easier when it's someone else's decision."

Marsha rose to her feet, a militant light in her do-gooder eyes. "Then I'll see it done." And she marched out.

Unfortunately, Karen and Marek were once again left with nothing to do... but wait.

"Hey, boss!" Karen looked out the door to see Walrus with her landline in his hand. "You've got a call."

Hope springs eternal. "From Larson?"

"No, The Seasons."

Karen got to her feet and tugged Marek to his, barely able to keep her balance. She'd been off balance most of this investigation, so nothing new there. "Put it on speakerphone."

CHAPTER 37

*F*ROM SEASONS SUCH AS THESE.

Marek sat down on his desk, thinking that Shakespeare had a line for anything and everything under the sun. Or Adam did. But he didn't think Karen, or The Seasons, would appreciate the reference. Then again, perhaps they would. He had met the FBI agents out of the Sioux Falls resident office: Wintersgill, a New Englander who walked with a limp, and Dakota native Sommervold. Male and female respectively. Their coloring—red hair, gray eyes; blonde hair, green eyes—covered all the seasons, hence their nickname.

What did they have for them this time, a fall guy or another fail?

Marek was getting tired of failure, all around. The case, the people. Times had been hard in the past in the Dakotas, but he didn't think that people had blamed those who were hit hardest as much as they did now. Or maybe they had. Blame games were always popular. And if it made you feel superior, smug in your good choices—or good luck—then all the better.

"Go ahead, Agent Sommervold." Karen settled on her own desk. "Detective Okerlund and Deputy Russell are here, too."

"Greetings," the FBI agent said. "Agent Wintersgill is on my end, as well. I'm sorry you weren't able to nab your Mountain Man this afternoon, Sheriff. I wish we could have provided backup for you, but it was a no-go on the weather front."

Glancing out, Marek saw that it had finally stopped raining, although a phalanx of trolling thunderclouds readied for another assault.

"It is what it is," Karen replied and got a sound of assent from the other Dakotan. "But since you're calling me, I'm guessing you've got something for us on the DNA?"

Wintersgill's clipped tones came over the airwaves. "We were able to pull down a priority on your duty shirt. All Native American rape cases have been flagged for immediate processing."

Several years ago, the national press had dinged the FBI for neglecting cases that involved the rape of Native American women by white men. Marek was glad that Two Fingers wasn't on shift yet. As it was, Walrus stoked his windsocks and eyed the exits, but Karen shook her head at him. "We're listening."

"Good news and bad news," Sommervold said. "Which do you want first?"

"Bad," Karen said as Walrus said, "Good."

"Detective Okerlund?" Wintersgill's wry, dry voice. "You're the tiebreaker."

He'd put up with more than enough bad news. "Good."

"Your deputy's blood type isn't compatible with Bunting's," Wintersgill informed them. "We got that from Dr. White just now. We can follow up with DNA but it's not a priority."

Walrus let out a whoosh. "Wonderful news. That would've sucked."

Marek picked his way through what Wintersgill hadn't said. "But the DNA on the duty shirt did belong to the rapist, to Two Fingers's father. Is that what you're trying not to say?"

"Very well put, Detective. Yes." Sommervold had taken over, seamlessly, like any longstanding partner did. "We weren't sure we'd get DNA off the duty shirt, to be honest, but the lab pulled it off. Multiple sources of DNA, but only one male profile. The others, seven in number, were are all female and, we presume, all his victims. We got hits on the three known victims of the patrol rapist. Since Two Fingers gave us the results of his own DNA test, we were able to make a match there as well. The lab says there is no doubt that Two Fingers is the product of two profiles, the male profile and your deputy's mother."

More careful wording. This time, Karen picked it up. "You know who this rapist is?"

"Yes, he was in the system, but not CODIS, which is why we didn't get a hit initially. Came from a state system that's still got a backlog. Your man was convicted of rape seventeen years ago in Idaho. He died in prison in a fight with an inmate he'd once put away. Karma, I'd say."

Marek and Karen exchanged a long look.

"Let me guess," Karen said. "Ed Johnson?"

After another pause, Sommervold returned the volley. "Sheriff, if you keep stealing our thunder, we don't get the payoff. Yes. Bunting's onetime stepfather."

Wintersgill's voice came out in ice shards. "Johnson killed a deputy and plugged another in the spine before they brought him down. His kind should be put down, like any rabid animal."

His kind? Meaning cops who abused their position to prey on those they were supposed to defend? Or any rapist or killer, period? Marek figured that life in a cage was a far better punishment. Never to see freedom again. But perhaps that was a cruelty worse than death.

"What we'd like to know," Sommervold went on, "is why your victim had the shirt."

Karen got up, looking ready to pace, but was constrained by the limits of the speakerphone. "A good question and one we don't have the answer to. Yet. Though how this old case might relate to what happened to Bunting, long after the fact, I can't say."

"For leverage?" Sommervold asked.

Marek had pondered that same angle. Bunting was in desperate straits, about to be evicted. But who would be his target, with Ed Johnson dead? Who would care? "Do you have any information on his family?"

They heard rapid typing. "Yes, there's a short list. He's got a stepmother in Boise, Idaho. Father, long dead. And he's got a much younger half-sister still living. A Mary Johnson, last address listed, Dutch Corners, South Dakota."

Johnson. Mary. Of Aleford and Dutch Corners. That wasn't coincidence.

With her gaze locked with Marek's, Karen said, "Mary Johnson was living at Grove Park the night that Bunting was killed. She's a big woman. And I'm guessing, despite what she told us, that she confronted Bunting that night in the parking lot. Slapped him and called him a piece of shit."

"There you go," Sommervold answered. "Hope it pans out. Even if I'd like to give her a star. Self-defense all the way. By the way, is it true that Alan Digges is up on charges?" The repressed glee was just audible under the studiously neutral tone.

"Not yet. But I have little doubt he will be. Everyone seems delighted."

"Digges spread his bullshit far and wide in our fair city," Sommervold confirmed. "I would love to have him in our sweatbox, but I'll take the win vicariously. Sheriff, thanks for the closed case."

Never closed for Two Fingers or his mother. Not really.

After the call ended, Walrus gave Karen a hangdog face. "Geez. What a mess. Do you really have to tell Two Fingers? I mean, about him being Ed Johnson's son? Seems cruel."

"He already knew he was the product of rape," Karen pointed out. "It's for him and his mother to decide whether they want to know anything more, other than that the rapist was found and is dead."

Walrus hauled himself to his feet as a call came up to report to a fender bender on Bluff Road. "And I'm off. Hopefully, that'll take me to end of shift."

As Walrus trundled off, Marek got to his feet. Lions Park wasn't far. "Walk or ride?"

Understanding immediately, Karen grabbed her radio. "Walk. I need it."

So they walked in rare silence—on her part—past the small community park and band shell where he'd sung a few times with a school chorus from Valeska, sticking out in the back row like a sore thumb.

As they made the turn down toward the even smaller park run by the Lions Club, he noted fewer cars than had been at Grove Park. He just hoped one in particular wasn't there. Figured that it was.

Lori Jansen was the first to see them. She froze between flight and fight. When Karen shook her head, Lori turned her back. Pointedly. Beside her, Bobby looked over at them, then at his mother, then slowly turned, as well. Marek didn't blame him for taking his cue from his mother. That was what kids did, at least up to a certain age, and in this case, it was entirely warranted.

He only hoped that the kid—or, more importantly, his mother—never connected Marek to Nikki, because he had no doubt Bobby was her wizard with computer graphics.

Not-Johnson greeted them, though not warmly. "You going to drive us off before time is out?"

"No, we want to talk to Mary Johnson." Marek saw Lori's shoulders relax. Then she tugged her son toward the ball field across the street. He went more than willingly, jumping around her like a pup, saying something that made her give a reluctant laugh and earned him a hair ruffling.

Yes, something about Bobby Jansen made you want to root for him. That his father, like Two Fingers's, had been a royal shit, made Marek wonder just where the boy got that spark.

Mary Johnson shuffled over from where she'd been sitting in her car and sank down to the picnic table, looking pleased when Not-Johnson joined her. "What now?"

Karen swung herself onto the picnic bench. Marek followed, less athletically, making sure he cleared his size-ginormous Blunnies first.

Going for the jugular, Karen laid out the punch line first. "You never told us that your brother Ed was a rapist and a killer. Or Bunting's stepfather."

"You didn't ask," Mary replied simply. "Rapist, I knew. Killer?

News to me. But it don't surprise me none. Is he in prison? Please God, tell me he is."

Marek didn't hear any sisterly love there. Nor did Karen, apparently. "He's dead."

Mary closed her eyes, nodded, and let out a huge breath.

Not-Johnson put a hand on her shoulder. "Mary? You okay?"

Her eyes popped open, and her smile could have lit countries with its wattage. "Good. Wonderful. I can stop worrying that someday he'll show up on my doorstep."

"You didn't know?" Marek asked. "It's been years since he died."

"Haven't heard head nor tail of him since he skedaddled... what? Twenty years ago or more? I can't keep track anymore. It all blurs. But that's good news."

Marek had never been a big brother, but he thought of Kaylee and Kyle. "You had no feelings for him, then?"

"Sure. Lots of 'em. All were bad. I hated him, Detective. The church says forgive. Maybe come eternity, I can, but I'll never forget. He was bad, through and through, and he took it out on whoever came to hand, myself included."

Marek wasn't sure where to take the interview, since it didn't appear that they had a family feud thing going on with Mary and Ed on one side and Bunting on the other. "Did Bunting know you, when you saw him that night?"

"You trying to pin murder on Mary?" Not-Johnson's easy features turned sharp, and for the first time, Marek saw a resemblance to Michelle Bayton. "She was in her tent the whole time."

But Mary patted his hand. "It's all right, Al. If I were gonna kill Bunting, I'd sic Daisy on him. Look, I tried to stay out of the whole thing. I didn't want no trouble. But I was up in the parking lot, coming off a sub job at the gas station in Fink."

That, at least, could be confirmed. "What was going on at the parking lot when you got there?"

"Just Bunting being Bunting. Throwing his weight around. Told everyone he'd won the election, told us to get out—or pay him the fine. But I'd heard on YRUN driving home that he lost the recount. He got pretty hot, saying I was a liar. So I slapped him, told him he'd always been a piece of shit. Then I hightailed it down the trail as fast as I could. He was still up there in the parking lot, alone by then. The rest, they didn't want to tangle with him, so they just left to park down the road. But I lied… about being woke up. But not any of the rest. I was scared to death that I'd finally managed to turn Bunting into a killer—and not just of myself but all of us."

Karen looked at Not-Johnson. "And you? Mr. Bayton?"

The wannabe Moses, leading his people out of the wilderness, looked pained. "I was right where I said. Asleep in my plywood home. As for why I hid my name? Precisely because of what I see on your faces. A Bayton. Homeless. I got tired of the double takes."

"You're the best of 'em," Mary said stoutly. "As for Bunting, he had a mean streak, no doubt about that. But really? Bob Bunting was a sad sack. A wannabe without the killer instinct. Ed? He was the real deal. Evil. Truly evil. Him and that Rachel Dutton were a pair. Yes, before you ask, Ed raped me, when I got old enough to make it worth his while. Only once. But you don't forget." Her chin wobbled, and Not-Johnson took her hand and gripped it hard. "You want to know why Ed left the highway patrol, the state, all of a sudden? Why despite everything, I'd never have laid a hand on Bunting other than that slap? You go ask Alice Dutton."

Marek looked at Karen, who said, "Guess we're going to need the ride after all."

But were they being taken for a ride? And if so, by whom?

CHAPTER 38

WHEN THE DOOR TO THE plain little ranch home opened, Karen was almost engulfed.

"Oh, Sheriff! I am so happy! Guess what?" Kaylee Early didn't wait for the answer. "I'm gonna have a baby." She squealed and clapped her hands together. "A real baby. Not a play one. I have lots of dolls. I hope it's a girl. Girls like dolls."

Some girls did. Karen hadn't. She'd used the few she'd gotten as target practice for the slingshot she'd made from scratch. But for Kaylee's sake, and the baby's future as Bunting's child, she hoped Kaylee was right. "That's wonderful. Where is your brother?"

"Kyle? He went to Sioux Falls. To work. He got a job with Jim."

"At a gym, dear." Alice came into view, wiping her hands on a dish towel. She looked a little tired, a little exasperated, but mostly... a lot happy. And much younger. "Now, why don't you go take a lie-down."

"Oh, I'm not tired. I could do jumping jacks all day long." Kaylee proceeded to do just that and finished it off with a cartwheel, narrowly missed a side table, and ended her routine with her hands flung up high, cheerleader style.

Alice shook her head at Kaylee. "Five minutes ago, you were throwing up. Now look at you. You know it's better for the baby to get some rest. The books say so. Go take a nap."

"Oh. Okay." Kaylee put her hand on her as-yet-slim waist. "Better for baby." She disappeared down the hallway into one of the two bedrooms.

Alice shook out her dish towel and began folding it. "She's an absolute joy, when she's not driving me crazy. I believe I have you to thank for her sudden appearance in my life. A second chance at a family." Alice gave Karen and Marek, a hovering presence, a searching look. "What's happened? Do you know who killed Robert? Is that why you're here?" Her face set as she put the dish towel on the stove handle. "Just tell me straight."

"Why don't we sit down," Karen suggested. When Alice balked, she said, "We don't know the identity of his killer yet, Ms.... Miss Dutton."

As guarded as Kaylee never would be, Alice took a seat at the kitchen table covered with baby books and paraphernalia. "Very well. What do you want to know? I wasn't there that night."

No, Alice hadn't been. Her call to him had been from her landline. Karen doubted Alice owned a cell phone at all, though that might change, with Kaylee in the mix. Karen picked her words with care. "We have some questions for you, not about your nephew, but his stepfather. Ed Johnson."

Alice looked all her age now. "Why bring him up, after all this time?" Then she lifted a hand. "Sorry, that was... cowardly... of me." Her guarded gaze went to Marek, who quietly got up and left.

"Your detective is a good man. But... I can't talk about it, with him present." Alice clasped her hands together in her lap. "Nor do I want to go into the details. I know Ed is dead. I know how he died. I was glad."

Just as Zoe had been when she'd found Bunting dead. He was the boogeyman of her childhood. Or one of them. But Ed Johnson had been much, much worse. "He raped you."

"Yes. After he won the custody suit. And he made Robert watch. Poor Robert. He tried to help me, jumped on Ed's back, but he got knocked out, backhanded into the wall, and I didn't move after that. Just let him... finish his business."

Karen had been expecting the first, not the second. Poor Baby Bunting.

"Ed said no one would believe me, no more than a judge had believed me fit to be Robert's guardian. When I came in to work the next day, with my eye battered, without taking the time to dress right, Mr. Logan, my boss, he knew. He wanted me to press charges. I think, truly, he would have killed Ed if he'd gotten his hands on him. But Ed left Eda County that day, took a job elsewhere. And I didn't see Robert for a very long time."

"When he came back to live with you, to work for my father."

"And then he moved to the highway patrol. Where he discovered, to his horror, that one of his new colleagues was Ed Johnson." Alice sniffed. "But he got his comeuppance. Robert found some kind of evidence against Ed, and he told Ed that if he ever, ever touched another woman against her will, he'd make sure that it went to the authorities, and he'd be done. I wish Robert had just done that, not holding it back. I presume you're here to tell me that you found that evidence?"

"We did. Ed's duty shirt. He raped several women while in the patrol, including a Native American woman, which made it an FBI matter."

"I'm so sorry." Alice began stacking the books into a neat pile. "Perhaps if I'd been stronger... done what Mr. Logan wanted."

"You were the victim, Miss Dutton. Coming forward, at that time, with that judge? They'd have spun it as a revenge ploy, paying Ed back for preventing you from taking Robert."

Alice laid her hand on the top of a book, one with a smiling baby. "Ed never cared about Robert. He took him, he took me, because he could. And that was that. Don't let people tell you, Sheriff Mehaffey, that the old days were better. They weren't. A lot of things were swept under the rug. Terrible things. You work for a lawyer, you hear some awful stories, and for most victims, Mr. Logan had to tell them that, in court, they wouldn't stand a chance."

From the bedroom, Karen could hear the tinkling sound of a

lullaby from a mobile, and Kaylee's soft, guileless voice singing, off tune.

"Thank you for letting us know. None of this goes in a report if you don't want it to."

"Sweeping it under a rug? No, Sheriff. You write your report. Putting it in black and white, even if Ed is long dead, makes a mark that won't ever go away. I want it there."

Karen nodded and rose to her feet. She turned, then turned back. "Miss Dutton?"

Wearily, Alice looked up, as if the conversation had taken all she had to give. "Yes?"

"You might take that picture out of the drawer. Of you and Robert. He was, shall we say, not always a good man. He learned the lesson of leverage, not love, because of who raised him. But... he was also a hero. That's what you, and Kaylee, and her child, should remember."

And so would Karen.

CHAPTER 39

Back in the office, Karen flopped into her seat and ditched the remains of her share of a Mex-Mix takeout into the trash. Marek did the same. Both of them were off their feed. Forcing people to recall terrible things from their past did that. Though they'd closed an FBI case, they weren't any closer to closing their own.

As Walrus had just arrived back from his fender bender, he looked down at the trash with horror. "Couldn't you have offered that to a starving man?" When they both looked at him, he sighed. "Geez. Can't you take a joke? You know, laughter is good for the soul? And for your information, I haven't eaten since lunch. I'm like a hobbit. I'm used to elevenses and two-ishes and whatever the heck else."

Though she knew very well that Walrus was too heavy by any chart she'd ever consulted, he'd also passed his last physical with flying colors—which went to show that the universe wasn't fair. Her own numbers weren't as good.

The doors to the office swung open, and Two Fingers walked in. She'd texted him to say that she knew who the rapist was and, if he wanted to know more, she could tell him in person. Right now, he was about as readable as the petroglyphs of the Ancient Puebloans she'd had occasion to see... only last week?

"Ah... I should go." Walrus—who'd been eyeing the trash as if trying to decide if the twenty-second rule applied or was even greater, say a minute, since the food was still in its packaging—got to his feet.

"Stay," Two Fingers said without inflection.

Walrus plopped back down and looked as serious as he ever did. "I'm here for you. Always. Just let me know what I can do."

A kick up at one side of the mouth was all the response he got. Two Fingers waited.

Karen got to her feet. "Well, Deputy? Do you want to know the identity of the rapist? Or do you want to say it's done?"

"It's done. Long ago. I'm the result. But I want him found, I want him locked up, and I want my mother not to have to ever look over her shoulder again."

"I can grant that last wish," she told him.

Something undefinable, something that might have been hope, died. "Bunting."

"No, not Bunting. His stepfather. Ed Johnson."

With the brisk tones she'd been resorting to during pretty much the entire investigation, Karen told him the whole story while Walrus fidgeted in distress. He might occasionally be clueless, but Walter Russell was a man who would take the shirt off his back—or the duty shirt off the evidence table—to keep from causing hurt to a friend. She knew that Taylor Peterson had a new home, courtesy of Walrus, and his debts were covered by the ministerial fund, so he could keep his truck—and his livelihood. Not to mention his life.

Marek cleared his throat. "I don't know if you're interested, but Ed Johnson does have a younger half-sister you might want to meet, also a victim of his..."

"No. Sorry. No."

"Maybe she's got Indian blood," Walrus put in. "You never know."

Two Fingers raised his brows. "You want me to move back to the Rez?"

Walrus shook his head like a beached... walrus. "You're one of us. But... do you want to?"

Two Fingers tipped his head back, as if to allow some thought, some revelation, to trickle down. "Maybe." When he tilted it down, he saw their faces. "Someday. But while I'm welcome to work there, I'll never be a part of the tribe, and that's... hard." He smiled, a slash of white. "Here, I get to arrest white boys. More fun."

"That's profiling," Walrus said gruffly, cuffing him as he went by. A phone ringing made him stop. "If that's Laura, tell her I'm on my way."

Laura wouldn't be calling her unless Walrus had turned off his cell—or lost it, which he'd been known to do. Karen snatched up the receiver. "Sheriff Mehaffey here."

"Didn't answer your cell."

Larson. Frowning, Karen pulled the cell phone out of her pocket. "It's dead. Sorry. It's been a busy day."

"Make it busier," he told her. "Got a hit. Fingerprint."

That would be on Mountain Man's pocketknife and the putative murder weapon. Karen stuck her tongue in her cheek. "Name?"

"Connor."

That threw her off for a second. But the name was common enough. "First?"

"Archibald. Hell of a tag." He paused. "Mehaffey?"

No one used Archibald unless they wanted their nose bloodied. "He went by Chee, not Archibald," she managed. That brought Walrus up short and Marek's head around.

Larson's tone flat-lined. "You knew him."

She held her deputy's shocked gaze. "Yes, I did. A long time ago."

"Robbing the cradle?" Larson asked.

Like Marek, Chee Connor was four years her junior. Marek would have gone to school with him, in the same grade, up until high school. "No, nothing like that. What've you got on him?"

"Faxing now."

Almost with his last word, the fax machine revved. That must be a record. She tilted her head at Marek, who got there one Blunnie step ahead of Walrus, and snatched it up. Then he stared at it as if it were written in Greek.

"Chee fell off the radar years back," Karen told Larson.

"Any family?"

Karen rubbed at the bridge of her nose. "I'm on that. I'll get back to you."

For once, Karen hung up before he could. And she snatched the fax from Marek, while Walrus crowded her. Two Fingers, looking off balance, waited.

One felony arrest. Dealing opioids. Just like Kyle Early. The rest, a very long list, were misdemeanors. But they told of a life on the edge. Trespassing. Driving without a license. Failure to appear. Vagrancy. Lots of those. Mostly in California. Point to Akio Miles. It had become a crime to be homeless. Chee had done time in Nevada for his felony arrest. That had been a couple years back. Nothing since then.

Walrus looked stricken. "Geez. That'll kill Laura. She'd always hoped..."

That he would come home again. Apparently, he had.

Two Fingers went to stand beside Walrus. Not touching. But there. "This is Mountain Man?"

"I hate to say it, but it makes sense." Walrus's mustache quivered until he gnawed on it. "Connor's father was Laura's dad's first cousin. Eldest son of an eldest son. Never got over the family losing their lands to the county. Connor Creek, you know? Geez." He sank heavily into his chair. "Chee spent a lot of time with Laura's family, off and on, when his father was in the drunk tank. How do I tell her?"

"You don't. I do." Before he could protest, Karen picked up her landline and called her best friend—as a child, at least. Until she'd returned to Reunion from Sioux Falls a couple years ago, they'd only maintained the polite fiction of friendship. Of late, it'd been real again, and it had felt good. "Hi, Laura. It's Karen."

"Walter?" came the immediate and predictable reply.

"Fine. Physically. Laura... it's about Archibald Connor."

After a very long pause, she asked, "Chee? Is he... is he dead, then?"

Karen wished she could say yes, because that hurt, while sharp, would be quick and clean. "No, he's living in Grove Park. Or was, he—"

"Mountain Man? He's Mountain Man?" The alarm in her voice went five-bell. "I'll be right there." Before Karen could stop her, Laura hung up. "She's coming."

Walrus rubbed his bald pate. "Always was his defender. She'll go for your throat."

But when the other Twin Tower of Reunion—Karen's high school basketball partner—arrived through punched doors and with a full head of steam, Laura Connor Russell flew straight for her husband. She topped him by a couple inches, but it was hard to say who hugged whom or who took and gave comfort most. Probably both. Karen felt sorry for them, but she was also envious of the relationship, the kind where nothing else mattered, appearances be damned.

Finally, Laura pushed away, dashing tears, and went for Karen's throat. "You're wrong. Chee can't be Mountain Man. He'd never hurt anybody." When she got silence from her audience, her shoulders slumped. "Okay, yes, he killed people. In combat. And that does something to guys. I know that. He's got PTSD. The Army admitted that, at least, before they kicked him to the curb. But Walter tracked him for me, and he's never been violent. When Chee was locked up in Nevada, I tried to contact him. But he wouldn't answer my calls, my letters. And now..."

Karen decided that her friend was starting to absorb reality. "Tell me about him. I mean, all my memories are from when Chee was still a mop-haired kid, always trailing after us, wanting to be a part of whatever we were doing. We ran him off most of the time."

Laura's mouth twisted. "Remember we called him dirtbag, because he was always getting dirty? Or Peewee Chee because we looked down at him from our great height? Or Chee-bacca when he'd bawl if we left him eating our dust?"

Karen winced. So much for taking the high road with the wolves. "Kids are cruel."

"Believe me, I'm well aware," the elementary-school teacher said dryly. "When Chee came to live with us, he had no clue how to do so many things we just... knew. Mom really got on us, to help him, not mock him. He'd had it rough. Not violence. Just neglect after his mom died when he was eight. Dead poor, really. His father, Ham—short for Hamilton, I believe—could barely hold a hammer, much less his liquor, after she died. Chee lived with us when he was drying out. Months at a time. Ham died just before Chee went into the military at eighteen." Laura gave Karen a tight smile. "Following your lead."

Except he was enlisted, not an officer. Karen had been ROTC and a college grad. Bosnia had been her war—and while she'd been in the line of fire a few times, she'd never been in combat per se.

"Connor knew Ted?" Marek asked.

Laura bit her lip then nodded. "Chee was raised as a wild thing, practically, living in the trailer park but spending most of his time in the woods, ones that he felt were rightfully his own. That is, when he wasn't living with us. He and Ted were tight. He often said he wished he were an Indian."

Two Fingers said, "Funny how that works. You tried to make us all white with your boarding schools, your laws that we couldn't do our sacred dances. Now you're all trying to be Indian, claiming to be Cherokee princesses."

That had been said lightly, in jest, but it backfired. Though Laura looked like she'd walked straight off the boat from Ireland, Karen knew that was only part of the story.

With an amusement that had been lacking in her green-as-Ireland eyes, Laura smiled at Two Fingers. "I actually do. Truly. Documented. Mixed-blood daughter of a Scotsman and Cherokee woman. No princess, though. Family ended up in Oklahoma after surviving the Trail of Tears, got their land taken by a swindler, and decided to hightail it up to Dakota Territory. A daughter of the family married the first Archibald Connor, a hunter and trapper in our fair woods. Their grandson lost the woods when the county took them back in the 1940s—by nefarious means, according to family legend. The documents say back taxes owed."

"Same thing," Walrus muttered.

"When did Chee start to go wrong?" Karen asked.

"Not for a good long time," Walrus said. "Chee—or just Connor as he preferred by then, as he said Chee was just too cheesy—came to our wedding, all dressed in his Army finery. He'd passed boot camp with flying colors, and the girls swooned. I was half afraid Laura would decide to kiss her cousin, not me."

"Oh, he was dashing, but really more like a little brother. A little too close even for us backwater Connors." Laura patted her husband's beefy arm. "I'd been worried that growing up as Chee had, with little structure, would put him at odds with his superiors. Instead, he was promoted. Lots of accolades. Then… I think it was his third deployment. Iraq? No, I think that was Afghanistan. He came back after that with a shoulder injury, and… well, he was on prescription meds. They were going to ship him off again, and he went a little crazy. Next thing I know, he's out. Dishonorably discharged. That just about killed him. Three tours. Brutal, brutal years. And they trashed him like garbage."

And Laura had called Karen to see if she could do anything, if she had any connections. She'd contacted a military defense lawyer who'd said, basically, that PTSD might grant Chee another hearing, but it would be costly, and he'd never had a case successfully appealed. That had been before public backlash had turned the tide and PTSD came into the lingo.

Leaning back against her husband, Laura swept a hand through her red hair. "I know you have to look at him. I get that. But what reason would Connor have to kill Bunting?"

That was a stumper. But Karen had at least an idea. "I think he may have been living a fantasy... of having a family. There was this woman and her boy, and—shit. Ted."

"I beg your pardon?" her friend said in her best teacher-on-the-playground voice. Why did people say that when what they really meant was: you'd better beg my pardon for your language. Right now.

"Just a minute." Hoping this brainstorm hit the jackpot, unlike the last, Karen rushed up the stairs, nearly taking out a late-leaving legal clerk. She rushed to the judge's chambers, where she stopped herself at the door. Calm, collected, she knocked and was granted entrance.

Without preamble, she said, "We have Mountain Man. It's Archibald Connor."

"Ah. I see. A pity. I saw far too much of his father in my court. Do you need a warrant, perhaps?"

"No. I need to see the will."

He raised his brows. "Because?"

"Connor. Was he the trustee for Bobby's inheritance? Not Conway?"

The judge unlocked a drawer in his desk and pulled out the will. After a moment, he said, "Yes, I believe you are correct. Connor, at least. But the first name starts also with C and is quite short, so..."

"Chee. C-H-E-E."

"Very good. Yes. 'I do appoint and nominate Chee Connor to be trustee of said properties until said minor comes of age.' The rest, I believe, is outlining various scenarios. I can only believe that this was meant as a draft, awaiting a better hand."

But the hand he'd been dealt had come up death. At least he'd written the will beforehand.

The judge steepled his fingers. "Speaking of the said property, as the current trustee, perhaps future trustee, as well, you might like to know that I am reviewing all relevant applications for return to the trailer park."

Thank God for Marsha Schaeffer. "Thank you, Judge."

"You know very well whom to thank. I believe you had a hand

in her plea. But as justice and charity align in this respect, I find myself inclined toward magnanimity." Seeing Karen fidgeting, he inclined his head. "Go. Find your killer."

Karen fled back downstairs, to be grilled. By all but Marek. And he was the one who said calmly, and correctly, "Chee Connor was named as trustee of the trailer park."

"Right. Ted knew he was back. He would have asked Connor first before making the will. And that means Connor knew that there was a will, or supposed to be one, even if not yet written. What if Bunting approached him, used the will as leverage, to get a piece of that park?"

"That's a motive," Marek finished.

A heated argument looked to ensue, until the phone rang. Karen snatched it up, hoping it was Larson again, with more forensics. But it wasn't.

"I've seen him. Mountain Man. In the park."

Karen had to backtrack. The voice was familiar. Barely. "Mr. Biester?"

"Yes. Sorry. I... I just ran back so I could call. I think we can set a trap for him, if you want."

She wanted.

CHAPTER 40

H UNCHED DOWN NEAR THE TOP of the trail that led to the abandoned encampment, Karen cursed the rain gods. Silently. If the storm hadn't prevented helicopter backup, they'd have Connor, and she wouldn't be trying to squat in the woods because she'd be swept down into the creek along with the runoff if she sat down. The moon, playing tease, kept flirting with them, on and off.

Marek shifted beside her, even more uncomfortable, she guessed, because of his bad ankle. Biester, on the other hand, seemed to not even notice. Why had she agreed to this?

Because she wanted it done. Impatient. That had always been the tag on her. She liked to think of it as being decisive. Now? Just stupid. If Connor was back in the woods, he would likely still be there in the morning. Of course, the whole plan to snare him was based on the cover of night, which thankfully, came much earlier than it had in the dog days of summer.

"The whole thing about a snare," Biester had told them as he outlined the strategy at his residence, "is that you place it where the animal will be—on their regular trail."

And Biester had seen Mountain Man walking away from the earth berm, which was built so that the rain was funneled around it. A smart move, really: take residence in the place everyone thought you'd abandoned for the open road. Long gone, she'd assumed. Off to collect more misdemeanors... unless and until her BOLO hit the airwaves, the websites, and the fax machines across the country.

Just as Karen was about to scream mercy and call it a night, Biester cocked his head and raised a finger to his mouth—which she could barely see as the moon was veiled. She'd heard noises ever since they'd squatted in place, so she wasn't sure what made this one any different.

Quietly, Biester fished into his jacket and pulled out his phone. She started to shake her head, worried it would make some sound to alert their prey. Then Biester took something else out of another pocket and, with a faint click, attached it to the phone and powered it up. The display of his phone showed them a grainy but surprisingly well-detailed picture of the muck. Cool. An IR attachment. They'd be able to see Connor even if the moon was behind clouds.

Karen as much felt as heard Marek's quick intake of breath beside her. He nodded at the IR light—the low but distinct glow of red.

An evil eye.

Mary Johnson wasn't mental. She'd seen a light that night. Biester's IR light.

Karen went cold. Biester had been *here*. Not in Sioux Falls as he claimed. The click in Karen's head was so loud, she was surprised Biester didn't hear it. So he'd been here, likely taking video of the encampment as evidence, but... what did that mean? Why hide it, unless he was a killer? But why would he kill Bunting? Seeing her expression, Marek turned over one hand and mimed a hovering insect.

"Drone?" she mouthed.

He nodded then pointed at the soles of his boots.

Boots?

He mouthed, "Glass."

And that did it. The evening before the murder, the drone had taken off from the park entrance, which was clear of any glass, metal, or plastic from a destroyed trail monitor. Yet by dawn the next morning, Walrus had picked it up in his boots. With his wireless phone connection, Biester would have been able to monitor the entrance that night—perhaps he even had an alert set up for any tampering. The soon-to-be-homeless Bunting, perhaps intending to scope out new digs in the encampment, might well have destroyed the entrance camera when he'd come back from the recount—and some kind of confrontation later ensued between the two men in the park, leaving Bunting dead. It all clicked.

Anger surged through her. If true, Biester had set up a sting operation, not just once, but twice. They'd been had. He'd helped them set up a snare for Connor—within a larger trap for them. And they'd walked right into it.

Perhaps realizing he'd lost their attention, Biester turned and looked at his frozen companions then down at what they were staring at—his camera. Potential evidence. "Shit."

Stealth forgotten, Karen leapt to her feet and fished for her gun with one hand while extending the other. "Can we see that phone, Mr. Biester?"

The moon came out in full force—and she saw the answer. He threw the phone as far as he could. She thought she heard a plop as it fell in water. Please, God, not the creek.

Then Biester ran.

A slow-rising Marek tried to stop him and got bowled over for his pains. Karen was swifter, but Biester knew the layout better. By the time she reached the trail that led down to the encampment, she could see he'd made his way nearly to the bottom, heading for the log bridge.

"Stop! Freeze!" she yelled. "I will shoot!"

But as she stepped onto the trail to get a good shot, she slid right down on her butt.

Right into a gully washer.

Her gun skittered out of her hand to God knew where. Cursing, she saw that she'd stepped on a long piece of bark—no doubt from one of those damned bur oaks of Biester's. Rough on one side, smooth as a baby's butt on the other. Wait. Smooth. Gully washer.

Grabbing the bark, she flipped the smooth side down, jumped up, and jumped on. As she'd hoped, her weight and the rushing water combined to propel her down the mud-slick trail. Mudboarding. Despite everything, she felt a rush. Her luck held out until the last few yards, when she hit a rock, and the bark broke in two underneath her. Using her momentum, she launched herself at Biester's back.

He rolled before she could grab his slick wrists and her cuffs... and she found herself looking down the barrel of a Sig Sauer.

CHAPTER 41

A S SHE SQUATTED THERE IN the mud, her muscles screaming, her mind racing, she could hear Marek crashing down the trail behind her. Slipping and sliding, a gentle bear of a man on the warpath.

"Call for backup!" she yelled, knowing her death was inevitable. "He's got a—"

Before she could finish, Biester pulled the trigger. The flash of fire. The hurt, oh God, the hurt. Her heart burst.

Because it wasn't her he'd aimed at. After a hoarse cry, a thud... and silence.

And she was next. She saw the feral smile, the calculating gleam, as death awaited. He'd talked about that awareness, the edge that the prospect of death gave to life, knowing you were prey, and she felt every beat of her heart. Last beats. He would have to look in her eyes. If he had even a shred of conscience, she hoped that would haunt him for the rest of his sorry life.

She saw the flash. She heard the cry.

But the flash had been from moonlight on gleaming metal, not from a gun. A knife? Relief flooded her. She whirled. "Marek?"

But as a cloud shifted to unveil the full light of the moon, she saw a tall, almost ethereal bearded figure. For a long, incredulous moment, she thought, *So I'm dead.* And this was what Saint Peter looked like. Like Gandalf. Or Treebeard, more fittingly, in the forest. Except... he wore camos.

Chee Connor. She had no words. They'd gone with her heart.

And in the silence, a man groaned. The wrong man. "Biester's not dead?"

"I was trained to kill," Chee told her. "But I got tired of it. I hit what I meant. Disabling strike to the shoulder."

Ignoring all her training, Karen tossed her cuffs at Connor and raced up the trail, grabbing tree branches to keep from falling. Marek lay a third of the way up. Unmoving. His gun was still in his hand.

Oh, God. He'd been shot in the head. She couldn't find where to staunch the flow. Lots of blood. Her hand was black with it.

"Take... Becca."

She stared at the slits of pale moonlight that were his eyes— until they closed with finality. "No! No, by God, no! I won't take her." She shook him. "Do you hear me, Marek? Talk to me!"

But all she heard were sirens approaching, then the screech of tires. Two Fingers had been stationed at the entrance to keep campers out. Marek must've called for backup before rushing to her aid. Something she should have done. Choices. Hers. Very, very bad.

They needed an ambulance ASAP. Where was her damned phone? Dead. She'd left it plugged in at the office, not wanting it to go off while they were setting the trap.

When the flashlight caught her full in the face, she yelled, "Call for an ambulance! Now!"

Behind her, Connor shouted up, "Too late!"

Karen cried out her denial. "No. It's bad. I know it's bad, but... he talked."

"Too late because I called for one already," Connor replied as he walked up to her. And to her shock, he held up a flip phone. "For emergencies. I have a solar charger to keep it charged. Dialing 9-1-1 always works."

Closing her eyes, Karen ran her fingers, slick with blood, over Marek's throat. And there, yes, there it was. A beat. Her fingers kept track as she willed the beats to continue.

As Two Fingers arrived, with more nimbleness than her as

she heard no slip or slide, she didn't look up. But she told him, in a reed-thin voice that she didn't recognize as her own, to watch their prisoner until the second ambulance arrived. And to find Biester's phone and its IR attachment—and her gun. In that order.

Not until the EMTs lifted Marek, with the help of Connor, onto the backboard, did she move her hand. She felt, somehow, that by releasing him, she'd doomed him. That only her will had kept him alive.

"Give me your keys," Connor said as the ambulance sped off.

"What?"

He held out a hand. "You're parked in the campground. I saw it earlier."

Of course he had. She fished out the keys then stared down at her fingers, at the blood. "I can drive." But she couldn't get her legs to move.

He just swiped the keys from her hand. "I'll be back in a jiffy." He loped up a trail and disappeared. A moment later, he reappeared in the Sub. "Trash ride," he commented as she finally got her legs to work and got in.

"It started. Often doesn't." Leaning over, Karen punched the sirens. "Just go."

He did. And within a span of minutes that seemed like years, she was standing beside Marek's gurney at the clinic. Doc Hudson had left him there, in the hallway, to attend Biester.

Karen had almost called Nikki, to let her know...but it was too late to make that call.

Hands in her back pockets, Karen knew the moment that awareness hit those pale-blue eyes. His face tightened, and he turned his head, even though it must've hurt.

She rounded the gurney. "Oh, no, you don't. Look at me, Marek." She trapped his head between her hands. "I'll take Becca if that's what you want. Though after tonight, you might want to rethink that. Nikki, even Dad and Clara, not to mention your New Mexico friends and family, might be better. Whatever you want, though. We'll do it up right and tight."

"Why...?" he croaked.

"Because I wanted you to fight!" Karen leaned down and hugged what she could, letting the relief, the tears, flow out onto his chest, where his heart beat steadily. "My God, Marek. I thought you were slipping away from me."

"Slipped..." He put a hand to his head. "Ouch."

"Concussion and laceration." She dashed her knuckles under her eyes. "Lots of blood."

"Can see that." He was looking at her hands. "Yours?"

"No, yours. You scared me to death."

Marek moved his head again, as if testing to make sure it was still attached. "Biester?"

"Chee Connor to the rescue. I lost my gun when I slipped. Connor nailed him with a knife. A little kiddie knife, if you can believe it. But he knew where to hit. Entire arm went numb. Doc Hudson is patching Biester up, Walrus is sitting on him, and I'm heading over to the office to talk to Connor. And I need to check with Two Fingers to see if he found Biester's phone. That's going to be key. Without you there, I want all the ammunition I can get against Biester, assuming he doesn't cry lawyer."

Marek gripped the sides of the gurney and pulled himself up.

"Hey, don't you dare—" she started, but he'd already swung his legs over. "No. Just, no. You nearly..."

"Didn't die," he finished.

Doc Hudson came in, stripped off bloodied gloves, and took a penlight to Marek's eyes. "Hard head. No obvious signs of subdural hematoma. I'd like to keep you over for observation..." As Marek slid his feet to the floor, he sighed. "But I'll have to settle for second best. Sheriff, be sure to keep him awake."

"Not a problem," she returned. "I'll slap him silly."

But Marek didn't sway, didn't even stumble, as he shook himself out like a dog.

With a sigh, Karen asked, "How's your patient?"

"My cooperative patient? He'll live. You can have him in an hour or so. Enough time for the two of you to get cleaned up. Thought I'd been invaded by a pack of zombies."

Karen looked down at her sodden, muddied, and bloodied self. Then at Marek. And she laughed. A real, unbridled laugh, like she hadn't done in… days? "That's a prescription that I promise we'll be filling."

CHAPTER 42

B Y THE TIME KAREN ARRIVED back at the courthouse with Marek, they weren't the only ones who'd cleaned up. A strangely familiar stranger awaited them, sitting in Walrus's chair, Laura's hand on his shoulder as she sat on Walrus's desk.

They turned together, rose together. Talk about the Twin Towers. Like his cousin, Connor had once had flaming-red hair. Unlike her darker titian, his had become more pepper, with plenty of salt. A hard life had left its marks. But in his steady eyes, the color of fall acorns, she saw something that she hadn't in most of the homeless: a deep well of acceptance—of himself, mostly, that led to acceptance of others. She saw no desperation, no bitterness, nothing but the moment. Good or bad, he'd take it.

Connor smiled at Marek. "Now that's a treat. Guess you're not at death's door."

Karen had texted Laura that an early Christmas present was arriving at the courthouse in her Sub. And that Marek was going to live. But nothing more. She'd had too much else to do.

So, too, had Laura, apparently. "You took Connor home?"

"He looked about a hundred years old and was twice as ripe." Laura bumped his arm. "Greybeard."

"Always was bossy," he said, fingering his beardless chin.

His filthy camos were gone, probably burned. Where Laura

had gotten him the jeans and sweatshirt, though, Karen had no clue. Neither Walrus nor any of their boys were of that build— though the younger boys might eventually get there. In another decade or so. Karen assumed that the boys were with their grandfather.... ah. That might well be the source of the clothes, though she had never seen the local jeweler slumming in jeans before.

Laura fisted her hands on her hips with mock outrage. "I was right. He wasn't your killer."

Echoing her friend's stance and tone, Karen bit out, "You are so right." She dropped her fists. "He was the hero of the piece."

For the first time, that self-acceptance slipped, to show scars that Karen thought would never truly heal. "I'm no hero."

"I beg to differ." Karen went tippy-toed to kiss him lightly on his newly bared cheek. "For my life, I thank you."

"And mine," Marek said, holding out his hand.

"Never thought to see you again in Reunion." Connor held his former classmate's hand for a long moment. "I missed you, you know, on the Island of Misfit Toys."

Karen lifted an eyebrow at Laura, who shrugged. That must be a reference to the broken toys looking for a home in *Rudolph the Red-Nosed Reindeer*. Both boys, broken, in different ways. A broken brain. A broken home.

Marek dropped his hand. "Misfits united. We'll need your testimony against Biester."

"I didn't see him kill Bunting. I'd have told you."

"But you saw him try to kill me, to kill Marek," Karen followed up. Enough sentiment. They would all be blubbering soon, and Biester would mud-board right over them.

Laura slapped her hands over her ears. "Lalalala. I didn't hear that. Go do your stuff. I'll wait for Walrus. Oh, and, Chee... I mean, Connor? Taylor Peterson's got the granny flat for now, but we've got a spare room for you."

"I don't need—"

"You are not going back to Grove Park. Not tonight. Not any night, if I have anything to do with it." She squeezed him until he cried uncle. "You are so... loved. Now go give the law what they need. Then I can put all my boys to bed." She pushed him toward the interview room, and Marek followed. After a second's hesitation, Karen sent a quick text then pocketed her phone.

When she closed the interview door behind her, Karen asked the first thing that popped into her head. "Why didn't you return Laura's calls, her letters, when you were in Nevada?"

The curse of his fair coloring was, of course, the dreaded flush that turned redder than the pepper in his hair. "I'd think that was pretty obvious. I was ashamed. Of what I'd done. What I'd become. That she bothered to keep track of me at all, though, was an eye-opener. That someone out there in the world was for me, not against me. I didn't think I had any family left, not the Army, not the Connors. I wanted to be worthy of that, if I ever returned."

"So where were you, after Nevada?" Marek asked.

"Here and there. Still homeless. But I no longer feared it. I did a lot of reading, of soul-searching, of talking to other veterans. I chucked all the meds, all the shrinks, and hooked up with a veterans group that did the Pacific Coast Trail. A sort of Mother-Nature-heals kind of thing. I was skeptical, given my track record, that I could be helped, that anything was worth saving. But I'd been happy, truly happy, when I was free to roam the woods as a kid, in the woods I always believed had been stolen from us Connors. So I figured that was going to be my last shot. If it didn't work... well, there was always the last shot."

Marek ran a fingernail down a joint in the table. "It worked."

"Somehow, someway, by the time my buddies and I made it to the end, I felt... like I'd come home. I don't know how else to describe it. I wasn't the only one. We bonded, but not really with each other, but with our true selves. Who we had been, who we could be again. Afterward, we all went our separate ways."

"Was Mountain Man your trail name?" Marek asked.

"No wonder you ended up a detective." Amusement crinkled Connor's eyes. "You ever read *The Seven Storey Mountain*?"

"Monks?" Karen hazarded, snagging a stray memory. Connor certainly had the life of poverty down pat.

"*A* monk. Thomas Merton. His autobiography. A battered hardback no one else wanted from the prison library in Nevada. Big, thick book. I figured I could use it to beat off any attackers. I put my nose in it, and by the time I stuck it out, I'd done my time. The mountain referred to purgatory. Seemed appropriate. Not that I was really a mountain man. I preferred the small woods, the long view, of our lands."

"So you came back home," Karen said. "But you met with Ted, not Laura, when you came back. Why?"

He cast a guilty look through the closed door. "It wasn't intentional. I ran into Ted in the woods. He recognized me, gave me a big hug, asked me how I was doing. We had a long talk. Several of them, actually. I didn't want to come back to Reunion, to family, until I could trust myself to stay clean."

Karen leaned forward. "Do you know what's in Ted's will? It involves Bobby and you, I know that much, but Ted had atrocious handwriting."

He looked startled. "I thought he didn't write the will, though we talked about it."

"He wrote it. Digges found it. He took it to Bunting to ask if it was valid. No witnesses, so he said no, but Judge Rudibaugh says it's legal."

"Ah... I see now why you might have questions for me." A rueful look crossed Connor's face. "Yes, I know what Ted intended, at least generally. He was very fond of Bobby—and it's not hard to figure out why. He's got an innocence to him, a purity, that so many of us lack. Ted was adamant that Alan Digges not get his hands on the trailer park. 'Bad seed,' was all he said when I asked why. Obviously, he didn't trust his nephew. At all. He thought about giving the park to Bobby's mother, Lori. Seemed no matter how hard she tried, she just kept going backward. But she didn't have a head for business." He pulled at his ear. "Before I went off the wagon, I got a solid base in business on the Army's dime. That's what I was going to do—start my own business. Something like whitewater rafting or working as a trail guide. Anything outdoors. I wanted to work for myself, since I didn't think anyone would hire me, with the black marks on my record."

The dishonorable discharge was the blackest. Karen wondered if, once his heroism hit the airwaves, whether she could get the Army to take another look. If she ever had the time. "So... Ted made you the trustee? What did you get out of the deal?"

"I believe I talked him down to ten percent of profit. I don't need much. And if I've gauged Lori Jansen right, she wants to work. Needs to work. It's her makeup. So while I might do the books, deal with the administration, profits and losses, she'd likely be out there doing what she did with her own trailer. Planting stuff, making a home. Fixing whatever she can and bartering for what she can't. And you're making a face at me, Karen. It's not sexist. It's what she does. It's why Bobby, for all that's happened, is what he is. Secure. Loved."

Marek said, "You seem to have made your own home at Grove Park."

"Yeah, I got a thrill out of making my own way on the old Connor lands."

"With the help of Biester's blind eye toward your poaching," Karen pointed out.

"Ah. Yes. He caught me at it. We got talking. Whatever he's done, whatever he tried to do, he knew how to live off these lands, appreciated them, wanted to preserve them." A deep sadness touched Connor's acorn eyes. Memories squirreled away. "We also had some good talks."

"Until Biester tried to frame you?" Karen prompted when he fell silent.

"Yeah. Until. Which I found out, apparently, just after you did. I thought he was in Sioux Falls that night. He let it be known far and wide so no one would be alarmed."

Alarmed. That was the word. Karen shook her head. "Biester *was* in Sioux Falls. Until he returned after midnight with a new trail monitor at the park entrance and his new IR attachment for his phone, so he could prove the identities of those in the encampment and get me to do something about it." And the thought that if she had, none of this would have happened, twisted her stomach. "He was afraid the state park board wouldn't get on board until that was done."

Connor still looked puzzled. "But why kill Bunting?"

"We hope to find out from the horse's mouth. All we know for sure is, one of the homeless saw the IR light. Evil eye, she called it. That's what finally clicked for us. When we were setting a trap for you, Biester was setting one for us. We're just hoping that his phone can be found." When she saw a blank look on Mountain Man's face, she clarified. "Biester had a wireless video feed set up. We've got good towers now. But he may well have deleted the good stuff, though maybe DCI can recover it. But... I heard a plop. Water. Not good."

Connor scratched at his shorn head. "You guys make me feel old. All this technology." He'd been living without it. Like Walden. Well, other than the emergency phone.

"And you make us feel frivolous."

"Why didn't you just come out from the get-go?" Marek asked.

"I've tried to stay away from your kind. Better for all of us."

"But you were in the woods that night?"

Connor nodded. "Caught a rabbit in a snare. I don't like to let them suffer long, if I can help it. When you live off your catch, you learn to be tuned to it. When I got there, I saw a man on the road, older, but he turned and went in the direction of the campground." That was Gus Farley out for a late-night walk. "I took the rabbit back to the lean-to to skin. Lots of arguing, drama in the parking lot, but I didn't know about Bunting's death until you did the next morning."

"No wonder I felt that itch between the shoulder blades. You were watching." Karen frowned at him. "Where were you, later, when we combed the woods?"

"In the creek."

She frowned at him. "But the tracks... ah. You doubled back.

We'll have to give Walrus grief over that. But why didn't we see you? The creek's not that deep."

He shivered. "Hid in the cattails and used snake grass to breathe through when I heard you all tromping around. Ever been nibbled on by carp? It tickles."

Getting down to business, they ran through the night's drama, for the record.

CHAPTER 43

WHEN THE THREE OF THEM eventually emerged, Karen found Walrus and Bobby playing tabletop football with wadded BOLOs. Looking like a rag doll flung into a corner, Lori was in Karen's chair, head back, either asleep or pretending to be.

Bobby hooted. "Touchdown!"

"You're too good at this," Walrus grumbled good-naturedly before looking up. "Ah, salvation. About time. Madden here was trouncing me."

Bobby flushed as he took in the tall stranger. He got to his feet and started forward. Then he stopped, until Connor broke the impasse. "Yes, it's me, Bobby. Mountain Man. Chee Connor. Most just call me Connor."

Bobby lurched forward, and Connor caught him in a bear hug.

When he was released, Bobby beamed up at him. "Mom said we had to come back to the Sheriff's Office 'cause there was a good surprise waiting."

Connor ruffled his hair. "Well, I hope I'm some of that, but that's not all of it."

But Bobby had turned on Karen and Marek, his face as fierce as only a child wronged could be. "I was right about Mountain Man... Mr. Connor."

"Yes, you were. I was wrong. Adults often are." Karen glanced at the rag doll, whose eyes had miraculously slitted open. "Even when they're trying their best."

But Bobby wasn't finished. "You told my mom that she was a killer."

"No, I tried to find out *if* she was a killer," Karen corrected. "That's my job, to find killers. She passed that test with flying colors."

"News to me," Lori muttered as she slid herself up in the chair. Like her son, she suddenly looked uncertain, and Karen thought she knew why. Mountain Man cleaned up well. Would the fantasy family that Karen had dreamed up as Connor's motivation for the attack on Lori become reality? The two of them were going to be thrown together at least for a time over managing the trailer park.

The heavy tread of footsteps ended the fraught silence, and the side door opened.

Judge Rudibaugh emerged in his black robes, and out of instinctual respect, anyone not already standing, immediately did so. Commissioner Dahl entered on his heels.

The judge took in the tableau and correctly assigned the players to the proper slots. "Sheriff, Detective, congratulations on being rescued. I hear it was a close thing. Finding your replacements would have been costly."

Talk about a backhanded slap. Nails must have gotten the story from the EMTs. The only surprise was that the judge listened to the radio, unless one of his clerks had been the messenger.

But she wasn't to know, as the judge turned to Chee. "Mr. Connor? As their rescuer, you are to be congratulated on saving the county endless amounts of aggravation, time, and money." Finally, the judge looked down his bulbous nose at his youngest target. "And you, young man, would be Robert Jansen."

His mother glued to his side, the boy gulped. "Yes, sir. Bobby."

"Your Honor," his mother coached, her face showing every ounce of her anxiety. Judges held an inordinate amount of power over the poor. A minor traffic ticket that most could pay and then drive off could land them in jail, often for good long chunks of time, in a downward spiral.

"Your Honor," Bobby repeated.

"You knew Ted Jorgenson."

The boy's bottom lip trembled. "He was awesome."

The judge's brows rose. "Ted Jorgenson was certainly a most estimable man. Except for his handwriting, that is." The judge glanced at Karen. "I believe I have now deciphered the whole will." His eyes dropped back down. "You, young man, have been given a gift—and a weighty responsibility. You will one day have the fate of others in your hands, never something to take lightly."

Bobby looked more confused than anything. "Did Ted leave me his gun? Or a knife?"

The brows rose higher. "No, though that is a good guess. I am glad to hear you understand that those are not items to be carried lightly."

So Lori hadn't told her son about the trailer park. She probably thought it was all bull, a tactic, no more. But the growing hope on the woman's face told Karen that what Lori wouldn't take from her, she would from the judge. But would she take it from Ted?

As if making his own assessment of the dynamics, Judge Rudibaugh placed his hands in his robe arms, all black, all serious, as he looked down at Bobby. "I knew Ted Jorgensen very well. We differed somewhat in our viewpoints on justice or mercy, but I never once doubted his very real concern about what would happen to his tenants when he died. He thought of them, perhaps in an outmoded paternalistic way, as his responsibility. He helped many, here and there, in some known and many unknown ways, to get their feet under them, to give them a rock to stand on—a home. You know what it feels like to lose yours. Alan Digges was not, as Ted apparently knew and that I discovered, alas, too late, the proper individual for that trust. Ted decided to leave the trailer park to you, in the trust of Mr. Connor and with the help of your mother."

While Lori appeared frozen, Bobby's nose wrinkled. "You mean... we get our trailer back?"

The judge cleared his throat. "Perhaps I should ask, young man, what you wish to be when you reach your majority." He got silence. "When you grow up."

"Oh. A graphic artist. I want to do animations for Disney." He bit his lip. "Or be a baseball player."

"I see. Well, normal enough for a boy your age. However, I would guess the first, and probably the second, require some postsecondary education." He paused. "College."

Lori looked far more excited about that prospect than her son, who made a face. "Oh. I guess. Maybe."

"The profits from the trailer park will enable you to do so without going into debt. Always something to avoid wherever possible. When you turn twenty-one, you will need to decide whether to run the trailer park yourself, to turn it over to your mother and Mr. Connor or some other combination thereof, or to sell it. You, or the trustee until your majority, will be deciding who gets to stay and who goes in the trailer park."

Bobby looked anxiously up at the judge. "Mr. Connor? We can give him a trailer?"

Before the judge could comment, Connor shook his head. "That's not how it works, Bobby. You need to make a profit."

"Ted gave us the trailer park," Bobby pointed out with perfect logic.

"And he's no longer in need of the profit. But you are. I expect growing boys cost a fortune in food, if I recall my own years." Connor's bittersweet smile told Karen that he'd often gone without.

"Ain't that the truth," Laura, the mother of three boys, muttered.

Harold Dahl cleared his throat. "We have a different proposition for Mr. Connor's housing."

Lori looked alarmed. "You're not putting him jail!"

"I sincerely hope not," the commissioner said. He looked at Karen, got her shake of the head, then he looked back at

Connor. "The county commissioners voted just now to pull the application with the state parks board for Grove Park."

Connor's face fell. "Why? I never had a problem with Biester's goal."

"We decided to offer the job of park manager to someone who might have a bit of trouble with the state's background check."

Connor looked stunned.

With a whoop of delight, Laura hugged her cousin then spun him around until he looked dizzy. "Connor lands—finally, back in Connor hands."

But her cousin, once released, held up a hand. "I have one condition."

Dahl looked taken aback. "What's that?"

"That you replace the vault toilet at the overlook."

Dahl gave him a pained look. "The park fund was pretty much depleted for the upgrades at the campground." But when Connor didn't so much as a blink, he sighed. "Done."

And that, apparently, was how you got things out of Dahl. You threatened to quit before you even got started. Too bad Karen had already burned that bridge and said yes without conditions.

Of course, she could still threaten to quit. But right now, he would see right through her ruse. Why had she taken this job, again?

Because of payoffs like that.

And the payoff to come, as Walrus finally entered with his sling-armed prisoner in tow. Two Fingers followed on his heels, holding up an evidence bag with a phone in it.

CHAPTER 44

MAREK'S HEAD HURT. AND HIS butt. All he wanted was to go home, retrieve Becca from Arne so he could hug her close enough to feel her heart against his, then invite Nikki over for a nightcap—or possibly more. He even wanted to get licked to death by his gun-shy dog.

But none of that would happen until they turned the key on Biester.

The former park manager seemed remarkably calm, though mildly stoic, as if merely awaiting release from the dentist chair. And that made Marek frown. A sane person facing murder charges and two attempted murder charges on police officers would usually be shaking in his booties. Either that, or asleep. He'd encountered the latter once or twice. They all knew the outcome.

With the formalities out of the way, Marek wasn't sure if he was pleased that Biester hadn't immediately cried for a lawyer, which was what he'd expected. No going home just yet.

Standing to the side of Marek's chair, Karen started the interview. They'd decided that might keep him off balance. "Mr. Biester, we are aware that, instead of staying in Sioux Falls last Friday night, you set up a sting operation to capture the evictees on camera."

His ruddy face reddened slightly. "If you'd done your job, none of this would've happened."

"If you'd waited, I would have done my job," Karen countered. "I had a few minor things to deal with in the last month, like an election loss with a side salad of murder, then a job hunt with same, only to come home to yet another homicide." Karen put her hands on the table and leaned into Biester's space. "You should've taken your pictures and left. Why didn't you?"

He lifted his chin, his square face set. "I tried to, but Bunting attacked me. Pure self-defense. Just like tonight. You both go batshit crazy on me, accusing me of murder of all things, when I was trying to help you with the *real* murderer, who you're treating like a returning hero. Typical small-town myopia. Just because you knew Connor, not me, I'm the bad guy? I had a right to protect myself. I only pulled the gun to stop you. That's all. No harm, no foul. I'm the one who got hurt."

A long night ahead, Marek thought. Or not. He pulled out the evidence bag with the phone.

Biester didn't bother to deny it was his. "So? I have a phone. That's not working. Another thing to add to a lawsuit for false arrest that will bankrupt this county."

"Make sure it's for the full value of the phone," Karen told him. "Because you apparently forgot that it's top-of-the-line."

"What does that have to do with..." Biester trailed off as Marek swiped the phone alive.

"It's waterproof," Captain Obvious—in the person of herself—gloated. "Play it again, Sam."

Marek started the video he'd queued up. Biester slumped as the chaotic scene unfolded.

On the trail, Bunting was barreling toward the encampment, intent unknown. But halfway down, he stopped, his head turning directly toward the camera lens, no doubt alerted by the red IR light. Then he changed direction toward the camera and charged.

The video continued. "What the hell are you doing?" Bunting demanded, trying to grab the phone, his sausage-sized fingers not quite quick enough as Biester pulled it out of reach.

"A present for the new sheriff," Biester returned.

Marek paused the video. "Despite pretending otherwise on the next morning, you knew that Bunting had lost the recount."

Head in hands, Biester nodded. "I heard it on the radio when I passed Reunion."

Marek hit play. Biester was still speaking. "Taking out the trail monitor I just installed at the entrance? Stupid. You're screwed."

They'd found that recording on the phone, as well. And that explained what Bunting had seen when on the phone with his aunt: the new trail monitor, just waiting to catch him evading the entrance fee. The last straw, he'd said. He'd used his nightstick on the trail monitor. All very damning. If only Biester had left it at that.

On the video, Bunting lunged for the phone as if it were a smoking gun—which it was. There was a tussle, a hand closed over the phone and its attachment, and the camera spun then hit ground, but the audio still worked. Bunting's throwing arm was weaker than a Ramen noodle. The audio still picked up the low, intense tones that hadn't carried all the way down to the encampment.

"Good luck finding your phone in this thicket," Bunting said. "But it doesn't matter. You want to clear the park? I can still do that for you. Only this time, it's going to cost you. Five hundred a month and a blind eye toward the earth berm, where I'll live and keep watch, earn you a trash-free state park."

Biester's response was quick. "Yes, I'll have the last."

A pause. "Well, okay, then—"

"I'll have the trash out of my park. You included. I don't take bribes. And the idea of you staying in that earth berm that Mountain Man built—that's just laughable. You wouldn't last a day, not now, certainly not come winter."

"I've survived worse," Bunting returned. "Much worse. And you're no saint. You want the county commissioners to hear what I dug up on you, Mr. High and Mighty Park Manager? You got fired from your last job. Got a little too aggressive with a tourist who crowded a bison calf that had to be put down.

Looks like the pot calling the kettle black. All I wanted out of this backwater county was a nice retirement job—and that's what you've got here. I want part of it."

A long silence ensued. Finally, Bunting spoke. "Yeah, that's what I thought. You won't get a better deal. Have the money for me by tomorrow. I gotta eat. And not rabbits."

Bunting must have turned his back, because there was an intake of air, a strangled sound, then a surprisingly soft thud. A minute later, something that sounded heavy was dragged away. Then the battery gave out, and the recording ended. Biester had obviously come back, found both phone and attachment in good shape, and instead of getting rid of them, he'd kept them and played clueless.

The pocketknife, though, was likely at the bottom of Connor Creek. He wasn't *that* stupid.

"Self-defense?" Karen challenged, putting her hands on the table. "Bullshit."

Biester started to cross his arms then winced. "He was threatening me. You heard him. I put my hand in my pocket, found my Swiss Army knife, and got it ready. I was within my rights there, defending myself. Just like I was with the tourist—some idiot with connections in DC, that's all. My supervisors took my side. But might makes right, and I was out."

Marek's head ached. "Survival of the fittest?"

"That's all that there is. All there ever was. When I stuck my knife into Bunting's back, I didn't think. I just acted. And you know what? After the shock wore off, I was elated. Like a weight had been lifted that I hadn't known was there. All those years living constricted by rules. I'd become one with the wild, just as we're meant to be. Bunting got it. Might makes right. I had the might, so I was in the right."

Marek wondered if that was how Biester would live with himself, with what he'd done. "Why attack Lori?"

Biester shrugged. "That wasn't personal. I didn't even know it was her, just that I was on the brink, the very cusp, of getting the park clear. When I realized someone was coming down the trail, I jumped them, intending to make sure they never returned. Then she started screaming, and Mountain Man came flying. Then Donahue."

Karen's lips pursed. "But Connor was the hero, not you."

His square face tightened. "Heroes are another name for the winner."

"That makes us the winners, not you," Karen needled him.

"Only a desperate throw by a washed up vet, a chance hit, made it so. Otherwise I'd have been the winner."

Marek asked, "You were going to blame it all on Connor? Our deaths?"

"Why not? I was the fittest to survive. The people in the trailer park? In the wild, they'd be dead, picked off by predators or by their own—or subservient. Not the ones reproducing. If Hitler hadn't messed up eugenics, we could have a much better citizenry. No more poor."

Karen settled back against the door. "There's this thing called civilization. Not perfect, but it beats the alternative. Of course, when you get banned from it? Prison. You can try out your survival theories there."

His face twitched.

"We've seen a lot of the poor this past weekend," Karen told him. "And you know what? I'd pit a Lori Jansen or Chee Connor against you, and they'd come up aces. Their guts, their resilience, their humanity beat the hell out of you. You could have, *should* have, walked away from Bunting, come back for your evidence, and brought it to us. Bunting would be in prison, and you'd have a state park."

His chin jutted out. "It'll still come."

"Not happening." Karen didn't bother to hide her pleasure, though Biester couldn't know that was only because Connor benefited. Biester would think it was all about winning. Well, in a manner of speaking, it was. "The county commissioners revoked the application for Grove Park."

"You're lying."

Marek stirred. "No, she's not. It'll soon be public knowledge."

That finally cracked him. Biester's head hit the table with a thud. "It was all for nothing."

Marek didn't take any pleasure in the man's shaking shoulders. Or the prospect of a man of nature caged for the rest of his life away from all he valued.

Where was Mother Nature in all this? Connor had been healed there, Biester had been bent there, and Bunting had been felled there. A toss-up.

As for Marek, he was going home.

CHAPTER 45

K AREN FOLLOWED MAREK OUT OF the interview room and directed Walrus to take their prisoner down to the jail.

"I'm going home," Marek told her when the downstairs door slammed shut. His tone brooked no opposition.

Karen grabbed his arm before he could leave. Doc Hudson had charged her with keeping Marek awake. But she decided that was a losing battle, so she looked for any sign of bleeding in the brain, like unequally dilated pupils. "Let me see your eyes."

Marek turned, and she looked into steady, if bloodshot, eyes that said: enough. But before she could give him her yea or nay, King Lear burst into the office in all his theatrical finery, his face drawn, his hair sticking up in tufts.

Karen checked her watch. Her reserve deputy had rushed his entrance. "It isn't midnight yet, your majesty. It's barely past ten. Was the show canceled for tonight?"

Adam cleared his throat. "No, I ran off right after curtain. Because I got a text from a friend of a friend who lives in Aleford asking me if I needed a new job, now my boss was dead." He pursed his lips. "Looks like reports of your death were exaggerated, Karen. What just happened here?"

With a few short sentences, Marek outlined the night's events. He had a knack for brevity that Karen lacked.

"'Allow not nature more than nature needs, man's life is cheap as beast's.'" Adam fingered his velvet cloak, back in character. "But the world's rid of Bunting, so that's all to the good."

"He wasn't as bad as billed," Karen said grudgingly.

"Do tell."

She did, still keeping a hold on Marek.

Adam mimed shock. "'The prince of darkness is a gentleman!'"

Karen rolled her eyes. "When does this run end? Be gone, evil spirit."

"That's not *King Lear*," Marek said wearily.

Karen dropped her hand from his arm. "Your marbles are still working. Go." When Marek headed straight for the door, she said to the mad king, "Since you're here, Two Fingers could use the support. Bork won't be back until next week."

"Gone. Exit, stage... down." Adam swirled his way down the stairs, the hinge-sprung door slamming shut behind him—but somehow, he managed to whisk the cloak away before it was caught. One of the tricks of the trade, she supposed.

Unlike Marek, Karen had gone beyond tired to wired. And she wasn't in the mood to do paperwork. That would wait for morning. She snapped on the radio to hear the tail end of Nails's on-the-hour recording.

—folks think that everyone gets what they deserve. The poor will always be with us. The more cynical among you will say that's just a statement of fact, nothing more, and dismiss the poor to their misery without another thought.

Used to be what elevated us beyond the animals was our minds... and our hearts. Ted Jorgenson had one. Alan Digges didn't. Biester lost one. Chee Connor gained his.

And Bunting? He's a mix, from what I hear. Good and bad. When all is said and done, though, what can I say but... poor Baby Bunting.

Karen turned off the radio when the cell phone charging on her desk pinged. She'd missed a number of texts, but the newest one was from Larson. That her heart could leap, could beat, was a treat that she wouldn't be tricked into almost losing again.

Blood on knife: animal. Sorry.

She texted back. *No. Good. Almost died tonight. Marek hurt but okay. Connor, the hero.*

A lengthy pause. *Coming with ball.*

My Cinderella, she texted back. He knew her so well. She needed to play. Hard. Of course, she'd prefer something a bit more primal than the hard floors of a basketball court. Well, why not? Almost dying put things in perspective in a hurry.

She typed in, *Come with slippers.*

Her finger hovered over Send. Choices, they were a killer. It was a school day. And when she'd agreed to take on Mary Hannah, there'd been an implicit contract with Elder Mock: don't shock the young girl's sensibilities. Booking into a hotel, which wasn't to be found in Reunion anyway, was just rife with problems.

And, really, just how well did she know Larson? Not very.

Like Biester's bur oaks, Larson wasn't pretty, but strong and resilient, with branches that twisted and turned down roads she hadn't yet traveled. Unlike her, he'd weathered the drought, the chilling cold, of poverty. Did that make him a poor second?

Or a second chance?

CAST OF CHARACTERS

Bayton, Albert Cram. Also known as Not-Johnson, as he gave his name as John Johnson, an obvious pseudonym. One of the homeless living in Grove Park.

Bayton, Michelle. Lawyer from a powerful Sioux Falls family. Wife of Alan Digges.

Bechtold, Kurt. Senior deputy in the Eda County Sheriff's Office. Unmarried. Lives with his unmarried sister, Eva, who bakes goodies to stave off her many phobias.

Biester, Jack. Park manager for Grove Park in Eda County. Formerly worked for the National Park Service.

Bjorkland, Travis "Bork." Swing-shift deputy in the Eda County Sheriff's Office. Unmarried. A native of Minnesota.

Bridges, Nancy Kubicek. Widow who waitresses at the truck stop in Aleford in Eda County. A cousin of Marek Okerlund and of Nadine Kubicek Bunting Early. Mother of Tanner Bridges, an aspiring veterinarian who attends college in Brookings.

Bullard, Mindy Hansen. Lost the family farm after her husband was sent to the state penitentiary. Mother of two children. Now lives with her brother Jeff Hansen near Fink in Eda County. Supported Bob Bunting at the recount.

Bunting, Robert Leonard "Baby." Also known as Bob. Elected sheriff of Eda County over Karen Okerlund Mehaffey until a recount gave her the victory. Former deputy under Arne Okerlund. Son of Rachel Dutton and nephew of Alice Dutton.

Cantor, Tricia. Pastor of the Congregational Church in Reunion. Former psychology professor from Chicago, Illinois, who lost her family in an accident. Informal profiler and consultant to the Eda County Sheriff's Office.

Connor, Archibald "Chee." Cousin of Laura Connor Russell.

Dahl, Harold. County commissioner for Eda County. Husband of Janet Dahl and son of Mayor Greta Dahl.

Dahl, Janet. Register of deeds for Eda County. Standing in for the ailing county auditor in this story. Wife of Harold Dahl.

Digges, Alan. Nephew of Ted Jorgenson and husband of Michelle Bayton. Lives in Sioux Falls and was appointed administrator of Ted's estate, including the trailer park.

Donahue, Pat. Rover of the highways and byways, a retired firefighter from San Diego, who parks his RV at the Grove Park overlook.

Dutton, Alice. Sister of Rachel Dutton and aunt of Bob Bunting. Retired legal secretary who lives in Aleford. Never married.

Dutton, Rachel. Deceased. Sister of Alice Dutton, mother of Bob Bunting, and ex-wife of Ed Johnson.

Early, Kaylee. A developmentally disabled young woman who works as a prostitute and lives with her brother Kyle in Valeska in Eda County.

Early, Kyle. A dealer of opioids and other vices who lives with his sister Kaylee in Valeska in Eda County.

Early, Nadine Kubicek Bunting. Ex-wife of Bob Bunting and of Jim Early. A cousin of Marek Okerlund and of Nancy Kubicek Bridges. An alcoholic who lives in the old Kubicek homestead near Valeska in Eda County.

Farley, Gus and Marlene. Campground visitors at Grove Park. Husband and wife living on Social Security. Natives of Chelsea, Vermont.

Fike, Jordan. Nightshift dispatcher and jailer for the Eda County Sheriff's Office.

Hageman, Blanche. Principal of kindergarten through 12th grades in Reunion schools.

Harkness, Doris. Disabled resident of the trailer park and grandmother of Zoe Harkness.

Harkness, Zoe. Teenage granddaughter of Doris Harkness and resident of the trailer park. Friend of Bobby Jansen.

Hudson, Doc. Longtime family doctor who works in Reunion at the only medical clinic in Eda County.

Jansen, Bobby. Son of Lori Jansen.

Jansen, Lori. Struggling single mother who works at a gas station and at Grove Park, cleaning the outhouses. Mother of Bobby Jansen.

Johnson, Ed. One of Rachel Dutton's husbands and stepfather of Bob Bunting. Worked for the South Dakota Highway Patrol at one time.

Johnson, Eyre. Archivist for the privately funded Eda County Archives housed in the old Carnegie Library in Reunion. Biological daughter of Karen Okerlund Mehaffey. Adopted by Karen's old basketball coach, Darrin Johnson, and his (now ex-) wife Professor Anne Leggett in Vermillion. After a fire destroyed her apartment, Eyre now lives with Karen at 22 Okerlund Road.

Johnson, Mary. One of the homeless living in Grove Park. Works in a school cafeteria.

Jorgenson, Ted. Deceased. Original owner of the trailer park adjoining Grove Park. Died from a stroke about three months prior to the start of the story. Uncle of Alan Digges.

Kubicek, Dr. Blaise. Professor of education at the University of South Dakota in Vermillion. Cousin of Janina Marek Okerlund.

Kubicek, Don. Farmer and brother of Nadine Kubicek Bunting Early and owner of the Kubicek homestead where she lives.

Larson, Dirk. Agent with the South Dakota Division of Criminal Investigation (DCI) in Sioux Falls. Divorced with children. Formerly a homicide detective in Chicago, Illinois. Once a professional basketball prospect. In a tentative relationship with Karen Okerlund Mehaffey.

Lindstrom, Josephine. A transplant from West River (South Dakota) who married a man from Reunion. He died in Vietnam and she became a secretary for the Eda County Sheriff's Office. After initially retiring, she has returned to work part-time. A champion barrel racer.

Marek, Jim. Deceased. Brother of Janina Marek Okerlund and uncle of Marek Okerlund. Worked as a carpenter for many years before he was killed in a traffic accident. Never married. Trained Marek early on in carpentry.

Marek, Lenny. Deceased. A carpenter and abusive alcoholic. Married Vera Kubicek. Father of Jim Marek and Janina Marek and grandfather of Marek Okerlund, who strongly resembles him. Killed two men in bar brawls. Convicted of manslaughter for the first and murder for the second. After being sentenced to life in prison for the latter, he jumped from the third floor of the courthouse, killing himself. Like his grandson, he likely had severe dyslexia.

Marek, Vera Kubicek. Deceased. Wife of Lenny Marek and mother of Jim Marek and Janina Marek and grandmother of Marek Okerlund. Worked as a seamstress and lived at the old Kubicek homestead until her death.

McGurdys. Campground visitors at Grove Park. Father, mother, and son Hugh, who plays ultimate Frisbee. Natives of Canada.

Mehaffey, Karen Okerlund. Acting sheriff of Eda County. Widow of Patrick Mehaffey, a Bosnian War casualty who lingered in a coma for many years. Daughter of former sheriff, Arne Okerlund, and half-niece of Detective Marek Okerlund, who is four years her junior. Biological mother of Eyre Johnson. Was an outstanding basketball player at the University of South Dakota in Vermillion. Former Army officer in Bosnia and police dispatcher in Sioux Falls. Took over as acting sheriff after her father's stroke. Lives at 22 Okerlund Road in the bungalow where she grew up.

Mehaffey, Patrick. Deceased husband of Karen Okerlund Mehaffey. An Army medic, he drove over a landmine in Bosnia and was in a coma for many years before his death.

Miles, Akio. Campground visitor at Grove Park. Works as a coder and travel blogger. Owns a drone. Native of Los Angeles.

Mock, Mary Hannah. Teenage cousin of Karen Okerlund Mehaffey. Daughter of Elder Sander Mock of the Eder Brethren, an Amish-like sect in Eda County. She is attending high school in Reunion and plans to eventually become a certified midwife. Lives weekdays during the school year with Karen at 22 Okerlund Road.

Mountain Man. Mysterious poacher living in Grove Park.

Nelson, Rusty "Nails." Disabled Vietnam veteran who lives above the old Carnegie Library in Reunion that now houses the county archives. Operates the low-power FM radio station YRUN and reports news from Eda County. Native of Bandit Ridge in Eda County.

Nylander, Tammy. Day-shift dispatcher and jailer for the Eda County Sheriff's Office.

Okerlund, Arne. Former sheriff of Eda County, son of Sheriff Leif Okerlund, father of Karen Okerlund Mehaffey, and half-brother of Marek Okerlund. First married to Hannah Mock and second to Clara, the widow of his childhood friend. A stroke ended his career as sheriff. He and Clara adopted Clara's grandson and babysit Marek's daughter, Becca. Lived at 22 Okerlund Road until his second marriage. Now lives on Okerlund Road in the old Stan Forsgren house.

Okerlund, Clara Gullick. Widow of Vern Gullick and mother of Deputy Rick Gullick (deceased). Grandmother of Joseph Jaramillo Okerlund. Married to Arne Okerlund after the deaths of her husband and son. Lives on Okerlund Road at the old Stan Forsgren house.

Okerlund, Hannah Mock. Deceased. First wife of Arne Okerlund and mother of Karen Okerlund Mehaffey. Died of ovarian cancer when Karen was in the Army. Raised among the Eder Brethren, she fled as a young woman.

Okerlund, Joseph Jaramillo. Toddler son of Rick Gullick (deceased) and Blanca Jaramillo (deceased). Grandson of Vern and Clara Gullick. Adopted by Arne Okerlund when he married the widow Clara Gullick. Becca Okerlund treats him as the brother she lost.

Okerlund, Joseph Leif Manuel. Deceased. Stillborn son of Marek Okerlund and his wife Valencia De Baca. Died with his mother in Albuquerque after their car was hit by a drunk driver.

Okerlund, Leif. Deceased. Former sheriff of Eda County and father of Arne Okerlund by first wife, Kari Halvorsen, and father of Marek Okerlund by second wife, Janina Marek. Grandfather of Karen Okerlund Mehaffey. World War II veteran. His second marriage caused a rift between himself and his elder son (Arne).

Okerlund, (Leif) Marek. Always called by his middle name. Part-time detective for Eda County. Part-time carpenter. Dyslexic. Son of Sheriff Leif Okerlund and second wife, Janina Marek. Half-brother of Arne Okerlund and half-uncle of Karen Okerlund Mehaffey, who is four years his elder. Moved from Reunion to Valeska in Eda County with his mother after his father's death. Left Eda County after high school and ended up in Albuquerque, New Mexico, where he was first a carpenter and then a cop, eventually rising to the rank of homicide detective. Lost his wife, Valencia De Baca, to a drunk driver. Their daughter, Becca, was in the car and survived. Lives at 21 Okerlund Road in the bungalow he spent his childhood in.

Okerlund, Rebecca "Becca" De Baca. Young daughter of Marek Okerlund and Valencia De Baca. A precocious artist, she was mute after losing her mother and unborn brother to a drunk driver but gradually recovered after the move to South Dakota.

Okerlund, Valencia "Val" De Baca. Deceased. Wife of Marek Okerlund. Daughter of Joseph De Baca and New York artist Adrienne Fiat. Killed with her unborn son by a drunk driver in Albuquerque.

Peterson, Taylor. Resident of the trailer park. Divorced. Works in construction. Childhood classmate of Marek Okerlund.

Redbird, Mary. Campground visitor at Grove Park. Elderly Native American woman from one of South Dakota's poorest reservations. Formerly a teacher and now works in the sugar beet fields in North Dakota and as a tour guide in the Black Hills.

Reicharts. Also known as "The Florids" from Florida. Campground visitors at Grove Park. Husband and wife on their way to their daughter's wedding in Seattle.

Rudibaugh, Judge John Franklin. Also known as "Judge Rudy." Presiding judge at the Eda County courthouse.

Russell, Laura Connor. Childhood friend, basketball teammate, and college roommate of Karen Okerlund Mehaffey. She is the wife of Deputy Walter Russell and mother of three boys. Works as an elementary-school teacher in Reunion.

Russell, Walter "Walrus." Day-shift deputy in the Eda County Sheriff's Office. Originally from Aleford in Eda County and married to Laura Connor. Father of three boys. Pheasant hunter and gun enthusiast.

Schaeffer, Marsha. Social worker based out of Sioux Falls. Visits Eda County only once a week.

Solberg, Annika "Nikki" Forsgren. Adopted daughter of Elmer Forsgren, a distant cousin of Karen and Marek. Biological daughter of the Eder Brethren. Made up her surname on leaving for California after high school. Artist and school teacher in Reunion. Lives off Okerlund Road in a former one-room schoolhouse. Tutors Becca Okerlund in art. In a tentative relationship with Marek Okerlund.

Sommervold, Agent. Female half of "The Seasons," top guns from the FBI resident agency in Sioux Falls. A native of South Dakota.

Tisher, Norm "Tish." He is the Eda County coroner, with no medical training other than that gleaned as a local mortician. A native of North Dakota.

Two Fingers, Deputy. Swing-shift deputy with the Eda County Sheriff's Office. Mixed maternal heritage of Dakota (Santee), Nakota (Yankton), Mandan, and Arikara. Father unknown (Caucasian). Mother enrolled at Flandreau Reservation in South Dakota but Two Fingers does not meet the blood quantum requirement. Dartmouth graduate and former Air Force pilot.

Van Eck, Adam. Reserve deputy on the night shift for the Eda County Sheriff's Office. Former Broadway actor who continues his passion in Sioux Falls.

White, Dr. Oscar Micheaux. Forensic pathologist and native of Sioux Falls. Named for African-American filmmaker Oscar Micheaux, who homesteaded in South Dakota.

Wintersgill, Agent. Male half of "The Seasons," top guns from the FBI resident agency in Sioux Falls. A New England native.

ABOUT THE AUTHOR

M.K. Coker grew up on a river bluff in southeastern South Dakota. Part of the Dakota diaspora, the author has lived in half a dozen states, but returns to the prairie at every opportunity.

Website: www.mkcoker.com

ACKNOWLEDGEMENTS

As always, my deepest thanks (and sympathies!) go to my long-suffering editor Stefanie Spangler Buswell, proofreader Susie Driver, and beta readers Marjory Coker, Kelli Lapour Cotter, Sheila Molony, and Cherié Wieble. And to Lynn McNamee of Red Adept Editing, who always seems to take missed deadlines in stride!

CPSIA information can be obtained
at www.ICGtesting.com
Printed in the USA
LVHW091751280319
612190LV00004B/858/P

8